His birth meant death for the world.

BAAL

His passion rages across time; his wrath
encircles the globe. he reappears at a time
when earth is in chaos, plotting a
climb to power that would eclipse Christ.

BAAL

'Take me with you, Baal. Please.'
Some call him the living Mohammed. Some
call him the Demon Prince. Millions of his
bloodthirsty disciples follow him to
the ends of the earth in a fury of mindless
violence and orgy from which there is
no escape. . . .

BAAL

It will turn your heart to ice.

Baal
ROBERT R. McCAMMON

SPHERE BOOKS LIMITED
30/32 Gray's Inn Road, London WC1X 8JL

First published in Great Britain by Sphere Books Ltd 1979
Reprinted 1980 (twice)
Copyright © Robert R. McCammon 1978

Set in Monotype Times

Printed in Great Britain by
William Collins Sons & Co Ltd
Glasgow

*For Michael, my brother
and Bill, my friend*

Prologue

Fury stung the sky.

Kul-Haziz smelled it. It had the odour of clashing weapons, of men's sweat, of new blood, of old sins.

Smelling it, he narrowed his eyes and looked over the backs of the grazing flock to the north. The sun hung high in a white sky, burning as it had for a thousand years. Its eye saw what was happening beyond the crags, beyond the flat plains, over meadows and hills in the distance. It saw what he could not. He could only smell.

His eyes fixed on the grim horizon, Kul-Haziz took his gnarled staff and walked slowly among his flock, softly nudging the flanks of the sheep. He was a man who, with his wife and young son, had always followed the rainfall because the rainfall meant new grass. Life for the flock. Now, in the distant north towards the city of Hazor, he saw the gathering of dark shapes that looked like rainclouds. But no. There was no odour of rain in the air. He would have smelled it days before. No, not rain. Only the smell of fury.

Behind him, inside a goatskin tent, his wife looked up from her mending. On the other side of the rolling slightly sloped plain his son had been striking his staff on the ground to urge straying animals back to the flock. Now he looked towards his father.

Kul-Haziz stood like stone on the hillside. He put his hand over his eyes to shield them from the sun. He didn't know what was happening. He had heard the stories from other nomadic families: the wrath of Yahweh has fallen upon us. We are a doomed race, they said with blabbering tongues. Yahweh will destroy us all for our wickedness. So said the shepherd prophets, the nomads of the grasslands, the kings of the hills. His heart beat within him. It sounded like someone crying out for knowledge.

His son reached him through the flock. He grasped his father's hand.

There was a flash like lightning, but no lightning. Far away in the distance, to the north, towards the city of Hazor. It was bright blue and blinding, intense, terrible. Kul-Haziz clapped a hand over his eyes. His son held to him, hiding his face. Behind him his wife cried out and the sheep scattered all around. Kul-Haziz felt the heat on his hand. When it had died away he looked again and saw nothing. His son was staring up at him, his eyes asking a question the man could not answer.

And then he saw it. Over the far crags, beyond the flat plains: trees bending in a fierce wind, breaking off and flying through the air, their branches turning to fire. And the grasslands beyond blackened as if an army were marching across them, leaving Hazor behind. The fire army crawled across the plains below, scorching them. Thornscrubs exploded in flame. Fire ripped the sands.

As the wind reached Kul-Haziz up on the grass-covered hill it woirled around him, tore at his rags, whispered the secrets into his ear. The flock bawled.

Only a short time now before the fire would come. It had consumed Hazor and was now devouring every living thing on all sides of that city. Kul-Haziz knew his family could take only a few more breaths before the warming air turned to raging white flame.

At his side his son said, 'Father?'

The prophets had been right. Their skulls and sticks, their writing across the sky had foretold the coming of the end. It had only been a matter of time.

Kul-Haziz said, 'The great god Baal is no more.'

He stood like stone.

Burning stone.

ONE

'Who is like unto the beast?'

—*Revelation* 13:4

1

On the television screen the newscaster was speaking of falling economies and the latest South American earthquakes.

Mary Kate slid a cup of coffee across the cigarette-burned countertop to the night's last customer. He looked at her through bleary eyes and mumbled a thank you.

Ernest was leaning against the counter watching the late-night news programme; he always did. She knew the routine. 'Holy Jesus Christ!' he said. 'They're killin' the city with all this tax shit! You can't make a decent livin' no more!'

'Man shouldn't even try,' said the customer. 'Should just be a bum and lay around in the park like all those kids do. The world has gone to hell.'

There was a clatter of plates as Mary Kate gathered them up. 'Watch that!' Ernest said. On the fly-blown black-and-white screen the solemn face said, '. . . fear another assassination attempt . . .'

She glanced at her wristwatch. Late! she thought. I'm running late! Joe's home by now and he'd be tired as hell. He'll want something to eat and I know how it is when he doesn't get his dinner on time. Damn it!

'You know what it is?' the customer was asking Ernest. 'It's time, that's what it is. The world has run the circle. You know what I'm talking about? The circle's been run and now, by God, it's time to pay up.'

'. . . kidnapped yesterday by members of Japan's Black Mask terrorist organization. Ransom demands have not yet . . .' said the newscaster.

'The circle's been run?' Ernest asked. He had turned his head to look at the other man and one side of his heavy-jowled face reflected the television's blue glow. 'What'd you mean by that?'

'You're only given so much time, y'know,' said the customer, his gaze flickering from Ernest to the newscaster and back again. 'When your time is up, you go. Same's true of cities, of

11

countries even. You know what happened to Rome, right? It reached its peak and then fell right over the edge.'

'So New York and Rome both got somethin' in common, huh?'

'Sure. I read about all this somewhere. Or maybe I saw it on the tube.'

Mary Kate had cradled greasy, cigarette-butt-littered plates in her arms. The odours repelled her. People are just like pigs, she mused. Oink oink oink just like pigs. She went through a pair of swinging doors into the kitchen and set the dirty dishes in a rack near the sink. The combination cook and dishwasher, a young black named Woodrow, lifted his chin and watched her intently, a cigarette dangling from a corner of his mouth.

'Do Baby Mary need a ride home tonight?' he asked her; he always did.

'I've asked you to stop calling me that.'

'It's right on my way. And I got me some good-lookin' rims last week.'

'I'll take the bus.'

'I can save you some money.'

She turned towards him and saw the heat simmering behind his eyes; that look of his always frightened her. 'I can save you some time. I don't need a ride. I'll take the bus like I always take the bus. You understand that now?'

Woodrow grinned around the cigarette. An ash fell like a block of marble from the Tower of Babel. 'I dig, sister. You don't go for the black meat is all.'

She swung the kitchen doors shut behind her and the sound made Ernest look up sharply. His gaze fixed on her for a few seconds and then turned again to the television, where a long-legged weathergirl was explaining that the heat wave would continue at least through Thursday.

That bastard! Mary Kate began methodically wiping the grime from ashtrays scattered along the counter. I've got to get a new job, she told herself; she always did. I've got to get a new job and get my ass out of here. I don't care what it is as long as I'm away from here!

Here I am, she said. Twenty years old and a waitress in a slop shop, married to an English-major dropout who drives a cab. Christ! I've got to get out of here even if it means . . .

12

doing something I don't want to do. She wondered what Joe's reaction would be if one night in their cramped steaming apartment she touched him gently and whispered, 'Joe my darling dearest one on earth, I think I'd be happier as a whore.'

There was a *click*! as Ernest switched off the television set. The customer had gone. A dime lay beside the coffee cup.

'Time to go home,' Ernest said. 'Another day, another dollar. Another lousy dollar. Hey! Woodrow! Hey! You locking up back there?'

Woodrow called back in his best slave imitation, 'I'se lockin' up, boss!'

Mary Kate folded her apron neatly and laid it beneath the counter. She said, 'I'm leaving now, okay? I've got to get home and cook something for Joe.'

Ernest was still propped against the counter, staring at the empty eye of the television. Without looking around, he said, 'So? Leave.'

She pushed through the frosted-glass door out into the street where a red neon sign flashed *Ernie's Grill* off and on, off and on a thousand times a day; once she'd actually counted.

The air was as thick and heavy as if she were standing in the centre of a steambath. She walked away from the grill towards her bus stop three blocks away, keeping her purse high on her shoulder to guard against hit-and-run thieves.

At one time she had wanted to go to secretarial school; she and Joe would be able to support each other and maybe save a little on the side. But then he had dropped out of school and his subsequent depression infected her as well. They were now like two survivors of a shipwreck in a leaking life raft. Too weak to live, too scared to die, just drifting, drifting. Things had to change.

And now she found herself doubting that she still loved him. She didn't know. No one had ever explained to her how she should feel; her father was the strict conservative type, a grease-handed mechanic in a New Jersey garage, and her mother was a chattering bingo addict who wore sunglasses after dark, as if she hoped to be discovered for the movies by talent scouts scrounging amid damaged canned goods in second-rate supermarkets.

She still felt attracted to Joe, yes. Of course she did. But love? Love? That thrilling passionate dip into the soul of someone else? She really couldn't put it into words, and if she asked Joe to help her articulate it she was certain he'd laugh. It wasn't that she was no longer healthy or pretty or anything like that, though when she stood before a mirror she had to admit she was far too thin and her face had taken on the blank stare of a well-worn woman. No, something was needed; something drastic.

The grill was far from her thoughts now. Ahead the streetlights glowed yellow all along the kerb. The empty scarred stone faces of apartment buildings watched her pass as solemnly as priests with bowed heads. Garbage cans overflowed into the gutter and newspaper headlines shrieked of murder and arson and the threat of war.

This heat, she said. This heat. The sweat had burst out across the bridge of her nose. It had collected under her arms and now trickled down her sides. How many more days of this? Already two weeks. How much longer? And only the beginning of summer, with the hottest months yet to come.

The bus stop. No, no, a block further. Her footsteps on the empty street echoed back and forth, back and forth between the stone walls. How much longer, she asked herself, can I take this?

Ahead she saw that the globe of one of the streetlights had been broken. Someone had thrown a stone or bottle and broken the glass, but not hard enough to completely shatter the bulb. It flickered wildly, buzzing like a great lost insect, yellow to black, yellow to black, yellow to black. It threw black shadows across the faces of the fearful watching priests.

'Come here,' someone said. It was a gentle, distant voice like that of a little child.

She turned and wiped her forearm across her face. It came away wet.

There was no one. The street was empty and quiet but for the noise of the bulb above her head. She pulled her purse higher on her arm, clamped it in her armpit. Hunching her head down, she walked on towards the bus stop. Her bus would be there soon.

'Come here,' said the voice, cool and startling as if a cube

14

of ice had been pressed suddenly against her forehead. She stopped abruptly and stood motionless.

Mary Kate glanced over her shoulder. Someone's playing a joke, she thought. Some little kid is playing a joke. 'That is not funny,' she said to no one. 'Go on home.'

But before she could move away the voice said softly, 'Here. I'm here.'

Something touched her; it was like smoke, grasping with whirling changing fingers. She felt it moving beneath her wet garments; her flesh crawled. The voice had walked up the skeletal staircase of her spine. And now it descended with measured steps.

'I'm here,' someone said, and she turned to peer into a black garbage-strewn alley that smelled of urine and sweat.

Someone was standing there, someone tall. Not a child. A man? Wearing a man's clothes, yes. A man. Who? A mugger? She felt an electric impulse to run. Above her head the broken bulb screamed in shades of yellow and black.

'Do I know you? Do I know you?' she found herself asking; a damned stupid question to ask a mugger, she angrily told herself. Her grip tightened around her purse. She was going to run and keep running until she'd lost him.

'No,' he said quietly. 'Don't run.'

He remained in shadow. She could see his shoes, a pair of battered black wingtips below dark trousers. He made no attempt to come closer to her. He simply stood framed in the alley entrance, with his arms at his sides, and she felt the urge to escape drained from her. No need to run, she told herself. This is someone I know.

'I'm someone you know,' he said in his childlike whisper. 'I'm someone you haven't seen for a long while. There is no need for fear.'

'What do you want with me?'

'Time. Just a moment out of all moments you will ever live. Is that too much to ask of a friend?'

'No. Not too much to ask.' She felt strange and heavy. Her head swam in a pool of yellow and black; her tongue was a plate of concrete jammed back into her mouth.

'If I reach out my hand for you,' he asked, 'will you take it?'

She shuddered. No. Yes. Yes. 'My bus,' she said in a helpless, unfamiliar voice.

His arm pierced the shadows. The fingers were long and thin; filth caked the nails.

The heat lay heavy about her shoulders and her hair, wet and stringy, clung to her neck. I can't breathe! she screamed inwardly. I'm drowning! I'm drowning. The mad buzzing streetlight drilled into her brain and lit it in glaring yellow neon. I don't want to, she said to herself.

And he answered, 'You will.'

His hand touched hers. The fingers locked around her knuckles, moved over her palm, clenched her wrist with a steadily rising force.

And then from the alley shadows a face yellow-illuminated burst its soundlessly screaming mouth open to devour her. She had no time to see him; she was overcome by a powerful high odour of something burning. His flesh was wet and soft – spongy – and hot. He bore down on her as she fell screaming and clawing to the concrete.

He smashed her head into the sidewalk. Again. Again. Something was bleeding; her ear was bleeding. The hot blood was streaming down her neck. 'YOU BITCH!' he shrieked in a voice that flailed her like a burning whip. 'YOU DAMNED COCKSUCKING BITCH AND ALL YOUR LOVERS DOGS!' The man's breath smelled foul and hot. She cringed as he beat at her breasts; he ripped her blouse and raked the smooth skin of her abdomen with his nails.

She screamed in agony and sang harmony with the streetlight. A window across the street slammed shut. Then another.

With both hands he tore away her skirt. Then he spread wide her thighs and drove in with a mad inhuman strength that ground her buttocks against the concrete. He pressed his fingers against her eyes and for an instant she thought, I'm dead oh God I'm dead.

'OOOOHHHH GODDDD!' she screamed aloud. Her mouth was filled suddenly by a greedy eager tongue.

'DIE YOU BITCH DIE YOU BITCH YOU CUNT DIE!' he screamed pounding and grinding and pounding and pounding until he climaxed with a fierce shudder that drew the breath from him and made her whine with pain.

16

'Hey! Hey! You! Get away from there!' Brakes squealed and rubber burned. She felt his weight rise from her and smelled him again; the odour made her vomit on the concrete. She heard someone running; no, two people running. Someone running away and someone running towards her. Oh God oh God oh God help me.

Mary Kate opened her eyes and saw a young man. Woodrow. Woodrow running towards her and behind him a fire-engine-red Buick with shining chrome wheel rims that caught the distorted reflections of streetlights. Woodrow reaching her and bending down and the cigarette dropping from his lips and . . .

2

He cracked the top off a can of beer and stood at an open window staring down at the dark quiet street. She's been late before but not like this. The bus never ran this late.

He'd tried the grill but it was past closing and no one answered the telephone. Maybe the bus had broken down. No, she would've called. Maybe she missed it and had to walk. No, that was a hell of a long way. Maybe she'd had an accident; or maybe she'd gotten crazy like she had before when she didn't come home for two days and they'd finally found her sitting in the park, doing nothing but just sitting.

Shit. Why does she do these things to me? He drank the beer down and placed the can on the splintery windowsill. She's more than two hours late. More than two hours and where can she be this time of night? He picked up the telephone and started to dial her parents' apartment in Jersey City but then he recalled her mother's whining voice. He put the receiver back on its cradle. Not yet.

Out in the distance, above the packed dirty rows of square-shouldered buildings, a police siren wailed. Or was it an ambulance? He'd never learned to tell the difference like some people could. Something had happened. Standing in the dark small fourth-floor apartment that inhaled the odours wafting from

17

beneath other doors, he was certain something had happened.

And he stood waiting and frozen until someone knocked at the door. But he knew it would not be her; no. The police officer with an impassive acne-scarred face simply said, 'I have a car outside.'

In the car on the way to the hospital he asked, 'Is she all right? I mean . . .'

'I'm sorry, Mr Raines,' the police officer said. 'They asked me to pick you up.'

He sat in an antiseptic-white waiting room on the seventh floor and clenched his hands. Hit by a car. That was it. Oh Jesus God hit by some drunk while she was walking to her bus stop.

Even at this early-morning hour, Bellevue moved at a frantic life-and-death pace. He watched the doctors and their nurses consulting charts in low-keyed, serious voices. And a sight that chilled him to the bone, a man in a suit sprinting down the hospital corridor, his shoes clat-clat-clatting on the linoleum. He sat and watched these private dramas until finally he was aware of someone standing beside him.

'Mr Joseph Raines?' someone asked. A tall gaunt man with tightly curled grey hair. He said, 'I'm Lt Hepelmann.' He flashed a NYPD badge and Joe rose from his seat.

'No, no. Sit down. Please.' Hepelmann put a hand on the younger man's shoulder and eased him back down into the chair. He sat beside him and drew his own chair closer, as if he were a friend about to advise him on a personal matter.

'I knew she was late and I knew something had happened,' said Joe, staring into his palms. 'I tried the grill but no one answered the phone.' He looked up. 'A hit-and-run driver?'

Hepelmann's deep-set blue eyes were calm and untroubled. He was used to scenes like this. 'No, Mr Raines. I don't know who told you that, but she was not struck by a car. Your wife has been . . . assaulted. She's safe now but still in shock. She might have died but some nigger saved her. Ran the guy off and chased him a block before he got away.'

'Assaulted? Assaulted? What does that mean?'

Hepelmann's jaw tightened. This was the moment that broke them to pieces, the mental image of some guy ramming himself in between thrashing thighs. 'There was sexual penetration, Mr Raines,' he said softly, as if sharing a secret.

Raped. Jesus Christ. Jesus Holy Christ. Raped. He looked directly into Hepelmann's eyes with a savage ferocity. 'You got the sonofabitch?'

'No. We haven't been able to get a description. Probably it's some nut who has a history of . . violations. When Mrs Raines recovers we'll get her to page through our mug files. We'll get the guy.'

'Oh man. Oh man oh man oh man.'

'Listen, you want a cup of coffee or something? Here. A cigarette.'

He took the cigarette the lieutenant offered. 'Christ,' he said weakly. 'But she's okay, right? I mean, no broken bones or anything?'

'No broken bones.' Hepelmann leaned forward until he might have been whispering in the other man's ear. 'I've worked a lot of these cases, Mr Raines. These things happen a hundred times a day. It's rough, yes. But you adjust to it. And usually the woman adjusts faster than the man. Everything's okay now. It's over.'

The man didn't react to this statement as Hepelmann had seen others react. He simply sat and smoked the cigarette, his eyes boring down the tunnel-like hospital corridor. Someone was paging a Dr Holland on the address system.

'Some people are just like animals,' Hepelmann said. 'They think of one thing and they go after it. Hell, they don't care who it is. I've investigated violation cases where the victims were eighty-year-old grandmothers! Hell, they don't care. Their minds are gone already.'

Joe sat quiet and still.

'You know what they ought to do? And I'm a firm believer in this. They ought to take these damned guys and cut their balls off. I'm sincere.'

Someone was walking towards them down the corridor. Joe watched the man approach. He presumed the man was either another police officer or a doctor because he carried a clipboard.

Hepelmann stood up and shook the man's hand. 'Dr Wynter,

this is Mr Raines. I've told him she's going to be okay.'

'That's correct Mr Raines,' the doctor said. There were deep lines of strain around his eyes. 'She's suffered some minor cuts and abrasions but otherwise she's physically sound. She's in a mild state of shock now; it's natural after something like this so don't be alarmed. Now you're going to have to be very strong for her. When she begins to recover she's going to have a little orientation disorder. And she may believe you think less of her. That's a problem many rape victims encounter.'

He was nodding. 'Can I see her?'

The doctor's eyes flashed over to Hepelmann and then back to the other man. 'I'd rather you didn't right now. We're trying to keep her sleeping under sedation. Tomorrow we can get you in to see her for a few minutes.'

'I'd like to see her now.'

Dr Wynter blinked.

'The doctor's right,' said Hepelmann, grasping the other man's elbow. 'Look. It's been a tough night. Go home and get some sleep. Okay? I'll even give you a ride.'

'Tomorrow,' Dr Wynter said. 'Check with me tomorrow.'

Joe ran a hand over his face. The men were right. She should sleep for a while and, anyway, there was nothing he could do. He said, 'Okay.'

'Here,' said Hepelmann, stepping towards the elevators on the other side of the corridor. 'I'll give you a ride home.'

Before the elevator doors closed on Raines and the policeman, Dr Wynter said, 'She's going to be all right.'

Wynter stood motionless for a moment after they had gone. He trembled inwardly from the confrontation with the man. What was he? A taxi driver, Hepelmann had told him. The man had looked intelligent; a high forehead, eyes that when not cold with fear would be warm and generous, moderately long dark hair that curled over his collar. An intelligent man. Thank God he had not pressed to see his wife.

Dr Wynter walked back up the corridor to the nurses' station. He asked one of them, 'Mrs Raines is resting now?'

'Yes, sir. She'll be calm for a while.'

'Very good. Now listen to me well. You make your nurses understand this ' He lowered his voice. 'No word on any other floor about her condition. This is our problem. Okay?'

'Yes, sir.'

He nodded and continued through the corridor around to her room. He stopped himself as he reached for the door. No need to look in on her again; no need to look at her body and ask himself and the skin specialist Dr Bertram what the hell it was. He knew the answer. But what in Christ's name would he tell Raines? What was the logical explanation for those burns on her body? Certainly not friction burns incurred as she was forced to the harsh concrete.

The burns were in the shape of human hands.

First-degree burns, yes. Nothing serious, but . . .

Handprints where the rapist had grasped her. Hands burned across stomach and arms and thighs as distinctly as if they had been dipped into red paint and then slapped against her smooth white flesh.

And two fingerprints.

One on each eyelid.

3

In the predawn hours the heat wafted high above the city and then, dropping down, wrapped itself like ropes around blocks of granite slugs. It waited for sunrise, to burn the city dry.

He had not slept. Bloated with beer, he sat in a cracked vinyl chair before the open window and watched the lights that never dimmed, very far away, towards the city's heart.

My God, he said to himself over and over until he thought there was someone else standing behind him and speaking. My God. How can a man be allowed to do something like this? He saw the scene in the reddened eye of his mind: the drunken gutter bum waiting in the shadows as Mary Kate approached. Then leaping from his hiding place to bear down on her like a heavy sack of filth. And pounding pounding pounding until he couldn't bear to think about it any more.

Things hadn't been the greatest in the world for a while; he knew that too well. And now this moved inside him like something trying to escape through the bars of his teeth, something to make him pick up a gun and roam the streets like a mad spittle-mouthed dog.

He had telephoned her parents earlier. Her mother choked back a cry. 'And where were you? You weren't where you were supposed to be! No, you were sitting on your ass at home! She could have been murdered!'

'I'm holding you responsible for this, Joe,' said her father, taking the phone away from the woman and bellowing into it. 'Now act like a man! What hospital did they take her to?'

'They're not going to let you see her,' he said quietly. 'They wouldn't even let me see her.'

'I don't give a damn about that! What hospital?'

He deliberately put the receiver on its cradle, cutting off the man's voice. He had expected there would soon be an angry knocking on the door but they didn't come. Maybe they'd checked the hospitals and found her, or maybe they meant to find him later on in the morning. He didn't care; for the moment he was glad he didn't have to face them.

He had come from the Midwest two years ago, hunting an education and a 'meaningful experience'. His family were people 'tied to the land', as his father put it. They had wanted him to root himself into the earth and grow like an ear of corn, rich with the good ways of the dirt. But that was not for him; he had known it for a long long time. He wanted to become a teacher, perhaps of Shakespeare and Renaissance Literature, but first he wanted to live, to break away from the flat land of his birth and perhaps in the city find himself born again. That was when he was so much younger and idealistic.

He'd found a part-time job driving a cab, enough to get by on with monthly allowances from his family, as he attended classes at night. And for a while he enjoyed *Othello* and Central Park concerts and the sweet strength of pot.

Then he met Mary Kate. He walked into a diner and there found himself attracted to a thin doe-eyed young girl who slapped plates down and feverishly wrote his check in a stilted, unschooled hand. They had nothing in common except an immature sexual yearning; she liked to read love novels in the afterglow. His parents had protested violently at the news of their impending marriage. Son, they'd written, if you do this

22

thing you can't count on us sending you money any more. Remember your education. He'd written back: Go to hell.

But then the plans had turned to smoke. Money was needed badly; driving the cab became a full-time occupation and the English courses went down the drain. Their dissimilarities became painfully obvious; her illiteracy made him wince. And here they were, like two roommates who suddenly discovered they got in each other's way. They barely made enough money to live on; a divorce was beyond their means.

Yet there had been good, close times. On their 'honeymoon', a trip to the movies to see a horror double bill, they sat together in the balcony and threw popcorn at the leering bloody faces, then slipped down under the seats and necked, smacking loudly like high-schoolers. They did have their friends in common; scatterbrained longhairs who supplied them with some good highs at low costs; a few married couples he had met in his classes. And sometimes a few buddies from the company would pop over for beer and poker and she would serve them sandwiches, writing them checks on paper napkins. That was always good for a laugh.

Sitting in the chair amid drained cans of beer, he realized how different the apartment was without her. At this time of the morning, usually, he would be awakened by her restless thrashings as she fought hash-house phantoms in her dreams. He sometimes sat up on their sofa-sleeper and watched her eyes dart beneath closed lids. Dreaming of what? Rush hour? The dinner trade? A hamburger fifty feet across?

He was responsible for her, for better or worse, as the vows had said. It was only right that he take care of her through this thing. He gathered up the cans and threw them into the trash. Outside, dawn was breaking behind a grey veil. It was odd, he thought, how at this time of morning the sky was so washed and featureless, neither holding the promise of sun nor rain. Blank like a staring impassive face.

He waited until visiting hours and then took a cross-town bus back to Bellevue.

On the seventh floor he stopped a nurse and enquired about his wife.

'I'm sorry, sir,' she told him. 'I can't let you see Mrs Raines

23

without an official okay from either Dr Wynter or Dr Bertram.'

'What? Listen, I'm her husband. I've got a right to see her. What room's she in?'

'I'm sorry, sir,' she repeated, and started to move away towards the nurses' station down the corridor.

Something was wrong. He had sensed it earlier and now he knew. He grasped her wrist. 'I am going to see my wife now,' he said, levelling his gaze at her. 'I am going to see her and you're going to take me to her.'

'Do you want me to call a security officer? I will.'

'All right then, goddamn it, you go ahead and call a damn security officer. But you're taking me to her room.' His voice had become unintentionally harsh. From the corner of his eye he saw the nurses at the station gawking. One of them reached for a telephone and pressed a button.

His threat had done its work. 'Room 712,' she said, and shook away from him.

He walked on down the corridor to room 712 and entered without hesitation.

Mary Kate was asleep. She had been placed in a private room with off-white walls and white half-closed window curtains. Through the blinds the sun cast three strips across her bed.

He closed the door behind him and approached her. The sheets were pulled up around her neck. She looked pale and wasted, frail and lost. Her eyelids were oddly red and swollen, probably, he thought, from crying. Here, surrounded by cloud-like walls, she seemed very far removed from both the harsh neon-painted grill and their forlorn apartment.

He lifted the sheets to take her hand.

And when he did he staggered back.

Splotched along her arm were the reddened marks of hands. Grasping and clawing, they crawled five-fingered along her flesh, disappearing beneath her hospital gown. The red hands tore open her thighs; a hand-print clutched at her throat. Fingers, like some strange faddish make-up, painted her cheek. He let the sheets fall, knowing that beneath her gown more hands moved, clutched, clawed in an obscene bit of choreography. Branded, he said. Like a piece of beef. Someone's tied her and branded her.

Someone touched him. Someone behind him. He caught his breath and whirled around. The touch had seared him.

It was Dr Wynter, with dark circles beneath his eyes that clearly indicated he, too, had gone without sleep. A severe-looking nurse stood behind him in the doorway.

'This is the man who caused the disturbance, Doctor,' the nurse was saying. 'We told him he couldn't just . . .'

'It's all right,' Dr Wynter said softly, searching the other man's eyes. 'Go back to your station and tell the security officer everything is under control. Go on, now.'

She looked from Dr Wynter to the ashen-faced man who stood limply over the bed and silently closed the door.

'I didn't want you to see her,' the doctor said. 'Not yet.'

'Not yet? Not yet?' He looked up, his lips spraying spittle, his confused eyes demanding a fierce vengeance. 'When? Jesus Christ! What's happened to my wife? You told me she'd been attacked . . . you didn't say a damned thing about this!'

Dr Wynter reached over and arranged the sheets neatly around the sleeping girl's throat. 'She's in no pain,' he said. 'The sedative is still in effect.' He turned to face the younger man. 'Mr Raines, I want to be candid with you. Lt Hepelmann asked me to withhold some things from you so as not to . . . overly excite you.'

'Jesus Christ!'

Dr Wynter held up a hand. 'Which I agreed with. I felt . . . telling you certain things would not be in order. These marks are first-degree burns. I've had two skin specialists examine her during the night. I called them out of bed. They both came to the same conclusion. Burns. Like a moderate sunburn. Mr Raines, I've been in medicine a very long time. Even probably before you were born. But never, never have I seen anything like this. These are the handprints of the man who attacked your wife.'

Dazed and suddenly very tired, he shook his head. 'Is that supposed to explain anything?'

'I'm sorry,' Dr Wynter said.

Joe had moved to the edge of the bed. He put his hand out and gingerly touched the print on his wife's cheek. It was still

25

hot. When he pressed the flesh the print whitened away, but when the blood flowed back it re-emerged in a sear of red.

'What could have caused this . . .? My God, the way these marks . . .?'

'I've never seen anything like it. Neither have the police. There should be no lasting tissue damage. It should peel within a few days, exactly as a sunburn would. But the heat from the man who attacked her left its mark, amazingly, on her flesh. And there is no way I can stand here and say that I understand it.'

'And you didn't want me to see until you could explain.'

'Or at the very least give an excuse why we couldn't. One theory has been offered by a psychologist friend of mine, though I tend to discount it because he said I woke him in the middle of a nightmare. He proposes that it's a psychological reaction to the attack, a mind-over-body sort of thing. But I am convinced that those are burns from some sort of . . . unnatural source of heat.

'So you can see for yourself,' Dr Wynter continued, 'why we must keep this as quiet as possible. Our observation will continue for another week or so at the very least. We wouldn't want any of those *National Enquirer* journalists nosing around, would we? All right?'

'Yes,' he said. 'All right. You say she's in no pain?'

'No pain.'

'Jesus,' he breathed, stunned by the patchwork of hands that violated her body, though their owner was now God knows where. 'The man,' he said after a moment. 'The man who attacked her. Did he . . . you know . . . did he . . .?'

'In emergency our usual procedure was followed. She was cleaned and probed. The nurses administered diethylstilbestrol. We'll conduct a thorough pelvic-vaginal exam. But from all indications there was no spermatozoal contact. Evidently the man was interrupted just prior to climax.'

'Oh man,' said Joe. 'Another week? I've got some insurance, but I don't know . . . I'm not a rich man.'

On the bed Mary Kate stirred. She whimpered and her arms weakly flailed the air above her.

He sat beside her and took both her hands. They were cold. 'Don't worry. I'm here,' he said. 'I'm here.'

She stirred again and finally looked up at him. Her face was swollen and her hair was dishevelled and dirty. She said, 'Joe? Joe?' and, reaching out, she clung to him and cried bitterly until the tears had wet the front of his shirt.

4

The summer moved like something alive. It weakened through August, losing days like scorching drops of blood.

The handprints peeled away, as the doctors had theorized, and Mary Kate came home from the hospital. She adjusted well to everyday life and no mention was made of the attack; in fact, it seemed to Joe that she was much more content with both her job and their life together. Once, though, they watched a television programme about a rapist on the loose in Manhattan and she suddenly began laughing, quietly at first but with a rising, frightening intensity, until she burst into tears and he held her as she trembled.

Lt Hepelmann telephoned to ask if she would come down to his precinct stationhouse to page through their mug files. She declined, explaining to Joe that if she ever saw the man again she felt sure she'd go into hysterics. He told Hepelmann and put down the phone before the policeman could protest.

There were other calls and visits: from Dr Wynter, who told them he wanted to check with Mary Kate every few weeks because the 'handprint symptom', as he now called it, was something he would not soon forget: from her parents, who brought her flowers and bottles of wine and who spoke to him with the tongues of serpents.

One night while they sat in the dark before black-and-white figures on the television screen, she looked at him and he saw the images reflected, glistening, in her eyes. 'I love you,' she said.

He sat still. The phrase was neither familiar nor easy for him.

'I do. I really do. It's just in the last few weeks that I've realized I love you so much.' She put her arms around his neck and kissed him lightly on the lips, her hair soft against his face.

He returned her kiss. Her tongue slipped into his mouth and explored it like a wet Columbus, though the world was hardly new. He felt his body answering the call. 'All right,' he said with a wry smile. 'You want something. I can always tell.'

She held him tight and kissed him again. She always smelled, he thought, like newly mown grass in a wide wet field. Probably his Midwest 'tied to the land' imagination showing. She leaned over and nibbled softly at his ear. 'I want,' she whispered, 'a child.'

She followed his eyes. They slid away from her towards the television screen. 'Mary Kate,' he said in a low, restrained voice, 'we've gone through all this before. There will be a time when a child will be welcome. You know that. But right now we have a hard enough time supporting ourselves, much less another mouth. And I wouldn't want to bring up a child in this neighbourhood.'

'That ivy-covered suburban cottage you've been dreaming about,' she said, 'is something we're never going to have. Can't you see that? Now we don't have anything. Don't look at me like that. You know I'm right. All we own right now is what we have in this apartment, things that are either yours or mine. We don't have anything we can call "ours".'

'Come on,' he said. 'A child is not a toy. You don't pick up a child and play with it like a doll. You'd have to quit your job, I'd have to work a double shift. Hell, no.'

She disentangled herself from him and stood staring through the open window, her arms folded across her chest. Finally she turned to him again. 'I need something,' she said softly. 'I really do. I want something to be different . . . I don't know what it is.'

'You're coming down off a traumatic experience.' He winced. Christ! Don't bring that up! 'You need some time to rest, baby. Don't get yourself all upset about this. We'll talk about it later.'

Mary Kate watched him, her dark brown eyes unyielding in a face suddenly pale and hard. She said, 'We could get a loan to cover my time off from work.'

'Mary Kate. Please.'

She came over beside him and put his hand to her cheek. He was amazed to feel tears. What the hell is this? he wondered. She'd never before gotten this emotional about a child. Usually, after he'd explained to her the economics of the thing, she would drop the subject without argument. This time she was hanging on with a tenacity he'd never seen before. 'It would be a beautiful child,' she said softly.

He eased her over the chair arm into his lap and whispered, 'I'm sure it would be,' kissing the tears away as they danced down the fine plains of her face.

'Now,' he said, nudging her chin to root her out of this mood, 'what is "it" going to be? Can't have them both ways, you know. Got to have one or another.'

She smiled and sniffled. 'You're teasing me. I don't like to be teased.'

'I'm not teasing. We're going to have a child someday. We should at least decide now what "it" is going to be.'

'A boy. I want a boy.'

'Everybody wants boys. What happens to girls when they're born and they find out their parents wanted boys? That's the beginnings of the inferiority feelings women have. A girl would be nice. Pink diapers scattered all over the floor, dolls lying on the chair so that when I sit down something squeaks and it scares hell out of me . . .'

'You're teasing again . . .'

'You want a boy, huh? That's all right. Then there are those little plastic soldiers that puncture your bare feet when you walk into the kitchen for a midnight snack. That's all right.'

Mary Kate snuggled closer to his chest and held tightly to him, her hands gently swirling at the back of his neck.

'A big businessman, maybe that's what he'll be,' he envisioned, kissing her forehead and then the closed lids of her eyes. 'Maybe the President.' He reconsidered for a few seconds. 'No, no. Scratch that. But somebody important.'

As the television continued flickering its shades of fantasy, he picked her up and carried her to the sofa that, when kicked in the right place, turned down into a spring-mattressed bed. He laid her down between the cool blue sheets and then, undressing, joined her there. She twined her arms and legs around him in a sweet captivity.

29

He made love to her in a soft, quiet way. Her body, always responsive, reacted to the caress of his finger-tips. She cried out and he took her cries deep into his throat. But always in his mind was the knowledge that someone else had enjoyed her warmth. Someone else, held between her thighs, had moved his body powerfully within her. The vision nagged relentlessly at him and he sought to control it by concentrating only on her body; the firm ripened breasts, the smooth light down on her arms and thighs, the barely healed scratches that ran the length of her belly . . .

And when he slept, enclosed by her limbs, he dreamed of those marks he had first seen beneath the crisp hospital sheets. Now they moved in red circles on her body, around and around until every inch of her flesh was burnt and swollen. And then a fiery hand planted itself on his face and sought to gouge out his eyes and hold them steaming on the tips of vapourish fingers.

When he awakened from his troubled sleep sweat was cold at his temples. He rose quietly from wet sheets and stood in the darkness, staring at her where she lay coiled on the mattress. Behind him the television's test pattern cast a black-shadowed grid on the opposite wall. He switched it off.

Those nightmates, he thought, are becoming too real. They had begun when Mary Kate returned from the hospital. When his mind was unguarded in sleep they crept out from their hiding places and sowed the seeds of hysteria. They now hid, rasping, in corners, listening, listening. Waiting for him to lose strength and return to the bed. And when his eyes had closed they would ooze from their crevices to touch hot fingers to his forehead. Against them he was defenceless. What was that theory, he asked himself, about the subconscious mind being the ruler of the body? That the subconscious mind, through dreams, spoke in cryptic scrawls of mental pain? Shit on it, he protested to himself. I'm just tired as hell.

He went into the bathroom and drank a glass of cold water, then returned to bed, and slipped against Mary Kate's warmth. As an afterthought he threw aside the sheets again and rechecked the door to make certain it was locked.

In the morning he was stirred by the sun as it lay in golden stripes across his face. She was cooking bacon and eggs for him – something she rarely did any more. Usually it was only cold cereal and a pot of reheated coffee. He made a conscious effort to be pleasant to her as she moved about the tiny nook of a kitchen. There was no mention of babies and he drank his fresh strong coffee while talking about the new dispatch man they'd hired at the cab company.

During the weeks that followed she ceased to talk about wanting children. He was honestly relieved not to have to answer her questions about why they couldn't afford a baby. The frequency of his nightmares diminished until, finally, he lost his fear of giving himself up to the darkness of sleep. Mary Kate settled back into a regular work schedule, though now she always left the diner before dusk, and it seemed to him that his tips were getting better. He was certain it was his imagination but he felt inspired and new all the same. He began, after a while, to entertain thoughts of returning to school.

He soon decided to do so without consulting Mary Kate, and telephoned a friend he had met in a literary criticism class three semesters before. 'Hello? Kenneth? This is Joe Raines. Right, from Marsh's class.'

'Oh yeah. Hey, I haven't seen you for a while. You've been hiding or something? What'd you come out with?'

'B. Just barely. Listen, I'm thinking about getting back into school next semester and I'd like to know what's going on, who's teaching what. I'm taking a day off Friday and I . . . we . . . wondered if you and Terri could drop over.'

'You're still hacking, huh?'

'Yeah. It's pretty rough but it beats working.'

'I know how it is. God, you and I have got a lot of ground to cover. It's been almost a year since I've seen you.'

'Well,' said Joe, 'I've gotten caught up in things, I guess.'

'Friday? Okay then, that sounds great. I'll pick up a semester catalogue for you and bring it over. What time? Do you want us to bring a bottle of wine?'

'We'll take care of that. Would seven be okay?'

'Fine. You're still at the same place? The sweat-box?'

'Right.' He laughed weakly. 'The sweatbox.'

'Okay then, we'll see you Friday. Thanks for calling.'

'Sure. Goodbye.'

The idea of returning to school excited him. For him attending classes was a release from the hot chrome crush of Manhattan traffic. The cavalier poets would sing in his ears instead of the metal voice of a taxi meter.

That night after work when he told Mary Kate of his decision, he was surprised at her genuine enthusiasm. On Friday afternoon they shopped for sandwich meats at the delicatessen on the next block, then went to the neighbourhood liquor store to look for two bottles of a good inexpensive wine. Their arms filled with packages, they kissed on the front steps of their building, and a small kid laughed at them from behind a fudge popsicle.

Kenneth Parks and his wife, Terri, were the kind who attended student-sponsored bonfires and campus Bogart festivals. He was tall and lean, the perfect build for a basketball player though he had told Joe he was never athletically inclined. She was his perfect complement, a girl of medium height with flashing green eyes and long chestnut-coloured hair. Dressed in clothes that were neither too old nor too new but just, as the rage demanded, 'lived in', they were a magazine couple, and Joe immediately felt a little insecure as they entered his cluttered, poster-walled apartment.

'The man is here,' said Parks, grasping his friend's hand. 'Haven't seen your face for a long time. I almost forgot what you looked like.'

Joe closed the door behind them and introduced his wife. She stood smiling and composed. 'Joe's told me about you,' she said to Parks. 'Aren't you the guy who explores the caves? A spe – ' she began hesitantly.

'Spelunker. Yeah, off and on I guess.' He took the glass of wine Joe offered and gave it to his wife. 'Used to do it every weekend when I was a kid.'

'What do you do for a living?'

'Well . . .' He glanced over at his wife, whose eyes were bright and empty over the rim of the wineglass. 'Terri's father is kind of . . . lending us the money we need until we finish school.' He playfully punched Joe's arm. 'Old buddy, only one more semester to go and then I pound my feet flat looking for a job.'

'And they're hard as hell to come by. I was lucky to get the one I have, believe me.'

Terri sat with the wineglass in her hand, transfixed by a poster on the opposite wall that showed King Kong atop the Empire

State Building, crushing a bullet-spitting biplane in a hairy fist. 'Do you like our apartment?' Mary Kate asked.

Parks had opened a semester catalogue on the scarred coffee table before him and indicated courses he had marked with a ballpoint pen. 'And Dr Ezell is teaching my European Lit Forum. That's supposed to be one of the major gut-grabbers this semester.'

'Oh yeah? I suppose Ezell hasn't eased up any?'

'Hell, no. That guy should've retired years ago. He mixes his lectures up, still. Like that final we had where he was asking us questions from another comparative lit course. My God.'

Joe grunted. 'Listen, can I get you a sandwich or something?'

'No, thanks. This is fine.' He glanced over to where Mary Kate and Terri had begun a conversation of their own. Terri's eyes were widening. 'So,' he said flatly, swinging his gaze back to Joe. 'You want to get back into it.'

'Yes, I do. I've got to. I need something more than what I'm doing. I mean, sure, driving a cab is okay. Really. I hear some fabulously funny stories and the tips are fair. But I don't want to stay there, like I'm locked behind the wheel or something. I've got to move in some kind of direction. I've got to take that first step.'

'And you want to complete your degree. You've only got two more semesters to go, right?'

'Three more.'

'The worst thing you can do,' Parks said, 'is to start and then quit. What happened? You didn't have the money?'

'Yeah. I don't know. I thought I could make it with what I had. And I was stupid. I wasn't prepared the way I should have been. My grades started falling off and I just lost interest in studying.' Mary Kate said something to him which he didn't hear. He nodded at her as if to say, Just a minute and I'll listen to you. Terri watched them as if she were frozen. 'I wasn't prepared for the grind of both school and work and it took me under.'

'I guess I'm lucky in that respect. Terri's father is making it very easy on – '

Terri was nudging her husband in the ribs. He looked at her and then at Mary Kate.

Mary Kate's eyes were fixed on Joe's face. 'What have we

decided to name our baby?' she asked again.

Terri said, 'She's been telling me all about it. I think that's great. Really.' Her voice was quiet and breathless, as if her lungs were grabbing for air. Joe thought something was wrong with her.

He asked, 'What?'

Mary Kate watched him silently. Terri grinned into his face with long horselike teeth.

'I'm pregnant,' Mary Kate said. She looked at Terri. 'He didn't know. This is a surprise.'

'I can tell it's knocked him on his ass,' said Parks, slapping his friend on the back. 'Here, here. Let's drink a toast. Everybody fill their glasses. Come on, Joe, drink up. You'll need your strength to open those diaper pins. Here's to the expectant mother. Come on, Joe, snap out of it.'

'How long have you been pregnant?' Terri asked. 'That's great. Isn't that great, Kenny?'

'A little less than a month,' Mary Kate said. She watched Joe as he stared into the depths of his wineglass, swirling the liquid round and round as his lips slowly tightened.

'A baby,' Terri was saying, as if mesmerized by the word, 'a baby. We want to have a baby sometime too, don't we, Kenny? Sometime when we finish school.'

He lifted the glass to his lips. 'Sure, sure,' he said. 'Damn. A kid. That's really something.'

Terri rambled on about sweet babies in cradles surrounded by squeaking Donald Ducks and pink rattles. Mary Kate's eyes never moved.

'This,' Joe said very quietly, 'finishes it.'

Parks hadn't heard him. He leaned over and said, 'What'd you say, old buddy?'

He could no longer contain the rage. It was blood-boiling, bursting behind his eyes; it was bile that gathered in his stomach and rocketed, geyserlike, towards his mouth. It overcame him and suddenly he was standing, his eyes hot and wild, the glass of wine leaving his hand. The glass shattered with a loud, pistol-like *crack*! and wine smeared along the wall like a thick track of blood. It ran down in rivulets to an oval pool on the floor.

Terri squealed as if someone had struck her. She sat, her

34

upper torso swaying slightly, giddy on her one glass of wine.

Joe stood staring at the eye of blood. His arms hung limply at his sides; he no longer seemed to have any muscle. The act of throwing the glass had drained him of all energy. Now even his speech was faint and weak: 'I . . . I've made a mess. I'll have to clean it up.'

A moment before, a candle had burned within him, something to warm him and give strength to go forward. Now someone had suddenly put it out; he seemed to smell the sharp odour of a smoking wick. He stared dumbly at the broken glass and the pool of wine until Mary Kate went to the kitchen and returned with paper towels and trash can and began to clean the floor.

Parks was struggling to maintain a smile. It was awkward and lopsided. His bewildered eyes made him look wild and embarrassed, as if he had just stepped onstage without knowing what the play was about. He took his wife's arm and stood up. 'We'd better go,' he said apologetically. 'Joe, call me, okay? About your classes?'

Joe nodded.

Terri said to Mary Kate, 'I think it's wonderful. I hope he's not too upset. Men are like that.'

'Good night,' said Parks, pushing his wife ahead of him, and Mary Kate closed the door after them.

She stood with her back to the wall, watching him as he continued nodding at his absent friend's last question.

'A month?' he asked her finally, avoiding her face. Instead he studied the red drops that slowly ran the length of the wall. 'A whole month and you didn't tell me before this?'

'I didn't know how to – '

He looked at her, his eyes burning. Over his shoulder King Kong glowered at her as well. 'That's impossible. Unless you've been lying to me about taking the Pill. You were lying to me, weren't you? Goddammit!'

'No,' she said softly. 'I haven't been lying.'

'I don't care about that now!' His anger sparked again. He took a step forward and she realized, with the harsh coldness of fear, that she was trapped against the wall. She had seen him lose his temper before. Once, after a heated telephone argument with her father over money, he had torn the telephone from the wall and smashed it to the floor; he had jerked lamps up off tables and hurled them crashing across the room until finally she left the apartment, wandering for two days until found by a police officer in the park. She had always been afraid of his unrestrained anger, though he had never before raised a hand to her. Now his red-rimmed eyes glared vengefully.

'I want to know,' he said in a loud, ragged voice, 'when you decided we'd have a child! I want to know when you decided to forget every goddamned thing I have ever told you about our having a child!'

'I always took my pills,' she said. 'Always. I promise.'

'Shit!' he yelled at her, and the word was like a hand across her cheek. She winced from the blow and stood breathless. He reached out for an ashtray, a ceramic bowl that had been given to them as a wedding gift by one of her uncles, and tensed to smash it across through the kitchen and into the far wall. The weight of it in his hand made him suddenly stop, realizing the utter futility of shattering bits of clay to avenge his bitter disappointment and, worse, to dispel his conviction that she had finally, utterly, overstepped her bounds. He let the ashtray drop to the floor and stood, his chest heaving, too confused and angry to do anything.

She sensed a gap in the tension. 'I swear to you,' she said quickly before his anger could peak again, 'I've never missed my pills. I don't know. I felt that I should have an examination about two weeks ago and the doctor told me. I got the bill out of the box before you could find it and paid it myself.'

'He's wrong!' said Joe. 'The doctor is wrong!'

'No,' she said. 'No.'

He sat down slowly on the sofa and put his face in his hands. 'You don't get pregnant unless you . . . Shit. Oh man. Mary Kate, I cannot afford this. I'll go under . . . I swear before God I'll go under!'

She waited until she felt certain that his anger had subsided. She came over and quietly knelt on the floor beside him, taking his hands and pressing them against her cheek. 'We can get a loan. Maybe from my father.'

'Sure,' he said. 'He won't let me have a dime!'

'I'll talk to him. I mean it.'

He shrugged. After a moment he said. 'You'll talk to him?'

'We can get a loan from him and we'll be okay,' Mary Kate said. 'It'll be rough; we know it will be. But other people have kids and they make it. They scrimp and save like hell but they do make it, Joe.'

He withdrew his hands and looked down into her innocent, wide-eyed face. Through tightly drawn lips he said, 'I don't mean a loan to keep the child, Mary Kate. I mean a loan for an abortion.'

'Goddamn you!' she cried out, drawing away from him. The tears burst from her eyes and streamed down over her cheeks. 'No abortion! Nobody in the world could make me go through that!'

'You're not going to break me,' he snarled bitterly at her. 'That's what you want to do! You want to finish my ass off!'

'No,' she said, her teeth clenched. 'No abortion. I mean it. I don't care what I have to do. I'll work a double shift, night and day. I'll sell my blood, I'll sell my body. I don't care. No abortion.'

Joe faced her, his lips working but no words coming out. He wondered if this was what made so many men just walk out the door and never come back, this sudden and terrible power she had obtained, this awesome force that came with the knowledge that she harboured a child in her body. The King is dead. Long live the Queen. But when the hell did I die? he asked himself. Two years ago? A minute ago? When?

Something was working its way out from a deep place of tissues and bone. It swam up through her blood and surfaced across her face. It distorted her features and left her glowering at him like an animal. She said, 'The baby is mine.'

He slumped back on the sofa, wanting instinctively to length-en the distance between himself and the woman whose white teeth glittered in the darkness. She had placed defeat like a crown of black thorns on his head. Her face, as lifeless and determined as some ancient concrete death mask, ate its way past his eyes and hung marionette-like in his brain, dancing there like a grim shade of what she had been only a few moments before. He shuddered suddenly and wondered why. In an empty, toneless voice he said, 'You're killing me, Mary Kate. I don't know why or how but you're killing me all the same. And this business about a child. This is the last nail in my coffin.'

'Then lie in it,' she said.

She rose and stood with her back to him. Her eyes, reflected in the window glass, were fierce and uncompromising. I will have my baby, she said to the wind that blew newspapers in the narrow street below. No one on earth will take my baby away from me now. And standing there she suddenly sensed someone standing beside her, a man whose pale thin hand touched her shoulder like a burning brand.

I will have my baby.

5

The child was born at the end of a turbulent March, while the wind outside Mary Kate's hospital room blew snow past the window in wild high flurries. She heard the scream of the storm both before and after labour, even as she was wheeled down linoleum corridors into Recovery.

The child was not beautiful. It was a boy with tight flat features and piercing, inquisitive blue eyes that she knew would dim to a much darker hue. But still she gratefully took the child from the nurse's arms and held him close to her breast to feed. The child was very quiet, barely moving except to grasp the flesh of her swollen teat with his tiny fists.

She didn't care for Joe's choice of a name for the baby, Edward, after one of his more obscure English poets. Instead, she wanted a name that had been in her family for years. So on the records of birth was written Jeffrey Harper Raines, over Joe's mild protests that the name Jeffrey currently belonged to one of his least favourite of her cousins.

When they brought him home from the hospital they lowered him into a crib he would share with red-lipped rubber animals. Above the crib, attached to the ceiling, was a hanging mobile of grinning plastic fish. She would move the fish in a tight circle and Jeffrey always sat in silence, watching. They arranged the crib so the child could see the television. It disturbed Mary

Kate in the first few weeks that Jeffrey was home, that the child so seldom cried. She complained about it to Joe, citing tears as a healthy response in children, and he replied, 'So? Maybe he's satisfied.'

But Jeffrey never laughed either. Even on Saturday mornings during cat-and-mouse cartoons and Howdy Doody reruns, Jeffrey's eyes roamed the tight confines of the apartment while his new teeth gripped at a pacifier. The lack of emotion in the child's eyes worried her; they were like the eyes of a fish or a snake, desiring either the cold sea or the depths of a den.

Sometimes when she held the child she thought it didn't seem to want to be near her. He would fight against her grasp and, when she pulled him closer, he would reach out to pinch her flesh between his fingers. Looking at Jeffrey, actually examining his features, unsettled her more and more as time went on. He didn't seem to resemble her at all, nor did he resemble Joe, as much as she imagined this to be the case. He would comment drily on how the baby would eventually look just like him but she knew it was far from the truth. And what was the truth? Was it perhaps locked away in her subconscious, lurking there where she remembered dimly a screaming ambulance and nurses white against emergency walls, groping, groping, groping?

Despite her disappointment, she never allowed herself to cry. She always stopped thinking about the child before the rush of tears, of mad whirling self-doubt, of figures framed in darkness, could begin.

Joe had begun working a double shift three days a week at the cab company. He came home on those days in the early morning hours, ready to drink a can or two of beer and fall into bed, sometimes without even undressing. Some days he went to work in the same clothes he had worn the day before and slept in; sometimes he went without shaving for days at a time; he had neither the time nor the energy to even consider a return to college, and always his sharp accusing eyes cut her to the quick. He barely spoke to her any more unless he found it necessary, and she learned to turn her back on him in bed.

In three month's time, as the apartment began to become cluttered with rubber toys and diapers and smelled of sourness and milk, Joe took to leaving on rambling walks, often not returning until Mary Kate had been asleep for some time.

Wakened by the opening door, she would hear him enter, often drunkenly, and mutter to himself things she couldn't quite hear. The bastard, she would say to herself. The stupid drunken bastard. And then she would say sharply, without looking at him, 'Take your clothes off before you come to bed.'

Joe's sleep was becoming more and more restless; often he cried out in the dark of night. Then she would hear him get out of bed, drink a glass of water in the bathroom and, oddly, rattle the door chain to make certain it held securely. But she never moved to show him she had awakened, and when he returned to bed she felt sure he lay for a very long while with his eyes open in the dark, just staring at her back.

More than once she awakened to see him framed in the square of light from the window, looking down into the crib at the sleeping child. He would stand rigid with his fists white-knuckled, staring down at the little quiet form in white baby pyjamas. In the mornings she would find Jeffrey already awake, his hands curled around the safety bars as if he wanted to escape the prison of infancy prematurely. His dark eyes pierced her; he seemed to be glaring through her at her sleeping husband. Once when Joe held the child in his arms in a rare show of fatherly affection, his eye was almost jabbed as Jeffrey pointed with a finger at the fish mobile. Joe said, 'Shit!' and eased the child back down into the crib, rubbing his injured eye.

She became fearful of Joe. He became increasingly short-tempered towards the child, as the hot summer fell upon them like a slavering animal. Jeffrey's eyes grew darker. They became black slits that gleamed with some sort of childish intelligence; his hair became straight and black. His nose lengthened and Mary Kate saw, with a rush of alarm, that there was going to be a cleft in the chin. There were no cleft chins in her family, as far as she knew, nor in Joe's. She traced the beginnings of the cleft with her finger, hearing somewhere the faint wail of a siren across the roof of the city. And Joe had noticed it as well. He would pop open a beer and watch the child as Jeffrey played on the floor. Mary Kate was certain that, if he could, Joe would lean forward and kick the child in the face.

As Jeffrey played with blocks strewn across the carpet one evening in late summer, she sat before him on the floor and examined his face. The black eye slits watched her incuriously, daring her to maintain a steady gaze, as he built towers of multicoloured blocks. The thin fingers moved not with the clumsiness of an infant, but instead with a practised adult grace.

'Jeffrey,' Mary Kate whispered.

The child slowly looked up from his blocks.

Mary Kate was forced to avert her gaze from his intense black stare. Looking into those eyes made her feel breathless and dizzy, as if she had been drinking. His eyes were as immobile as those in a painting.

Mary Kate reached out to smooth his swirling mass of black hair. 'My Jeffrey,' she said.

With one arm Jeffrey swung out and through the tower of building blocks. They scattered across the room, and one of them struck Mary Kate in the mouth. She cried out, startled.

Jeffrey leaned forward, his eyes wide and entranced, and Mary Kate shivered. She took his hand and slapped it, saying, 'Bad baby! Bad baby!' but Jeffrey paid no attention. Instead, with his free hand, he touched his mother's lip. The fingers came away with a single drop of blood.

Horrified and hypnotized by his black, unwavering stare, she watched him put his fingers to his mouth, saw the tongue dart from between lips to lick the red liquid, saw the eyes gleam briefly like a light shining far away in the night. She recovered herself and said, 'Bad for baby!' trying to slap his hand again, but he turned his back on her and began gathering up the building blocks.

Autumn came, then winter. Outside the wind was unnervingly shrill, day after day. Leaves clattered along the gutters. Ice and snow caked the lids of garbage cans. Throughout the winter bleakness Mary Kate grew more distant from Joe. It was as if he had given up; now he ceased even to try to communicate with her at all. He had long since forgotten that she shared a bed with him and now she knew it was only a matter of time before he would leave the apartment one night for 'a walk' and never come back. Already he was sometimes gone for a day at a time and, afterwards, when she would scream at him about having to make up excuses for the cab dispatcher, he would simply spin around on his heel and disappear again through the doorway. And then, finally, he would come home unshaven and dirty, his body reeking of beer and sweat, stumbling through the doorway muttering something about the child. 'You fool,' she would tell him. 'You pitiful fool.'

And one night less than a week before the child's first birthday, after leaving Jeffrey with Joe for a few moments while she went down to the delicatessen for groceries, she returned home to find him calmly undressing the child over a tub of steaming water. The child's hands were gripped around his shoulders; the eyes were narrowed and cunning. Across Joe's unshaven face were red marks that looked like scratches. An empty wine bottle lay broken on the yellow bathroom tiles.

She dropped the sack. A glass broke. 'What do you think you're doing?' she screamed as Joe held the struggling child over the hot water. He looked around, his eyes bleary and frightened, and she twisted Jeffrey away from him to hug the child to her breast.

'My God!' she said, her shrill voice echoing from the tiles. 'You're crazy! My God!'

He sat, his shoulders sagging, on the edge of the tub. His face seemed drained of blood, the only colour the grey circles beneath his eyes. 'One more minute,' he said in a distant, dead, emotionless voice. 'If you'd only stayed away one minute more. Just one.'

'My God!'

'Just one,' he said, 'and it would've been over.'

She screamed at him, 'You're crazy! My God! Oh my God Jesus!'

'Yes,' he said. 'You call out for Jesus. You do that. But it's too late. Oh God it's too late for that. You look at me. *Look at me, I said!* I'm dying . . . inch by inch . . . I'm dying, and you know it.' He looked around and saw the fragments of glass on the floor. 'Oh no,' he whimpered. 'My last bottle.'

As he stood up and began walking towards her, she backed away with the child in her arms. He caught himself in the bathroom doorway and stood there with his head down and mouth open, as if he were about to be sick. 'I have good dreams at night, Mary Kate. Oh those dreams I have. You know what I dream about? You really want to know? I dream of faces that come flying around me screaming my name. A thousand . . .

42

ten thousand times a night they wake me. And I dream of a child's gouging out my eyes until I'm blind. Oh Jesus Christ I need a drink!'

'You're crazy,' said Mary Kate, her tongue slowly going numb so she had to concentrate to get the two words out.

'I thought maybe if I got away from here, if I slept somewhere else, it would help. If I slept in the subway, or in a movie, or even in a church, I thought it would help. But no. You know what else I dream, Mary Kate? My sweet Mary Kate . . . you want to know? I dream of finding you on your knees, my sweet wife, sucking the penis of a man with the face of a child. *That child in your arms now.*'

She caught back a cry and saw his mad eyes darting at the long shadows in the room. 'That child is not mine, Mary Kate,' he said. 'I'm certain of that now. And you've known all along. I don't care how it's done, Mary Kate, I don't care who does it. That child must die. We can put the body in a trash can somewhere across town; we can throw the body in the river.'

He stood staring at her, pleading, and she saw him through eyes that suddenly filled with tears. 'Oh God you need help, Joe. You need help.'

'No one can give me help.' He staggered weakly to the window and stood with his forehead steaming the cold glass as his hands scratched across the cracked walls. He closed his eyes. 'Oh Jesus Christ.'

Jeffrey stirred in her arms and moved against her. 'I love you I love you I love you,' she murmured inaudibly to the child. 'He's crazy. This man is crazy and he's going to try to kill you. Oh God.'

The child's hands moved at her face. It burrowed against her for warmth and when she looked down she saw his strange hot stare.

Joe leaned against the window, breathing harshly. She saw his breath fan out in a mist across the dirty glass. Tears streaming hotly down her face, she put Jeffrey back into his crib and listened to Joe's wild muttering. Jeffrey sat up, squeezing his face against the safety bars. He'll try to kill both of us, she said to herself. Both of us. Goddamn his soul! He's going to kill my baby . . . and then me so I'll never tell anyone what happened!

43

Going back into the bathroom, she watched her tears splash the long jagged shards of the broken wine bottle on the floor. He'll kill us both. Both both both. He's gone crazy.

She picked up the neck of the bottle and stepped towards him.

Joe started to turn away from the window and opened his mouth to say something.

She took two quick steps and was upon him, driving the jagged glass into his chest, beneath the collarbone. He grunted with the shock of the blow and stood, his mouth still open, looking down at the front of his shirt. When the racing pain had arrived at his brain, he cried out wildly and pushed her away. She dislodged the broken bottle and struck again; his drink-slowed hand was not enough to stop her. The glass pierced through the rib cage into lung tissue. He coughed a shower of red droplets that sprayed across her face and blouse. She struck at his face. He frantically backed away, bleeding from his chest and cheeks, and still she attacked, like something wild and relentless, her arm upraised for a second thrust at his face.

His panic carried him backward and, his arms flailing, smashed him through the window. His face, white and with terror-stricken eyes, went over the ledge and the last thing she saw before he fell were his fingertips, reaching desperately for the windowsill.

Below the window his body lay sprawled wildly on the concrete, the neck twisted at an angle to the torso.

Someone, a man in a brown overcoat, stood over the corpse and stared up at her with frightened eyes.

Behind her, in his crib, Jeffrey pointed up at the dancing mobile. 'Mommy,' he said in a saliva-thick voice, 'see pretty fish?'

6

The boys, chattering and rough-housing like young jungle-fresh monkeys, filed into the lunchroom with a burst of noise, taking their usual seats around a long table scarred with the initials of those who had come before them.

Sister Miriam watched them from behind her severe black-rimmed eye glasses, waiting patiently until all thirty were seated. Even sitting around the table, waiting for grace to be said before lunch, the children still poked each other with the rough curious hands of ten-year-olds. She said above their noise, 'All right. Can I have quiet, please?'

They settled like food bubbling in a pot and watched her as she stood before them, a dark grandmother in her black habit. She held up her clipboard. It was her responsibility to make certain they'd all returned from their recreation period. She knew their names and faces well, but still there was the possibility that one of them, perhaps one of the less bright ones, had managed to straggle into the forest around the orphanage. It had happened once before, many years ago when she had first begun her work here, before the fence was put up, and there had almost been serious consequences for the child. Now she took no chances.

'We'll have roll call before our lunch,' she told them, as she always told them. 'James Patterson Antonelli?'

'Here.'

'Thomas Keene Billings?'

'Here.'

'Edward Andrew Bayless?'

'Present.'

'Jerome Darkowski?'

'President.' Giggles and howls from the children. Sister Miriam looked up sharply.

'You have half an hour for lunch before the next group comes in, children. If you choose to be silly you simply waste your time. Now I asked for silence, didn't I?' She turned back to her clipboard. 'Gregory Holt Frazier?'

'Here.'

She went through the alphabet, nearing his name. Sometimes she wished that he would leave, that he would turn his back on the home and disappear like a wraith into the thicket, leaving perhaps only a shred of torn clothing on the fence to indicate that he had ever been there at all. No, no, she said inwardly. Forgive me. I don't mean to think such things. She glanced up, her eyes nervous behind the glasses, and saw him sitting there, at the head of the table where he always sat, waiting for her to get on to his name. He was smiling faintly, as if he knew what unprofessional disorder lay behind her mask-like features.

'Jeffrey Harper Raines.'

He didn't answer.

The children had stopped moving.

They waited.

He waited.

She cleared her throat and kept her head down, away from them. She caught the odour of hamburgers cooking back in the kitchen. 'Jeffrey Harper Raines,' she repeated.

He sat in silence, his hands folded before him on the table. His black eyes, narrow slits in a pale face, challenged her to challenge him.

Sister Miriam dropped the clipboard down by her side. Really! This nonsense had gone on quite long enough! 'Jeffrey, I called your name out twice. You failed to answer. You will write your name two hundred times during your study hour and present that paper to me.' She looked to the next name on the list. 'Edgar Oliver Tortorelli.'

But it was not that child who answered. This was the voice of another child. Him.

'I didn't hear my name called, Sister,' he said, hissing the word Sister so she thought at first he was going to utter a profanity.

She blinked. She felt suddenly hot. Trays and plates clattered in the kitchen. She said, 'I called your name. Children, didn't I call Jeffrey's name?' She winced. No, no. Don't bring the other children into this. This is something between him and me, not them.

They squirmed in their chairs, their eyes moving like little

46

dark marbles between the boy and the woman.

'My name is Baal,' the boy said. 'I do not answer to any other name.'

'Now don't start that nonsense again, young – '

The crack of his voice stopped her short. 'I will not write a paper. I will not answer to any name but my own.'

She stood helpless under his steady gaze. And she saw the grin slowly spread over his mouth, lifting the lips into a cruel smile, yet those eyes . . . those eyes remained as cold and deadly as upraised rifle barrels. Sister Miriam slammed the clipboard down on the table. The other children jumped and giggled nervously, but not him. He sat motionless with his hands folded before him.

Sister Miriam looked through a doorway and called to the sisters in the kitchen, 'They're ready for their lunches now.' Without another glance at the children, she pushed through the heavy doors that led out of the dining hall. Down dim corridors lined with classrooms, through the main corridor, past the reception area, out stained-glass doors on to the great wide porch and past a grey-metal sign near the steps that read *The Valiant Saints Home for Boys*. Out in the far playground, rimmed by the forest that was beginning to lose its late-autumn colours of red and yellow, another group of boys ran round and round in circles like bees about a hive.

She traversed the courtyard and started across the concrete drive for a small brick building, so dissimilar in its construction to the rambling gable-eyed hulk of the orphanage, that housed the administrative offices. Beside that building, ringed by trees that glowed bright yellow in the sunlight, was the orphanage chapel.

Sister Miriam entered the brick building and continued through quiet wine-carpeted hallways to a small office with the name *Emory T. Dunn* in gold script on the door. His receptionist, a frail woman with a bitter face. looked up at her. 'Sister Miriam? Can I help you?'

'Yes. I'd like to see Father Dunn, please.'

'I'm sorry. He has an appointment in ten minutes. I believe we have a nice family for the Latta child.'

'I have to see him,' Sister Miriam said, and the receptionist watched, astonished, as the other woman knocked on the door without listening to what she, an orphanage legend as Father Dunn's receptionist for twenty-one years, had said.

'Come in,' said a voice from behind the door.

'Really, Sister Miriam,' the receptionist said indignantly. 'I don't see why . . .'

Sister Miriam closed the door behind her.

Father Dunn, seated behind a wide blotter-topped desk, looked at her with his quizzical grey eyes. He was a middle-aged man with grey hair that still held, here and there, traces of a glossy black. Behind him, on an oak-panelled wall, were a score of citations for his theological and humanitarian work; he was an intelligent man who had brought his degree in sociology from Harvard into the priesthood with him. Sister Miriam had wondered about him at times. He was certainly a well-kept and dignified man, though there was often a brief flash of ill temper in his eyes.

He said, 'Isn't this rather irregular? I have an appointment shortly. Could you come back later this afternoon?'

'Please, Father. I do need to talk with you for a moment.'

'Perhaps Father Cary can help you? Or Sister Rosamond?'

'No, sir,' she replied, unwilling to give any ground. She had talked to all the others before. They had listened politely and made their suggestions, some liberal and some harsh. But none of them had worked. Now it was time for Father Dunn's opinion and she was not going to be cut short before she'd spoken her piece. 'I need to speak with you about the Raines child.'

Dunn's eyes narrowed fractionally; she thought they even became icy as he stared up at her. He said, 'Very well, then. Please sit down.' He motioned towards a black leather chair and with the other hand switched on his intercom. 'Mrs Beamon, ask Mr and Mrs Scheer to wait a few moments, please.'

'Yes, sir.'

He sat back in his chair, fingers tapping steadily on the blotter. 'I believe I'm familiar with this problem, Sister Miriam,' he said. 'Any new developments?'

'Sir . . . this child. This child is so . . . different. I cannot control him. He hates me with such an intensity that – well, I can almost physically feel the hate.'

Father Dunn reached again for the intercom. 'Mrs Beamon, will you find the records for me on Jeffrey Harper Raines? Ten years old.'

'Yes, sir.'

'I believe you've seen his records?' Father Dunn asked.

'Yes, I have,' Sister Miriam said.

'Then you're familiar with his history?'

'His history, yes; not his motivations.'

'Well,' Father Dunn said, 'you might be familiar also with my theories on infant stress. Are you?'

'Not directly. I believe I overheard you and Father Robson discussing the subject.'

'Well then,' he said, 'consider the fact that the infant is the most superbly sensitive of all God's creations. From the moment of birth the infant is reaching out, touching, exploring a new environment. And he reacts to that environment; the environment moulds him to a certain degree. Infants, or children of any age for that matter, are remarkably perceptive of emotions, passions.' He held up a finger. 'And hatred in particular. An infant can carry those disruptive passions, those emotions that seethe on the edge of violence, with him for the rest of his life. The child we're speaking of, as you're aware, has had a history of . . . unpleasantness. The rape of his mother ignited in her a small spark of hatred that, growing unchecked, finally culminated in the murder of her husband with the child present. I believe this is the seed of hatred, of agony perhaps, that Jeffrey carries within him. He's been affected by a scene of brutal violence that repeats itself just on the fringe of his memory . . .'

Mrs Beamon came through the door and put a yellow folder marked *Raines, Jeffrey Harper*, on Father Dunn's desk. He thanked her and then silently turned pages for a moment. 'Jeffrey probably doesn't even remember that night, at least not in his conscious memory. But in his subconscious mind he can recall every angry word, every brutal blow.' He glanced up for a second to see if she were paying attention. 'And then, Sister Miriam, there's the psychology of the orphan to consider, and what we have here are those who are continual orphans, children no one wants, children who cause problems, children who are problems. They didn't ask to be brought into the world.

They think it was some kind of a mistake, someone forgot to take their birth control pills, and so here they are. We're managing – very slowly and with minimum return on maximum effort – to break through to some of them. But this Raines child . . . has not yet let us in.'

'He unnerves me,' she said.

Father Dunn grunted and looked back to the yellow folder. 'He's been here four months, transferred to us from the St Francis School for Boys in Trenton. Before that he was transferred from the Home of the Holy Mother in New York City, before that the St Vincent Boys' Centre, also in New York City. He's been in several foster homes, all of which in one way or another have not seemed to work out. The parents have repeatedly cited his unwillingness to co-operate, his – ' he glanced up at Sister Miriam ' – foul language and habits, his defiance of parental authority. And then this thing . . . this recurring insistence on denying his Christian name.' He raised his brow and looked at the woman. 'What do you make of that?'

'He refuses now to even answer to his real name. He calls himself Baal and I've heard several of the others address him also by that name.'

'Yes,' said Father Dunn, swinging his chair around to stare out an open-curtained window at the children playing in the recreation yard. 'Yes. And I understand he refuses to attend chapel. Is that correct?'

'Yes, sir. That's correct. He refuses to even set foot in the chapel. We've taken away his playground privileges, his movie privileges, everything, but nothing works. Father Robson told us to reinstate his privileges and go about our business as usual.'

'I think that's best,' Father Dunn said. 'Very strange, very strange. I wonder if his father was a religious man?'

Sister Miriam shook her head and Father Dunn said, 'Well, I don't know either. I only know what's written here in his file. He doesn't socialize very much with the others, does he?'

'There are a few I believe he's taken into his confidence, but they're all like him, silent and suspicious. Still, for all his misbehaviour, he's a very good student. He reads a great deal, especially history and geography texts, and biography. I might add that he has a rather morbid interest in Hitler. Once in the library I heard him grinding his teeth. He was reading an old *Life* magazine article on the Dachau ovens. He shut the magazine when he saw me looking.'

Father Dunn grunted. 'Well, I suspect he's more intelligent than he pretends to be.'

'Sir?'

He tapped a finger on a page of the file. 'His standard test results give him a phenomenal IQ score and still Father Robson, after examining the answer forms, feels Jeffrey was hedging. Some of the answers, he feels, were deliberate mistakes. Can you give me an answer to that?'

'No, sir.'

'I don't understand it myself,' he said, then muttered something under his breath.

'Sir?' she asked, leaning forward. She hadn't heard him.

'Baal . . . Baal,' he repeated softly. Then, as if he'd made up his mind about something, he turned towards her once again. 'He's playing a game with us, Sister Miriam. It's a game he subconsciously wants to lose; I'll grant you that. Father Robson has an aptitude with these . . . difficult cases. I'll have him speak with Jeffrey. But, Sister Miriam, we must not give up. It's for the child's own welfare that we're as strong,' he paused, searching for the correct phrasing, 'as we have to be. All right?' He looked questioningly at Sister Miriam.

'Yes, sir,' she said. 'I hope Father Robson can understand him much better than I.'

'Agreed then. I'll ask him to talk with the child at the first opportunity. Good day, then, Sister Miriam.'

'Good day, Father,' she said, nodding her head respectfully and rising from her chair.

When Sister Miriam had closed the door behind her, Father Dunn sat perfectly still for a moment more, looking through the window at the yard where children flew in the autumn sunlight like aimless tattered bats. He started to reach for a cigar from the humidor in his desk drawer but stopped himself; no, not another one until late afternoon. Doctor's orders. He reached instead for a book on mental disorders in pre-teenagers from a shelf behind his desk. But as his eyes scanned the cold logical information his mind sparred with the name Baal.

The prince of demons.

Father Dunn closed the book and peered out the window. Such enigmas children are, he told himself. Leading their secret lives and shutting the door on those who try to come in; children are jealous of their mysterious identities, they become different people after nightfall. So different even their own parents wouldn't know them.

7

The child walked slowly along the high mesh fence where the playground and the thick belt of vari-coloured woodland met. He stood for a moment, his back to the others who ran and screamed in the dusty yard; he stood staring out to where the trees surrendered to the highway that went through Albany and on to the city. Then he turned and, leaning against the fence, watched the others scrambling after a wildly thrown football.

Two other children approached him. One was heavy-set with thick black hair and prominent teeth, the other was a thinner child with hair the colour of dirty sand and deep-set, hollow blue eyes. The sandy-haired child said, 'That four-eyes is a bitch.'

Baal remained silent. He wove his thin fingers through the metal mesh. 'This place is a prison,' he said after another moment. 'They're frightened of us. Can't you feel it? So in their fear they hope to cage us. But they cannot keep us here much longer.'

'How can we get away?' the sandy-haired child asked.

His black eyes glittered. 'Already you doubt me?'

'No. No, Baal. I believe you.'

'All in its time,' Baal said quietly. 'I will choose my friends and take them with me. The rest will perish.'

'Take me with you, Baal,' the heavy-set child whined. 'Please.'

Baal grinned but his black eyes remained lifeless. He reached out and, tangling his fingers in the boy's curly black hair, drew his face towards him until his glistening eyes were only inches away. 'Love me, Thomas,' whispered Baal. 'Love me and follow what I say. If you do this I can save you.'

Thomas was trembling. Saliva dribbled from his open mouth, hung from his chin by a silvery thread. His eyes blinked back tears that threatened to break over his cheeks. He said, 'I love you, Baal. I don't want you to leave me.'

'Saying you love me is not enough. You must show me; and you will.'

'I will,' Thomas said. 'I will.'

The two children stood transfixed. His eyes would not free them.

Someone called, 'Jeffrey! Jeffrey!'

Baal blinked. The two boys lowered their heads and ran away across the playground.

Someone approached him; a nun in a flowing black habit, Sister Rosamond. She reached him and, smiling, said, 'Jeffrey, you're going to be excused from your reading class. Father Robson would like to see you.'

Baal nodded. He followed her silently as she walked across the yard, through a screaming knot of boys who instantly parted when they saw him, and into the dark corridors of the rambling orphanage. He watched her buttocks as they swayed beneath the material of the habit.

Sister Rosamond was probably in her early thirties. She had a high-browed oval face and very clear greenish-blue eyes. Her hair would probably be golden with a slight tinge of red. She was very much unlike the other grey-fleshed, thick-glassed women at the boys' home; she was, in Baal's eyes, attainable. She was the one sister who encouraged the children to come to her with their personal problems; with wide, reassuring eyes, she would sit and listen to their stories of drunken fathers and whorish mothers and beatings and drugs and on and on. Baal wondered if she ever fucked.

They climbed the wide stairway. Sister Rosamond looked to make sure he was following; she saw his eyes flicker from her haunches up to her face and back again.

She didn't want to look at him. She could feel his eyes ripping away the habit and running up and down her full thighs like fingers on a keyboard, pressure here, pressure here, pressure here. Her lips were drawn and white; her hands trembled at her sides. Beneath her habit the eyes of the child reached her

53

undergarments and slid relentlessly towards the triangle between her legs. She whirled, finally unable to maintain her composure, and said, 'Stop that!'

'Stop what?' the child asked.

Sister Rosamond stood shaking, her lips moving without making sounds. She was new to the orphanage, yet she understood the harmless pranks and dirty street language of the children. She understood all that. But this child . . . this child she could not understand. There was something intangible about him that both attracted and repelled her. His incurious gaze and coldly calculating eyes now sent chills of fear skittering towards her throat.

They stood before the closed doors of the upper-floor library. Wincing at the sound of her own strained voice, Sister Rosamond said, 'Father Robson wants to speak with you.'

She watched as he stepped through the doorway and then turned to smile faintly into her face, like the cat that stalks a caged canary. She caught her breath and let the door swing shut.

In the library Baal breathed the smell of old paper and book bindings. Library period had not yet begun; the bookshelves were undisturbed, everything in its proper place. Chairs were arranged neatly around circular reading tables. After sweeping the room, Baal's eyes finally came to rest on the back of a man who stood in a corner, his finger brushing the spines of books on a shelf.

Father Robson had heard the door close. He had watched the child from the corner of his eye; now he turned slowly from his appraisal of the bookshelves and said, 'Hello, Jeffrey. How are you today?'

The child remained motionless. Somewhere in the library a clock ticked; a pendulum swung back and forth, back and forth.

'Come sit down, Jeffrey. I'd like to talk with you.'

The child still didn't move. Father Robson had no indication at all that what he'd said had even registered with Jeffrey.

'I won't bite,' Father Robson said. 'Come over here.'

'Why?' the child asked.

'Because I don't like to talk over a distance. If I did I would've called you on the downstairs telephone.'

'You should have. Then you wouldn't have wasted your time.'

Father Robson grunted. Damn. Hard as nails. He managed another smile and said, 'I understand you're quite interested in books. I thought you'd be comfortable here.'

'I would be,' the child said, 'if you would leave.'

'Aren't you at all curious as to why I wanted to speak with you?'

'No.'

'Why not?'

The child didn't answer for a moment. Father Robson, peering through the shadows thrown across the library floor, was almost certain he saw a brief flash of red in the eyes of the child. It was so sharp and sudden that he was momentarily dizzied. He blinked and looked again, but the child had lowered his gaze. 'I already know,' Baal said. He stepped towards a bookshelf and began looking at the illustrations on the dust jackets. 'You were sent here to talk to me because I am what you call an "incorrigible". Sister Miriam calls me a "delinquent". Father Cary calls me a "troublemaker". Isn't that right?'

'It's right that they call you those things, yes,' said Father Robson, moving a step closer to the child. 'But I don't believe it's right that you are those things.'

Baal's head swivelled around and his eyes flashed briefly, an illumination so uncanny that Father Robson stopped as surely as if he had walked into a wall. 'Don't approach me,' the child said quietly. When he saw that the man was going to obey, Baal turned back to the bookshelves. 'You're a psychologist. What do you see in me?'

'I'm a psychologist but not a mind reader,' he said, his eyes narrowed. Had he imagined that glimmer of red? Maybe the shadows had something to do with it, playing tricks with his vision. 'If I cannot move towards you physically I certainly can't move towards you mentally.'

'Then I will tell you what you see in me,' Baal said. 'You think I have a mental disorder; you think some experience or series of experiences in my past has affected me. Is that correct?'

'Yes. How did you know?'

'I'm quite interested in books,' said Baal, glancing up. 'Didn't you say so yourself?'

Father Robson nodded. This child was different from any

he had ever seen before. He wondered at the strangeness of him; the body was that of a normal ten-year-old, clad in patched jeans and a sweater, but the extraordinarily intelligent mind was possessed of a clarity that suggested extrasensory perception. And this aura around the child, this aura of a heavy, demanding power. A presence, Father Robson told himself, that was utterly without precedent in his own experience. He said, 'Why do you persist in denying your name, Jeffrey? Do you wish to deny your past?'

'My name is Baal. That is my one and only name. I do not deny it. You're referring also to an incident in my past that you believe has affected me. You believe I underwent a trauma that made me want to bury any recollection of the period in which it happened.'

Father Robson took note of something behind the face of this child that, for all his years as a child psychologist, he could not identify. 'What incident do you refer to?'

Baal looked at him steadily; a grin flickered across his face, and then was gone. 'I seem to have . . . forgotten.'

'You're playing games now.'

'No,' Baal said. 'Only playing out the game you've begun.'

'You're an intelligent young man,' Father Robson said. 'I won't talk to you as I would talk to the others. I'll lay it on the line for you. You've been with a half-dozen families and every time you've been returned to a children's home because of your disruptive attitude. I don't believe you want to go out.'

Baal was silent, listening.

'What do you want? What is it you're waiting for? The time will come when you're old enough to leave the children's home system. What then?'

'Then . . .' said Baal, and Father Robson thought he was going to continue but the child's mouth closed slowly; he stood without saying another word, just watching the man across the shadow-dappled, musty library.

No, this will not work, Father Robson said to himself. This child needs professional, full-time guidance. To build a bridge towards the child was a futile hope. He was not getting through at all. As a last effort, a throwaway attempt, he asked, 'Why do you not attend chapel with the others?'

'I choose not to,' Baal said.

'You're not religious?'

'I'm religious.'

The answer surprised him. He had expected a curse instead of a curt reply. 'Then you believe in God?' he asked.

'A god,' said Baal, his eyes scanning the packed bookshelves. 'Perhaps not yours.'

'Is yours a different God?'

The child's head turned slowly. His lips were twisted into a cold grin. 'Your god,' said the child, 'is one of white-steepled churches. That's all; beyond the chapel doors He has no strength. Mine is the god of the alley, the whorehouse, the world. Mine is the true king.'

'My God, Jeffrey,' said Father Robson, astonished at the outburst. 'What's made you like this? Who planted these terrible things inside you?' He took a step forward to see the child's face more clearly.

Baal growled, 'Stay back.'

But he would not listen. He was going to move close enough to touch the child. He said, 'Jeffrey . . .'

And that was all he said, for in the next second the child shrieked '*Stay back I said!*' in a voice that slammed the man back into the bookshelves, sending volumes toppling him to the floor. Father Robson struggled against something that seemed to be choking him, pinning him physically so that he could not move, could not breathe, could not think.

With one hand the child ripped books from their places and scattered them through the air, yellowed pages flying, bindings breaking. His teeth clenched and his breath rasping like that of an enraged animal, he tore into the shelves. Father Robson saw that he had reached the section of the library that housed religious books. As if in a mad frenzy, a terrible uncontrolled anger because the man had not obeyed, he tore the books to shreds and let their remains fall around him.

Father Robson tried to shout but his voice, weakened and strangled by the force that held him, came out only as a barely audible croak. His eyes were swimming in their sockets and his head felt bloated with blood, distorted like a freak's, ballooning and ready to explode.

But the child stopped. He stood amid the carnage of books and grinned at him with a savage ferocity that froze the blood in Father Robson's veins.

Baal slowly, gracefully, lifted his arm. Clutched in the hand was a Bible with a white binding. As Father Robson watched, the book seemed to smoke; vapours whirled around the child's head and moved up towards the ceiling lights. Baal opened his hand and let the book fall into the scattered heaps around him.

Baal said, 'This conversation is ended.' He turned abruptly and shut the doors behind him.

When the child left it seemed that the heavy force fell away from Father Robson. He felt his neck, certain that a hand had grasped his throat but knowing there would be no bruises. He waited for a moment until a spasm of trembling had passed and then he picked carefully through the litter of paper and bindings. The smell of heat, of burned paper, was still strong. He searched for its source.

He found the white-bound Bible the child had held above his head. There, scorched brown and curled around the front cover, was a sight that made him catch his breath as sharply as if the floor had suddenly given way beneath him.

A handprint.

8

In mottled shadows cast by the late-afternoon sun, Father Robson thrust his hands into his pockets and walked the orphanage grounds. He had completed what little paperwork he could concentrate on and finally, after filing it away in his office, emerged to breathe the crisp fall air that smelled of cold Canadian winds and leaves burning in Albany backyards. The Bible he had locked securely away in a safe.

He studied the ground as he walked. Above him wind suddenly swept through the brilliant trees and showered him with leaves that clung briefly to his coat before falling to the ground.

In his years with the orphanage, in his years as a man who observed the mentality of children, he had never before en-

58

countered anything like this. The child's hatred, the name he had chosen, his savage unnatural intelligence, the scorched handprint: perhaps they were, he thought, beyond any experience. There had been a child a few years before whose hatred was similar; this had been a child of the streets who had learned early to fight for his survival. He had hated everything and everybody. Father Robson could understand his motivation; in the instance of Jeffrey Harper Raines, or Baal or whatever, there was no simple explanation. Perhaps there was a persecution complex that manifested itself in anger, a desire to strike out, but that scorched handprint across the book . . .? No, there was no explanation.

He'd kept the incident to himself. After he'd composed himself in the ravaged library he calmly put as many books as he could back into their proper places. He would talk later with the librarian about the books that needed to be replaced. He had returned to his office with the Bible underneath his arm. And after lighting a cigarette, he sat staring at the handprint until his vision was clouded by smoke.

Now, walking the grounds, he decided he could not yet tell Father Dunn. He would have to begin a quiet examination of the child; then, when his findings were complete, some explanation might offer itself. But until that moment arrived the questions were knots that ate at his guts.

As he crossed the paved parking area towards the administration building someone reached out a pale hand from the shadow of a tree and grasped his arm.

He whirled to face a woman in black. One of the sisters. 'Oh!' he said, recognizing her. 'Sister Rosamond.'

'I'm sorry. Is something bothering you? I saw you walking . . .'

'No, no.' He kept his head down. They walked together, two figures in flowing black, along the line of trees. 'Aren't you cold? The wind's coming up.'

She walked in silence. Ahead loomed the dark structure of the orphanage; lights in the windows made it seem like some kind of great dark bulldog, watching them with hooded eyes, crouched on powerful hind legs. 'I overheard you and the Raines child in the library this afternoon,' she said after a moment. 'I didn't mean to be listening.'

Father Robson nodded. She glanced over and saw the deep creases in his face, the spider-web lines around his cautious eyes. He said, 'I don't know how to deal with this child. Over a hundred children here and I can handle all of them. All of them. But this one? No. I don't even think he wants any help.'

'I think he does. Down deep, perhaps.'

He grunted. 'Buried maybe. Well. You've been with us two months now. Is this what you expected?'

'Yes, it is.'

'Working with orphans appeals to you?'

She smiled, thinking that his psychologist's curiosity was working overtime. He returned her smile but his eyes were intent and watchful. 'I'm attracted to them because of their helplessness,' she said. 'They need a shoulder on which to lean and I enjoy providing that shoulder. I couldn't bear the thought of them turned out in the world with nowhere to go.'

'And yet many of them would prefer the street to being here,' he said.

'Because they're still afraid of us. It's very difficult to shake our image of severe, black-robed instructors who strike rulers across the palms of children.'

Father Robson nodded, intrigued by her passionate criticism of the sisterhood's past. 'Agreed. You overheard the Raines child this afternoon; would you say a ruler across the palm would work in his case?'

'No.'

'What, then?'

'Respect and understanding. He has a human core but it's going to take a great deal of effort to uncover it.'

Yes, Father Robson thought, like digging with a pick-axe. 'You seem to be interested in him. Are you?'

'Yes,' she said without hesitation, 'I am, and I don't know why.' She glanced over at the man. 'He seems so out of place here.'

'Oh?'

'All the others are simply helpless, drifting; you can see it in their eyes. Jeffrey is different. His eyes reflect, to me, some sort of purpose, something he wants to keep hidden from any of us. If you ask any of the other children what they might like to become when they grow up you'll get the usual answers: firemen, detectives, things like that. But Jeffrey never says anything because for some reason he doesn't want us to know.'

Father Robson nodded. 'Good observation. Very good.'

They neared the broad porch of the orphanage. Father Robson stopped walking and she looked at him.

'Would you like to help me?' he asked. 'Jeffrey is not going to communicate with me at all. He's shut the door on me. I need someone who can talk with him, who can find out what's troubling him. I'd appreciate it very much if you would look in on him from time to time, as your schedule permits.'

'Something torments him,' she said. 'He frightens me.'

'I think he frightens everyone.'

'Do you feel he's . . . mentally unbalanced?'

'I can't say. I need more information and that's where you can do me a great favour.'

'Why do you think he might respond to me?'

'He came with you to the library, didn't he? Believe me, if you'd been Sister Miriam the best you could've hoped for was a curse or a rock. Anything but obedience.'

The wind disturbed fallen leaves around their feet, making them crackle with the sound of a sudden brush-fire. 'Yes,' she said, the lights from windows shining across her face. 'I'll try to make some sort of contact with him.'

'Good,' he said. 'I'd appreciate it very much. I'll say good night, then.' He smiled at her and started back towards his office, wishing that he could have told her more, and damning himself for bringing her into this. He turned and said, 'Be careful he doesn't . . . bite you,' and then he disappeared into the deepening shadows.

She watched until she could no longer see him. On the ground before her was a yellow square of light, streaming from a window on the third floor, the floor that served as a dormitory for the children. She was abruptly jolted from her dreamy state of mind and stared at the square of light as a new gust of whirling leaves blew past. She thought she had seen someone move away from the window; a shadow had swept across the light at her feet. She walked out into the yard and looked up at the window as the wind wrenched violently at her habit. The curtains were open but no one was there. She shivered, thinking how cold the air had suddenly become, and climbed the steps to the doorway.

Sister Rosamond had almost seen him where he stood watching from the window. He had seen both of them, Sister Rosamond and Father Robson, as they approached across the grounds. He had watched as they spoke, surrounded by a swirling carpet of leaves. They had been talking about him. Father Robson would have been intrigued by what he'd done to the book; he was a stupid man, the child thought, who believed himself intelligent. And Sister Rosamond was no better; she thought herself a guiding angel of mercy when she was nothing but a whore in holy black.

He stood amid the rows of metal-framed bunk beds, cluttered with clothes and toys and comic books. He stood staring into the night that fell like the blow of an axe.

Behind him one of the sisters called in a shrill voice, 'Jeffrey! Aren't you going downstairs for your dinner?'

He remained motionless. In another moment he heard her walk heavily through the corridor and down the staircase. Then the only sounds were of the wind and the muffled voices of the children, downstairs in the dining hall.

From the other end of the room someone, a child, said, 'Baal?'

He turned slowly and saw that it was Peter Francis, a pale-fleshed, frail child who walked with an aggravated limp from an accident as an infant. The child, his eyes wide and pleading, made his way through the tangle of beds towards Baal.

Peter said, 'You haven't talked to me today, Baal. Have I done something wrong?'

Baal said nothing.

'I have? What have I done?'

Baal said softly, 'Come here.'

The child approached, fear swimming in his eyes like darting red fish in dark waters.

Baal said, 'You almost told, didn't you?'

'No! I swear I didn't! Whoever told you that is a liar! I swear I didn't!'

'I was told by someone who did not lie. He never lies to me. You almost told Sister Miriam, didn't you?'

Peter saw Baal's eyes change, from a thick terrible black

through grey and on to a burning, uncontrollable red that froze his blood and scorched his flesh at the same time. He shuddered and, in a mindless panic, looked about for help before realizing that everyone, the children and the sisters, was now downstairs in the dining hall. He was beyond help. Baal's eyes became as red as pooling blood; they became white-hot, like molten steel.

Peter said, 'I swear she made me! She wanted to know all about you and everything! She wanted to know about you and she said she could trust me!'

The power and heat from those eyes made his tongue bloat like a frog in a stagnant pond; it filled his mouth so he could do nothing but blubber unintelligibly. He tried desperately to cry out for the sisters, for anyone who would hear him, but the words were strangled in his throat.

Baal said, 'I've seen your records, Peter. Did you know that? Yes, I have. They keep them in a dark cave beneath this place. I broke in there once and read all the records. Do you know how you got that limp, Peter?'

'No . . .' – the child choked – '. . . please . . .' He fell to his knees and wrapped his arms around Baal's legs, but the other stepped back quickly and let him drop forward. Peter whimpered, waiting for the crack of the whip.

'They never told you, did they?' Baal whispered. 'Then remember, Peter . . . remember . . . remember.'

'No . . . please . . .'

'Yesssss. Remember. They never wanted you at all, did they, Peter? And your father – your drunken old father – picked you up . . . remember?'

'No . . .' He held his hands over his ears and crouched down on the floor. In his mind's eye he saw a man with a leering crooked grin and red-veined eyes lifting him up. Then, with a harsh and desperate curse, the man threw him at a blank white expanse that would have looked like snow but for the cracks. And then falling falling with a searing pain in his hip and a smear of red across the white. 'No!' he screamed aloud, feeling again the pain of broken bones tearing through infant flesh.

Peter sobbed on the floor, holding his hands over his ears but knowing that alone would not stop the pain.

'That never . . . that never happened . . . happened,' he

sobbed brokenly, in heaving shudders. 'It never did . . .'

Baal reached out and savagely clutched the child's face in one hand; until the flesh was white, the eyes devoid of hope. 'It happened,' Baal said, 'if I say it did. You are mine now. I have your past and your future.'

Peter was hunched over, his crying now without tears or noise.

Slowly, the red intensity drained from Baal's eyes and they went back to the deep black of a bottomless cavern. His fierce grip softened; he stroked the child as one would stroke a dog after whipping it. 'No, Peter, now you can forget those things that harmed you. You're safe. They can't reach you here.'

The child grasped Baal's legs. 'They can't? They can't?' he asked through swollen, blubbering lips.

'No. Those shadows are gone. If you belong to me they can never reach you.'

'I do . . . I do . . .'

'Peter,' Baal said softly, 'Sister Miriam must not know. No one must know except us. If they find out they'll try to kill us. Do you understand?'

'Yes.'

'And if Sister Miriam – if anyone asks about me you must not tell them. I want you to stay away from Sister Miriam. When she speaks to you again you will not even answer. She is evil, Peter. She can bring the shadows back.'

The child at his feet tensed. 'No!'

'It's all right now,' Baal said. 'It's all right. Stand up.'

The child stood on trembling legs. One tear hung, ready to drop, from the point of his chin. Peter looked up sharply, over Baal's shoulder and past him, and Baal stood as motionless as if he had suddenly turned to stone. Someone was standing behind them; someone had been there for several moments, watching.

Baal turned to gaze at Sister Rosamond in the corridor doorway, her arms hanging limply by her sides and her face questioning. He had been too engrossed with Peter to sense her there.

'Jeffrey?' she asked. 'You didn't come down for your dinner. I wanted to see if anything was wrong.' There was the faintest tremor in her voice, an uncertainty in the eyes.

'Peter . . . stumbled and hurt himself,' Baal said. He held his hand beneath the child's chin to catch in his palm the falling teardrop. He offered the glistening intact tear to Sister Rosamond. 'He's been crying. You see?'

'Yes,' she said. 'I see. Peter, are you all right? Are you hurt?'

'I'm okay,' he said, wiping his face with a shirt-sleeve. 'I tripped over something.'

She moved closer so she could see the two boys clearly beneath the globe lights that studded the ceiling. She said, 'You're going to miss your dinner, Peter. Go downstairs now and eat.'

'Yes, ma'am,' he said obediently, and with a final glance over his shoulder at Baal he went past Sister Rosamond. In another moment they heard him descending the corridor staircase.

'I'm missing my dinner too,' Baal said. 'I'd better go.'

'No,' she said quickly

He looked her fully in the face, his eyes narrowing. 'Isn't that what you're here for? To ask me to come downstairs to dinner?'

'That's why I came here, yes. But I saw you and Peter. And I know he didn't fall.'

'Didn't I say he fell?'

'I was standing there watching, Jeffrey.'

'Then perhaps,' Baal whispered, so low she had to strain to hear, 'your eyes are at fault.'

She realized that her breathing had quickened. She felt suddenly cold though the window was closed. The window; yes. This was the window she'd seen from the ground. She rubbed her eyes because they'd filled with water; her eyes stung as if she had rinsed them in sea brine. She said, 'My eyes . . .'

'Perhaps your vision is fading, Sister,' Baal said. 'Surely your sweet Jesus would not rob the sight of one of his ladies-in-waiting?'

The pain was increasing. She gasped, pushing her palms against her eye sockets. When she took her hands away she found that her vision was hazy, confused, as if what she saw was reflected by fun-house mirrors. Where the child's head should have been there was an intense white glow like the globe lights on the ceiling. She blinked, water fell from her lashes. I've gotten something in my eyes, she thought. Some dust or something. When I wash them with water they'll be all right. But the pain . . . 'My eyes,' she said aloud, and her trembling voice shamed her as it echoed off the walls.

She reached out both arms to feel her path through the beds and towards the doorway. But his hand clamped itself firmly around her wrist. He would not let her go.

Through the murky tears she saw him step forward and felt him run his fingers lightly across her eyelids; she felt a strange heat that, penetrating her skull, seemed to burn at the back of her head.

'There is no need to be afraid,' he told her. 'Not now.'

She blinked her eyes.

She was standing on a street corner. No, it was a bus stop. Around her the city was absorbing the blue tinge of early evening. Lights, garish neon, flickering bulbs, hot white, gleamed off mounds of dirty snow piled in gutters and around alleyways. She was dressed not in the black habit but, instead, in a long dark coat and dark gloves. She knew what she wore under the coat. A dark blue dress with a striped belt. Her birthday present.

Christopher stood beside her. He blew into his hands to warm them. His eyes, normally so carefree and laughing, now were as cold as the bitter February wind that sliced across the avenue. He said, 'This is a hell of a time to tell me. Jesus Christ what a time to tell me!'

'I'm sorry, Chris,' she said, and instantly chided herself because she had said she was sorry so many times. She was tired of explaining her decision. In the last few days she had had endless long-distance telephone conversations, tearful ones, with her parents in Hartford. They had finally, she hoped, come to understand the reasons for her decision. Now this man with whom she had fallen in and out of love again and again demanded once more to know why.

'I was hoping you would understand,' she said. 'I really thought you would.'

'Is it that you feel useless or something? Do I make you feel useless? Is that it?'

'No,' she said, and inwardly winced. Yes, that was part of it. The love she felt for him was for the most part physical. Emotionally and intellectually, she had come to realize, he

66

left her untouched. 'There are things I want to do that perhaps I can do by making this vow. We've talked about this before, Chris. You know we have.'

'Talked about it, yes. Talked about it. But now you've actually contacted them and you're going to go through with it? I mean, hell, that's putting your neck in the rope, isn't it?'

'Rope? I don't consider it a rope. I consider it an opportunity.'

He shook his head and kicked at a frozen mound of snow with one foot. 'Right. Right. An opportunity. Listen, you want to be an old lady in a convent somewhere? You want to give up everything? You want to give up . . . us?'

She turned around and looked directly into his face. My God, she thought. He's actually serious. 'I have decided,' she said flatly, 'that my life belongs to me.'

'To throw away,' he said.

'I will take the vows because I believe in some small way I can do something for someone else. I've been considering this for quite some time and it is the right choice to make.'

He stood looking at her to see if she would suddenly start laughing and nudge him in the ribs to let him know this was all a joke. He mumbled, 'I don't understand. You don't have to run from anything.'

She glanced up the avenue. Her bus, its tyres throwing slush, had made its turn and would be there shortly. 'I am not running from anything, Chris. I'm running towards something.'

'I don't understand,' he said, rubbing the back of his neck. 'I never knew anybody who wanted to be a nun before.'

Her bus came closer and slowed. She could hear the crunch of the tyres on packed gutter snow. She had her fare ready, as she always did, clutched tightly in her hand. Christopher kept his head down, seemingly absorbed by the pattern the dirty slush made as it ran through a sewer grating. She unconsciously jingled the coins in her hand.

He looked up suddenly. 'I'll marry you. Is that what you want? Really. I mean it. I'll marry you.'

The bus braked to a halt. The doors hissed open and the driver peered out at her.

She stepped up into the bus.

'I'll marry you,' he said again. 'I'll call you tonight, Rose. Okay? We'll get together for a little while. Okay?'

She dropped her coins into the fare box; they fell like shells exploding on some foreign battlefield. Behind her the doors closed, cutting off his voice as surely as if they were cutting off his head. When she sat down and the bus pulled away from the kerb, she looked back again and saw Christopher standing in a floating white cloud of bus exhaust.

The child dropped his hand from her eyes; no, not the child. Christopher. She saw him standing beneath the harsh white light of the ceiling globes. Christopher smiling, his eyes clear and untroubled. He'd come to see her! After all this time he'd finally found her!

Baal's hand fell to his side. Slowly her vision cleared until she recognized his black, slitted eyes. Her breath was forced and rasping, her flesh cold as if she had just stepped indoors from the snow.

He said, 'You should have married him. You broke his heart, Sister. He would have been good for you.'

No, no, she screamed inwardly. This is not happening. 'He didn't understand what I needed,' she said weakly. 'Not really.'

'That's a shame,' Baal said, 'because he loved you so much. And now it's just too late.'

'What?' she asked, her head throbbing. 'What?'

'Didn't you know? That's why he never looked for you. That's why he never called your parents to find you. He's dead, Sister. He was killed in an automobile accident – '

Her hand went to her mouth. She choked.

' – that mangled him horribly. Oh you wouldn't have recognized him, the way he was. He had to be cut . . . piece by piece . . . out of his car.'

'You're lying!' she screamed. 'You're lying!'

'Then why,' Baal asked, 'do you believe me?'

'My parents would have called and told me. You're lying!' Clapping her hand over her mouth because she knew her lips were as white, as brittle as dried bones, she backed away from him towards the corridor. And she saw him grinning and the grin became a wide smile on Christopher's face. Christopher held out his arms for her and said in a soft, distant voice, 'Rose? I'm here. I know how much you need me now. And I need you, darling. I keep falling asleep at the wheel.'

She screamed, a long thin scream that cracked and left her throat raw, and bolted from the dormitory into the corridor. As she ran down the stairway, her habit flowing, her feet missing stairs, she saw the faces of the sisters looking up the stairwell at her. They were whisperings.

She stopped to steady herself, her hands gripping the bannister to prevent a fall as a thick wave of nausea suddenly shuddered its way through her. Am I going insane? she wondered. Am I going insane? Her hands were clenched so tightly around the bannister she could see the blood as it raced through the veins towards her wildly pumping heart.

9

Sister Rosamond avoided the child during the next few weeks; she couldn't bear to be near him because of the memory of Christopher's smiling face atop his body.

Sometimes, even while teaching her basic history pupils or at chapel with the other nuns, she would begin trembling uncontrollably. Once it happened during dinner and she dropped her tray, shattering the plates on the floor. More and more often she caught the inquisitive sidelong glances of her colleagues.

She had telephoned her parents for any news they might have about Christopher, but they'd heard nothing from him in years. That left only one other person she could call, his brother who lived in Detroit. But dialling the Detroit information operator she caught herself and slammed the receiver down. She was uncertain as to whether or not she really wanted to know; perhaps finding out it was true would be too much for her. She was caught between two poles – wanting to know yet fearing the knowledge – and at night she tossed and turned in her bed until the sheets were wet.

Perhaps this was wrong after all, she told herself in the silent darkness so many times. Yes, she'd turned her back on him when he needed her. Now she was tied in the black bindings of her mistake. He'd been right. She'd been running from something and, worse, had known it all along. She had wished to avoid the harsh trappings of reality; she'd wanted to find security somewhere, anywhere, and cling to it as if it were her dying breath.

And now she realized how she missed the physical intimacies of love. She missed the strong tender hands touching her on a wide rumpled bed in his apartment; she missed curling up in his arms while he tucked his face down and whispered into her ear about how beautiful he thought her body was. She missed the act almost as much as she missed him. This is so very unfair, she told herself, to deny myself those things I need. And here, surrounded by austere black and holy contemplation, she felt suddenly out of place and lost; she was suddenly surrounded by freaks who also denied themselves and who, if she were to dare to tell them of her feelings, would scold her severely and probably also send her to see Father Robson.

I am still young, she told herself in the middle of the night. I am growing old here before it's time, and for the rest of my life I'll wear black and have to hide my feelings. Oh God oh God it isn't fair.

Each day that drifted by reminded her of the time she could never regain; she tried to immerse herself totally in her work and she spent her free hours alone, reading, but she couldn't quell the rising insecurities. She expected every morning to look into a mirror and see tiny lines criss-crossing the plains beneath her eyes. She expected to find herself resembling the older sisters who had forgotten anything existed beyond the orphanage grounds. Soon she ate her meals in her room, refusing to participate in the little birthday parties and movie nights. She began to question the judgement of a God who would trap her here like a sleek animal, to rot and die in a bleak-walled cage.

One morning she dismissed her history pupils and, after the children had filed from the room to go to their next period class, Father Robson came through the door and quietly shut it behind him.

She sat at her desk, watching him approach. So, she thought, it's finally come to this. When he smiled she busied herself by arranging stacks of test papers.

He said, 'Good morning, Sister Rosamond. Are you busy?'

'We've had a test this morning.'

'Yes, I see.' He looked around at the bulletin board with its exhibit on Thomas Jefferson, drawings done by the children. In one of the portraits of that esteemed statesman Father Robson saw that his hair was green and his teeth blackened. On the blackboard were Sister Rosamond's handwritten questions on the American Constitution. He recognized the stress in the squeezed, disarrayed lettering, in the sentences that climbed from the middle of the board up towards the top. He made a mental note. 'You know, I was quite a history scholar myself. Made all the history clubs in prep school, even won a few scholastic awards. I was always interested in ancient history, the beginnings of civilization and all that. Fascinating subject.'

'I'm afraid the children aren't quite prepared for that.'

'Well,' he said, 'probably not.'

'I'm very busy,' Sister Rosamond said. 'My next class will be in a few minutes.'

He nodded. 'Can I talk with you for just a moment?'

She didn't reply.

He stood over her until she had glanced up. Catching her eyes, he said, 'Sister Rosamond, is something bothering you?'

'Why should anything be bothering me?'

'I didn't say anything was bothering you,' he said softly. 'I only asked. And you know it's not fair to answer a question with a question.'

'Things are not always fair,' she said, and immediately dropped her eyes.

He had caught the sarcasm and now he knew that the sisters' concern for her behaviour during the past weeks had some sort of basis. 'No,' he said. 'I don't suppose so. Would you like to talk about it?'

'You're confusing me with the children. Did someone ask you to talk with me? Father Dunn?'

'No. I've noticed a sharp change in your behaviour. Everyone has, even the children. And I simply wanted to know if I could be of help.'

'No,' she said flatly, 'you can't.'

'All right then,' he said. 'I'm sorry if I disturbed you. One more thing and then I'll go. You remember I spoke with you about the Raines child?'

She looked up from her papers and Father Robson saw the blood drain from her face for a few seconds. The sight chilled him. 'I'm sorry,' she said after a moment. 'I'd forgotten that you'd asked me to look in on him.'

'No, no, don't be. I understand. You have enough work to do and, besides, the child should really be my responsibility.'

She opened a drawer and began to file the papers away.

Pursue this, Father Robson told himself. Something is very wrong. 'Have your feelings changed about him? Do you still think he can be touched?'

She closed the drawer. 'He's a . . . very difficult child.'

He grunted in agreement. The stress in her face was so defined it could have been etched by a sculptor; her fingers continually clenched and unclenched. He realized with a sudden start that she had become, strangely, like the child, distant and remote and bitterly cold. He said, 'Does the child have anything to do with your problem, Sister?' and instantly regretted the bluntness of the question.

A gleam of heat flashed briefly in her eyes. Just as suddenly she controlled herself and Father Robson felt the boil of anger, of confusion, subsiding. For a moment he thought she wouldn't reply but then she said, 'What makes you think that?'

'There you are,' he said, trying to maintain a smile, 'answering a question with a question. I asked you to speak with him; almost immediately after that you began acting very . . . depressed and withdrawn. I believe the child radiates a disturbing presence. So . . .'

'I told you,' she said. 'I haven't spoken with him.' She tried to look him in the eye but her gaze wavered.

'You're holding back on me, Sister,' he said, 'and if you can't talk with me about it then you might speak with one of the others. I don't like to see you upset.'

Several children had begun to come in for the next period's history class. They ground their pencils into the sharpener on the wall and took their seats in the classroom.

'I have to give a test,' she said.

'Very well, then,' Father Robson said, exploring her eyes once more in a final attempt to discover what was hidden there. 'If you need me you know where I am.' He smiled one last time at her and then stepped towards the door.

'Father Robson,' she said as he reached for the knob.

The desperation in her voice stopped him. There was something in it that was about to break like a fragile bit of glass. The grinding of the pencil sharpener abruptly ceased.

His hand on the doorknob, he turned to look at her.

'Do you think I'm an attractive woman?' she asked. She trembled; beneath her desk her leg struck wood.

He said very softly, 'Yes, Sister Rosamond. I think you're attractive in many different ways. You're a very kindhearted woman.'

The children sat still, listening.

'I don't mean that. I mean . . .' But suddenly she didn't know what she meant. She let the sentence falter and die on trembling lips. Her face burned. Several of the children giggled.

Father Robson said, 'Yes?'

'I have a test to give,' she said abruptly, looking away from him. 'If you'll excuse me now . . .'

'Of course,' he said. 'Forgive me for taking up so much of your time.'

She shuffled through a stack of papers and he knew she would say nothing else.

In the corridor he wondered if her involvement with the children was too much of a responsibility for her; perhaps her emotional nature was such that the orphans were depressing her. Or it could be something else entirely . . . He remembered the way her face had become ashen at the mention of the child. Something was wrong, terribly, possibly irreversibly wrong. All is not as it seems, he told himself. All is not as it seems. He thrust his hands into his pockets and walked away down the dimly lit corridor, unconsciously counting the linoleum tiles on the floor.

And soon, locking herself away from the curious stares and whispers of the others, Sister Rosamond began to fear herself. She had trouble sleeping; often she dreamed that Christopher was shrouded in a white robe and standing amid high golden dunes in a swirling desert. His arms reached out for her and, as she approached, she was nude and wet. As their fingers entwined she saw his skin turn the cold grey of wet sand, his lips draw back in an obscene grimace. And then he drew away his robe to reveal his grotesque nakedness and, throwing her down across the golden expanse, wrenched her thighs apart. And slowly slowly the features changed from those of Christopher to someone else, someone with pale flesh and burning dark eyes like fires at the bottom of black wells. She recognized the child and awakened with her breast heaving for air; he had been heavy as he lay across her belly with slavering tongue lapping at her swollen nipples.

Autumn lost its colours for the bleakness of winter. The trees gave up their leaves with a desperate finality and stood fragile under grey snow-laden skies. The grass became brown and harsh; the orphanage itself was a dark stone capped with glistening frost.

She suspected she was losing her mind. She was increasingly forgetful and would sometimes, in mid-sentence, forget what she was talking about. Her dreams became more intense; the child and Christopher became interchangeable. Sometimes she thought she had always known Jeffrey's face; she dreamed she was stepping on to a bus on a street in some city and as the bus pulled away she looked back to see the child, she thought, waving from the kerb, but she wasn't certain. She was never certain. She shuddered and burned and knew she was insane.

Sister Rosamond would have to be assigned somewhere else; Father Robson observed that her dark moods, her preoccupation and listlessness, had affected the children. Now it seemed to him that the children whispered behind his back; it seemed to him that they had grown older, more secretive, even in a few months. Their childish horseplay natural at this age had almost entirely ceased. Now they spoke and moved as if on the brink of manhood and their eyes mirrored a feverish intelligence that seemed to him terribly, terribly out of place.

And apart from them all, above them all, was the child. He walked alone in the bitter wind on the playground, his hands slowly clenching and unclenching at his sides. He spoke to no one, at least as far as Father Robson could tell, and no one spoke to him. But Father Robson saw the child's eyes sweep the faces of the others. When they drew back, cowering, Father Robson dropped his own eyes and pretended not to see.

There was only one word for it. Father Robson knew it: power. He sat behind his desk in his paper-cluttered office and chewed a pencil as he flipped through psychological journals

74

he had already read and reread. Power. Power. Power. Rising, rising up like a shadow, intangible. Perhaps, like – and the thought chilled him – the shadow he had seen in the eyes of Sister Rosamond.

And the child's power was growing. Father Robson could sense it rising like a cobra from a wicker basket, undulating in the dirty sunlight. Inevitably it would strike. But . . . at what? At what?

He put aside his journals and sat with his hands folded. The numb disbelief when the child had forced him back with a single sentence, the cold terror when the child had burned his handprint into the bookcover with an eerie inexplicable force had returned. Perhaps now it was time to send the child into New York for examination by a psychiatrist who had experience with problem children, who could explain the things that had haunted Father Robson for so long. And perhaps also it was time to unlock the safe, to disclose the scorched Bible. Yes. It was time. It was past time.

Out in the yard he stood alone.

The freezing wind whipped around him. He watched them approach; two children, one limping, nearing him from across the yard. They shivered in their coats and hunched to warm themselves from the wind. He waited without moving.

The weather was wild, unsettled, vicious. The thick layer of clouds alternated white and black, all washed-out bright and deep bottomless pits. They reached him, the wind tangling their hair.

They did not speak.

Baal caught their eyes. He said, 'Tonight.'

75

10

Sister Rosamond was wet. She threw aside the blankets feverishly, though across the room harsh wind scratched the windows. Rolling and tossing between sodden sheets, she dreamed of beautiful animals trapped in cages, pacing back and forth back and forth until they were forgotten and their flesh rotted. Oh God oh Christ my mistake my mistake where is my faith? Where is my faith?

Your faith, someone said, *seeks now to save you. Your faith grows stronger now, stronger now. Beyond these walls you will be strong and free.*

Can I be? Can I be?

Yes. But not here. Oh misguided misguided come to me.

Tangled in the sheets, she put her hands to her ears.

Someone, very close to her now, said, *You try to hide. Your fear breeds another mistake. There is a man here who wants you. He wants to take you away with him. His name is . . .*

Christopher.

Christopher. He waits here for you, but he cannot wait long. His time is limited, as is yours. And in this place of rot and dark walls you have no time at all. Come to me.

The sheets, clinging to her, would not let her go. She wrenched at them and the tearing of cloth awakened her from sleep. She lay still until her breathing was measured and calm. Who is calling me? Who is calling me?

There was no answer.

She knew the voice had come from the opposite side of the floor, from the dormitory where the children slept. She rose from her bed, quietly so as not to disturb any of the others, and started to reach for the light switch but caught herself. No, no, she thought. They'll want to know what I'm doing. They'll want to stop me and they'll say I'm crazy and should not be up in the night. She fumbled in a bureau drawer for a candle and matches; she lit the wick and watched the small flame climb to the white point of a blade. Barefoot and clad in her grey nightgown, she let the circle of the candle lead her through the corridors towards the children's dormitory, towards . . . Christopher. Yes, yes. Christopher who had come to take her away with him, back to life and the city. He'd learned how unhappy she was and he'd come to take her back with him. The candle, sputtering, dripped hot wax down over her hand. She didn't feel any pain.

Father Robson typed the final page of notes and rubbed his eyes. He reached for his cup of coffee and realized, to his chagrin, that he must have finished it some time before. The late-night work in his office had been rewarding; he'd completed the compilation of notes on the behaviour of both Jeffrey Harper Raines and Sister Rosamond for presentation to Father Dunn the following morning. He knew what Dunn was going to say. What? Hogwash! And then it would be up to him to convince the man that Sister Rosamond would best be helped by being given a different assignment, and that, in the child's case, a thorough professional examination was necessary. The evidence of the Bible would be a point in his favour; indeed, it was practically the case itself. Even someone as stubborn and opinionated as Dunn would see the need for outside aid when confronted by that handprint on the Bible. They would have to send the child to the city for a few weeks while the examinations were conducted. He felt relieved to have come to a positive decision on the matter. At the same time he realized his own shortcomings; he was just not able to deal with this case as he would have liked. No, it was better this way. Call for the services of a professional and send the child to the city. Then, possibly, the dark mood that had descended on the orphans with the winter would dissipate somewhat. Yes, he told himself finally as he switched off the lights and locked his office door, this is the right thing to do.

He left the brick building and made his way against the cold swirling wind to his car in the parking lot. Now an exhausting thirty minute drive to his home; he'd lost all track of time when he sat down to organize and write out his thoughts. He realized that still he knew no more than when he'd first begun, only now he could see the frightening questions on the page in black type.

He wished he'd had another cup of coffee before starting the drive.

Reaching his car, he stopped abruptly.

What was that he'd just seen? Passing before the window up there? That was the third floor, the children's dormitory. There were no lights, everyone was certainly sleeping at this hour of the morning, and yet . . . and yet . . .

He'd seen something pass the window, like a flashlight or the flame of a candle. And now – or was it his imagination stirred by shadows thrown by the moonlight on dancing bare limbs – did he see figures moving there, darting past the dark glass? He stood motionless for a moment and then, as the chill began to gnaw at him, he pulled his coat up around his neck. Yes! There! The flame of a candle passing the window!

He walked back across the parking area and up on to the orphanage porch, where the wind sang through cracks in the wood. He unlocked the doors with his master key.

There was no sound on the lower floor. After his eyes had grown accustomed to the dark, the empty corridors and classrooms seemed haunted by long shadows that suddenly leaped from his path or slid soundlessly along the papered walls. He climbed the stairs, past the second-floor landing with its tattered carpet and mothball odour, on up the stairway towards the third floor. He walked with one hand grasping the smooth bannister, mindful of his footing in the dark. He was careful to make as little noise as possible; he did not, for some reason he was reluctant to admit, want to announce his presence to whomever was walking amid the children as they slept.

On the third floor he could smell the path in the air where a burning candle had passed; the thick odour of wax led directly down the corridor to the dormitory's closed doors. He moved through the corridor, stopping once and wincing as a loose board squealed beneath him, and then his hand touched the dormitory doors. The crack at the bottom betrayed no light and there was no sound of movement beyond. He listened. He hoped to confront a sister who had perhaps gotten up to attend to a sick child but the relentless hammering of his heart, the fearful pounding of blood through his veins, reminded him that he already knew this was not the case.

Behind that door something waited. Behind that door was the child.

He thought he felt vibrations with his hand, as if someone – or more than one? – were on the other side of the door and heard his heartbeats, counted them while laughing into cupped hands. Go away, he told himself, go away. Get away from this door, this place. Get into your car and drive home and come back in the morning as if nothing had happened, as if you had never seen a white trace of flame flicker briefly by the glass. Get away. Get away while you can.

But no. No.

He opened the doors and stepped through into the dormitory.

It seemed darker than the corridor. His eyes strained to make out the jigsaw of bunk beds. A thin sliver of moonlight zigzagged across the floor from a window, cut in thirds and quarters by the shadows of tree limbs. A branch scraped across glass and made the flesh crawl at the back of his neck; the sound reminded him of fingernails on blackboards.

And then he noticed something – too late, and with a sudden rush of fear that made his eyes widen involuntarily, made him back towards the doors that had now shut behind him.

The beds.

The beds were empty.

Hands clawed at his legs; dozens of hands moved over him like cold ants. He tripped and threw out his arms for support but he was falling, falling, falling to the floor as the bodies leaped at him from the blackness around the doorway. He saw gleaming teeth, eyes round and wild, fingers curled into awful tearing claws. He opened his mouth to cry out but one of them jammed a fist between his teeth; other hands grasped at his hair, scratched at his eyes, held him down against the floor. He thrashed wildly in an effort to escape but the bodies he shook off returned like angry wasps. And finally, bruised and beaten, he lay quiet knowing it was not yet over.

One of them wrenched his head to the right.

In the corner, standing with his back against the wall, was the child. He held a candle; Father Robson watched wax splatter to the floor in a round puddle. The flame, swaying to a silent rhythm, cast red shadows on the wall around the child's head. The child's eyes were in shadow still, but his lips were tight and grim in the dim candle glow. The lips, Father Robson thought, of a man.

And then the child whispered, 'We've been waiting for you, Dog Father. Now we can begin.'

The children waited. Eyes glittered in the candlelight. Father Robson heard the boys' harsh breath and saw it beginning to fog the cold glass of the windows. Begin? Begin? Now he knew; he was too late. The power and madness of this child had taken them over, had mesmerized them until they were all echoes of his own black rage. Father Robson wanted to scream, loudly scream scream scream for help without shame. For anyone. For God. But he was afraid to try to scream; he was afraid he would not be heard and the realization of his fate would drive him mad.

Baal hadn't moved. He stood holding the candle, watching the pale face of the man on the floor beneath him, as the thin flame sharpened into a burning knife and illuminated a pair of eyes that tore bloodily through the soul of the holy man and emerged, grinning, with his heart.

There was a movement from the other side of the room, from among a jumble of metal bed frames. Someone was being held there by three of the children, someone moving, shaking a head from side to side, someone with eyes wide and glistening. A woman. A woman in a gown with her hair tangled behind her as she lay outstretched on a bed. Father Robson struggled to see her face but he could not. Their grip on him was too strong. He saw her fragile white limbs outspread; the hands clutched helplessly at the metal bars above her head.

Baal said to one of the children, 'Richard. You will go through the corridor and lock the sisters' wing off from the stairway. Go.' The child nodded and slipped away into the darkness. In a moment he had returned and Baal saw that it had been done. 'Good,' he said. 'My good Richard.'

Baal cast his eyes on the man and Father Robson saw a thin smile on his lips, as if he had already declared himself the victor in this vile game of blindman's buff. Baal said, 'The time for struggle is past, Dog Father. Things are simply as they are. Each passing day has seen my strength increase. Now these are my children. This has been my testing ground; the ultimate test was this . . .' He held forth the candle. 'The minds of children are simple and innocent. The mind of an adult is somewhat more . . . complex. My angel of light came bearing gifts, Dog Father. The gift of life; the gift of freedom. And I give freedom to my faithful. Oh yes. One touch and I make them kings. One touch and I destroy them. I hold them. I hold you.'

The man's face was contorted with fear. Tears began to well in his eyes and mucous dripped from his nose to the floor. Baal said, 'No tears, Dog Father. You will go to your ever-lasting reward; isn't that so? Or have you sinned and been fucking the sisters in the closets? Man of God, where is your God? Where is He?' Baal bent towards the offered, blood-drained face. 'Where is He now, Dog Father? I'll tell you . . . He cringes and hides. He holds up a cross and hides in the darkness.'

Baal straightened. 'And now I consummate my angel of light,' he said mockingly, and the children around him moved aside to let him pass. Father Robson worked his head around to watch.

Baal, his face gaunt and purposeful in the light of the flame, stood over the bed where the woman lay and gave the candle to one of the others. Father Robson saw that the woman had stopped moving. She lay still even when the children released her. Baal unhurriedly removed his pants and with groping hands spread apart the woman's legs. He moved upon her and then, with a maddened intensity, tore at her gown, clawing red rents in her flesh. Father Robson ground his teeth and closed his eyes to escape the awful moment but he could not shut out the sounds; the flesh against flesh, the moaning of the woman, the urgent breathing of the child. Then he exhaled finally with a noise that made Father Robson sick to his stomach. The bedsprings creaked as the child stood and put on his pants again. And there was another sound, a sound that made Father Robson spray tears and sweat as he jerked his head up against the force of the children.

He had heard the sound of licking flames. The child had set the mattress afire with the candle. Fire crept towards the spent, naked body of the woman. Dark smoke began to billow up. Oh God, the holy man thought, the child will kill us all. He thrashed and bit his lips but to no purpose.

Baal stepped back, his red eyes reflecting tongues of flame. He moved to another bed and, extending both hands, grasped the sheets. Father Robson watched, horrified. It had not been the candle that had set the bed afire, as he'd thought. It had been the hands, the body of the child. Baal grew rigid and the sheets began to char where his hands touched. On the already burning mattress the woman hadn't moved; Father Robson turned his head away as he saw flames catch the remnants of her gown and spread into her fan of hair.

The child moved through the dormitory, his hands outspread as if conducting a symphony of flame, touching the sheets and pillows and mattresses, setting hungry fires racing. Smoke choked them. Father Robson had difficulty breathing and he heard the children around him coughing, yet none of them moved to extinguish the fires. A glass shattered with the heat. The ceiling began to char and blacken. Flames weaved like cobras before Father Robson's face. He thought he could smell his own flesh burning.

And he was aware, as well, that the smoke was spreading through the cracks of the doors out into the corridor. Soon the sisters would be alerted by the smoke and heat. But something tensed in his throat, choking him. He gagged on his wild hopes of rescue. The wing where they slept . . . had been locked off from the corridor. They would not be able to smell the smoke until flames had reached the stairway.

Baal, framed by wild raging fire, stood over him. The eyes of the others were on him; their clothing smoked. Baal said over the noise, 'Rend him to pieces,' and the children fell upon Father Robson like greedy rats on a bloating carcass, savage teeth sinking for veins. When they had finished they stood in crimson pools and held out their hands for Baal's approval.

The child moved among them, mindless of the heat searching their eyes. Some he touched gently, a finger to the forehead. When he withdrew the finger, it left in its place a small burned print like a whirling design. With the marking of each uplifted face Baal spoke a name:

'Verin.'

'Cresil.'

'Ashtaroth.'

They seemed to feel no pain but rather to welcome his searing touch. Their eyes glittered; the finger descended.

'Carreau.'

'Sonneilton.'

'Asmodeus.'

Windows shattered from the heat all along the dormitory. Flames pulsated like a great fiery heartbeat.

'Olivier.'

'Verrier.'

'Carnivean.'

Those Baal passed unmarked cast down their eyes and fell to their knees before him. He cast a final glance along the mass of huddled bodies and threw open the doors; smoke and sparks rushed past him, driven by the wind through broken glass. The chosen nine followed him from the fiery dormitory and the last one, a hobbling Sonneilton whose name had once been Peter, quietly closed and locked the doors on the other children.

The chosen followed Baal to the stairway. From the other wing came muffled cries for help; glass broke as someone tried to climb from a window. Pulled by the wind, the smoke whirled beneath locked doors to choke the trapped women.

They crossed the porch and reached the fringe of trees. Baal held up a hand and turned to watch the final act of his performance of flame.

The wind, roaring in, spewed sparks into the sky. Flames had completely engulfed the third floor; as the children watched there was a sound of sagging timber and the fourth floor, the library with its aged volumes, caved in, sending new fire tongues lapping. The gabled roof caught; tiles burst into flame, lighting a thin smile on the face of Baal. Someone from inside the structure screamed, a long and piercing scream that shattered, for an instant, the noise of the fires. Someone else cried out for God and then there were no more cries.

The groaning roof collapsed. Burning timbers exploded into the sky. Flames leaped at the roof of the administration building and in another moment it too had caught afire.

Against the cacophony of crashing timber and bursting glass, against the framework of black sky and whirling white smoke, Baal turned to his chosen nine. He did not raise his voice but still they could hear him above the flames. He said, 'We are now men in a world of children. We will teach them what to see, what to say, what to think. They will follow because they have no choice; and if we choose we will set the world afire.'

His black eyes passed from one to the other; they stood in smoking garments and on their foreheads the fingerprint glowed red. Baal moved into the dark veil of forest and the others followed without a backward glance.

The orphanage shuddered on fire-weakened legs; its blood had flowed away in the smoke that leaped up and up, dancing like the smoke of pagan fires. With a final hopeless cry as from a scorched open mouth, the structure trembled and crashed down in an explosion of flames that would burn the forest into ashes before the coming of dawn.

TWO

'. . . and who is able to war with him?'

—*Revelation* 13:4

11

He had woken at six o'clock and was now sitting in the breakfast nook of his quiet apartment, reading the morning newspaper as the sun threw purple shadows along the cobblestoned street below.

This was his time of the day, before the noise of awakening Boston reached him, urging him forward with a note-filled briefcase. Now he sipped at a cup of hot dark tea and watched the day brighten, thinking how beautiful and distant the furry cirrus clouds looked over the towers of the city. In the last few years he had found that he enjoyed the little things so much. The tea's sharp taste, the blues and whites that stretched the sky and gave it life, the peaceful silence of the apartment with its shelves of books and busts of Moses and Solomon: he wished so much, as he did always these early mornings, that Katherine could be here to share these things with him. But death, he knew, was never the end. Her death had made him re-analyse his own life; he knew she was at a blessed peace that he had finally learned to share.

He scanned the newspaper's front page. Here was a catalogue of what had happened in the world while he'd slept. The headlines screamed of a world hungry for either relief or destruction. Every morning it was the same; in fact, the horrible had become common place. There had been more than a dozen murders in Boston alone. Kidnappings, arson, robberies and beatings spread across the nation like a thread of blood from a ripped-open wound. A bombing in Los Angeles had killed ten and wounded thrice that many, perhaps, he thought, at the same time he'd rolled over in his sleep; a mass murder in Atlanta while he pulled the blanket up around him; gang warfare in New York while his eyes darted beneath closed lids in pursuit of dreams. Here at the top of the page a suicide pact, in the lower column abandoned children. A tramway explosion in London, a burning monk in the streets of New Delhi, a terrorist group in Prague holding captives and vowing to murder them slowly, one by one, in the name of God.

During the night, while he slept, the world had moved and agonized. It had writhed in fits of passion. Old wounds had been reopened, old hatreds stirred, until bullets and bombs were the only voices to be heard. Indeed, even the bullets and bombs spoke softly now. Soon, perhaps, the loudest voice of all, that blasting voice that rocked nations and burned cities to rubble, would descend screaming through the night. And when he awakened the next morning and looked at the headlines, perhaps he would see no headlines there at all, just a question mark because then all the words in the world would be powerless.

He finished his tea and pushed the cup aside. The pain of the night had settled within him. And the pain of the nights ahead was already unbearable. He knew that his feeling of awful frustration also tormented many of his colleagues at the university, the frustration of speaking out but never being heard.

Many years before he'd had great hopes for his books on philosophy and theology, and though they had been academic successes, they had all died quiet deaths in that limited literary arena. He realized now that no book could ever change a man, no book ever quiet the rush or violent fever on the streets. Perhaps they'd been wrong; the sword now was much mightier than the pen. The sword wrote in red passages of carnage and violence that seemed now to outweigh by far the black words on white pages. Soon, he thought, the time for thinking would be past and men, like automatons, would grasp guns to scrawl their signatures in flesh.

He looked at the grandfather clock in the hallway and noted the time. Today, fittingly, he was lecturing to his morning class on the Book of Job and the theme of human suffering. It had begun to concern him that time was passing very swiftly indeed; he'd been lecturing day in and day out for almost sixteen years with only a few visits to the Holy Land to break the routine. It had begun to concern him that he should always be either travelling or working wholeheartedly on another book. After all, he told himself, he was past sixty-five – he would be sixty-seven in three months – and time was passing. He was afraid of senility, that disease of old minds, that horrible thing of drooling lips and uncaring eyes, partly because in the last few years he'd already observed the ageing process in several of the theology professors at the university. As head of the department, it had been his responsibility to cut back their teaching assignments or, as tactfully as possible, suggest they work on independent studies. He'd hated being administrative hatchet-man but there was no use in arguing with the Board of Review. He was afraid that, in a few years, he would find himself on that scholarly chopping block.

He drove his accustomed route to the university and saw it awakening in the golden morning as he walked, briefcase in hand, up the wide stone steps, flanked by time-scarred statues of angels about to spring towards the sky, of the Theology and Philosophy Building. He walked across the marble-floored hallway and took the elevator to his office on the third floor.

His secretary said good morning. She was a good worker, always there before him in the morning to straighten his papers and arrange his appointments around his classroom schedule. He made small talk with her for a few moments, asking her about the trip to Canada he knew she was going to take in two weeks, and then went on through the frosted-glass door bearing in black letters the name *James N. Virga* and, in smaller letters, *Professor of Theology, Department Head.* In his comfortable dark-blue-carpeted office, he sat at his desk and arranged his notes on the Book of Job. His secretary knocked at the door and entered with his appointment agenda.

He scanned the names to get an idea of what was ahead for the day. There was a coffee meeting with the Rev. Thomas Griffith of the First Methodist Church of Boston; in mid-morning a session with the University Financial Board to compile budget information for the coming fiscal year; in early afternoon a special seminar on the Crucifixion with Professors Landon and O'Dannis in preparation of a public television taping; in late afternoon a conference with Donald Naughton, one of the younger professors who was also a close personal friend. He thanked his secretary and asked her if she would leave Friday afternoon clear of appointments.

An hour later, he moved back and forth behind his podium, framed by the blackboard that bore his distinguished hand-writing tracing the probable lineage of Job, identifying him as Jobab the second king of Edom.

The faces of the students in the amphitheatre watched him, dipped as notes were made, watched him again as he emphasized his words with sweeping gestures.

'It was at a very early time,' he was saying, 'that man began wondering why he must suffer. Why?' He threw up his hands. 'Why me, Lord? I haven't done anything wrong! So why should it be me? Why not that guy who lives over across the chasm?'

There was a murmur of respectful laughter.

'That's right!' he continued. 'And that's an attitude and question that lingers today. We cannot understand the type of God who is represented to us as a kind Father yet who does nothing – at least in our limited perception – to turn back the tide of suffering from innocents. Now look at Job, or Jobab. He maintained he was always a moral, upright man, as much a sinner as anyone else but certainly no more so. And yet when he was at the height of his power he was struck with what we believe to be a form of leprosy, complicated also by what was most probably elephantiasis. He was afflicted with swollen flesh that broke and tore with every movement; his herds of camels were stolen by Chaldean thieves; his seven thousand sheep were killed in a thunderstorm, his ten children were wiped out by a cyclone. And yet Job knows himself; he proclaims his innocence. He says, "'Till I die I hold fast my integrity." Our minds boggle at this vast reserve of faith despite his ordeal.

'The Book of Job,' he said, 'is primarily a philosophic meditation on the mysterious ways of God. It is also a book that explores the relationship between God and Satan; God observes as Satan experiments with the strength of Job's faith. So then this is the question: Does human suffering come about because of an eternal game between God and Satan? Are we simply pawns in a game that would stagger the imagination? Do we exist only as flesh to hold the sores?'

Eyes flickered up from notebooks, then back down again.

He held up a hand. 'If this is true then the whole world, the universe, the cosmos, is Job. And we either endure the sores, which are certain to come, crying for help, or we say, like the Biblical Job, *integrity*. And this is the philosophic core of the book. Integrity. Bravery. Self-knowledge.'

He lunched on a ham sandwich and a cup of coffee in his

office while he worked up an outline on the Crucifixion seminar. After his last class he returned and began reading a newly published work entitled *The Christians versus The Lions*, a lengthy account of early Christianity in Rome, written by a scholarly friend who taught at the College of the Bible. He sat with the afternoon sun glinting through the window over his shoulder, carefully reading page after page and wondering how he'd let his communication with the man grow so lax. He'd heard nothing about the publication of this book and here it had shown up in the morning mails. He made a mental note to telephone the man the following day.

His secretary looked in. 'Dr Virga?'

'Yes?'

'Dr Naughton is here.'

He glanced up from the book. 'Oh? Yes. Show him in, please.'

Naughton was in his mid-thirties, a tall lean man with inquisitive blue eyes and fair hair that had begun to retreat further and further up his forehead during three years at the university. He was a quiet man who rarely attended faculty luncheons or teas, preferring instead to work alone in his office down the corridor. Virga liked him, seeing in him a conservatism that made a steady, conscientious teacher. The man had been working of late on a history of messianic cults; the research involved was very time-consuming and Virga hadn't seen much of Naughton in the past few weeks.

'Hello, Donald,' said Virga, motioning towards a chair before his desk. 'How is everything?'

'Fine, sir,' he said, taking the seat.

Virga relit his pipe. 'I've been meaning to take you and Judith to lunch sometime soon, but it seems you're so busy these days even your own wife can't keep track of you.'

He smiled. 'I'm afraid the research has kept me tied up. I've been spending so much time in libraries I'm beginning to feel like a fixture.'

'I know the feeling.' Virga looked across the desk into the man's eyes. 'But I know it's worth it. When can I see a first draft?'

'Sometime soon, I hope. I also hope that after you've read it you'll still feel it's academically justified.'

'Oh?'

'Well,' he said, leaning forward fractionally, 'I've gathered a great deal of information on latter-day cults, those originating towards the end of the eighteenth century up until the present. Almost without fail these cults are based not on the deeds of the messianic figure, but instead on his personality, his ability to attract converts into his flock. The mass worshipped his talent for domination instead of any true God-given vision. So the more recent cults evolved around strong-willed fanatics who were adept at impressing their beliefs on to others.'

Virga grunted. 'And you've stumbled into a religious viper's nest?'

'Viper is the correct term,' Naughton said. 'The "messiahs" shared two common motives: money and sexual power. In Great Britain in the early nineteenth century the Rev. Henry Prince announced he was the prophet Elijah and became the master of a religious movement that regarded all female disciples as members of a huge harem; Aleister Crowley built a castle on Loch Ness and proclaimed himself "The Great Beast", converting hundreds of women into his concubines; Francis Pencovic, Krishna Venta, established the Fountain of the World in the San Fernando Valley and was later blown up by a rebellious disciple; Paul Baumann, Grand Master of Methernitha, a cult based in Switzerland, advocated the purification of female converts by sexual intercourse; Charles Manson held his Family on a threat of sexuality and murder. The list, unbelievably, goes on and on.'

A line of blue smoke rose from the bowl of Virga's pipe. Naughton continued: 'It might interest you to know that on one occasion Crowley pulled down his trousers and defecated in the midst of a formal dinner; then he urged the guests to preserve his excreta because, he said, it was divine.'

'Mankind under the direction of madmen,' Virga mused. 'Well, Donald, it's a book that needs to be written. I'm afraid men are only too willing to be led by those who proclaim themselves divine but who are, in essence, only as divine as Mr Crowley's . . . offerings.'

Naughton nodded. Virga's cool grey eyes were sharp and intelligent through a thin curtain of smoke. Naughton was amazed, as always, at how little Virga reflected his advancing age. There were heavy lines around the eyes; a fringe of white was all that was left of his hair. But the expression on the face, the way the man carried himself, the way he expressed himself, all these were controlled and precise. There was none of the confusion, both mental and physical, that plagued many other men his age. Naughton respected him greatly. Virga smiled faintly and placed his hands on the desk before him. 'Did you want to see me this afternoon about anything in particular? Anything pressing?'

Naughton said, 'Yes there is. A mutual friend of ours, Dr Deagan of the Holy Catholic Centre, has been helping me compile information in the last few weeks.'

'Has he? How is Raymond?'

'Fine. And he wishes you'd call him. But I received a message from him two days ago concerning a report from a missionary family in Iran. It seems they understand a new messianic figure is being financed by oil money in Kuwait. They weren't able to supply details, but Dr Deagan tells me a great number of people are making pilgrimages into Kuwait City.'

'I hadn't heard anything about that,' Virga said, 'but I suppose it's because I have my nose in a book all the time.'

'So far the missionary family believes it to be an underground movement,' Naughton said, 'with little or no publicity. They only learned of it when they discovered the members of their own village were leaving for Kuwait. These people simply left their belongings and that was it.'

'Throughout history, as you well know,' Virga said, 'that sort of thing has gone on. A powerful man gains financial backing and converts the unfortunately ignorant to a religious fervour. It's not new. What's this one teaching?'

'No information,' Naughton said. 'The missionaries can't even supply a name or nationality. Evidently, though, the movement involves children in some way.'

'How do you know?'

'Our missionary friends report that the influx of children into the area from Iran, Iraq, and Saudia Arabia is phenomenal. But they're at a loss to explain how the children are involved. Anyway, the missionaries are travelling to Kuwait themselves in order to report further.'

'Well,' said Virga, shrugging, 'in the past these men have

thrust children up as the vanguard of their flock in imitation of Christ. The pattern seems the same.'

'But intriguing, none the less, due to the utter lack of publicity. You'll recall that one of the most recent messianic figures purchased a full-page advertisement in the *New York Times*. In this case the man, if it is indeed a man, prefers secrecy.'

'Yes,' Virga said. He struck a match and held it above the bowl of his pipe. 'Yes, that's intriguing. That doesn't quite follow the usual outburst of "spiritual resurgence" when a "messiah" begins to take some sort of control over the mass. Usually the name is shouted from the lips of poor followers who find out too late they're being used.'

Naughton cleared his throat. 'Up until now I've buried myself in libraries, digging through books for the observations of others on messianic cults. Up until now I've only been able to compile second-hand information. Now I feel this is an excellent opportunity to document a gathering of this nature personally. So I'd like to request from you a leave of absence.'

'Oh?'

'Yes sir. I want to go to Kuwait myself. I'd like to request a leave now in order to make the arrangements.'

Virga had leaned forward, his eyes shining. He wished he could be undertaking the trip himself. 'Can you afford it?'

'Well,' Naughton said, 'Judith wanted to go as well but I told her no. I can afford myself.'

Virga smiled and turned his chair around slightly so the afternoon sun streaked across his face. Beyond the window the sky was a muted blue that held pink-edged clouds. 'I'll arrange a leave for you,' he said after a moment. 'Off into the sky.'

'Sir?'

'I'm thinking aloud. I'd go with you if I could. I need some foreign air. But someone's got to mind the store.' He swung back around to face Naughton. 'Can I ask that you keep me informed of your progress? I'll be very interested in your findings.'

'I will,' said the other man, rising from his seat. 'Thank you.'

'Just remember me in your acknowledgements,' Virga said. 'I'd like for my name to appear in print again one last time.

And I still want to take you and Judith to lunch one day before you leave.'

'All right,' Naughton said. 'I'll be in touch.' He moved towards the door and reached for the knob. Virga reopened the book and leaned back in his chair.

Naughton turned again and Virga looked up. 'You know, sir, I find myself puzzling over the same question that men have asked themselves ever since the time of Jesus Christ. What if this one is . . . different? What if this one isn't false? What then?'

'If this is a false messiah,' Virga said after a moment, 'you'll be there to see how men can be tricked. If this is not a false messiah, then,' he smiled, 'you'll have a fascinating last chapter for your book, won't you?'

Naughton stood at the door for a few seconds. He nodded and closed the door behind him.

12

In the dirty desert city with its fringe of tin-walled tenements Naughton thought he was still asleep, that perhaps when he had imagined awakening at the rude kiss of rubber tyres on concrete runway he had been sleeping and that was part of the nightmare as well. But no. The blazing white sun in a diamond-blue sky told him no. This was not a nightmare from which he could struggle away through the watery folds of sleep. This was real. Very real.

His cab, driven by a middle-aged man with blackened front teeth and dark sunken circles beneath the eyes, had stopped on a suburban street where traffic was snarled by an accident up ahead. Someone had been run off the road into a gully and voices were raised in a frantic Arabic chatter. Hands waved in the air. The two drivers involved, both as burly as black slabs of meat, squared off in an argument that bordered on hysteria. But Naughton was not concerned by all that. He was staring fixedly out the back window at something on the side of the street, a patchwork of broken concrete and sand that, beyond the stinking sores of tenements, became a dark ribbon through the towers of Kuwait City proper.

There in the gutter, held by sticks planted into firm sand, the skinned carcass of a dog rotated over and over, over and over above a fire of newspaper and rags. Two half-naked children watched the meat turn, choosing a spot at which to rip when the feast was done, and the eyes of the dog stared back, popping from their sockets like white marbles. The smell of it reached Naughton and he instinctively recoiled. He would have rolled up the window but the heat was too much and the smell would have finally reached him anyway through the cab's broken windshield.

A loud *crack!* like the backfiring of a car very near made him start violently. Up ahead there was a haze of smoke in the air.

The driver muttered an oath and pulled out of the line of traffic and up over the kerb. As they swept around the accident Naughton looked out to see what had happened. One of the drivers lay on the concrete, bleeding profusely from a stomach wound. The other stood over him, one foot on each side of the body, and in his right hand was a smoking pistol. The man on the ground clutched out weakly for the tyres of the cab as it passed him to regain the street.

Naughton said over the howl of the engine, 'That man was shot back there!'

The driver half-turned his squat head.

'Shot! Do you understand? Can't you stop and help him?'

The driver laughed harshly. 'Ha! You Americans!'

Naughton looked back and saw that the man with the gun was still standing over his fallen victim. Cars pulled around the accident to continue down the street and their movement whirled smoke around the man's head in a lazy blue circle.

The cab moved over gouged concrete towards the outskirts of the city, through a maze of makeshift dwellings. There were people everywhere, dark people in flowing rags who grinned at him and tried to reach him through the open window before he could slide away. They sprawled in gutters, their eyes open and cautious but their faces already dead. They stepped out into the street from between the tenement houses and eagerly watched the approach of the cab, as if he rode the engine of

96

destruction and destruction here was the guest of honour.

Naughton had been prepared for the poverty but not quite enough. This land bothered him greatly; he felt as if something were about to crash down on his head without warning. He seemed to sense it in the acid pall over the city. The smoke began to drift in during the early-morning hours, out of the west where the desert dipped and swayed like a lissome brown woman. And during the night he stood on the mosaic-tiled terrace of his hotel room and saw them there; the thousands of blinking fire eyes that matched the cold silver starlids above. He was amazed at their number; he was awestruck. Some of the reports had counted upwards of three thousand and that had been days before. Now Naughton felt certain that over five thousand people crowded together there between the walls of sand.

He had immediately, on viewing the great sprawling assembly, written to both Dr Virga and Judith.

To Dr Virga he had written of the horrible paradox of this country: on one side the beggars pulled and cried on the garments of tourists, on the other the thin spires of oil derricks shot up from the desert and dishdashah-clad sheiks drove gleaming Ferraris on palm-lined avenues. Here the line dividing the rich and poor was so sharp as to be utterly appalling. He had written Dr Virga of the gathering people and the still-nameless messiah figure, a man who was completely unreachable; Naughton had still not even been able to learn his nationality. But there on the desert they waited for him. Each day saw them kneeling towards the sun and shrieking out lamentations because he had not seen fit to address them yet.

To Judith he had written of the country itself, its mysterious facelessness and the colours of the desert, the gold shimmering waves of midday and the thick black snake shadows cast by the setting sun.

But there was something he'd kept to himself. The number of violent incidents he'd witnessed since his arrival two weeks before unnerved him; it seemed that this country seethed with growing hatred. There was the smoke of guns and fires in the air; this was a land at war with itself.

He realized he was being affected as well. He was being hardened by the unconcern with poverty and violent death; at one time he would have demanded that the cabdriver stop to call an ambulance for the wounded man they'd left behind. Now – and he wondered why – he really didn't give a damn and felt no shame about it. It had shocked him, yes, as any raw act of violence would shock him, but he rationalized that there was nothing he could do and left it at that. This land breeds violence, he told himself. This was a hard land, so different from America that it made him feel truly alien, cold, and detached. Perhaps the natives lived in poverty and died by the gun or knife because it was their destiny; to order anything else would cause a disharmony, a disorder in the world like ripples spreading across a pond. People died here because they got in the way. Their way of life nursed violence until it was as prevalent and bitter as the hot overhead sun.

Now the cab had left the rows of tenements. The road smoothed, stretching long and empty over a flat expanse of shimmering desert. The country was still in the midst of hurried growth. Oil derricks stood gaunt on the horizon. Superhighways cut the desert only to die sand-covered deaths far from where they had begun. Many roads led nowhere, just winding and winding in circles as if someone had built them as playthings to while away the hours and then, tiring of the game, simply abandoned them unfinished.

Ahead, between desert dunes that shifted like the tails of dragons, lay the encampment. He had visited it daily, moving in among the goatskin tents and aluminium huts with his tape recorder over his shoulder, watching his footing on the hard-packed, excrement-covered sand and stopping now and then to speak with the Bedouins and Kuwaitis who, after eyeing him suspiciously, always turned their backs on him. Packs of howling dogs roamed the encampment fighting over scraps from garbage piles; flies by the thousands had followed people from all parts of this land and now circled in dark clouds, landing to pick at festered sores. The sick who had hobbled from the desert villages kept to themselves; Naughton had seen them kicked and beaten to the ground when they begged food from others.

In the encampment, as in the city, a firm line was drawn.

On one side the poor made their beds in simple tents or on the sand; on the other the wealthy sheiks constructed elaborate flowing tents with rich carpets, employing servants with fans to beat away the flies and servants with guns to beat away the beggars. For one of the wealthy to cross that invisible line was suicide. Naughton, on his fifth day as an observer, had seen one of them, drunken with hashish, stumble over that boundary into the realm of the poor. At once he had been seized and thrown to the ground by a score of men as others watched with glaring eyes and the women screamed in wild laughter. The man had tried to get away but they tore his robes and kicked him back, naked and bruised, like a thin dark dog turned from the house. Naughton watched it all silently, realizing from the burning faces that his interference would mean his death.

The cab turned on to a long unpaved road that led directly into the midst of the encampment. Naughton could see the sun glinting fiercely off the aluminium-walled huts. He could smell the stench of the human specimens gathered there, waiting for . . . whom?

Naughton asked his driver. 'Who is this man?'

He didn t answer. His eyes in the rearview mirror never acknowledged a question.

Naughton leaned forward. Perhaps the man hadn't heard. He said in a louder voice, 'This man they've assembled to see? What do you know of him?'

When there was still no answer Naughton muttered a curse. Try another tack. 'Is he a prophet?' he asked.

Backward bunch of bastards, Naughton thought. Bastards all. This bastard was just as uncommunicative as the rest had been. He settled back on the seat, feeling the hard springs beneath him, and watched the line of huts come up to meet them.

It was worse than it had been the day before. The huts were packed side by side like sudden slums constructed in the desert. Lines of clothes hung from roof to roof. The beggars assailed his cab as it wound its way through the haphazard dwellings; they grinned through broken teeth and shouted foul curses at him after he'd passed. The sand was churned as two beggars fought, rolling over and over into the road as a crowd of people screamed with delight and passed money from hand to hand. Naughton's driver blasted them with a horn and swerved. Naked children moved through the tents in the quarters of the sick, throwing rocks or sand at the bedridden. Everywhere clusters of ragged people swarmed like mad frothing animals and Naughton saw a man with a knife, stalking a woman who fell to her knees and screamed for mercy. Naughton wanted to strike out at them, to wipe them from the face of the earth as cleanly as if he had created them to begin with.

The cab slowed as a group of beggars hammered at the hood. The driver shouted, 'Get away or I'll run you down!'

Naughton reached over to roll up his window, heat or no. When he did someone caught his hand and squeezed it tightly. He looked up into the pleading dark eyes of a young girl, possibly fifteen or sixteen, who stood pressed against the door of the cab.

She said in a faint, tired voice, 'Money, please.'

Naughton saw that she might have been pretty but for her protruding bones, sunken gums, and listless eyes that made her appear already a corpse. She must have gone without food for days. She whined, 'Money, please.'

Her fingers were digging viciously into the flesh of his hand. He reached into a pocket for a few coins and gave them to her. 'Here,' he said. 'For food.'

The girl caught up the money and stared directly into his eyes; he felt a tremor of panic at the point-blank gaze. She suddenly hoisted up her long dirt-edged skirt so that he was staring into the dark triangle between her bony thighs. Across her legs were rough-handed scratches, blue-black bruises; scores of open sores gave forth a yellowish liquid that had flowed almost down to her knees. He started in horror and when she saw his eyes she laughed wildly, spraying spittle. And she was still laughing, her skirt up like a whore's banner, as the cab pulled away. Naughton shivered with the bestiality of this place.

At the other side of the encampment they came to clean tents of the wealthy, scattered across the flatland and up on a rock bluff over the assembly. Here there were the odours of spices and rich perfumes, of burning incense and flowing silks. Great gleaming cars, their back sides raked by the rocks and bodies of the poor, stood attended by armed servants. Naughton

100

noticed the dented front grill and shattered headlamp of a nearby Mercedes-Benz. Dried blood was smeared along a fender where something or someone had been struck down.

Naughton paid the driver and asked him to come back to pick him up at dusk. The driver's eyes were impassive and Naughton knew he would again have to walk back to the highway before finding a ride. He slammed the door shut and the cab roared away in a flurry of sand and dark exhaust.

You bastard, Naughton said to his back. All of them bastards. He plugged the tape recorder's microphone into its jack and strung its cord around his hand. Moving among the tents of the wealthy, he saw the suspicious eyes of the armed servants. He started to approach one but when the man dropped his hand to his pistol Naughton moved away towards the stench of the packed dwellings.

It was then that he noticed a new addition to the encampment, something that must have gone up during the night. It was a huge oval tent staked out on a clean white spot of sand, removed from the encampment's dirty rectangle. Trucks with electrical equipment had moved around it and Naughton saw workmen fencing in a generator. The folds of the great tent undulated sluggishly in a hot breeze from the Persian Gulf. There were no other dwellings near it and Naughton was drawn by its solitariness. His boots sinking in the sand, he started walking towards the equipment trucks.

'Hey! Sorry, old boy! I've already tried that. No luck.'

Naughton turned.

A man wearing a khaki desert suit had come from between two of the tents. He was a stocky, broad-shouldered specimen; his exposed arms showed cords of muscle. Two cameras were slung around his neck and clicked together as he approached Naughton. In his late thirties at least, the man had a tangle of light hair and grey eyes that had become red-rimmed from too much sun. He'd been badly sunburned; some sort of greasy ointment was applied to his forehead and the bridge of his nose. He said, 'I've already tried the workmen. But they don't know anything. They're only employees.'

Naughton said, 'I was hoping they might tell me something about what's going on here.'

The man shrugged. 'They were sent from the city. They don't know anything.' He held out a hand. 'I'm George Kaspar from the BBC. Scouting a documentary. About to burn alive in this damned sun. Who you working for?'

'Working for?'

'Yes. Your paper. You're an American, aren't you? Don't tell me the networks want something on this.'

'Oh. No, no. I'm Donald Naughton; I'm a professor of theology at Boston City University. I'm doing field research for a book on messianic figures. And you're right about the sun. I never thought it would be like this.'

'The eye of the beast,' said Kaspar, nodding up towards that blazing spot of fire. 'Look at me. Fried alive and raw in a dozen places. You're here with a group?'

'No, regrettably alone. Had to finance the trip myself.'

Kaspar grunted. 'Goddamn,' he said, brushing at a fly that had attached itself to his forearm. 'Bloody things just suck at you until you're as dry as a bone.' He held out a canteen. 'Here. Better take this.'

'Thanks. I've got water,' said Naughton, indicating the canteen beneath his jacket.

Kaspar laughed and took a drink. 'Water, hell,' he said. 'That's good whisky. And God knows I need it. Here I am up to my ass in sand and God knows where the rest of them are. A cameraman and two assistants, out fucking around somewhere in our van. They up and left me out here. Fucking buggers. Three days out here and I've had it.' He narrowed his eyes seriously. 'I mean it. Fucking had it. All this sprawled out here, this stink and . . . you're a writer? You're writing a book on this bloody mess?'

'A professor,' Naughton corrected him, shielding his eyes from the sun to look over his shoulder at the men connecting the generator cables. 'I wonder what they're up to over there. Have you heard?'

'Hell, yes. I've heard this and that and this and that and all of it lies.' Kaspar slapped at a fly circling his head. 'The BBC tried to find out what was going on through diplomatic contacts. No luck. Then through personal friends. Nothing. Just a great mess of these buggers out in the desert waiting. That's all they're doing . . . just waiting. I saw a couple of fellows from *The*

Times here yesterday, a correspondent from one of your magazines, and a few others from area publications. But this mass of humanity is sickening. I was told to get my ass out here; I wouldn't have fucking come if it were left to me. I'm going to have to go to the hospital when I get back.'

Naughton started walking away from the huge tent towards the smoking expanse of huts. Kaspar walked with him. 'You're not going into that mess, are you? Hell, it's a risk of life in that bloody cauldron.'

They left the opulent tents and crossed that invisible line over into the other side. The odours of excrement, both animal and human, and the odour of something else, indescribable in its baseness, hit them full in the face. Kaspar drew back but then followed Naughton when he saw the other man was going on.

'What's this about a book?' Kaspar asked. 'You're working on a book?'

'Yes. I needed first-hand contact with a mass religious assembly like this to – '

'Fucking buggers,' Kaspar said. 'Fucking buggers to leave me out here. I'll fix their asses.'

They walked shoulder to shoulder among the walls of goatskin and hot blinding aluminium, hearing everywhere sobs and shouts, screams of wrath and wild uncontained laughter. They ran into a whirling black cloud of flies. The fires of burning garbage piles glowed orange around them; the smoke drifted down like a yellow door cutting off retreat. Rounding a cluster of aluminium huts Kaspar gasped audibly and stepped back, bumping into Naughton. Before them a pack of dogs spun in a mad death fight, their slavering jaws snapping the air, over a thick piece of tattered bloody meat. Neither Kaspar nor Naughton dared even guess what the mauled bit of flesh had been; they made a wide circle of the dogs and heard their growling fade in the distance.

'I'm going back,' Kaspar said after another moment. 'This is too bloody much for me.'

'Go ahead. But it'll be easy to get lost back there,' Naughton replied.

'The hell with that,' the other man said. He waved a hand and turned to retrace his steps in the opposite direction.

But then he had stopped, frozen in the sun, and Naughton heard the click-click-click of his cameras bumping together.

Naughton looked to see what was wrong. As he spun around, he was aware of figures darting amid the murky haze of yellow smoke, shadows hiding behind walls and water barrels. The smoke began to burn the back of Naughton's throat.

Kaspar said, 'Great Jesus! Who is that there? Did you see them?'

Naughton stood still and watched but they were hiding. Around the two men the yellow walls dropped until they were as close and tight as those of any prison.

'They're following us,' Naughton said finally. 'Come on.' He grasped the man's shoulder and pulled him along as they ducked through the narrow alleys. When Kaspar looked back Naughton felt him go tense as he realized they – whoever they were – were still behind them, following just out of reach and then hiding when the two men turned to see.

And finally Kaspar turned and shouted, 'Get away you bloody bastards!' and was answered by a thin piercing laugh that came to them through the silence of the smoke.

They went on. At all sides they were haunted by shrill laughter, mutterings, and screams. Dark faces watched them; the dark faces held red eyes and had gleaming yellow teeth as sharp as those of the dogs that battled for garbage and human refuse.

At last they came to the far side of the encampment where the sick were banished from the rest of the assembly. The sun burned down on pitiful bodies coughing thick liquids and blood into the sand. Some lay on cots, others sprawled out on the ground as if claiming the right to die on a particular spot. Stepping among the huts and bodies, the two men continued to look back to make sure they were not still being tracked.

Kaspar said, 'What is this place? What's going on here?'

'I don't know,' Naughton said. 'Something's gone wrong – this is madness.'

'Madness?' someone asked. 'Madness? Who is there?'

Naughton looked around. An old man, so thin his bones seemed to bear no flesh at all, sat in the sand with his back to an aluminium wall. His skin was almost black while the hair on his head was white and clean. The old man sat cross-legged, his frail straw arms in his naked lap, and Naughton saw that he was staring directly into the afternoon sun. His eyes were incredibly black hollows. Naughton knew the eyeballs had retreated from the sun's power; the old man had been burned blind.

'Madness?' the old man asked again, tilting his head to catch the voice he'd heard. 'Is someone there?'

Naughton bent down, squinting against the sun reflected off the metal wall, and softly touched the old man's hard cheeks. The old man started at the touch and jerked back but Naughton said, 'I mean you no harm.'

'Where'd those fucking buggers go?' Kaspar asked.

'Who is there?' asked the old man, fumbling weakly for Naughton's hand, his own hard fingers searching, searching, then finally lacing with the young American's.

'A soft man,' he said as he felt Naughton's hands. 'No work against the weather. I'm blind.'

'Yes,' said Naughton, staring into those deep sockets. 'You've blinded yourself.'

'Just up and left my ass here,' said Kaspar, his expensive Nikons cracking together like pistol shots. 'I'll kill them.'

'There were men following us,' Naughton said.

'Yes. I hear the beating of your heart. I smell your fear.'

'I'm an American,' Naughton said. 'I want to know what's happening here. Have these people gone mad?'

The old man smiled, showing yellowed teeth broken and ground into stubs, and shook his head as if he had just heard a joke. 'Mad? Mad? No. There is no longer any madness. There is now only what is.' He turned his face towards the heat of the sun and its golden fire settled in his sightless eyes. 'I can still see the sun; I am not yet blind after all. And while I can still see there is no hope.'

'What?' Naughton asked. 'What?'

Kaspar said, 'Let's get out of here, old boy. Take to the desert and get back to the highway.'

'I came to this place with my daughter and her husband,' the old man was saying. 'A new life, they said. Here we will find a new life, they said. And here they left me. I don't know where they are. She was my daughter until she reached this place; then I knew her no longer. I must burn it out. I must burn it out.'

'Huh?' Kaspar said. 'What's that old cock talking about?'

Naughton leaned forward. 'Who have these people assembled to see? Who will give your daughter a new life?'

The old man nodded. 'Yes. A new life is what she said.'

'Who will give her a new life?'

The old man groped for Naughton's face; his fingers traced the lips and nose, felt along his cheeks. 'Can you help me find them? Perhaps they will still go back with me. Help me.'

'Come on, Naughton. He's crazy.'

'No!' Naughton said harshly over his shoulder. He turned back to the old man. 'I'll help you. But who . . . what is the name of the man you've come to find?'

The old man smiled again. 'Baal,' he said. 'Baal.'

Something clattered off the wall of the aluminium hut and fell to Naughton's feet. A rock.

He looked up to see Kaspar ducking, shielding the lens of his cameras with one hand. And beyond Kaspar ragged hollow-eyed men and women stood in a semicircle. Naughton could hear their breathing, coarse and hot. They held jagged stones. A thin Bedouin in gaily coloured rags reared back and threw his weapon. Naughton dodged; the rock sang past his head and cracked off the metal.

'Jesus Christ!' Kaspar shouted. 'Have you people gone fucking nuts? I'm a British citizen!'

Someone else, a woman, threw her stone and Naughton heard Kaspar grunt. Then the air was filled with them, clattering off the metal wall and striking Naughton on the arms he had brought up to protect his head. He looked down and saw that a stone had struck the old man; his head was gashed above the empty pools of his eyes. Kaspar shouted out in pain and staggered back holding his chest where a shattered camera dangled, the lens dripping glass. Then Naughton saw another stone strike Kaspar directly on the head and he fell to his knees, his head dragging.

The beggars moved forward. Someone threw an arm back to fling another stone and Naughton knew already where it would strike, on the forehead over his right eye, as if he had seen this in a dozen sweating dreams. He tensed his back against the scorching metal wall.

A long gleaming black limousine roared between Naughton and the beggars. Sand spattered across his shins. He heard the solid *thunk !* as the stone, meant for him, struck the window jamb of the car and bounced off. He dropped down and saw that Kaspar was barely breathing.

The car doors opened. Two white-robed Kuwaitis herded the beggars back. They obeyed, muttering in menacing tones but subservient all the same. Someone took Naughton's arm and lifted him up.

'Are you injured?' the man asked. Dark darting eyes beneath the traditional head-dress, a thin moustache above pouting feminine lips.

Naughton shook his head to clear it. 'No. No, I'm all right. Another thirty seconds and it might have been different.'

The man grunted and nodded. He looked across and saw the old man but did not move to give aid. He said, 'This scum is difficult. I am Haiber Talat Musallim. You're an American?'

'Yes. My friend there . . . he's hurt badly, I'm afraid.'

The man glanced down. Kaspar was lying in a pool of blood. 'This scum is difficult,' he said. He motioned with a thick hand. 'Please . . . my car.'

Naughton shook his head; he felt overcome and off balance. Leaning against Musallim, he staggered to the limousine. In the air-conditioned, perfume-reeking car was a white-uniformed driver and another man, blond and pale, in a dark blue suit. Naughton said drunkenly, 'My friend is hurt. I've got to see about my friend.' He made a move to climb out of the car, but Musallim grasped him clawlike on the upper arm.

The man in the blue suit was staring at him with vacant eyes. He slowly opened the car door, rose to his feet, and said, 'I'll take care of your friend.'

Naughton said, 'No, I .. .'

'I'll take care of your friend,' said the pale man in the blue suit, and as he approached the figure on the ground Naughton saw that he walked with an aggravated limp as if something was wrong with his hip joint.

Musallim patted Naughton's hand and said calmly, 'You're all right now. You're among friends.'

And as the limousine roared off through the tangle of blinding walls and emaciated bodies, Naughton turned in his seat as weakly as if he had been suddenly drained of his lifeblood. He was almost certain that he saw the group of beggars moving forward again towards Kaspar, creeping creeping with their hands tight around new stones.

And the man in the blue suit stood watching.

13

'Here,' Musallim said as he took two thimble-sized silver cups from a tray held by a white-uniformed servant, 'some tea would cool you. This heat, I know, must be unbearable to foreigners. Me, I was born in the desert.'

Naughton took the proffered cup and drank. The tea was black and very strong, with an aftertaste of cloves. The two men sat within Musallim's magnificent gold-embroidered tent at the fringe of the encampment. Rich red and gold carpets were spread across the sand. Musallim sat behind a wide ornate desk and Naughton occupied one of two canvas armchairs in the tent's blessed shade. Naughton said, 'This is very good.'

'Someday I'll control the desert,' Musallim said. 'Already I've cut across it like the most skilled surgeon of your country. Water lines, gas lines . . . I've strung them through the sand as if I were,' he made a needle-and-thread gesture, 'sewing stitches. The people appreciate me for that.'

Naughton nodded. In the distance, over Musallim's droning voice, he could still hear the din of the people bubbling in the pot of the encampment. 'Could you find out about my friend, please?' he asked.

'Your friend?'

'Yes, the man I was with. Mr Kaspar.'

Musallim waved a hand and leaned back in his chair. Against the startling white of his dishdashah the man's flesh was the colour of rust. 'He's well taken care of. That rabble out there can be quite annoying. It is hot, isn't it?'

Naughton finished the tea and put the cup down on a circular table beside his chair. He looked up into the flat, hooded eyes of the man across the desk. 'I don't understand what's going on here,' he said. 'I've been researching my book for several weeks and I've watched this crowd grow. Now it seems as though they've finally gotten out of control. I don't know . . .' he ran a hand across his forehead to soak up the droplets of sweat that hung, eager to break, over his eyebrows, 'I've never seen anything like this before. It's ugly. It – I don't know.'

Musallim sat in silence for a moment, his ring-laden fingers toying with the golden scrolls that decorated the arms of his chair. 'Mr Naughton,' he said finally, 'there are many things in this life that seem ugly. But later, on close and logical scrutiny, they begin to take on a special beauty. You're disturbed by what is happening here because you do not yet understand. I'm at ease because I do. And I would not have donated this land for such a purpose if I did not feel it was worth while and very important. You'll see, Mr Naughton. History will record this flat plain of sand as a place of exquisite and divine purpose.'

Naughton had looked up sharply. 'You own this land?'

'Yes, this land and miles beyond. Would you like more tea?'

'No. Thank you.' From the corner of his eye Naughton caught the sudden brilliance of a diamond as it gleamed from Musallim's hand. 'Please explain this to me. I see madness and death here. Do you see something else?'

'I see everything else,' the other man said. He gazed at Naughton for a few seconds and then his dark eyes flickered around the confines of the tent. He seemed to be choosing the correct words. 'My family was of very poor stock, Mr Naughton . . . or so I thought at the time.' He held up a finger for emphasis. 'They were Bedouins, nomads of the desert. My father – oh I remember my father, his teeth flashing in the sun, astride a great foaming white horse. He was a strong-willed man who took what he wanted when he wanted and who,' he glanced at Naughton and smiled self-consciously, 'beat his wife and children when he felt the need. He was a man of the desert, Mr Naughton, and more important, he was a man of the spirit.'

'The spirit . . .?' Naughton asked.

'When he was still a young man he controlled six families and their water wells. He was a man to be reckoned with. Of course he . . . had his enemies. They despised him as cowardly dogs fear all noble wolves. And even his own family moved against him. I remember one night our camp was set up on stone bluffs where he could stand and look out to the gulf . . . I remember there was a full moon. And I remember our tents stirring in the breeze and the gulf crashing beyond. It was his brother Assaid who was the enemy . . . his own brother. He came to tell my father that he'd gone too far. Too far, said Assaid. Like telling the gulf to stop its gnawing of the land.

'My father had killed someone – one of the well-keepers who had cheated him – and he'd left his head on a stake to drip blood into the water, to poison it as a message to those who would not give my father the respect he deserved. And his brother had come to tell him that his family was through with him. He had disgraced their name, said Assaid. And he spit at my father's feet. I remember that because I saw the spit gleam in the moonlight.'

The man's eyes were shining. He leaned forward, his fingers tracing pictures in the air before Naughton's face.

'Assaid turned to walk back to his horse,' Musallim said, 'but that was not the end of it. Oh no. That could never be the end of it. My father, as I said, was a strong-willed man. There was a knife at his belt. He unsheathed it and my mother put her hands over my eyes but I pulled away. And around the fire the rest of the men grinned as they saw the naked blade. My father never drew a knife and sheathed it clean. So he struck at his brother and the knife caught him here, up above the shoulder blade. But Assaid was a strong man too, though weak in the ways of the world. He turned and grasped my father around the throat; they battled there in the moonlight, my father cursing and Assaid gasping for air with the knife in him up to its black hilt. They reached the edge of the bluff and my father, with a twist of the knife that scraped against bone – I remember hearing that – tossed Assaid over on to the rocks at the foot of the gulf.' He looked up suddenly into Naughton's eyes. 'With no regrets.'

Naughton was shocked by the unconcern in Musallim's tone of voice. The man didn't seem to realize he had been witness to a cold-blooded murder. Naughton said, 'He killed his brother? Why?'

Musallim smiled faintly, cruelly, and there was something about his smile that mirrored a strange satisfaction. 'Why? Why does a lion hunt a lamb? Why does a vulture wait for the last gasp of death? It's the nature of the beast, Mr Naughton; the glorious beast stalks, waits for the right moment, then – ' he reached out as if catching something in the air ' – the prize. The world spins on that circle of victims, Mr Naughton. All of us either stalk or are stalked. It's an inescapable fact.'

'But,' Naughton said, 'hopefully a man has progressed far enough over the lions and vultures that he no longer needs to stalk.'

'Ah,' said Musallim, holding up a hand. 'The God that created this earth and all on it was wise. He created the natural rhythm of life and death, the circle of victim and survivor. We act in blasphemy if we fail to observe His sacred wisdom.'

Naughton sat still. The din outside was rising. It seemed to thrash the folds of the tent.

'What noble creatures the lions are,' Musallim said, 'to make themselves stronger over the bodies of the weak. How wise and kind are the talons of vultures, to rend away the dead and dying flesh and in so doing clear the way for the strong. The struggle of life and death is not a purposeless game, Mr Naughton, it's a thing of special beauty. Do you understand?'

Naughton reached for the cup of tea and swirled the residue at the bottom. He did not want to look into the face of the man before him because a strange and terrible philosophy glittered in Musallim's eyes.

'The land my father left to me wasn't much,' Musallim said, 'but the secrets hidden from him were revealed to me. One day I found my land swimming in a thick dark pool that had flowed up from the depths. I scooped it up by the bucketful. I smeared it over my face and rolled in it. On that day I traded my modest clothing for the raiment of a wealthy man. On that day I finally knew the power my father had left to me. And now I can build cities and move mountains and change the course of water. Now I finally have the opportunity to communicate to the world the logic of my father.'

'I don't understand.'

Musallim motioned for the servant to carry away the two silver cups. The man bowed and backed out of the tent. 'I

111

have met a man,' Musallim said after another moment, 'who has taught me what I failed to see before. Through him I have grasped the beauty of power. It's so clear to me, Mr Naughton. He is the tooth of the lion, the talon of the vulture. I have given myself to him in order to live in glorious honour.'

The name the old man had spoken. Naughton couldn't remember it. What had it been?

'At first I thought him only a prophet. Now I see him as so much more, so much more. The old prophets spoke of a god who saw things as they could never be. Baal sees what is and what shall always be.'

Naughton tensed involuntarily. Baal. Baal. That was it. He'd read something about it somewhere before. The word Canaan briefly came into his mind.

Naughton said, 'Baal.'

'Yes,' Musallim said. 'Baal. The living Muhammad.'

The other man stood up abruptly and walked to the tent opening. He could see the mad dancing figures in the encampment beyond; the rising smoke dimmed the setting sun. He was breathing heavily though he didn't know why; he wondered if it was safe to try to get back to the city. He said, 'This is madness. This is . . . madness.'

'No, my friend. The madness lies in not accepting the reality of the world as it is. To suddenly find oneself seeing life for the first time after so long being deceived . . . that is a recovery from madness, isn't it?'

He was silent. He could see, in the shadows cast by the dying sun, the great oval tent erected beyond the encampment. He said, 'This man has taken the name of a heathen god. No more, no less.'

'Has he?' the other man whispered. Musallim had moved quietly up behind Naughton. He touched the American gently, up over the shoulder blade, and the fingers reminded Naughton, oddly, of the touch of a knife. 'That was my reaction also, until I saw evidence of his miracles. I've seen the holy fire leap from his fingers. I've seen him kiss the sand and cause a flower to grow. You'll soon discover a truth that will silence all the lying voices. The crowd waits for Baal. His disciples have roamed this land whispering his name to those who would hear. I've seen the converts arriving, in increasing numbers, day after day. But this night, Mr Naughton, Baal breaks his silence . . . there.' He pointed beyond to the huge tent and the humming generator. 'And tomorrow will be the first day of a new world.'

Naughton turned and said hurriedly, 'I need to send a cable immediately. Is there a telegraph office this far from the city?'

Musallim held up his hand to quiet the other man. 'No time, my friend. No time.' And almost with the end of his sentence there began the deep hollow clamour of a bell somewhere in the encampment, over and over until it seemed as if first one person moaned with the bell, then a dozen, then a hundred, until the encampment reverberated with the sound.

'He is come,' said Musallim, his voice trembling with excitement. 'He is come!'

14

The day held on to life by a thin red thread gashed along the horizon. Above it the sky was starless as a lowered blackout curtain.

All across the wide encampment the fires flickered, the lights of a city perched on the brink of a desert no-man's-land. At the tolling of the bell the noise of the assembly, their howls and curses, suddenly rumbled to a halt until there was only the barking of the camp dogs.

And then, as Naughton stood cold and transfixed at the mouth of Musallim's tent, the mass of humanity began to rise up from the smoke-enshrouded encampment. They had thrown all consideration of dignity away; Naughton saw them running for the tent beyond as if they were a pack of maddened animals, snarling and snapping at each other, most of them in filthy rags and many entirely nude. They called out the name over and over, shrieking and begging, as they sent a cloud of sand that spun whipping through tents like desert devil spirals. Naughton saw many of them trampled; one would fall, tripping a score of others, and then there would be a crush of bodies, all arms and legs and heads, fighting to get free and find room inside

113

the great tent ahead. The wealthy ones, clad in shining gold robes and dazzling jewellery, ran shrieking with the rabble; their servants, in the lead, struck down people right and left with the butts of rifles. And still the bell boomed on and on like a great commanding voice and the assembly shrieked the answer *Baal Baal Baal* until it became so loud and terrible Naughton put his hands to his ears.

Wherever the main body of the assembly had passed, the torn ground was littered with the broken bodies of those dead and dying. Then came the sick, struggling through the thick sand on crutches and crawling on their bellies like snake skeletons while angry-eyed dogs nipped at their heels and, taking hold of ripped clothes, worried the wasted bodies mercilessly.

Musallim said quietly, 'It is time for us to go, Mr Naughton. Our place is waiting.' He opened a desk drawer and reached inside. His hand emerged with a shining ruby-encrusted revolver.

Naughton was watching a fight that had broken out at the tent's aperture; men and women battled with each other to gain entrance and finally vanished in a swirl of sand. Musallim caught his elbow and urged him from his safe refuge into a maddened hoard beyond.

As they neared the tent Naughton saw how huge it really was; its appearance had been deceptive. Now the wind beat at its billowing sides and the entrance swallowed swarms of ragged figures. Naughton heard a *click!* as Musallim eased back the hammer of his revolver. Around them the masses churned with glittering teeth and grasping hands, their voices calling out the name even as they battered each other. Musallim shouted at a group of beggars to make way and one of the men, a cruel savagery in his eyes, leaped for Naughton. Musallim's arm jerked out and a pistol shot flung the man away.

They reached the tent entrance, which was clogged by the shouting hordes, and to Naughton's horror Musallim began indiscriminately firing into the dark clot of bodies until a path was made and the two men were able to slip through.

Inside more than one thousand people crowded shoulder to shoulder, kneeling in the sand. Glittering golden chandeliers hung suspended by cables from the ceiling, illuminating in harsh white a sea of heads and bodies in motion like waves. Naughton followed Musallim as he elbowed his way through

114

the mob, brandishing his gun and shouting threats, but the American kept a careful watch over his shoulder in case of an attack from behind. They reached the front of the shouting, sobbing mass and then Naughton saw the immense statue to which the assembly seemed to be praying. High atop a pedestal of gold was a primitive statue of a man. The arms were thrown across the chest in an attitude of superiority and the elongated head, almost triangular, showed thin slits of eyes and a cruel slash of lips. One of the most remarkable, and certainly most disturbing, aspects of the strange artifact was its sexual organs; the penis jutted forward almost four feet and the testes were great black spheres. Naughton stood motionless for a moment, staring at the figure; beside him Musallim fell to his knees and blended his own pleading voice with those of the others. The figure had been carved by a time-lost master; beneath the black stone actual rippling muscles bulged. The features were fierce and demanding. Its eyes seemed to follow Naughton as he stepped forth from the throng and reached out to touch the stone.

It was then that he almost tripped over something that cried out and scuttled away. He looked down and saw an Arab child in rags, its eyes wide and frightened and its body reduced to the merest house of bone. The elbows looked as sharp as daggers and the knees were flat pads on rails of legs. Naughton decided the child was male and that he had probably fallen and been injured in the rush of the crowd. As he looked closer he saw a metal collar around the child's neck, attached to a chain that let out about three feet of slack, then joined to a metal spike driven firmly into the sand. The child seemed on the verge of hysteria; he cringed, holding up his hands for mercy from the man towering over him.

Naughton stepped back a few paces, realizing with a curious and alien sense of power that, if he had so desired, he could have crushed the child with one well-placed slam of his boot.

The great clamour of the bell stopped so abruptly that the sudden silence made Naughton's ears ring. The assembly was quieted; figures lay prone on the ground or kneeled in deference to the glowering statue. Naughton, breaking out in a sweat of absolute fear, looked around for Musallim, but the man had been sucked into the maelstrom. It was not so much the man

115

Naughton sought as the safety of his revolver. Now, standing amid the sour smells of sweat and anticipation, Naughton again felt compelled to seek the eyes of the idol. Its gaze rooted him to the spot. He heard a roar in his head like someone shouting at him from a great distance and he said, *No no this cannot be!*

He was awed by the utter power of the figure as it stood triumphant over the child. How strong and firm it was, he thought. It was the master of them all. When they'd all died and their flesh had decayed back to the dust it would still be there, haughty and sure, in its stone body that had worn the coats of countless ages. He was suddenly ashamed of his frailty. He wanted to fall to his knees and hide his face, but he could not. He trembled, caught between the statue and the mob and unable to turn his back on either.

Naughton was aware of a new sound. The wind had risen to a high-pitched wail that ripped past the great tent. Around him the walls were beaten by the fists of those who had not found room inside. The tent shuddered and rippled. Ropes and support beams groaned. Naughton thought for an instant that the entire enclosure and all in it would be ravaged by the force of the gathering sandstorm.

From behind him, at the rear of the mass, someone screamed brokenly, a strangling sound. Naughton turned to look over the assembly but he couldn't see back as far as the source of the sound. He thought another fight had broken out. And then a Bedouin very near him cried out and put his hands over his ears, throwing himself to the ground and rolling amid the other bodies.

Naughton stood as if in a trance, the sweat beading on his face and dripping softly to his collar.

He watched as the throes began to spread. The wealthy Kuwaitis and Bedouin beggars alike took up the same moan, the same terrible cry of hatred. Scattered fights erupted. Naughton saw the gleam of blood-lust in their eyes as they sprang at each other's throats. He drew back against the statue, feeling somehow protected by its bulk. When the men and women struggled to their feet and attacked each other without hesitation the screaming, moaning din rose and rose until Naughton thought he was going mad. The noise pounded at his temples and he cringed, unable to protect himself.

He saw men ripping the clothes from women and then copulating with them in the churned sand. Women threw their skirts over their heads and spread their legs for anyone who would take them. Gradually the fighting altered itself into an endless series of private sexual combats, but here and there new fights began over partners. Naughton saw men and women wildly hammering each other with no shame nor guilt; women used brutally and then thrown aside for the next pair of ready thighs. He was sickened but could not turn away; it was beyond his power to turn away. A copulating pair rolled against him and he stepped back out of their way. Someone, a Bedouin, screamed something in his ear and leaped for him. He wrestled away from the man and saw the Bedouin dragged down into a heap of struggling bodies. He moved back to get away from sweating nude figures plastered with sand and as he did he stumbled again over the child. He said, 'Goddammit!' and kicked out blindly, hearing a grunt as his boot struck flesh. A hollow-eyed woman with grey decaying teeth groped at his crotch. He swung out at her, his stomach reeling, and caught her solidly beneath the chin. Another woman clutched at his back, her nails raking open his shirt while her teeth tore at his ear. Naughton cursed and pushed her off, his chest heaving and blood dripping down from his ravaged earlobe. A gaunt man in stained robes kicked at his groin, but Naughton caught the man's ankle and heaved him backward on to a stuporous nude couple.

He had no time to think; the blood boiled in his brain. Goddamn them, he said. Goddamn all of them to hell. They were going to kill both themselves and him too; that was it. This would go on until they were all dead. He heard pistol shots and wondered if he could find Musallim. He could hardly breathe for the awful stink. He was choking. Goddamn them, he said. They're trying to kill me. He stumbled against two Bedouins embroiled in a knife fight; one of the men bled from a long gash across his chest and his weak eyes mirrored the loss of blood. The draining man saw Naughton and, turning towards him with a foul curse, lifted his arm to strike with his weapon. At once his opponent took advantage; his arm flashed as he drove his weapon into the small of the wounded man's back.

Naughton picked up the fallen man's knife and backed away

as the victor approached like a dark juggernaut. Naughton screamed, 'Get away!' but his voice was lost in the raging din. He saw murder in the eyes of the other man. Someone behind Naughton shrieked loudly into his ear, and as he spun around to strike he tripped over a body and fell heavily, at the same time tearing the knife back and forth with new-found strength to save his own life.

And then the moaning ceased.

Those fighting in bloody sand stared as if someone had abruptly startled them from their anger. The copulating bodies slowed their sexual throes. Naughton saw Musallim standing halfway across the tent, the gun still in his hand. Their eyes met.

Naughton trembled in rage and confusion. His arms and chest were sticky and warm, but he was only dimly aware that he had bitten into his lower lip. He felt feverish, on the verge of collapse. As the sweet smell of blood reached him he dropped the knife and, like a wounded animal, pressed his face against the wet sand.

He had slashed the throat of the child.

With a cry Naughton pushed at the slack body and dragged himself through the sand. The child's eyes were open above its horrible mauled throat; they stared blankly at Naughton and the wound made him think the child was laughing through blood-caked lips. Naughton dragged over bodies that sought to touch him, to clutch at his drawn face and tear strips from his tattered shirt. He hid his face from them and cringed at the kiss of crawling hands.

And then the sound grew even louder; they were calling the name over and over. He felt as if he were encased in a vault with fleshy walls. He reached out and touched a woman's bare thigh. She sucked eagerly at his mouth. Around him they lifted their arms to the ceiling and the name *Baal Baal Baal* whirled about his head. When he took a breath it was the breath of Baal. When he clutched at slippery flesh it was the flesh of Baal. When he kissed a pair of straining lips they were the lips of Baal.

Sweat filled his eyes. His vision became cloudily dreamlike. He suddenly felt elated and free, caressed intimately by a woman – or more than one woman – he had never even seen before. The smell of blood had seemed to heighten his general sensory awareness. He ripped at the remnants of his shirt, suddenly wishing to be rid of it, and a woman bit like a wild thing at his stomach. The voices around him reached a fever pitch and he let the fever take him. The name throbbed within him. It had already filled his mouth before he could speak. He said, 'Baal.'

Through his blurred eyes he saw men moving among the assembly. One of them he seemed to recognize though he couldn't remember from where. The multitude shrieked in a frenzy. He tried to rise up but was too weak; he remained where he was, his head down. And then someone took his arm and began to pull him steadily to his feet. The grip was tight and strong. Naughton could feel nails biting into his flesh. He tried to see who it was but he could not; the man towered over him like the bulbous-organed statue.

A finger touched his forehead.

He felt a sensation like a mild electric shock course through him; it set him on fire and made the blood tingle He opened his mouth to cry out in an ecstatic agony as his blood turned to liquid fire. Then the man released him and was gone in the crush of the assembly.

Someone else moved beside him and held him as his knees sagged. He looked across and through the mist could make out the placid, drained face of Musallim. His chest was marked with the paths of riotous fingernails and his head-dress had been torn away. Naughton blinked. On the man's forehead, directly between his eyes, was a small red mark that looked like some sort of stain. No, Naughton told himself, no stain. No stain. A fingerprint. A fingerprint.

When he reached out to touch it with grasping empty fingers his knees finally buckled.

15

While he was packing Virga came across the copy of *Time* magazine that had arrived in the mail some days before. He had read it cover to cover, concentrating on the article that had first attracted his interest. Now he took the magazine and walked through the grey-carpeted hallway into his study. He switched on the lights and sat at his desk to re-read the article because in the space of a few days it had become more meaningful than he could have imagined.

It was under the heading *Religion*. Two words, in the magazine's bold typeface, began the article: The Messiah? There was a picture of ragged men and women huddled around a fire, leering and gesturing towards the camera. And another picture, enlarged and very grainy, showed a figure standing on the balcony of a great turreted palace. The caption read 'Baal'.

Virga reached for a pipe from the rack on his desk and lit it thoughtfully. The article contained a piecemeal picture of the swarm of people who had flooded into Kuwait and gathered at a religious shrine erected in the desert. The correspondent had evidently been able to work only with second-hand sources and thus the philosophy of the 'Baalism movement' was not clear; the article indicated that 'Baalism' sought to reinstate individual power. But the primary figure, this mysterious man who called himself Baal, granted no interviews and gave out no public relations material. Kuwait City and its surrounding desert villages, said the article, 'are on the verge of an uncontained religious hysteria due to the very presence of this man, whom some recognize as the living Muhammad, the chosen one, the Messiah.' Virga closed the magazine and pushed it across the desk.

He sat motionlessly. This was certainly a madman who had taken the name of an ancient Canaanite god of sexuality and sacrifice. But why? For what purpose? The worship of Baal, some fifteen hundred years before Christ, involved extravagant and loathsome orgies, child sacrifice, and the transformation of the temple into a house of sodomy and prostitution. It was unbelievable to Virga that any sane man should hope to identify himself with a figure whom Jehovah had ordered banished from the land of Canaan. Under the worship of Baal, primarily a god of fertility, Canaan became a market-place of flesh and savagery; Virga knew that archaeologists who dug the ruined Canaanite cities at Hazor and Megiddo found abominations shocking to a modern world: skeletons of infants stuffed into rude earthen jars for sacrificial burial, idols with warrior-like features and hugely exaggerated sexual organs. There were other times and places, as well, in which the name Baal had surfaced: about three thousand years before Christ he was the 'storm-god' of the Amorites; in the sixteenth century, having fallen from grace by the hand of Jehovah so long before, he preferred to cast his lot with the darker fates and was identified by demon-ologist Jean Wier as a demon prince with three heads: of a man, a toad, and a cat.

And this man, this 'Baal', was the one whom Naughton had gone to find.

Judith Naughton had telephoned Virga one afternoon at his office.

'I was wondering,' she said calmly, 'if you had heard anything from Donald in the last week or so?'

'No, I haven't,' said Virga. 'I expected him to be back by now. He isn't?'

'No.'

Virga waited for her to say something more. When she didn't he said, uncomfortably, 'Well, he's probably all wrapped up in his project. You know how we so-called men of learning act like children when we're working. We lose all sense of time. By the way, wasn't Timmy's birthday last week? What is he now? Seven?'

'Yes. Seven. Donald bought him a present before he left.'

'Oh. Anyway, I really expected to hear more from Donald by now. I received a few letters, just general information on how he was progressing. But nothing in the last three weeks. Actually I need him back to give me an idea of the content of his courses for next semester. Any notion when he's returning?'

'No,' she said. Virga heard her suddenly choke.

'Judith?' he asked. 'Is anything wrong?'

121

And when he met her at lunch the following afternoon he noticed her trembling hands and the swollen pouches beneath her eyes. He ordered a drink for her and said, 'Now. You haven't told me what the problem is. Here I am doing my best to cheer you and you won't give me an inch.' He smiled gently. 'I don't understand the modern woman. I suppose I should give up trying.'

She returned his smile, awkwardly, and Virga saw that she was extremely disturbed. He leaned forward slightly and said, 'I'd like to help you if I can.'

Judith looked into her drink; Virga knew she was deliberately avoiding his gaze. She toyed with the stem of the glass and said, 'I did receive a letter from Donald. A week or so ago. I didn't know what to do; I didn't know whom to talk to. I thought maybe it was some kind of joke or something; I don't know what I thought.' She reached into her handbag. The letter was folded and refolded and bore the stains of a long journey. She slid it across the table to Virga. 'Here,' she said.

He opened the envelope and carefully unfolded a piece of tattered paper. There was only one word on it, scribbled in an almost illegible handwriting. The word *Goodbye*.

Virga said, 'This isn't Donald's handwriting. He didn't send this.'

'Yes,' she said. 'I recognize the handwriting except it's distorted and hurried.' She put a hand to her face. 'I don't know what I've done.' She began to tremble and caught back a sob.

'Did he tell you where he was staying?'

'Yes. I called them but they told me he'd left all his clothes and suitcases and just . . . gone.' She looked up, suddenly pleading with him. 'We never had any trouble. Honestly. Just, you know, arguments over little things. But never anything to make him just decide to leave me with no warning. This is not like him . . .' She dropped her eyes, ashamed at having dragged him into this. 'What am I going to do?'

Virga sat with his hands folded beneath his chin. The *Time* magazine lay on the desk beside him. Judith's eyes, lost and hopeless, had forced his decision. He had discussed with Dr Landon the possibilities of his assuming the duties of department head for a week or so; he had made his airline connections and hotel reservations in advance.

Judith had been correct; such an action was not in line with Naughton's cool, restrained character. And Virga remembered the handwriting, like the mad scratching of an animal's claw on paper. And now this . . . this madman who called himself Baal and who was perhaps responsible, directly or indirectly, for Naughton's letter. He felt the heat of challenge course through his blood. A madman, a false messiah who had encouraged thousands to pay homage to him there on the desert. A man of reason and intelligence suddenly throwing away with a scrawled word his wife, his work, his life. Was there a connection? Virga stood up, filled with new resolve, and went back to his bedroom to finish packing.

On the following day Virga was flying into the rising sun in a TWA Boeing bound for Lisbon, still hours away. From there would be a connection to Cairo, then across the jutting triangle of Saudi Arabia to Kuwait. He drank two scotches and tried to concentrate on *The God-Myths*, a book he had brought along, to sharpen his recall of the pre-Christ Canaan fertility rites and the significance of the warrior-god Baal. Baal, as he'd remembered from his own education on pre-Christ cults, was vanquished from the land by Jehovah, in that period of history called Yahweh. From that time the people of Yahweh grew to despise the memory of Baal.

It interested Virga how the god Baal had become the demon Baal. Perhaps it was only man's memory, reacting to the vile orgies and sacrifices of children performed in Baal's temple; perhaps it was the memory of Yahweh's destruction of Canaan, passed down from mouth to mouth over tribal campfires and finally depicted in Joshua in the Old Testament. But a question haunted him: was Baal only a myth? If Jehovah was a true entity, as Virga believed, then what about the minor gods, like Baal and Seth, Mot and Mithras? But in any event, this man had taken the name Baal for a purpose and Virga was intrigued to find out why.

He was unprepared for the pandemonium at Kuwait's International Airport. Bone-weary and afflicted with jet lag, he took his suitcases and hailed a taxi to get away as soon as possible from the crush of journalists with their cameras and sound rigs. On the highway into the city the sun shimmered in hot waves that rolled and broke across the barren flats. He had visited the Middle East many times before and was well-versed in both customs and language; he found always that the land looked either very old or very new, either ravaged by time or just awakening from a sleep that had spanned the centuries. He reached into his coat and from a tube spread a balm over his forehead and the bridge of his nose to prevent sunburn. The highway seemed congested with all manner of vehicles from limousine on down, and Virga saw scattered accidents here and there. On each side of the highway wrecked and abandoned car hulks had been set afire. In the distance the towers of the city undulated in the heat and, south of them, smoke rose up to the sky in a thousand dark banners. Virga knew it was the encampment Naughton had described.

As they neared the city Virga saw that ramshackle tenements had been constructed to handle an overflow of people. Prefabricated houses and goatskin tents simmered side by side on the flat landscape. And in the sky there was always a slow whirl of smoke that at times drifted across the concrete and made the driver skitter into the sand to avoid heaps of rotting food and bundles of clothing.

In the city Virga felt he had finally caught up with the war; he was appalled. Groups of angry-eyed beggars heaved stones through car windows and uniformed Kuwaiti police officers, armed with revolvers and batons, surged into them to force them away from the roadway. The beggars rocked parked automobiles back and forth, flipped them over on their sides. Fires burned through tenement sections; in the midst of the city several buildings had been set afire. Twice Virga's driver cursed and swerved to miss a body sprawled in the car's path.

The driver put his foot to the floor and roared through a group of Arabs expecting him to slow. They leaped back, cursing, and one of them threw a stone that glanced off the fender. Virga knew that he had entered the land of the insane. Here the insanity was brother to the smoke. Blown by the wind off the gulf, it was everywhere, and he was fearful that if he inhaled it too deeply it would bring on madness.

They arrived at his hotel. Virga took his suitcases in through the shattered glass doors of the lobby. Fragments glittered on the rich dark carpets. One wall, he noted, was punctured by two neat round bullet holes.

The Kuwaiti at the reception desk, a young man in a cream-coloured suit, rang for a boy to carry the cases. 'Dr Virga, yes? It's good you reserved a suite. The Americans have landed, yes?'

'I was unaware there was a war on,' he said, motioning to the smashed windows.

'Last night the scum overflowed the streets. The Holiday Inn and the Hilton were set afire. Nothing left now but hulks. There's not much we can do.'

'I see the police are out.'

'They have to be,' said the Kuwaiti, shrugging. 'If they weren't we'd have no order at all. And three-fourths of the officers have deserted their jobs. Military units are stationed in the city and there are curfews, but there's not much that can be done to stop the property destruction. The jails and hospitals are crowded. What can be done with these people? I've even started carrying a gun.'

Virga looked around the lobby. It was deserted. Chairs were overturned, mirrors broken, ornamental pottery ground into bits. A gold and green tapestry had been ripped down from the ceiling. A small fountain, now drained of water, was filled with glass.

'I apologize for the condition of our vestibule,' the man said. 'Too many stones and no one able to control these people.'

'No,' Virga said, 'that's all right. I understand.'

'You have come, of course,' he said, 'to seek Baal?'

Virga raised his brow. Beside him a slim young man bent to pick up his suitcases.

'All the rest of them have. The airport has been jammed; the highways are almost impassable. I understand the airport will be closed by military order soon. They've come here from all over: Greece, Italy, Spain. The wealthy ones arrived early. They moored their yachts in the harbour or brought their own aircraft; the poor got here any way they could. Of course no one stays in the city. They're all out . . . there.'

'Have you seen this man yourself?' Virga asked.

'Oh no. Not myself. But I know people who have. And of

course the place is packed with journalists seeking interviews.'

Virga reached into the inside pocket of his jacket and unfolded the *Time* magazine page with its photograph of the man standing on a balcony. 'Do you know this place?'

The Kuwaiti leaned over and looked at it carefully. In the far distance Virga heard gunfire that seemed to go on and on, then stopped with disturbing suddenness. The man said, 'In the ancient section. The estate of Haiber Talat Musallim. You've heard of him?'

'No.'

'Ah. The new prophet and disciple of Baal. I'm surprised at this photograph. I didn't know the sentries allowed cameras near the walls.' He looked up from the photographs. 'So. You are here to seek him.'

Virga said, 'Yes,' and took the key he was offered. 'And now I want to take a hot bath and wash this smell of smoke off me.'

'The flow of water is erratic,' the man called. 'Something's wrong with the pipes.'

Virga followed the young man across the lobby to the elevators. He stopped suddenly, staring at a dark wide crust of blood that spread out in a circle on the smooth marble floor. The young man carrying the suitcases looked back at him incuriously.

'Please forgive us,' said the Kuwaiti behind the reception desk. 'We haven't been able to be as clean as we would like. I was forced to shoot a man last night. That is where he bled to death.'

Virga looked up. 'Bled to death?'

'There was no need to call an ambulance. As I told you, the hospitals are crowded.'

Virga blinked, suddenly sick to his stomach.

'If it offends you, we'll clean it up,' the man said.

Behind Virga the elevator doors opened.

16

From his room Virga telephoned the hotel in which Naughton had stayed. A man there explained to him basically what he'd already learned from Judith. Naughton had simply left his belongings and vanished. No word, no trace. Perhaps, the man enquired, if he were a friend of Mr Naughton he would care to pay the remainder of his bill and pick up his suitcases? Virga said he would be in touch again and hung up the receiver.

He tried to rest to alleviate his jet lag but he couldn't fall asleep. Instead he tossed in bed and finally lay staring fixedly up at the ornate ceiling. Through the open windows that looked out on a small balcony the waves of heat were stubborn and brutal, but to close the windows would mean no air circulation. The air conditioning wasn't working. So he lay on the bed, the sweat slowly gathering under his arms and at his temples, and he listened to the raucous noise in the streets below: the honking of automobile horns, the screech of tyres, the cursing and shouting, the occasional blast that might have been either a backfire or the report of a gun. He watched the noise swirl up at the ceiling, there among the ornate gilt-edged scroll-work the Arabs use to excess. It hung there like cobwebs.

He rolled over and unfolded the magazine photograph. The figure was thin and tall; the features were only a shapeless blur. Virga wondered what this man who called himself Baal looked like. He found himself mentally piecing together fragments of faces, though none of them seemed quite right. Whatever he looked like, whoever he was, his presence had thrown this land crazily off balance. And, Virga realized, this man's strength was now stretching across the land's boundaries infecting, as the Kuwaiti had told him, those in other countries as well. The idea of one man wielding the power to throw people into savagery, like the god he had named himself after, was as unsettling and frightening as a nightmare in which one must run but is trapped in an invisible mire.

And another thing disturbed him. He could see no good in

this movement whatsoever. Behind the facade of its promise of 'individual power' was the extreme of violence and rule by mob. All order in this land was on the verge of being overthrown.

He rose up from the bed. He had loosened his tie earlier, and now he took it off. He stripped off his shirt and walked into the bathroom to draw bathwater. After he had turned on the taps he caught a glimpse of himself in the mirror: almost completely bald, dark circles of age under his eyes, the mouth slack and tired. Age had crept upon him line by line, night by night, year by year. He didn't remember growing old. Around his neck hung the small golden crucifix, a gift from Katherine.

Katherine.

He took the crucifix off and laid it carefully on a table in the other room. When he returned to the bathroom he saw a residue of sand at the bottom of the tub.

When he had dressed in a cool blue suit and reapplied the sunburn balm to his face he locked the door and took the elevator down to the lobby. The pool of blood was still there.

Outside the hotel he stood in the heat and watched the erratic flow of traffic while waiting for a taxi.

The cab driver had a ragged grey beard and wore a dirty white cap pulled low. Virga slipped into the rear seat and showed him the magazine photograph. 'Do you recognize this place?'

'I recognize it,' the man said.

'Can you take me there?'

He re-entered the stream of traffic. He drove for a while without speaking, sometimes detouring streets that had been closed off by police officers. Here and there Virga saw groups of uniformed soldiers on patrol; once they passed the body of a soldier, sprawled and bloated on the sidewalk. Once the cab was waved away from a street of ravaged, bullet-torn shops by three soldiers who appeared to be fresh from battle; one of them had a bandage wrapped around his head and another supported himself weakly on his rifle.

They drove on through narrow deserted side streets and alleys.

The driver said, 'Everyone wants to go out there. Why do you wish to see him?'

'I'm very curious,' Virga said.

'You won't get in.'

'Why not?'

'He sees no one.'

'Have you taken many others there?' Virga asked.

'And brought them back when they were turned away. You're no different. I'll be bringing you back as well.'

'Perhaps.'

The driver grunted. 'No perhaps. You're an American? A journalist?'

'Yes, an American. But not a journalist.'

'Then what do you want to see him for?'

'I'm a professor of theology,' Virga said. 'I've heard a great deal about him.'

'No one,' the driver said, 'sees him.'

Virga decided there was no point in arguing. Something caught his eye, a white-painted slogan, in Arabic, on the wall of an empty building: KILL THE JEWS.

They passed the jumble of beggars' shanties and continued out towards the city edge. Then they were in the older part of the city where the stone walls twisted like serpents and the stones of the road were rough and broken. Beyond the square, flat dwellings Virga could see high walls surrounding a structure with imposing, time-worn turrets. As they neared he saw a cluster of automobiles and vans and a swarm of men with cameras and microphones. Around the walls people, in all manner of clothing, either milled about or sat on the ground with their foreheads pressed against the stone. An iron gate was closed across a driveway through the wall and Virga saw it was guarded by two Bedouins in white dishdashahs. He also saw they carried submachine-guns.

The driver stopped the cab along the wall and said without looking back, 'I'll leave the meter running.'

Virga looked at him disdainfully and walked the fifteen yards or so along the wall to where the main body of journalists packed around the barred gate. He was able to see the turreted structure beyond; he had the immediate impression of great wealth and grandeur. The driveway continued on, split around an island of carefully manicured shrubs, then became a short stairway of stone leading up to a massive canopy-shaded doorway. The structure was more tall than it was broad; windows in the turrets gave no sign of life and Virga noted that much of the glass had been broken out. On all sides the lawn was green and immaculate and there was even a small pond. Beyond the landscaped shrubbery there was a metal-walled hangar and a hint of heat waves rolling across tarmac.

Someone jostled into him. Someone dropped a camera; Virga heard it shatter on the stones. There were curses and shouts and suddenly he realized he was in the midst of a group of journalists, none of them appearing to be American. Someone started shouting in French at the Bedouin guards and Virga saw, with an alarm bordering on panic, one of the men swing his submachine-gun up, smoothly and coldly, with the air of a seasoned killer. The angrily shouting Frenchman continued his verbal abuse. One of the guards stepped forward and grabbed at a man in a loud green jacket. Another man said something sharply in a language Virga didn't recognize, and a scuffle began between two or three men at the front of the group. Fists were flying. The Bedouin guard staggered back away from the gate and at that moment the crowd of journalists saw their opportunity and surged forward with their cameras ready, moving towards the gate in hopes of getting through. The other guard backed away.

Virga struggled against them. He was carried forward and almost went down. Someone beside him was shrieking in Arabic, 'One picture! One picture!' A man ahead of Virga fell down and Virga tripped over his legs. He reached out a hand for support and found himself grasping the bars of the gate, his face pressed against the scorching iron.

He caught his breath and tried to pull away but there were others behind him, pressed forward by the group of wild journalists.

Something growled, low and with utter menace.

Virga was looking into the bared maw of a Doberman Pinscher on the other side of the gate. Its eyes were wide with a fury that signalled attack; the gleaming white teeth, stake-sharp, were only inches from Virga's face. The animal strained on a chain leash.

'My God,' Virga said.

Behind him the journalists were snapping pictures one after another. They pressed against the gate, their cameras whirring.

The man holding the Doberman let his grip go slack on the chain.

Virga jerked his head away just as the animal charged the gate. It sprang up on its hind legs, snapping and snarling at the men who cringed but still kept taking pictures even as they backed away. Another Doberman sprang from nowhere. It remained crouched, growling, with eyes that watched for any new threat.

The Bedouin guards tore into the journalists, pushing them back with their weapons. One of them fired his gun over their heads by only a few inches and spent shells clattered to the ground. Another Bedouin reached down and roughly grabbed Virga around the collar, dragging him back away from the gate.

'No,' said a man standing on the other side, the man whose fingers had released the dog chain. 'Not him.'

The Bedouin looked up. He immediately let Virga go and turned to push the other men back with the butt of his gun.

The man behind the gate grabbed hold of the dangling chain and drew the dog towards him. Someone else, another man, retrieved his animal as well.

Virga shook his head. He had bumped it on the gate and he felt dizzy. He slowly brushed himself off and got to his feet. He looked through the bars at a tall blond man whose flesh was the colour of paste. His eyes seemed dead; they stared through Virga. Beside him stood a darker man with curly hair and broad shoulders. Both of them shared the same incurious expression, the same air of superiority. And both of them, Virga saw, had some sort of mark on their foreheads. He couldn't tell what it was.

The blond man said in English, 'I heard you say something. You're an American.'

'Yes,' Virga said, his head beginning to ache. 'I am.'

'You're a journalist?' the man asked. At his side the eyes of the Doberman yearned for Virga.

'No.' He thought for a moment of what he was but the ache in his head prevented him from remembering.

'Your name?'

'Virga,' he said. 'My name is James Virga.'

The man nodded. He glanced over at the darker man, who turned without a word and walked up the drive towards the structure beyond.

And suddenly he remembered. 'I'm a professor of theology,' he said.

'I know,' the man replied. He threw a bolt on the gate, then another, and finally he swung it open.

Behind Virga the crowd surged forward again towards the opened gate. The blond man grasped Virga's shoulder and pulled him through, then let the Doberman stand guard while he hurriedly rebolted the gate. The Bedouins were knocked aside, cursing. Men crushed up against the iron bars, shouting and pleading.

Over the noise of the journalists, the man said, 'Rashid. Kill three of them.'

The words took effect. The journalists scrambled away from the gate, clawing at each other so as to get someone in front of them in the line of fire. Several of them fell to the ground and were trampled senseless.

But already one of the guards had stepped forward, satisfaction and pleasure on his face. His weapon came up with an excruciating delicacy. In the next moment it rattled in an arc across the front line of the terrified men. Shell casings hissed in all directions.

The blond man drew the Doberman close and began walking up the drive. When he saw that Virga wasn't following he turned and said softly, 'Are you coming?'

Virga was staring at the dead men on the other side of the bars. The crowd of journalists had scattered; some were still taking pictures as they ran. One of the Bedouins kicked a corpse squarely in the face. Virga turned away. 'Yes,' he said. 'I'm coming.'

17

Down the dim corridors Virga followed the blond man who had moments before ordered the execution of three men.

They climbed a long marble staircase where Virga saw food and excrement smeared about; he wondered if the dogs were allowed to run free. They reached a narrow hallway that stretched on past a dozen closed doors. Here and there the hallway turned off into huge rooms or widened into alcoves. They moved through an area that had been decorated with elaborate Islamic art; Virga saw the remnants of pictures, now shredded as if by maddened claws, and of bits of ancient and probably priceless pottery. Now the once beautiful objects crunched beneath their feet.

Virga felt alarm at being in a hostile environment. Everywhere eyes seemed to be following him; he was conscious of being watched from all sides, though they never passed anyone or saw anyone. He had felt, or rather sensed, the ominous presence that was part of this place. The notion of something lurking, something staring from the shadows at his back, was unshakable. And he noticed, in the dankness of the hallway, things scrawled on the walls, on the floor, on the ceiling. Triangles and circles and strange scribblings that made no sense to him at all, yet filled him with a dread he could not even begin to grasp. He was trembling and he hoped the other man would not notice.

And there was something else. An odour, a stench. Part of it was the excrement smeared everywhere, even on the walls; part of it was rotted food. But there was something else, something that was whirling around his head, clinging to his clothes as if it were a solid but decaying presence. It was the stench of death, of something perhaps long past death.

'Are you also an American?' Virga asked the man. His voice echoed in the hallway.

'I was born in America,' the man said without turning.

Virga had hoped he would. He wanted to see what it was up

on the man's forehead. 'What's your name?'

'Olivier,' the man said.

'That's all?'

'Yes. That's all.'

Ahead the hallway ended at a pair of gold-ornamented closed doors. On the walls and ceiling were the same strange symbols, triangles and circles. Centred directly above the doorway, Virga noted, was an inverted cross.

The man turned abruptly. 'I assume we'll be meeting again. I'll leave you now.' He opened the doors and Virga stepped through, his eyes trying to pierce the gloom that leaped at him from the silent chamber. The man firmly shut the doors behind him.

He felt, with the closing of the door, a tremendous and awful sense of being imprisoned in a place from which he had no chance of escape. He shivered; it was actually cold in the room. As his eyes grew accustomed to the dimness he saw that he stood in a library of some sort. Around him were shelves packed with books, thousands and thousands of them. Not wanting to betray his fear, he attempted to control his trembling. He checked his initial impulse to turn towards the doorway and retrace his steps, if that were possible, out into the sweet hot sun. In this room the presence was fierce and heavy, bearing down on his back like the teeth of the snarling Dobermans.

And he realized, as the flesh tingled at the back of his neck, that he was not alone.

He heard the breathing, steady and soft, from the opposite side of the room. A single thin beam of sunlight was thrown through the narrow slit of a window. It fell across the shoulders of a man.

The man sat motionless, his hands folded before him on a wide desk topped with the alternating squares of a chessboard. The two opposing camps had been set up; they glowered at each other across their battlefield. Virga stepped forward. He could not see the man's face quite yet; it was covered by a broad band of shadow. But he could see clearly the man's hands, skeletal and white as if carved of either ivory or ice. They never moved, but as Virga approached he was aware of the man's head turning slightly, very slightly, to watch him. He was aware of eyes cutting into his brain, though he couldn't see them at all. He felt open and defenceless.

Baal said softly, 'Dr Virga?'

He was surprised. Had the man been aware of his presence? He was fearful of moving any closer. He stopped where he was.

'It is Dr Virga, isn't it?' the man asked.

'Yes. That's right.'

The man was nodding. He gestured with a thin finger to the shelves of books. 'Your works are here. I've read them. I've read every volume in this library.'

Virga grunted. Impossible.

'Is it?'

He froze. Had he spoken the words? Had he? The choking presence in the room made it difficult to think clearly. Yes, he decided momentarily, he'd spoken aloud.

'Your colleague Dr Naughton,' Baal said, 'has told me a great deal about you. And of course your reputation as a man of intellect precedes you.'

'Naughton? He's here?'

'Of course. Isn't that why you've come to this place? To seek Dr Naughton? Yes, I think it is. Dr Naughton is also a man of great intellect, a man of great foresight. He recognizes opportunities and thus controls his destiny.'

Virga was straining to see through the shadows that obscured the man's face. He had the impression of sharp features, of high cheekbones and narrow eyes. 'I've come a long way. I'd like to see him.'

Baal smiled; Virga saw the teeth flash in an obscene grimace. Something oppressive radiated from this man that filled him with alarm. 'Dr Naughton has been working day and night on his research. His book will be completed shortly.'

'His book?'

'I believe he discussed it with you before he left America. His book on the false messiahs that distorted the truth before I came to cleanse it. His final chapter is devoted to my philosophy.'

'I'd like to see him. Surely you won't turn me away after I've come all this distance. He's here, isn't he?'

'He's here,' Baal said. 'But working.'

135

Virga waited but Baal sat without speaking. As a final effort Virga said, 'I have a message from his wife.'

'He has no wife.'

Virga had decided he would have to see Baal more clearly. He stepped forward, almost to the edge of the chessboard.

The power, the menace, in Baal's eyes almost staggered him. He found he couldn't gaze into them; he had to avert his own eyes. They were dark and deep-set with a cruel intelligence, a glimmer of utter hatred. The man was lean but there was a suggestion of raw physical strength in his wide firm shoulders. Virga guessed that he was in his late twenties, possibly thirty but certainly no more. He spoke perfect English with no trace of an accent. Indeed, his voice was as soft and soothing as the first wave on the shore of sleep. It was only those eyes, those terrible things moving in a white firm-jawed face, that gave him the aspect of a death's head.

'You're an American?' Virga asked.

'I am Baal,' the man said, as if in some way this answered his question.

Virga suddenly noticed the chess pieces, carved of a fine and lustrous stone. The white pieces, on the side on which Virga stood, were monks in flowing robes, demure nuns, sombre priests, thin towers of cathedrals. The queen was represented by a woman in a shawl, her eyes cast to heaven. The king, a bearded image of Christ, stood with hands imploring the Father. On the opposite side, and Virga saw now that the man had moved some of the black pieces to begin the game, were sorcerers, sword-wielding barbarians, hunch-backed demons; the king and queen were, respectively, a thin crouching figure with a beckoning forefinger and a woman with the tongue of a snake.

Baal had noticed his interest. 'You're a chess player?' he asked.

'Occasionally. I see you're attacking. But you lack an opponent.'

'Attacking?' he asked quietly. He leaned forward. His eyes were burning through Virga's forehead. 'Oh no, not yet. I'm still learning the art of manoeuvre.'

'A time-consuming art.'

'I have time.'

136

Virga raised his eyes from the chessboard and looked into Baal's face; he held his gaze as long as he dared. 'Tell me,' he said, 'who you really are. Why have you chosen the name of a god of savagery and sacrifice?'

'My name is . . . my name. It has always been Baal; Baal it will always be. And in this world, my good Dr Virga, savagery and sacrifice are the wine and bread of the true God.'

'Then who is the true God?'

Baal smiled again, as if he knew some secret Virga could never hope to fathom. 'You have eyes. You've seen the forces at work in this land, even in the entire world. Now you can answer your own senseless question. Who is the true God?'

'I see here men becoming less than men. I've seen brutality and murder and I want to know the part you're playing in it all. I want to know your motives. Is it political power you seek? Money?'

Baal's eyes had become more threatening. Virga felt the need to back away a few paces. 'I have all the money I want at my disposal. Political power is worthless. No. Mine is the power to reinforce the will of the true God of this world. And reinforce it I will. They listen; they listen. They've grown sick of a teaching for mindless children. Real men must live in the real world and the real world teaches one law – survive. Survive if you must break the bodies of those who hope to break yours. It is a world of the living and the dead, the wise and the foolish.'

'Yours is a dog-eat-dog philosophy that leads to . . . what I've seen happening here. This city has gone mad. I've seen what I never thought was possible in a civilized country.'

'This city has regained its senses.'

'Then,' Virga said, 'you're the one who must be mad. You advocate death and destruction, fire and hatred. Your name is well-chosen. The Baal who preceded you was a festering sore to Jehovah.'

Baal sat without moving. Virga thought he felt something clutch at his throat, something cold and solid. Baal's head slowly, slowly came up; in his white face were the eyes of a snake. 'No Baal,' he said, 'preceded me. I know Jehovah,' he spat the name out as if it were pus, 'better than you dream. Bethel, Ai, Jericho, Hazor . . . all the glorious cities ash.' His face suddenly distorted. His voice changed from silken smoothness to the rough guttural voice of the storm. 'War,' he breathed, 'war is the sceptre of my God and he wields it so very very well. To take the name of Jehovah and induce men to betray their cardinal nature is the sin. To distort the world with lies is the fall of Jehovah. He wishes to hide the truth.'

Baal's eyes flashed. 'Enough games,' he said.

'My God,' Virga said, transfixed. 'You actually want havoc and death. Who are you?'

'I am Baal,' said the man across the chessboard, and Virga caught a brief, frightening glimmer of red in the man's gaze, 'and I hold you between my fingers.'

With one arm Baal swept across the chessboard, scattering the white pieces around Virga's feet. Virga's head pounded fiercely; he wondered vaguely if he could have a concussion from striking the gate. But there was something else, the thing that he thought had grasped him around the throat. Now he was certain that something was there, squeezing with icy disembodied fingers. He put his hand to his forehead; he was sweating and seemed to be running a sudden fever. He staggered and shook his head, aware of the man's eyes burning, burning, burning. Oh God the pain, the pain.

'Yes,' said the man softly. 'The pain.'

Black smoke whirled inside Virga's head. His brain had caught fire; the smoke clogged his sight and breathing. He shook his head to clear it but it was no good. He stumbled backward, away from Baal, and almost fell to the floor.

'It is no accident,' Baal said, 'that you're here. You were expected. Naughton's letter brought you.'

It seemed as though Baal were speaking in more than one voice. The voices merged together and then split into hundreds of distinct sounds, strained through the kaleidoscope of whirling smoke that brought tears to Virga's eyes.

Baal said, 'You are a respected theologian, known as a man of sound and logical intellect. I can use you . . .'

The pounding within Virga's head continued. He could not free himself of it. The voice shouted into his ears; he could hear nothing but the voice, the commands, of Baal.

'. . . to bring others to me. You will tell the story of how I was born in poverty in America, how the image of God came

138

to me in a dream and commanded that I lead the people through the labyrinth of knowledge. This you will do and more. Much much more. You will publicly proclaim your faith to me and your rejection of the Jew disease. I am the cleansing fire.'

'No,' said Virga, struggling to keep his balance. He closed his eyes but still the voices hammered at him brutally. 'No . . . I . . . won't . . .'

'Yesssss,' hissed the thousand voices. They echoed from the library walls and tore through him like bullets from all directions. 'Yesssss.'

Virga struggled and shook his head. The black smoke was choking him. No. No. 'Yes,' he said, falling to his knees. 'Yes. The pain. The pain.'

Baal was standing. He moved around the desk and Virga saw him reaching as if in a slow-motion nightmare, his thin fingers outspread. 'Yesssss,' said Baal, almost in his ear. 'Yesssss.'

Virga couldn't breathe. He was choking, gasping for air in the stinking chamber. He wrenched loose his tie, tore open his collar, and the sunlight glinted from the crucifix as it hung free.

Baal didn't move. 'Take that off,' he said very quietly. 'Did you hear what I said?' There was something of the knife's edge in his voice.

Virga stirred, feeling that the disembodied fingers around his throat had, at least fractionally, weakened. He tried to rise but couldn't.

Baal stood his ground but still did not move. 'Take that off,' he said, his eyes red and widened.

'No,' said Virga, bile burning within him. 'No.'

'DOG! YOU DAMNED WHORESON BASTARD!' Baal snarled, his teeth clenched like a ravening animal. 'DAMN YOU TO HELL! DAMN YOU!'

Virga frantically shook his head to clear it. Baal kicked at him and then drew back; he would not move any closer to the crucifix. Virga tore it from around his neck and held it in the palm of his outstretched hand, defying Baal with the object's gleaming golden surface.

And he was aware too late that the doors had been violently flung open, that two men, one dark and the other fair, had

139

burst behind him into the library. Baal motioned with a hand and Virga turned to meet the fist that slammed solidly into the side of his head. He groaned in pain and fell forward, gripping the crucifix with ebbing strength.

'GET THAT OUT OF HIS HAND!' commanded Baal, maintaining his distance.

The two disciples picked at Virga's closed hand as if it were red-hot; they worked at the fingers, trying to loosen the man's grip. Virga, in semiconsciousness, held on to it knowing that if he lost it he too was lost. The power of the man would swallow him into a bestial maw without its protection.

Virga's fingers would not open. The dark-haired disciple cursed violently and stamped down on the man's hand with his booted foot. There was the sound of shattering bone and Virga immediately lost consciousness. The man who had broken his hand found the crucifix and with the toe of his boot kicked it away into a dark corner.

'Bastard,' said Baal, whispering close to Virga's head. 'You thought it would be easy. No, my friend, it is not. You will come to love me and despise that. Its touch, the mere sight of it, will be hot like the diseased bowels from which it dropped. You weak bastard.' Baal paused, glancing down to where a smear of blood showed on the palm of Virga's injured hand. Baal roughly spread the broken fingers and stared into the wound inflicted when a booted foot had smashed flesh against a golden object.

The wound was in the shape of a crucifix.

Baal dropped the hand with a shouted oath and wrenched away. 'HIS HAND!' he said. 'CLOSE IT! CLOSE IT!'

The fair-haired disciple hauled Virga up by his collar and then let him fall so he was lying on the offending wound. Then he too backed away, trembling, from the fallen man.

'We have come far,' Baal said, 'but not far enough. Some day we can withstand that, but not now . . . not now. Our good Dr Virga – our fucking bastard Dr Virga was to provide our passage. And now . . .' his eyes narrowed. 'There is another way. There is another way.'

'What about him?' the dark-haired disciple asked.

Baal turned, keeping his eyes averted from the far corner of the library. He towered over the motionless body. 'He's contaminated by that mark. With the stub of a hand he'll do us no good. I don't want his corpse found near this place. Do you understand, Verin?'

'Yes,' the other man said.

'Then you and Cresil do what you will with him; afterwards leave the corpse for the vultures in the desert.'

The fair-haired man, Cresil, bent and dragged Virga across the floor and through the doorway, leaving a trail of blood, while Verin followed like a jackal smelling death.

18

Virga regained consciousness when a sponge was thrown across his face. No, not a sponge, he decided momentarily, but rather his swollen and bloody hand. He remembered the awful sound of bones giving way, like sticks broken by powerful hands, and wanted to be sick but could not move. He forced down the bile that rose, burning, to the top of his throat and tried to get his bearings.

He looked up at the bright stars as they whirled their divine patterns. But the night was not old; a faint tinge of purple in the sky showed the path on which the sun had slipped the horizon. He was moving, being jostled and bounced on thick tyres, and there was the loud roar of an engine. There was no longer the smell of gulf salt in the air. Now there was only the dry, bitter smell of the desert cooling into night.

Virga's knees were drawn up tightly, his legs cramped. He had been slammed on to the rear floorboard of a Land-Rover and it was only when he twisted his head to the side that he realized his mouth was gagged with coarse cloth. At the driver's seat was a man Virga had to concentrate to recognize. Yes. The fair-haired man from Baal's library. And in the other seat was the darker disciple. He had seen them for only a split second before his vision was blocked out by a fist. Both of the men wore pistols at their belts.

How far into the desert they were Virga had no way of knowing. He didn't know where they were headed or why, but he made no noise or motion to indicate to the disciples that he had awakened.

His head pounded fiercely. It was a fiery ache that raged just behind his eyes. The pain of his head and the pain of his shattered hand were two brothers who met somewhere at his shoulder.

He realized that the crucifix had saved him, had amazingly repelled the man, as if he were a vampire. Another moment and Virga would have been swept away by an awesome combination of horror and euphoria, sweating and screaming. The man's eyes remained in his mind, circling in mockery of the stars.

The Land-Rover dipped and swayed over desert dunes like a craft at sea. The two men never spoke or moved; the guns they wore spoke for them. Virga thought he was either going to be killed or held somewhere until he agreed to aid Baal. Perhaps he would even be tortured. These were men like their eerie master, without shame, without guilt, without mercy.

Virga fought off a new wave of unconsciousness that crept subtly over him. His fingers, crushed and crooked, had turned blue. Veins throbbed in his wrist and the injured hand had swollen hideously to twice its size. Like Job's disease, Virga thought, almost humoured by that recollection. The Land-Rover, jarred by rocks, brought him back into the terrible present and the realization that he must at least try to escape.

He stretched slowly, watching the men's profiles. There seemed to be no injuries other than the hand. But his legs were very stiff. If he could leap from the Land-Rover and find a hiding place in the darkness, perhaps . . . but he feared that his legs might not hold against the shock. If his knees buckled they would simply run him down, if they meant to kill him, or jam him into the vehicle again if they meant to hold him captive. He worked his shoulders free, painfully, and was able to glance about in the darkness. On all sides the desert was bare and forbidding. The only lights he saw were cast by the headlamps of the vehicle, revealing flat sand and outcroppings of rock. He drew his head back down.

He would not get two chances. The element of surprise would have to carry him. He would have to take the risk of not being able to find a hiding place. If they meant to kill him it was the logical thing to do; if they meant to torture him it was the logical thing to do because he would rather be dead than help this madman who called himself Baal. His breath hissing under the cloth, he worked his legs free. He tensed to jump and then untensed, tensed and untensed, waiting for a rush of adrenalin to boost him. His heart pounded almost audibly.

The Land-Rover was climbing a bluff. Rocks thumped beneath the tyres. This was the moment.

Virga grit his teeth and, shoving out with his legs, dived over the side of the vehicle.

He cradled his injured hand but his elbows hit rocks when he fell, shredding his jacket. He cried out involuntarily and knew that the muffled sound had carried. As he slid across rocks to smooth sand at the base of the bluff, he saw the two men look down at the Land-Rover's empty rear floorboard.

The Land-Rover turned sharply, its yellow headlamps searching like spider eyes.

Virga scrambled to his feet, sweating with the awful pain, and ran. The sand, sucking at his shoes, slowed him. Behind him the vehicle roared louder and louder. He did not dare look around. Suddenly there came the *crack!* of a pistol shot and sand kicked up viciously to his right, less than a foot away. Virga knew they meant to murder him. Before him stretched a plain of sand and rock; the Land-Rover would soon reach him on this terrain. Already his silhouette ran ahead of him, framed in the headlamps that were rapidly gaining distance. He cursed and felt cold panic rising. There was no place to hide!

But no! Virga ducked his head and ran, smelling the swirl of sand from the heavy-ribbed tyres. Ahead, the plain suddenly dropped off into jagged darkness: a narrow chasm. If he could reach it the Land-Rover couldn't follow without turning turtle. But there was no way of judging its depth. It could be a fall of only ten feet to deep sand, or it could be a fall of twenty-five feet to razor-edged rocks. There was no time to weigh a death by bullet against a death in free-fall. The Land-Rover roared at his heels; the next bullet screamed past his left ear. Virga took a deep breath and, reaching the edge, leaped out into space.

The length of the fall made him shriek into the cloth. Brush and rocks ripped at him. And then, finally, he hit sand peppered with stone. His knees and elbows scraped raw, he rolled for cover against the chasm wall. With his good hand he ripped away the gag and panted heavily, listening for another shot.

Dozens of feet above him, the lights of the Land-Rover prowled the opposite wall. He could see the men looking over the precipice into the chasm's depths. Virga flattened himself against the wall of sand and stone, afraid that they might pinpoint him by his heartbeat. He tried to control his ragged breathing. After a few endless moments Virga watched the Land-Rover's headlamps move a dozen yards along the rim.

Virga's senses stirred. Perhaps they had lost him entirely. Perhaps they thought he was moving at the bottom of the chasm, or perhaps they even thought that he might be dead and now they were searching for the body. The Land-Rover slowly, slowly followed the winding course of the chasm. Virga watched the yellow headlamps move away. Yes! They'd lost him! But still he crouched in the darkness, ignoring the swollen agony of his hand; his eyes were narrowed and probing the depths around him, wary of some kind of trick. Perhaps one of the men had come down into the chasm and was now, gun in hand, stalking him.

But then he saw the two men begin to fire randomly down from the Land-Rover, spraying bullets in haphazard patterns. Slugs whined around him; he cringed and saw sparks fly along the chasm wall as bullets ricocheted off rock. The men continued firing until Virga heard the clicking of empty chambers. They arranged themselves back into their seats and the Land-Rover tore away across the desert, leaving a trail of spinning sand.

It was a very long time before Virga reached the rim. Losing a foothold on rocks or a grip on brush, he fell twice before hauling himself over the edge. Very far away but still visible on the desert were the red tail-lights of the vehicle.

Watching the Land-Rover vanish in the night, Virga was aware of the pain that had crawled up his shoulder and spread across his chest, sending out razors as reconnaissance over the fields of flesh. It gradually and insidiously claimed his neck, numbing it, and when it reached his temples he slumped forward and lay with his lips pressed into the sand.

When he awakened he realized why they had not made a

stronger effort to find him. In the harsh crimson light of the predawn sky he struggled to his feet, his hand hanging like a sack of concrete, and saw the immense empty expanse of desert that even now shifted and danced in veils of heat. For miles and miles and miles beyond stretched only the white dunes and sun-baked flats. God only knew how far it would be to a highway or a Bedouin waterhole. Soon the sun would burst over the far dam of land and drown him in an ocean of his own salt sweat. Around him, with the first blinding arc, came a solid drone of insects awakening in their sand nests. Flies began circling his head, darting down to suck at the sweat; they smelled the blood and attached themselves greedily to the crusted wound on his palm.

They had left him, not caring whether he was dead or not, because out here it was only a matter of time. He had no water and no hope of shade, though tyre tracks were still clear in the direction in which the Land-Rover travelled. He blessed the deep indentations that stretched on, on, on out of sight, seeing in them at least the correct direction in which to walk. Virga pulled his jacket up like a makeshift Arab head-dress to protect his face and bald head. He started walking, squinting as the sun whitened above the horizon.

The sun climbed. Maddening insects bit at his exposed flesh. When he ducked his head to escape their whirling cloud they descended too; they filled his eyes and clogged his nostrils. They smashed themselves to death against his face. He moved on, across rock flats and across dunes in which he sank to his knees. Overhead the sun was both a staring inflamed eye and an open bloody mouth.

Fever boiled in his brain. His legs cramped and knotted again and again; he had to sit in the sand and knead the muscles with his good hand until he could walk again. Soon he found himself dazed by the heat and drifting off the tyre track. Shaking himself awake, he stared into the distance hoping to see telephone lines or the rise of derricks, but nothing altered the desolation. His lips cracked with the unbearable midday sun; the thought of cool water was driving him mad but it was difficult to think of anything else. He was past the point of either pain or fear; he concentrated on what seemed to be the blue shimmer of a river far, far ahead.

He remembered sailing the *Charles* with Katherine clutching his arm, her nose and cheeks windburned, her dark hair wild in the bracing wind. Above them the canvas billowed dramatically and he caught the fresh scent of the wide wonderful river; he wondered now, thousands of miles from that time and place, why he hadn't cupped his hand in the water and pressed it to his lips, gently, just like . . . this.

And when he opened his eyes he staggered and spat out sand.

Katherine, he said, closing his eyes to blot away the sun. Katherine. The world had revolved around her face, the centre of the universe. He had watched her grow from a tomboyish Irish girl into a woman of charm and grace. He remembered that she spoke with her hands. They were always in motion like white butterflies and it intrigued him to watch their performance. She said it was a trait passed down from generation to generation on her mother's side, that constant conversation of weaving fingers. Katherine had been a fine woman; the memory of her was still fine. She had been energy and life, beauty and hope.

He remembered her joy at realizing she was pregnant. When she'd first thought, after two miscarriages, that she was destined to remain childless she had purposefully kept a tight grip on her emotions. Maybe, she had whispered to him while they lay beneath the blankets listening to the crack of logs in the fireplace, the muted music of rain against the windows, she was not meant to bear children.

'And how can you be a judge of that?' he asked her.

'I don't know. I feel it, that's all.'

'Mrs Virga,' he said, taking on the tone of mock gravity, 'beware. You're dabbling in theories of predestination.'

'No. I'm serious.'

He gazed into her placid eyes, those orbs of fathomless blue, and saw that she was. He said, 'They say the third time is the charm.'

'This is the last time,' she said. 'If something happens this time I don't know what I'll do. I don't think I could go through that again.'

'Nothing,' he said firmly, 'is going to happen.'

146

'I'm frightened,' she said, drawing close to him. In the fireplace a log squealed. 'Really I am. I've never been so frightened about anything before.'

'I'm not.' He looked deep into her eyes. 'I'm not frightened because I know it'll be all right. Whatever happens, everything will be all right.'

But everything was not 'all right'. It ceased being all right when, months later as she was swollen and radiant, she tripped on loose carpeting at the top of the stairway and, screaming out, plunged helplessly down the stairs.

He wondered what the child would have been like. A boy. Perhaps like Naughton.

He opened his eyes, the movement of his lids scattering flies. He'd been walking in his sleep. The sun was still as hot; the desert was still as empty. He might have been walking for days; he might have been walking in circles. He didn't know. Looking towards the horizon, he felt the knot of tension in his stomach explode in a burst of bitter pain.

Ahead the sand was endless and unchanging.

He had lost the Land-Rover trail.

In all directions there was only the blinding white. Nothing else. He reached into a pocket of his tattered jacket and found the small bottle of sunburn balm. He applied it to his face, feeling cracked skin and the beginnings of large watery blisters. Several broke when he touched them and fluids leaked down his face, attracting new hordes of insects. Still he moved on, stumbling along what he thought was a straight line leading directly towards the gulf, but after a while he decided no, this was not the right way. He turned and retraced his path; after several minutes he decided this was again wrong and began walking in yet another direction. His flesh burned, blistered, burst and then reburned all over again.

The sun ate through his skull to the brain. The great white circle darkened, darkened, darkened until it was as black as the eye of Baal. Virga saw the man's head as huge as a solar system, with one eye the sun and the other the moon. His captive planet was always beneath his gaze. Virga saw him in black robes towering over the cities of man. And he grew larger and larger, his shadow spreading across the face of the earth. Finally his awful form darkened the stars and all creation was pitched into the black stagnation of the abyss. Virga shook his head to free himself of the maddening visions but he could still see Baal's gigantic head suspended in the sky and his mouth opening to swallow museums and libraries and all the wonderful works of man.

Virga fell to his hands and knees. The flies swarmed thickly about his head; he waved them off weakly with a hand swollen black. This is the moment. He saw it scrawled on the sand, in the blazing sky, on the undulating horizon. Of all the hundreds who had proclaimed themselves messiah, all the madmen, all the cheats, this one was different.

Fluids from broken blisters dripped down his chin. He watched the pattern they made as they splattered in the sand.

This one was different. An animal and a man. The intelligence and cunning of a man, the savagery and power of a brute beast. This one . . . was different. He had already infected thousands; how many more? And thus the slaughter and chaos would continue until that final finger moved towards a button in an unlocked steel cylinder. And the blast would moan on four winds *Baal Baal Baal*. It would scrawl his name on ravaged concrete and scorched flesh. And then it would be too late. Could it be too late already? Could it? Virga trembled violently and shook his head from side to side. The Antichrist. He looked up to the sun for flaming mercy but it only burned him the more. The Antichrist. The insects' torment had his sanity hanging by a thread. Filled with his blood, they would fly to their nests to disgorge it and then return, newly hungry. They shrieked in his ears. Against the silence of the desert was a great multitude of people shouting at him from a distance: *Antichrist Antichrist*.

Virga could not hold on. Beneath his face there was a puddle of liquid, his liquid. His life. He saw himself reflected in it.

He loosened his grip on consciousness. As he fell forward the noise of the multitude rose in his ears until he was completely, totally deafened.

19

Out of the depths of darkness came a hand that circled his face. Its fingers were poised to rip out his eyes; Virga tried desperately to move his head but he couldn't. It seemed that he was pinned down, helpless to protect himself. He thrashed and moaned, trying to avoid the awful claw that now lowered itself, twitching sporadically towards his open eyes. He could see nothing but the hand as it gradually grew larger and larger, broader and more sinewy, and he saw the shudder through the tendons that foretold the coming pain of plucked-out eyes. He fought against whatever was confining him and cried out 'NO!' at the top of his lungs.

The hand suddenly burst into flame. Within seconds it had burned itself out and fallen into ashen pieces. He saw the outline of another hand pressing against his forehead. Its touch soothed him; he felt mercifully released from the pain that tormented his every breath. He tried to see who it was but the palm touched his eyelids and made him forget everything but the softness of rest.

A man said, 'The fever is gone. Sleep now.'

And Virga slipped away to dream of sailing the *Charles* with Katherine, smelling of cinnamon, clutching tightly to his arm.

When he opened his eyes again it seemed that he could still smell the warm timber of his sloop, the soft suppleness of the river. But it was still dark and he thought at first he was still dreaming. He lay, his eyes open, and listened.

Insects hummed in the distance; the thought of them made him wince. Something was burning. Virga heard the gentle crackling of wood and smelled smoke. He was lying on a frame cot within a tent of goatskin. He could see a small fire of brush and sticks burning just outside the tent entrance. Night had fallen but he had no idea how long it had been since he found himself lost in the desert. When he tried to struggle up he realized his hand had been splinted with sticks and wrapped in a cloth bandage.

Virga quietly pushed back the blanket and got to his feet. He staggered, drunk with the sudden rush of blood to his head, and waited until he could walk steadily to the tent entrance. Outside there was a battered jeep, its windshield cobwebbed with cracks. On the fire there was a spit impaling the roasting meat of some sort of fowl. He was about to cross through the tent opening when a tall, slender man in a bush suit walked into his field of vision. The man bent down over the fire, adding to it bits of brush and sticks he'd been carrying in his arms. He tended the meat, turning the spit to make certain it wasn't burning. Virga watched, his eyes narrowed, as the man sat before the flames, crossed his legs beneath him, and stared motionlessly out towards the glittering fires that burned far away across the desert.

The man seemed to be watching for something. His expression an intense composure, never altered. He seemed to be a young man but in the flicker of the fires it was hard for Virga to tell his exact age. He had light hair and a fair complexion; he wasn't Arabic, there was no doubt about that. But for all this man's fair, even fragile, appearance his eyes were strangely disturbing and Virga was uncertain if he could withstand his direct gaze. They glistened in the firelight; they seemed to absorb the golden hue of the flames before becoming darker, as if they were no fixed colour at all. He reached out to turn the spit again and at the same time his head came around a few inches to the left. He looked directly at Virga as if he'd known all along the other man had been standing there. The force and abruptness of his gaze made Virga step back, his heart hammering.

He rose up. The man was well over six feet; his lean frame made him appear even taller. When he saw Virga's apprehension his fierce eyes slowly gave way to a controlled concern. He turned and without speaking sat before the fire again.

Virga stood at the mouth of the tent, aware that his hand was throbbing painfully. The man had seemed not to notice him; he sat staring out, as he had before, at the small dots of fires in the black distance. Hunger was churning in Virga's stomach, enough to make him risk any threat this man might pose. After another moment he said through still swollen lips,

'Are you going to eat that or let it burn?'

The man's eyes flickered towards the fire. He took the spit off and, with a knife from his belt, cut a hunk of stringy meat. He said in a very distinct voice, 'Be careful. You've been throwing up everything I've fed you.'

Virga took the meat and tore into it thankfully. He wiped his greasy hands along the sides of his trousers. He painfully sat down across from the man, shielding his face from the flames because the heat made his blistered flesh feel as if it were puckering.

'Your hand was infected,' said the man, not looking at Virga but rather through him. 'I cleaned the wound and bound it.'

'Thank you.'

'I found you a few miles away. What were you doing out here?'

Virga didn't know if he could trust this man or not. He averted his eyes from the man's, but that had little effect. He could feel the man watching him. He said, 'Someone left me there.'

The man said, 'I see.'

He looked away from Virga, directing his attention towards the fires. When Virga turned to look he saw a great orange tongue of flame leap up amid the smaller fires. 'Is that an explosion?' he asked.

'They're burning books,' the man answered softly. 'They began yesterday, first raiding the libraries and then the private residences. Soon they'll turn to other things.'

Virga gave a tired sigh of frustration. He fearfully touched the healing blisters on his cheeks and forehead. 'They've gone too far. There's no stopping them.'

'Who are you?'

'My name is James Virga. I'm a professor of theology.'

The man raised a brow. 'Oh?'

'And you? I'd like to know who saved my life.'

'I didn't save your life. I only found you.'

'Isn't that the same thing?'

The man paused and then said, 'My name is Michael.'

'You're an American also?'

'No,' he said, 'not an American.'

Virga chewed at a bone. The heat of the fire made him draw away a few feet. He threw aside the bone and said, 'Why are you out here? Why aren't you in the city?'

The man smiled faintly and motioned towards the jeep. 'I did go into the city,' he said, 'but I couldn't get through the crowd without . . . injuring someone, and that was over two weeks ago. So I decided it might be best to make camp out here. In the city the forces of violence are building too rapidly.'

'I never saw anything like it before. Never.'

'Then be prepared to see more of it,' said the man with a bluntness that made Virga look up from his new piece of meat, 'because it's only begun.'

Virga stared at him.

'This place is not the worst, only the most well-publicized. There are villages and settlements all over the Middle East that have been burned to the ground by their own inhabitants. After they'd turned on everything in sight they finally, ultimately, turned on themselves and destroyed each other. Al Ahmadi, Al Jahra, Safwan, even Abadan and Basra. Up into Iran and Iraq, crawling towards Turkey. I know because I've seen.'

'It's all happened so suddenly,' Virga said. 'No one had any idea this was going on.'

'Suddenly?' Michael asked. 'No, not suddenly. This has been building since the beginning of time, this mad last struggle, this legacy of destruction. No, not suddenly.'

'What about the Holy Land?'

Michael glanced over at him, through him. 'Soon,' he said.

'My God,' Virga said. 'If this insanity ever spread into America . . .'

The man was quiet for a moment, watching the last embers of a million ideas. Then he said, 'You've been in delirium for the last four days. I thought at first you were going to die but you were gradually able to keep down small amounts of water. For that space of time – four days – you hung on the edge of death. Yesterday your fever broke and you regained consciousness for only a moment.'

'Four days . . .' Virga repeated.

'I've met stragglers here and there,' Michael said. 'Those

who have somehow maintained their senses in this onslaught and who are trying to leave the country. But there are not very many. The police force and the military have been severely weakened. Four days can be a very long time; in this place there is not much more time left. Having used all he could here, Baal will go elsewhere.'

At the mention of that obscene name, Virga shuddered. He remembered the figure that sat in darkness on the other side of a chessboard. 'How do you know all this?' he asked.

'I have my sources.'

'What sources?'

The man said, 'You ask too many questions.'

'Because I want to understand,' Virga said. 'I have to understand . . . Dear God, I have to . . .'

Michael had leaned forward slightly. His eyes cut Virga to the bone. 'What you've seen here pains you,' he stated matter-of-factly.

'Yes. I've seen murder and savagery. I've met Baal and escaped with my life.'

Michael seemed surprised. He narrowed his eyes very slightly. 'You've met Baal?'

'He has one of my colleagues, a Dr Naughton.'

'As a disciple?'

'Hell, no!' cried Virga, realizing as soon as he said it that he didn't know for certain. 'He's probably a prisoner . . . I don't know. But Baal told me he had Naughton.'

'If he's not dead,' Michael said, 'he's given his life to Baal. Those were his two alternatives. How was it that you managed to get away?' There was a hint of caution, of distrust, in the man's voice.

'I don't know. I can't understand it. I had a crucifix – '

Michael nodded.

' – and he couldn't touch me as long as I held it where he could see it. Yet above his doorway there was the drawing of a crucifix, in plain view.'

'But,' Michael said, 'wasn't it upside down?'

He remembered. 'Yes. It was.'

Michael sat back, seemingly satisfied.

'I want to know,' Virga said, 'how you can know so much about this man.'

Virga waited for an answer. From the corner of his eye he saw orange flames explode into the sky again.

Michael said, 'I've been following Baal. I have been tracking him across the world. I won't stop, not until I have him. I know his past and present; I will write his future.'

'For what purpose? To kill him?'

The other man paused, his eyes still guarded and wary. 'No. No, not to kill him. But to stop him before this Godless disease overpowers the centres of humanity. To destroy is enough, justified perhaps, though that is not for me to say. But to strip the creation of all intelligence and dignity, like a cat that slowly strips a wounded mouse, is too much.'

'Have you ever met the man?'

'We've met,' Michael said.

'Then you believe there are no limits to his power?'

'He has his limits, though they are only temporary. As his power develops he will be able to overcome those limitations.'

'My God,' Virga breathed, 'you mean to say he hasn't fully developed his capabilities?'

The man looked up. 'By no means.'

'I felt his power even when I was in the same room with him. I still don't know what it was. Some sort of hypnotism or something, some sort of brainwashing technique.'

'Yes,' Michael said, 'that was what it was.'

'He almost had me,' Virga said. 'God only knows what he's done to Naughton.'

'Remember that moment. Remember that Baal has no mercy. He exists only to shame the creation in the sight of God.'

Virga noted the use of the word creation again. He began to think that this man might be some sort of fanatic. 'If you won't kill him,' he asked after a moment, 'how can you stop him? His disciples would rip you to pieces if you even got near.'

Michael seemed to disregard the question. He sat as motionless as if he were part of the desert itself, perhaps a clump of camel's-thorn. Then he said, very quietly, 'His influence must be contained.'

'It's not quite that simple.'

'No. Not quite.'

A taut, dry silence stretched between them. Virga expected

154

the man to say more, but he seemed preoccupied with the book-burning miles away. He winced, almost imperceptibly, with every new thrust of fire.

Virga's hand was hurting. He wanted to keep the conversation going so he wouldn't have to be alone with the pain. 'You said you've been following Baal. Where from?'

'It's not important. What's important is the here and now.'

'I'd like to know.'

'No you wouldn't,' the man said.

Virga said, 'Yes. I want to know.'

The man's eyes shifted from the fires to Virga and back again. With an effort he said, 'I came across his trail in California some years ago. He and his disciples, a small group then, had taken control of a town called Borja, near the Mexican border. The townspeople, the law officers, the ministers, at first everyone thought them only a commune of fanatics; they were affected by the same powers you see working here. Soon they'd turned against each other. Some of them Baal induced into his circle. The others he destroyed. Then it was only a matter of time; the word spread underground to every madman who would listen. The motorcycle gangs, the Satan-worshippers, the drug- and power-obsessed: Baal held sway over all these. When Baal was prepared, the commune, now over five hundred strong, split into four groups, and all of them gained notoriety. They became murderers and terrorists and they neither knew why nor cared. They were tainted. But they were only part of Baal's education.'

'His education?' asked Virga, watching the shadows the dying fire scrawled across the man's face.

'His power grew by degrees, as his followers increased. And those he claimed added their forces to the movement to make it possible to influence thousands of people very quietly. He wanted no fanfare nor banners, not yet. He was not prepared for that. His commune left California and in Nevada sought out a group of Satanists financed on a desert estate by a woman named Van Lynn. Within weeks he had taken control of both the group and the money; they worshipped him as their master's prince. Baal remained with Mrs Van Lynn for several years while his followers quietly made more converts in both America

155

and Europe. From the very beginning he had always known what to do: appeal to man's baser desires, tap the capacity for violence and the lust for power. Make them drunk with illusion. He impressed upon his converts that the God they had been following is dead; His ideas of peace and harmony are no longer valid in this world. Thus, Baal said, the only recourse for the survival of man is a battle of the animals, a survival of the strongest.'

'From reason to chaos,' Virga said, 'is not a very long step.'

Michael shook his head. 'No, unfortunately not. Baal took the remainder of Mrs Van Lynn's money and left America. In Europe he began the same procedure of selecting converts and spreading them out to influence others. But he needed more money, more power, and thus he came to the oil fields.'

'So in the midst of all this Baal is the manipulator?'

'Yes.'

'Leading us towards . . .' Virga let his voice trail off; the answer was too terrible to consider.

'Yes,' Michael said. 'A complete breakdown of order. Death and destruction.'

'But what is his motive? And why has he named himself after a god of sacrifice?'

Michael did not answer.

'We have our sanity,' Virga said, 'and while we do we cannot just sit here and let these things happen. There must be someone we can warn . . . there must be someone we can tell.'

'We? We?' Michael looked sharply at him over the last of the fire. 'You have no part in this.'

Virga leaned forward, defying the man's gaze. He said, 'No. I owe Naughton that much. I'm going to do what I can to help him.'

'You're a fool. You don't understand what you're dealing with here.'

Virga said, 'I'm a fool, then.'

Michael fixed his gaze firmly on the other man. After a moment Michael's eyes softened only a fraction. 'All men are fools,' he said. 'And fools are dangerous.'

'You said you've met Baal before,' Virga said. 'Where?'

At first he thought the man would refuse to answer. Then he slowly unbuttoned the collar of his bush jacket and thrust his chin into the dim light of the embers. 'Where is not your concern,' he said. 'It's enough to say we've met.'

Virga recoiled.

Splayed across the fair flesh of Michael's throat, two deeply burned handprints sought to strangle him.

20

In the morning Virga awakened with nerves on edge, afraid that the nightmares he'd endured were about to become realities.

He swung himself into a sitting position on the cot and gingerly tested his injured hand. It was completely numb from the wrist down. When he tried to move the crushed fingers pain began somewhere deep within his forearm and raced through agonized nerves up his shoulder and neck to the brain. He was afraid the hand was beyond repair. He stepped through the tent opening out into the white sunlight, where the desert stretched flat and dry forever, and saw Michael sitting on the ground in almost the same spot as the night before. The man's eyes were narrowed against the glare; he looked out across the vast expanse.

Virga looked around. No words were needed.

Far out, where they had watched the fires, the sky was filled with a brooding black smoke that coiled around and around like vipers twisting amid the clouds. It was like the smoke of a gigantic bomb blast, thick and heavy. Virga shivered at the ominous sight, the preview of things to come. He watched it moving with the currents of air and knew the sickening odour of it would soon reach them.

'What is it?' he asked.

'The city,' Michael said.

'They've destroyed their homes? How could they?'

'No man has a home any longer,' the other man said quietly. 'They've gone to join Baal and the city has been set afire, possibly as an offering.'

Virga stood, his arms at his sides, and watched the smoke

fill the sky. He had never in his life felt as helpless as he did now; no, he corrected himself, there was one other time, but he kept that so far back in his mind that it hardly ever hurt any more. Now he was one little speck on the world and he was helpless against the man whose power grew against the heavens like the columns of black smoke. No words could save them, not the philosophic wisdom of the saints nor even the teachings of Christ. Baal had given them what they wanted; they had been granted permission to smash at the guiding forces of reason, and they would snarl in the streets like wild dogs until they were mastered by the frenzy.

The smoke had almost reached them. It hovered across the desert. Virga watched it coming. He said, 'I've got to know whether Naughton is dead or alive.'

'He's dead.'

'How do you know that?'

'I know,' Michael said. 'Perhaps he still walks and breathes and perhaps his brain still functions, but the man is dead.'

'I don't believe that,' said Virga, hearing the lie as he spoke it. If he had fallen into Baal's grasp there was nothing that could save him.

Michael stood up, towering over Virga. He said, 'You know who Baal is, you know what he represents. You sense it. Don't look away; I can read it in your eyes. Soon Baal will be capable of burning this land to a cinder. Can a man stand against power of that nature?'

'Can a man turn his back?' Virga asked. 'No. To turn my back would be my surrender to him. And if I can tear anything from him, even Naughton's corpse, I will.'

The smoke touched the white desert sand and immediately blackened it with its filth. Soon the rolling darkness would engulf them like a fog at sea. Virga smelled a high, acrid odour that made his stomach churn.

Michael said, 'You're an old man.'

'I'm a man!' Virga said sharply. He trembled, trying to control himself. 'Don't ever say that to me again.'

Michael paused to let the man's anger subside. Then he said, 'You want to find your friend?'

'I'm going to find my friend.'

'All right then. We'll go into the city, or rather what's left of it, and I don't think that's much. Perhaps we'll find your friend with Baal.' He looked directly into Virga's eyes. 'Or perhaps it will not be your friend we find.'

Michael stepped past Virga towards the jeep. He started to climb in and then stopped, listening for something. He looked around, his eyes scanning the horizon. Virga looked also but could see nothing beyond the silent wall of smoke. He felt the other man's tension. Michael said, 'This place is haunted. I hear the mad gods shrieking for revenge. Listen.'

Virga couldn't hear anything. He thought the man was insane. He said, 'There's nothing.'

'Oh yes,' the other man replied softly. 'Oh yes there is.'

He took his place behind the wheel, and Virga took the seat beside him. They roared away into the smoke, throwing sand. Twenty minutes later, on the city's outskirts, they had not seen a living soul. Bodies of men and animals lay scattered everywhere as if a terrible storm had ripped through, but nothing moved. Ahead of them fires gutted the city, modern and ancient sections alike, and the entire sky was a maelstrom of searing red and whirling black smoke, a chaotic kaleidoscope.

The roar of the fires was deafening. It was as if some giant with torch in hand had walked the streets setting everything in sight ablaze. To Virga it was revolting; he had never seen so much carnage and waste. Michael drove on, his hands tight around the wheel, his narrowed eyes flickering right and left to pierce the gloom. The human storm had torn through the city's commercial district without mercy. Windows were shattered and stores had been looted. Merchandise littered the streets and Michael swept through it as if running an obstacle course.

Michael heard it first. Virga saw him lean forward almost imperceptibly, and then he also heard the loud static-garbled Arabic voice:

'. . . impossible to accurately count this mass of people . . . also members of the press from the United States, the Soviet Union, England, Germany, and Japan . . . the officials cannot maintain order. Already the ambulances have been . . . but the medical centres that have been set up here are being ravaged by those in search of drugs. I don't know if transmission is getting through . . .'

Michael swung the jeep to the kerb and cut the engine.

In the broken window of a housewares store, amid shattered goods and displays, were three televisions. Two of them were overturned and useless but the third was still operating, though the picture faded in and out. The volume had been turned up to full. The voice of a man on the brink of panic blared out into the street.

'. . . but we'll try to keep you informed.' The newsman, a slim sunglassed Arab, stood on a platform over what appeared to be an endless sea of heads. As he spoke into a microphone he kept looking over his shoulder at the mass of humanity beneath him. Virga saw that the platform shook as bodies crushed around its base.

The newsman said, '. . . some call him the living Muhammad, some call him devil, but there is no mistaking the strength of this man. He has declared himself the unreachable, the untouchable saviour of man and hundreds of thousands have gathered here to pay him homage. Even now I can look across and see . . . I can see the fires of the old city. On this site he has proclaimed the beginnings of the new age of Baal and the Baalians gathered here will soon strike the first stone into the foundations of his city. Now he . . .' Static overpowered the voice and Virga put his hands to his ears. When the picture had cleared the camera was panning and he saw the horrible mass of them, some grovelling in the sand and others dancing wildly, both clothed and nude. In the distance there were trucks with emblems of both Middle Eastern and foreign television networks. The camera towers rose up like derricks.

'. . . I have never witnessed anything like this,' the newsman said. The platform shook. He put a hand to the railing for support. 'I feel a mixture of elation and fear. I can't describe it. I only pray that what is happening here is indeed for the good of all mankind . . .'

Michael sat rigid in his seat. He was motionless, staring at the television. Behind the two men, across the street, flames burst along the roof of a building and timbers cracked.

'There are people here from around the world,' the Arab was saying. 'This is totally without parallel. There are those who say that Baal was born with the mark of heaven. From birth, they say, he was destined to lead men to the gates of greatness.

It is only for the future to decide. This is without a doubt the beginning of a new age . . .' He touched his earphones and listened for a moment. The picture became unfocussed as tubes cracked suddenly, then regained its sharpness. 'Yes . . . yes. It's been verified now. Yes. He is walking among the crowd now! Look at them! You can see them falling to their knees, wave after wave of them, as he passes into their midst! I can see him!' The camera panned, jerking crazily, until it had picked up the tableau of kneeling figures. People were lifting up their faces for his touch as he passed. Virga recognized the tall frame of the man who had faced him over the chessboard. Baal, though still in the distance and almost obscured, touched his fingertip to upturned faces and Virga saw the forms collapse in a writhing ecstasy.

'He's out there among the masses now!' the newsman said. 'This is the first time we've been able to get a good picture, though we still can't quite see – ' The platform suddenly shook violently. The newsman shouted, 'Watch that boom! Get away from there!' Someone in the background, a technician, shouted, 'Move away from the platform!'

The newsman was still trying to regain his composure. 'The officials cannot control this crowd,' he was saying, 'and to move among them is a great risk . . . I saw someone fall a moment ago and he was trampled; the power of the crowd is too much . . .' He swung around and watched the moving figures as the camera photographed over his shoulder.

Suddenly Michael leaned forward. His eyes had caught something Virga had not seen.

'*What was that?*' the newsman shrieked. The platform shook. The crowd was pushing forward and Virga heard something like a low moan, growing in intensity. '*I've just heard something!*' said the newsman. '*I don't know what it was!*' He tapped on his earphones. 'Hey! What was that? Hassan! Do you hear me?'

He listened through the earphones. Behind him the crowd surged forward. Screams and moans drowned out the voice of the newsman as he frantically shouted into his microphone. His face had suddenly become gaunt and ashen.

Virga was only peripherally aware that the row of buildings on the opposite side of the street were completely afire and smoking timbers were crashing down on to the pavement all around.

'. . . a few moments ago. We still don't know who or why . . .' The newsman looked up as if he were not certain he was still on the air. He nodded at someone. 'Hassan is out there with an audio unit but he's having trouble communicating . . . I can't hear very well. Right now . . . I think only two bullets were fired . . . The crowd is still moving forward. GRAB THAT EQUIPMENT!' The platform shuddered and swayed. Something crashed. 'IT'S GOING OVER!'

Behind Michael and Virga one of the buildings exploded in a belch of black smoke. Bits of concrete skittered along the broken sidewalk. Virga ducked his head instinctively.

The newsman was leaning over the railing. 'THEY'RE TEARING HIM TO PIECES! THE MAN IS BEGGING FOR MERCY BUT THEY'RE TEARING HIM TO PIECES!' He put his hand to the headset. 'What? Get out of there! Those people will tear you apart!' Then, directed back into the microphone,' Someone, a Jew, has fired two bullets into Baal at point-blank range! They're lifting Baal . . . they're taking him somewhere . . . I can't see for the people crowded around him . . . They're putting him in a car but the people are still crowded around. GET AWAY FROM HIM! GIVE HIM ROOM!' The Arab stopped to catch his breath. Tears of either rage or frustration were glittering on his cheeks. Static blurred his voice when he spoke again.

'. . . I have a report . . . he is seriously injured . . . I repeat, Baal is seriously injured. There is no controlling this crowd now . . . They're ripping at each other . . . The Jew who held the gun is – he's been torn and scattered . . . We're going to have to radio a helicopter to get us out of here! The car is pulling away . . . I don't know where they're going to take him, I don't know who fired the shots, I don't know . . .' He suddenly pitched forward and caught the handrail again. Beneath him fights were erupting; the screaming of the crowd was loud and bloodthirsty. The newsman cried out, 'GET AWAY FROM THE PLATFORM! WATCH THAT CABLE! GET AWAY FROM THE – ' and the television screen was suddenly a solid blank, cracked occasionally with a black line of static.

Michael started the engine and jammed it into gear. Across

the street another building exploded. Ashes were raining down. Virga had to grab hold of the dash with his good hand to steady himself. Michael drove through the holocaust as if pursuing something, or as if something were pursuing him. He drove over kerbs and down narrow stinking side streets and across the charred remains of elegant homes. Virga gritted his teeth and held on for life. The jeep plunged through the ruins of the modern section into the ancient section of the city, where already the ashes were cold and only occasional red flames lit the way in a morass of black earth and grey sky. Virga glimpsed, for an instant, the scorched walls and towers of Musallim's palace in the distance, above the burned remains of other dwellings.

They swerved on to a long street paved with rough, broken squares of stone. On both sides were high walls, veined with cracks and bearing painted Arabic slogans. Doorways were cut directly into the stone; here and there Virga saw sprawled corpses.

The engine suddenly screamed. Michael was ramming his foot down on the accelerator. Virga cried out, 'What the hell are you doing?'

Ahead of them was a gleaming black limousine with closed blinds across the rear window. It was racing across the rough stones, its wheels trembling from the impact of crashing down again and again. Michael was bearing down on the limousine; his eyes were purposeful, his jaw clenched. They roared up on the left side of the car and Virga saw that closed blinds obscured the rear seat. The driver of the limousine had been unaware of their presence; he looked over and his eyes widened.

And Virga saw it was the man named Olivier.

Michael swerved the jeep to the right. Metal crashed against metal. Rubber burned. Virga shouted out, realizing that Michael was deliberately trying to run them into a wall. Virga saw fingers pull down a blind. The eyes that stared through were black, something from a nightmare. The fingers let go and the blind snapped back.

Michael wrenched at the wheel over Virga's shouted protests. This time Olivier met him in the middle of the street and the two vehicles, like bulls with locked horns, roared together. Something, a small piece of metal like a hubcap, flew up from beneath the limousine and went spinning past Virga's head. He crouched down, hearing the wail of metal beside his ear.

Olivier was trying to drive the jeep into the wall now. The limousine was screaming, forcing the other vehicle closer and closer to those stones. They were going so fast that the hand-written slogans on the ancient walls were now only a solid smear of primary colours. Metal crashed again; the jeep shuddered and Michael's hands were bone-white on the wheel. The limousine was driving them towards the wall. A head-lamp smashed and glass went flying. Virga caught a glimpse of Olivier's face, grinning like a bleached skull. The jeep hit the far wall and the noise of rending metal sounded like the shriek-ing of a man's voice. And Virga realized it was his own.

Michael slammed on the brakes. The limousine scraped along the side of the jeep, then regained the middle of the street and roared away. The veins in his neck throbbing, Michael fought the wheel to stave off a headlong crash; he pulled the jeep away from the wall with only a slight reduction of speed, then he too had reached the middle of the street. Far ahead the limousine swerved sharply and disappeared around a corner.

They followed, seeing the limousine as it turned into a side street ahead. They lost sight of it again as it made another sharp turn.

In another few moments they came into full view of Musal-lim's palace. Masonry had crumbled until the place looked unused and decrepit; ashes had settled everywhere like a layer of dust. It seemed to be deserted; Virga could see neither guards nor dogs. The gate had been torn from its hinges. The jeep raced through into the courtyard. Michael skidded the vehicle up across the driveway and on to the scorched ground where it spun in a fishtail circle. The engine died.

He took the key from the ignition and looked around. There was no sign that anyone had ever been here. It could have been a mass of charred brick and shattered glass a thousand years before and no one would have known the difference. Virga saw that the huge door of the palace had been wrenched open. Now the entrance yawned obscenely.

Michael stepped out of the jeep. Before he could move there came a whine of engines gathering power and in another moment, before either Michael or Virga could cross the grounds to the private airstrip, a gleaming white aircraft burst along the black tarmac and took to the sky. A last correction of the rudder, a minor shudder along the tail, and the banshee wail of the engines had lifted, along with the aircraft, towards the north-west.

Michael stared at its slipstream. Then he said, as quietly as if he were speaking to himself, 'I'm too late.'

'What did you expect to find here,' Virga asked. 'This place has been destroyed. They've all gone.'

'Yes. Now they've all gone.'

'Where would they take Baal? With the hospitals afire there would be no one to treat the wounds.'

Michael seemed not to be listening. He ran a hand along his forehead and then looked at the black ash his fingers had accumulated.

'Did you hear me? We've got to find where they've taken Baal.'

'What?' he asked, then seemed to remember what Virga had said. 'Baal was on board that aircraft. Probably they're leaving the country. Even the continent.'

'What? How do you know?'

'I know,' Michael said.

'Surely he'll bleed to death without medical attention. Where are they taking him?'

Michael turned away without answering. He walked back across the barren grounds to the open entrance with Virga following. Michael stopped just short of the doorway and stood peering into the dank, filth-walled interior. 'Something is wrong,' he said quietly.

'A trap?'

'I'm not sure. It seems that no one is here . . . and yet . . . Follow directly behind me and walk quietly. All right?'

'Yes,' Virga said. 'All right.'

Michael stepped through and Virga followed, minding his footing on shards of broken glass and burned tapestries. The interior was ruined. The walls were scarred and burned black, carpets torn to pieces, huge mirrors shattered, exquisitely ornamented furniture ripped apart as if by axes. There was the heavy pall of smoke, the thick garbage stench of it; this place had been murdered and already smelled of decaying flesh. Michael turned to him to make certain he could go on and then they continued together through the corridors past huge rooms and marble staircases. Beneath them their feet slipped on human excrement and glass.

There was no sound. They're all gone, Virga thought. All of them. The disciples as well as their wounded master had vanished. They moved silently through the darkness; the corridors wound about them as if they crawled in the intestines of a burned carcass.

And then there was the sharp noise of glass breaking from behind closed doors on one side of the corridor. Michael tensed and waited, his hand gripping Virga's forearm to prevent him from moving, but the noise did not repeat itself.

Michael set himself and kicked through into the room beyond. The doors collapsed from their battered hinges and fell with a resounding crash to a floor of cracked stone.

They stood in the remains of what had been a dining hall. Chairs were overturned, scattered wildly about a charred, ash-topped table. There were still food-smeared dishes and pewter goblets arranged as if for a banquet. Three of the goblets had overturned and the liquid had collected in slimy puddles. Blue clouds of smoke still wafted about the room, swirling like spirits of the dead. Above the odours of smoke and decay there was something else, something that made Virga grind his teeth against its presence. It was the sickly sweet smell of the burial vault. He felt Michael tense beside him.

Someone sat at the table.

Someone who had slumped forward, overturning a crystal decanter, and whose face was now hidden in shadows. The figure, dressed in a man's ragged clothes, was emaciated and pale-fleshed. Virga gasped as he saw the terrible dark blotches on one of the exposed arms. The figure stirred, turning his face towards the muddy light that streamed through shattered doors.

'My God,' Virga said. 'It's Naughton.'

But he knew immediately it was also not Naughton. The man who sat there perhaps resembled Naughton, in a high fine forehead now covered with festering sores, in the shape of a nose now partially eaten away by some cancerous disease,

166

in fair hair that had been ripped away in spots to expose bloody scalp, but this was also not Donald Naughton.

The man's eyes glittered with a savage ferocity. He scooped up a goblet and, shouting out in incomprehensive rage, threw it directly at the two men.

Michael ducked. The goblet clattered against the far wall. Naughton struggled to his feet. He lifted a chair high and threw it at them; the effort made him stagger back and he fell to all fours. He growled and scurried into a corner, where his eyes glowed red in the midst of shadows.

'My God,' Virga said. 'They've made him into some sort of animal! Oh Jesus Christ!'

'Stay back!' Michael commanded. He stepped forward and Naughton howled like a maddened dog. Naughton reached out for dinner-ware and pieces of glass scattered about him, throwing them at the men. Michael asked Virga quietly, 'What was his first name?'

'Donald,' Virga said. 'Was'? Had the man said 'was'?

Naughton settled down on his haunches.

When Michael took another step forward Naughton bared his teeth.

'Be quiet,' Michael said in a voice that resounded with calm authority. 'Be quiet. Your name is Donald Naughton. Do you remember that name?'

Naughton cocked his head to one side, listening. He put both hands to his ears and sank his chin down against his chest.

'Donald Naughton, listen to me,' Michael said. 'You're still a man. You can still fight this; I want you to fight it. FIGHT IT!'

Naughton growled and looked for something else to throw.

Michael stepped forward again and bent to look across into the man's eyes. 'Fight it,' he commanded. He thrust his arm out, offered his palm. 'Trust me. Trust me. You can fight it.'

Naughton seemed confused. He shook his head back and forth in a mindless frenzy. He turned and scratched at the walls, seeking some kind of escape.

'DONALD NAUGHTON!' Michael said.

'NOOOOOO!' moaned the animal on the floor. 'NOT DONALD NAUGHTON ANY MORE!'

'Jesus Christ,' Virga said under his breath.

Michael sprang up from his bent position. As the diseased figure turned from the wall he was upon him. Naughton screamed, a wild cry of rage and fear. Michael clapped both hands to Naughton's temples. Virga could see the veins stand out in Michael's hands. 'DONALD NAUGHTON!' he said.

The man shook himself; saliva drooled from his open mouth. Slowly, very slowly, his eyes changed. There was the brief glimmer of recognition. His entire body seemed to unwind, as if giving itself up to Michael's touch. Then he breathed, a harsh awful rattle that filled the hall with stinking breath, and collapsed in Michael's arms. Michael held him as he was racked with sobbing and gently, gently lay him down on the stone. He motioned for Virga to come forward.

Virga leaned over his friend. The sores were even more terrible than he had thought. Some unimaginable disease had ripped across the flesh, tearing like the teeth of dogs. Michael, cradling Naughton's head, said, 'This man is dying. It will be his only release from the pain.'

'No help now,' Naughton muttered, his eyes glazed. 'Too late. Now too late . . .' He looked up, unbelieving. 'You . . . are . . . Dr Virga . . .?'

'Yes. My God, my God. What have they done to you?'

He moaned, tormented by the pain. He could fight it off only for moments at a time and when it returned it was always stronger. 'All of them have left this place,' he whispered weakly, haltingly. 'Cresil, Verin, Sonneilton, Carreau . . . all of them. Baal has taken them away.'

'Baal was shot,' Virga said. 'Where was he taken?'

Naughton looked up. Virga thought the man was smiling, just a trace of it, but he couldn't be sure. 'Shot . . .' the man said. 'No.'

'Where was he taken?' Virga asked again.

Naughton was breathing harshly. The pain was coming back. It caressed him with red-hot fingers. He shuddered and Michael put his hand on the man's forehead.

'Gone,' said Naughton, gasping around the agony.

'What?' Michael bent his head down to hear. 'Gone where?'

'That child that child,' Naughton was saying. Tears filled his eyes, streamed down his cheeks. 'Oh God I held the knife

168

'... I didn't know ... I couldn't think ...' Michael brushed the tears away with a fingertip. 'No one can stop him now,' Naughton whispered.

'Baal was shot,' Virga said. He glanced over at Michael. 'Wasn't he?'

'Twice . . .' Naughton said, 'shot twice. The Arabs will rise up to avenge the murder of the living Mu – oh God the pain the pain the pain – ooohhhhh!' He fought it, his teeth clenched.

Virga felt the tears on his face. 'For what purpose?' he heard himself asking. Naughton looked up at him through a haze of pain.

'The destruction of the Jews . . . total destruction . . . no Jew left alive . . . terrorism across the world . . . total . . .'

'Why?'

Michael was staring at Virga. 'Revenge,' he said, answering even as Naughton whispered the word.

The breath rattled in Naughton's throat. 'He plans a resurrection from death . . . while his disciples spread chaos and war . . . he waits . . . and . . . oh Jesus the pain ooohhhhh!'

Dear God in Heaven, breathed Virga. Dear God in Heaven.

'And when he returns the master will come with him . . .'

The man was insane, his senses destroyed. Dear God in Heaven. Vipers vipers vipers. 'I don't understand,' Virga said, almost to himself. 'Baal was shot . . . he was shot . . .'

Michael asked softly, 'Where has Baal gone?'

'No one can find him,' Naughton said. He choked and dribbled a vile-smelling liquid. 'Too far . . .'

'Where?' Michael asked. His eyes frightened Virga; they had become fierce and weirdly golden in the dim light.

Naughton blinked his eyes to regain focus. Virga could see him slipping away. 'I saw . . . the maps,' he said finally. 'I heard them talking. They left me here to die . . . but I saw the maps . . .'

Michael leaned forward.

'Greenland,' Naughton said, 'gathering supplies at an Eskimo settlement . . . Avatik . . . then across the ice cap . . .' He looked away from Michael, searching for Virga. He touched Virga's hand. 'Judith . . . she's all right?'

'Yes. Judith is well.'

169

'They made me write the letter . . . They were going to use you . . .'

'I know.'

The pale light in Naughton's eyes had almost burned away. His face was white and his lips barely moved when he spoke. Whimpering in pain, he looked up suddenly, appealingly, at Virga and his eyes were filled with tears. 'I don't want to die like this,' he said, 'not like this . . .'

Virga couldn't reply. The helplessness on the man's face had taken his breath away. He stammered.

Michael pressed his hand against Naughton's forehead. 'It's all right,' he whispered. 'Rest now. Just close your eyes and rest for a while.'

'Oh . . .' Naughton said. He gave a small sigh and as Virga watched, the light of life flickered and vanished from his eyes. Michael folded the man's arms across the chest.

He stood up. 'You should take his body back home with you. This place will be burned to the ground and the ashes buried.'

'He was a very fine man.'

'And now at peace.'

Virga suddenly looked up sharply. 'I'll ship his body to his wife for proper burial. I'm not going back yet.'

Michael slowly turned on the other man and the force of his presence was almost palpable. He said, 'Your part in this is done. You've found your friend. What lies ahead will not be for you.'

'And how can you track him alone? Answer me that.'

'I have done so for . . . years before this day. Alone.'

'I'm going with you.'

'No.'

'Yes.'

Michael said, 'I could make you stay, you know.'

'I don't know who you are but I'll tell you one thing. I am fully aware of Baal's capabilities and I am not going to go back to Boston and sit on my ass.'

Michael looked at him through the gloom for a silent moment. He abruptly shrugged his shoulders. 'As you wish. I don't care, I'm not going to look after you. And I repeat my sentiments that you're a fool.'

'So be it,' Virga said.

'Yes,' Michael said. 'The winter night is about to begin in Greenland – I assume you're aware of that fact – so I suggest you take along more than what you're wearing now. We will not be travelling together. If you haven't met me in the place called Avatik in three days I leave without you.'

'I'll meet you.'

'Yes. I believe you will. Then you'd best make your air connections and leave this country as soon as possible. I don't think it has much future. Here. I'll help you carry your friend out of this place.'

THREE

'And I saw . . . a sea of glass mingled with fire'

—*Revelation* 15:2

21

Across sprawling white sands in the lands of simmering heat, across winter-canopied Europe, across great blue threads of rivers and wide valleys marked with man's cities Virga thought of Baal and Baal alone.

Baal was the disease of madness, carried through the bodies of once-sane men to infect the world; he was the end of man. And why Virga desired to confront Baal again was a question he could not answer. Michael had been right. He had no part in this, no place in what was to unfold. He was only a man, yes, and an old man; he had the awesome and frightening premonition that what was to come would be beyond his comprehension. Michael's glittering golden eyes disturbed him as much as the darker visage of Baal. The two would finally meet face to face, if not in Greenland then somewhere else, somewhere hidden from all eyes but his own. He would have to see it; he had made up his mind he would have to see it and this, he concluded, was what drove him on.

Through a succession of airline connections he steadily moved towards the top of the world. He watched the sun lower on the horizon; it hung blood-red and sinking in a sky of ice. Through the airports and the flights that carried him further north he watched the faces of people and wondered how they could be so unaware. The businessmen with their eternal black briefcases and dark suits, the young tourists, the solitary travellers: all of them so unaware. And everywhere, in every language, he saw magazines and newspapers with front-page photographs of murders and bombings and faces eager for war. Baal, though hidden perhaps from even the eye of God, was still at work. Virga turned his head from the smiling SAS stewardess in the aisle and looked through the oval window at a sea of darkening clouds. Where is God? he asked himself. Has man lost himself so hopelessly now that God allows this moment without a single merciful breath? Has Baal grown so strong that even He is struck with terror? The thought chilled him. Now it seemed that the great mechanism that governed the last moments of man had been set in motion; it ticked the seconds away like a gigantic pendulum clock.

Virga was wasted. The constant pressure of the travel schedule necessary to meet the time limit imposed by Michael had worn him down until he was so tired he couldn't even sleep. The stubble of whiskers he'd seen in the lavatory mirror made him look dismal and forlorn and the new lines around his eyes added years to his appearance.

In glittering, frost-encrusted Copenhagen he'd purchased boots and warm clothing for the colder climate ahead. Now, in the final hours, there would be a landing at Reykjavik and then at the commercial air facilities at Søndre Strømfjord. From there he would have to arrange a charter flight up the western coast to Avatik, a pinhead on the map of Greenland.

When they had left Iceland, Virga saw the sun vanish beneath the horizon, leaving only a faint trace of angry red in the sky. They were outracing its brilliance, climbing towards the dark Pole.

Virga drank a final scotch and wondered if Michael had lied to him. Perhaps he would not wait at all; perhaps he would be gone when Virga arrived there. Then the long journey would have been for nothing. He would be lost and alone and not know whether to remain in Avatik or return, without hope, to the United States. Both of them would seem foreign to him now.

But he found himself wondering, while a knot of tension steadily grew in his stomach, what they would do when, and if, they found Baal. Short of murder, they could do nothing to stop the man and, in murdering him, they would only be strengthening the philosophy of violence that had grown in his shadow. No, he was not yet prepared to view himself as a religious assassin; there was enough bloodshed in the world already.

At the air facility at Søndre Strømfjord, Virga found that the violence had arrived with Baal. Danish authorities were carefully checking passports and baggage. A bomb, one of them told a man ahead of Virga, had been hidden in a suitcase and left among the seats in a waiting area. The resultant blast had killed four people and wounded six more. The authorities

176

checked through the one bag Virga carried and waved him through. Virga passed the area that had been damaged; he saw the remaining metal stumps where seats had been ripped away. There were dark stains on the linoleum floor. Virga wondered briefly who the people had been.

With little difficulty, which surprised him because he knew none of the language, Virga learned from the attractive dark-haired girl at the information centre that, yes, there were private planes for charter up the coast but he would have to arrange for a pilot some days in advance. No, Virga said, that would not do. He would be willing to pay anything the man asked. It was crucial that he get to Avatik by the following morning, he said, and watched as she winced and reached for a directory of carter agents. Virga chose one at random, Helmer Ingestahl. It was only when he heard the sleepy voice on the other end of the telephones that Virga realized he was calling in the middle of the night; he was that disoriented and bone-weary.

'Avatik?' the man asked in a thick Danish accent. 'I know the settlement. There's an airstrip. Who has given you this number?'

'I'm at the airfield now,' said Virga, speaking slowly so the man would understand. 'I cannot tell you how much it means to me to reach Avatik immediately.'

'Why?' he asked. 'Something you're doing is against the law?'

'No. I'll pay as much as you ask.'

Silence. Then, 'You will?'

'Yes,' Virga said.

The man grunted. 'Well then,' he said, 'maybe I forgive you for awakening me.'

Ingestahl was a burly, broad-shouldered Dane with reddish-brown hair and a thick bull neck. Out on the airfield, as they walked across the crust of snow towards his hangar, he laughed at the wolfskin coat Virga had bought in Copenhagen. 'You going to wear that thing?' he asked. 'Ha! Your balls will freeze off!'

His plane was an old United States Army recon job that Ingestahl said he'd bought from the junkpile and refitted. Virga took little comfort in the way he kicked the studded rubber tyres and wrenched at the wing slats. 'Fine old lady,' Ingestah said. 'Good American labour.'

Within twenty minutes they were lifting off from the frozen airfield. With a final shudder and groan the plane left the ground. Swirling snow threatened for a moment to obscure visibility; then they were free of it and climbing, climbing, climbing into the darkness.

Ingestahl cursed and slammed violently at the heater; it sputtered and refused to operate. Virga pulled his collar up around his frost-burning ears and breathed slowly and shallowly to protect his lungs as the craft continued to gain altitude. When they levelled off Ingestahl unscrewed a thermos of coffee and drank from it. He offered a swig to Virga.

'You never said what you were going there for,' the man said. 'You don't plan to?'

Virga saw the dark caps of mountains around them. The sun had completely gone now, though the sky still clung to the faintest trace of grey at the horizon. Below them were stretched miles and miles of snow-covered land, dotted infrequently with the lights of settlements. The land was rough. Virga could see its harshness even at this height. He pulled the hood of his coat up and laced it beneath his chin. The cold across his cheeks lay as heavy as freezing metal. In the darkness Virga could look over and see the blinking light at the wingtip on his side; as he sat in the cockpit steam rose from the open thermos in his hand and Ingestahl's face was daubed green by the glow of his instrument panel.

'I'm going to meet someone,' Virga said.

'Well. None of my business. You're paying me. Looks like you had a fall.'

'What?'

'Looks like you had a fall. Your hand.'

'Oh. An accident.'

The man nodded. 'Had a fall like that once myself. Broke my shoulder, my collarbone and my left leg. Ha!' His laugh was a clearing of the throat. 'Crash-landing when I was a bush pilot in Manitoba.'

Virga drank from the thermos. The taste was terrible. It had obviously been sitting for some time, but he needed the warmth. He peered out through the ice-glazed window at

178

forbidding glaciers as they slid their inevitable way to the sea. The expanse of snow was now completely unbroken except for dark outcroppings of rock. And when they had passed over the mountainous land, beneath them was nothing but a flat stretch of solid ice. There seemed to be no end to it. It stretched in every direction and at the horizon seemed to merge into the sky. Beyond the wingtip light and the green of the panel Virga could see no colours but black and white, black and white, black and white, merging and yet startlingly separate.

'I don't know what you're travelling to this place for,' Ingestahl said, 'but I'll tell you something. This is a hard land. It lulls you to sleep and when you fall asleep it kills you. I can tell by your face you don't live in the weather. And I don't know if you know the Eskimo or not. Do you?'

'No.'

'As I thought. You're a stranger, *kraslunas*. You have no place here. You'd better keep your eyes open.'

Between them they drank the thermos dry. On the last leg of the journey, over a new series of black rock and white wind-tossed snow, the heater abruptly clicked on and the glorious warmth filled the cockpit. Virga took off his gloves and thrust his hands before the vent.

'You're going to be returning soon?' the man asked. 'You'll have to pay me for my waiting time.'

'No,' Virga said. 'I'm not sure. It won't be necessary for you to wait.'

Ingestahl nodded. 'There's a Danish family living with the Eskimos in Avatik. A Lutheran minister and his wife who came up about four years ago. You'll be just in time for breakfast.' He motioned ahead. Far below and off to the left there were lights on the icepack. 'That's Avatik. The Eskimo there is in the middle: too far south to be nomadic, too far north to be part of modern Greenland. You'll see.'

He swung the plane around in a wide arc. Virga could see two rows of widely spaced oil drums, the contents of which had been set afire, marking the boundaries of a short airstrip. Ingestahl steadily lost altitude until Virga could make out pale yellow lights in the windows of what appeared to be shanty-like dwellings. Beyond Avatik the ice mountains loomed like bleached bodies, supine in the snow. Ingestahl hit the airstrip, calmly corrected a threatening skid, and stopped the craft in a wild flurry of snow and chips of ice.

Ingestahl kept the engine alive and reached behind the cockpit for Virga's case. He waited until the other man had stepped out into the snow and then tossed it to him. Ingestahl made a thumbs-up gesture, and shouted over the roar of the prop, 'Good luck!'

Virga stepped back out of the way and, snow stinging his face, stood watching the old craft tear away between the rows of bright burning drums until it finally lifted from the ice and headed into the veil of darkness.

He pulled his coat up against the bitter wind and, his boots crunching snow, walked towards the settlement. A metal-walled supply hut, ringed with broken stones, stood at one end of the airstrip. The doors had been thrown open and empty crates were scattered about. Across the ice were the prefabricated dwellings of Avatik. Lanterns gleamed behind windows that Virga thought must be of double thickness to withstand the below-zero temperatures.

Ahead he could hear dogs howling and barking. There came a sudden series of yips as if one, or more than one, had been injured. Then the dogs quieted and there was only the sound of the wind as it hissed through the thick snow underneath his feet.

A figure clad in furs appeared suddenly from between two of the prefabricated dwellings. Startled, Virga stood where he was and watched the bundled figure approach. Virga heard the crunch of snow beneath heavy boots. Beyond the figure the howling started up again; there was the sound of churning bodies as if some of the dogs had begun fighting.

Michael reached him. He said, 'You're late.'

22

They walked together between the crude huts. Virga saw that if the ground had not been smoothed by heavy snow it would have turned his stomach. Everywhere there was frozen garbage, frayed ropes, dog excrement, cans and crates. They stepped across pools of icy blood that glimmered black in the lantern light shining through hut windows; Virga was startled by the frozen gaping maw of a huge seal whose puckered protuberant eyes looked like softballs.

Near many of the prefab huts dogs were tied to steel poles driven into the ground. As the two men passed, the huge, intelligent-eyed animals struggled to their feet, tangling each other in their ropes as they did so. Virga saw that several of them were sick and several had been severely bitten in dog-fights; these misfits curled up into balls of white fur and let the stronger animals walk about over their bodies as they pleased.

'How long have you been here?' he asked Michael.

'Yesterday. I arrived by charter flight. I had them set up the oil drums for you.'

Virga nodded. He was aware now of the eyes that peered through windows and then darted away. He heard the creaking of doors; he turned once and a door slammed shut with a noise that made a pack of sledge dogs near by leap to their feet, expecting the hiss of the whip.

Ahead there was the tall timber spire of a church, battered by the subzero winds. A plaster image of Jesus had been nailed above the arched doorway and the figure's eyes looked plaintively down at the approaching men. With only the traditional robes of Nazareth to shield it from the awful wind, the image looked odd to Virga.

To the left of the church was a prefab dwelling with a number of windows and a stone chimney that now showed a brief column of white smoke. Someone passed a window and in another moment the door was opened.

A lean-framed elderly man in a dark brown sweater said,

'Dr Virga, yes? We've been waiting for you. Please come in.'

Virga entered a room lit with kerosene lamps. The walls were plastered with newspaper for extra insulation; there was a crude painting of a halo-crowned Jesus. On the floor were animal skins. There was a fire in a wide stone hearth and Virga immediately stepped to it to soak up the warmth. The man took Virga's coat and gloves and said, 'You've come a long way?'

'Yes. A very long way.'

'My name is Thomas Lahr; I am minister to the Eskimo in this settlement.'

Virga shook the offered hand, finding that the man's palm was as hard as the toughest leather. He said, 'You're a Lutheran minister?'

'That is right. We came here when the man before me took ill and died. His grave is just beyond the village.' He called into the next room, 'Dorte, we have a new visitor. Is the tea brewing?'

A woman as old as Lahr came into the room and said hello. Her face was weather-beaten and heavily lined, though in her eyes there was a tremendous and refreshing hope. 'Dr Virga?' she asked.

'Yes.'

'Can I prepare something for you to eat? Some broth?'

'Yes, that would be fine. Thank you.'

She smiled and, nodding, stepped back into what Virga presumed was a small kitchen.

Michael was slowly and methodically peeling off first his bulky fur coat and then a lighter parka. He hung them to dry over a wooden rack near the fire.

Through a window Virga saw beams of light and shadowy figures moving in the darkness. He stared.

'They're very curious people,' Lahr said. 'They mean no offence; they were frightened of you and now they feel safe to gather up ice to melt for water. It's just that the noise of the airplane and the activity in this area has unsettled them.'

'They won't harm the crate, will they?' Michael asked.

'Oh no, oh no,' Lahr said. 'Don't worry about that.'

'What crate?' asked Virga, looking around at Michael.

'Something I brought with me.'

'I didn't see it.'

Lahr said, 'It's perfectly safe where we left it, out in the storage shed. No one will harm it.'

Virga was still looking at Michael. 'What is it?' he asked.

Lahr's wife came through the doorway with tea. It was thick, black stuff that clung to the sides of clay cups. Michael and Virga drank it in silence.

Lahr stretched out in a chair before the fire and said, 'So. Your friend and I have been discussing the problems of teaching Christianity to the nomadic Eskimo, Dr Virga. I find his views very interesting.'

'You're the only Danish family here?' Virga asked.

'Oh yes. Actually the Eskimos have taken to us quite well and vice versa. They're fascinating people. When I decided I would like to be a missionary in the North I read books and books on their customs; I even attended classes on Eskimo culture in Copenhagen. But nothing is as revealing as observing their way of life first-hand. They have a perfect communion with the land.'

'In some ways,' said Michael from his position in the corner of the room, 'they've been damaged by the white men who came here to teach Christianity.'

The elderly minister smiled and waved a hand. 'Yes, yes. I couldn't agree with you more. There were some unscrupulous men posing as missionaries. With them, unfortunately, came venereal disease and alcoholism. Now the Danish government has to ration beer and liquor on a monthly basis to these people: one bottle of spirits, two bottles of wine, or twenty small bottles of beer. That's the Greenlandic disease, that and suicide. This year we've had six. I don't know what it is. Their moods change so quickly. They're difficult to predict. Did you know,' he turned to Virga, 'that many many years ago, after listening to the Christian missionaries from the Netherlands, some Eskimo fathers killed their sons to make a religious gesture? Yes, it's true. Unbelievable. But of course then the Eskimo was much more naïve.

'Still,' he continued, 'there are elements of the primitive that linger. During the summer months when the sun begins to thaw the bay the *piniartorssuit* – the best hunters – pray to their individual and very personal deities before taking to the

183

ice. The animals, the winds, the tides: all of them have spirits. And all of them, like the Eskimo, have their moods.'

'Your task must be very difficult,' said Virga, finishing his tea and putting the cup aside.

'I consider it a learning experience. We'll be here until we die. I couldn't conceive of living again in Copenhagen. Now all that seems too distant to be real. This,' he motioned in a circle with his hard brown hands, 'is real. These are the real people. For four years I've settled family disputes, I've laughed and cried with them, I've seen them give birth and lower coffins. Yes; we'll die here. It would be a fine place. Ah! Here's your broth. Drink it while it's hot.'

As Virga lifted the steaming mug to his lips Lahr leaned forward in his chair and said quietly, 'So you two men are going northward, uh? That's the way their helicopters went.'

Virga looked up. Michael had not moved from his corner.

Lahr said, 'Oh,' and glanced over at Michael. 'You didn't tell him, did you?'

'No.'

'Well.' He turned back around to Virga. 'They came less than seven days ago. They dropped prefab materials and supplies down and built that shed out on the airstrip to keep them dry. I don't know who they were but . . . well, I kept to my business and advised the elders to do the same. I had a very strange feeling about these men. The Eskimos stayed in their huts and even the dogs cringed from them. I thought about sending a message to the Ice Patrol that maybe these men were up to no good, but one of the younger hunters, Ingsavik, came to me and said he had spoken with these men, that they were part of a weather-research team. He said everything was all right and I should not try to alert the authorities. I did as he asked and the men left soon afterward.

'I thought nothing more of it,' the minister said, 'but they returned only a few days ago and recovered their supplies. Then the helicopters flew to the north, towards the barren ice flats, and that was the end of it except . . .'

The man paused. Virga said, 'Yes?'

'Perhaps there's no connection. I had noticed he was drinking heavily and beating his wife and that probably had a great deal to do with it. But Ingsavik stripped and walked away into the snow. His wife screamed and begged him not to go but he struck her in the face until she was senseless and let her drop. I walked with him for almost a kilometre asking him if I could help, but he turned on me in a rage. Then he begged my forgiveness and ran away across the flat. It's a time-honoured method of suicide.'

Virga sat motionless. Behind him the fire cracked.

Lahr said, 'Who were these men? You know, don't you?'

'Yes,' Michael replied, 'we know.'

'And you cannot tell me?'

'No. We cannot tell you. But if you understand that our search is just, then possibly you can help us. Dr Virga and I want to leave as soon as we can; it may even be too late now. We need someone who knows the ice flats to guide us. We need a sledge and dogs.'

The other man shrugged. 'All of them know the ice flats, but they're wary of strangers by nature. And certainly no one would take the trouble of guiding two *kraslunas* into the North. Bad country. You men don't know the ice; the man who took you would be considered a fool by his peers.'

'We can bargain with them?'

'Perhaps.' Lahr looked over as the door opened and a young Eskimo boy entered, glancing nervously at Virga and Michael. He was carrying two buckets of chunk ice. Lahr said, 'Come on, don't be afraid. This is Chinauganuk, a young man who brings us fresh ice every morning. Yes, take those into the kitchen, will you? Dorte helped deliver Chinauganuk's little brother a year ago and in this way he hopes to repay the debt.'

The boy, buried in thick dirty furs and his eyes rolling in fleshy folds, said a few words to Lahr in the Eskimo language that sounded to Virga like clickings of the tongue and a sudden clearing of the throat. Lahr shook his head and replied. The boy looked at the two strangers and backed warily towards the door. Lahr said, 'He's afraid you're *piktaungitok* – evil – as he believes the men with the helicopters were.' He said something in a soothing voice to calm Chinauganuk, and the Eskimo, after glancing with visible fear into Michael's radiant eyes, scurried through the door and into the darkness.

'Well,' Lahr said after another moment, 'the old superstitions persist and there is not much I can do to change them. I can

185

tell them about a forgiving and powerful God and the glory of Christ but I cannot take away the teachings of the ancients. And I do not know if it is wise to try.'

Lahr looked into the fire as if attempting to read there some answer to the question he had asked himself. Then he turned again towards Virga. 'I've asked Chinauganuk to send his father, Migatuk, around to see us. He's one of the settlement elders and he may suggest a guide for you, though I doubt seriously that he will wish to regard your journey as anything but a hazard. That may sound rude, but unfortunately it's a reality.'

'We understand,' Michael said.

'I expect my friend Migatuk will take his time in paying us a visit,' the elderly minister said. He took the empty cups and stepped towards the kitchen. 'I'll pour more tea and then you men can tell me what's happening down below. I'm afraid most of the news I get here is very dated.'

When Lahr left the room Virga said to Michael, 'I don't see how you reached this place before me.'

Michael looked at him and said nothing.

'Thank you for waiting,' Virga said, and the other man nodded his head.

After another round of tea and more conversation between the three men, Lahr listening and then reacting with disgust at the news of murders and bombings, the door came open again.

With the bitter gust of wind and snow that blew in across the floor came a heavy-set Eskimo man, bare-headed, with narrow inquisitive eyes and cautious lips compressed tight. The stub of a cigarette burned at his mouth and Virga caught the scent of harsh tobacco and sweat. The man closed the door behind him and nodded respectfully to Lahr. 'My son brought your request,' the man said in a stiff Danish-influenced English.

'Sit down, Migatuk. Over by the fire. That's right. Would you like a brew?'

'No.' The man's eyes flickered back and forth between the two strangers.

'Your family is well?'

'Yes.'

'And your wife no longer has her trouble sleeping?'

186

'No.'

Lahr said to Virga, 'Migatuk's wife was experiencing some very upsetting nightmares there for a while.' He turned again to the stocky Eskimo. 'You're my friend, Migatuk. I value your friendship highly. Because you're my friend I know I can make a request of you that I ask you to consider carefully.'

Migatuk cocked his head to one side.

'These men want to journey up into the flats,' Lahr said. The Eskimo nodded. Now there was the beginning of a mocking smile, though the eyes remained carefully controlled. He took his cigarette stub and flicked it into the hearth. 'These men have come a very long way,' the minister was saying. 'They know nothing about ice travel.'

'*Nuna sutakasuitok*,' the Eskimo said. 'Why do you wish to go up there? Nothing is there but a few small settlements and ice. In the darkness the hunting is bad. So why?'

'It has to do with the men who gathered their supplies here,' Michael said. 'We must find them.'

Migatuk shrugged. 'They left. They flew into the north, yes, but can you be certain they did not fly also in some other direction?'

'A possibility. But someone in a northward settlement might have seen their helicopters.'

Lahr said, 'What I would like to ask of you, Migatuk, is that you recommend someone as a guide to these men. Yes, I know. Their not knowing the ice would make it very dangerous. But I have faith in their cause, though they've felt it best to keep their reasons to themselves.'

'There is something I do not understand about this,' Migatuk said in a firm voice. He looked for a few seconds at Michael and then back at Lahr. 'I would not ask any other man to do this thing; I would not do it myself.'

Lahr looked disappointed. He nodded and said after a pause, 'All right then. I understand your feelings. But I have another request to make, if my friends allow. Perhaps the two-headed man can help them?'

The mocking smile vanished off Migatuk's face. He slowly lit another cigarette and shrugged.

'Would you take them to the two-headed man?' Lahr asked. 'I would consider it the greatest personal favour.'

The man muttered something in his native language and Lahr replied. They talked back and forth for a few moments and Virga could see the restrained fear in the Eskimo's dark eyes. Migatūk sat examining his calloused knuckles for a long while, then he looked around at Virga and Michael and said in an authoritative tone, 'I will take you to the two-headed man. But no further. We leave in the morning. I will ask the women to find for you kamiks and dogskin mitts.' He took a final drag at the cigarette and flicked it with the other smouldering butt. Then he nodded at Lahr and went through the door.

'He's a very fine man,' Lahr said. 'Not many of them would have done this for you.'

'What's this about a two-headed man?' Virga asked.

'A shaman,' Michael said. 'A sorcerer.'

Lahr looked at him in surprise. 'I didn't know you knew the language. Well then, as you overheard, these people hold the two-headed man in great esteem. He lives a few kilometres to the north and has for several years, all alone. One rarely hears the word shaman anymore. It's rather something the elders talk about when they relive the ancient past. I've never seen the man, though once last summer I went up there with a group of very reluctant hunters. I saw his hut but his dogs and sledge were gone.'

'Why is he called that?'

'I don't know. A shaman, according to the legends, is traditionally deformed in some way or another, but I draw the line at believing he actually has two heads. I do understand that he's a very fine hunter. Once a year, before the thaw, a chosen elder is allowed to visit him to ask his opinion of what the season's hunting will produce. Perhaps he can help you in determining the route of the helicopters; his eye, they say, is everywhere. But there is also the possibility that he will refuse to talk with you because you are white men, and therefore considered less than perfect by the Eskimo.'

Lahr looked out the window. Following his gaze, Virga saw someone approaching through the gloom, a kerosene lamp swinging from one hand. 'Ah!' Lahr said. 'Chinauganuk is coming to take you to be fitted. Please don't be offended by any sexual comments the women may make about you to each other. They see *kraslunas* so rarely.'

188

23

For hours they travelled into harsh winds wailing down from the bitter ice-cap. They were slowed to a crawl by its force and now Migatuk only cracked his whip over the heads of the struggling dogs to change their course a few degrees. Piled atop the wide iron-runnered Eskimo sledge were enough supplies to maintain them should an ice storm pin them down. There were fresh parkas and kamiks, boots of seal flesh with dog-skin liners, and a tent of sewn polar-bear hides that could be hammered into the ice with small steel pegs. Lashed down as well was the long canvas-covered crate Michael had brought along with him. The three men had strained against its weight as they lifted it on to the sledge; Migatuk had voiced his displeasure at forcing his dogs to haul such an impediment, but Michael remained silent as to its contents.

Ahead of them was only blackness as if they were either climbing or falling headlong into a gigantic hole. Even the ice seemed black. Migatuk had warned them to rub their cheeks and the bridge of the nose vigourously if the flesh felt as if it might be deadening. That, he said, was the first sign of frostbite. The small white sores would come later. So after every fierce howl of wind swept past, staggering him, Virga gingerly felt his exposed flesh, fearful of what he might discover.

At Avatik the strong-armed, heavy-bellied Eskimo women had giggled and made snide comments about the men as they were fitted with the kamiks. They were given thermal underwear and heavier trousers, though not nearly so warm as the polar-bear pants worn proudly by the Eskimo men. Then, while they sat with Migatuk and he carefully cleaned his rifle, explaining how the oil and grit would freeze in only a few moments on the ice flats, he told them bluntly what he expected. They would not talk without purpose, they would not stray out from behind the sledge track, and they would under no circumstances go near the dogs. Michael agreed and, after the men and a group of other Eskimos had loaded the sledge, they had slept soundly before the fire in Lahr's hut.

In the morning – and the only way Virga could tell it was morning was because Lahr said it was – the winds had increased, slapping intermittent snow aganst the windows. After a fortifying cup of tea the two men stepped into the cold and found Migatuk and his son untangling the dogs' traces before hooking them in place on the sledge. Then, with a final wave from Lahr and Migatuk's cry of *'Gamma! Gamma!'* to his team, they moved away from the settlement until its warm lights were lost across the plain.

The cold was numbing but not as bad as Virga had expected. The subzero winds could not penetrate either his trousers or parka. His feet and hands were warm with the coverings provided by Migatuk; his face was the only flesh exposed to the weather and he felt ice collecting in his eyebrows and in the stubble on his chin.

Michael, walking beside and a pace in front of Virga, seemed oblivious to the cold.

After a while Virga thought that Migatuk had lost the way. Virga himself had no sense of direction here. Everything was bleak and alien; there were no landmarks, not even rocks or abandoned huts, on which to base a path. But occasionally the dogs would yip at the crack of the whip and the sledge, its runners hissing through the packed snow, would slide a fraction to the left or right. And still they climbed, without speaking, into the wind.

Without warning the land erupted from a flat plain to rocks dappled with ice. They seemed to be going down an incline and the dogs slowed to keep their footing on the slope. Great black rocks rose up on all sides. They were shielded from the direct blast of the wind but Virga could hear it whining eerily through cracks and crevices, to explode high over their heads. Migatuk snapped his whip and called to the dogs to give them confidence.

Virga looked into the distance. There seemed to be a glimmering light very far ahead. He could feel his heart racing. Migatuk called to the dogs again and Virga thought, but was not certain, that he heard the man's voice tremble. They continued on, the Eskimo's whip cracking on all sides to keep the dogs on a straight path.

At the base of the incline they were again on a solid sheet of smooth snow and ice, but here the wind was not so fierce. Ahead on the plain, Virga could recognize the squat rectangular shape of a prefab hut. A light shone through a solitary window. Beyond the hut there was nothing but a solid black curtain.

Migatuk called out and the sledge ground to a halt far short of the prefab dwelling. Then there was no sound but the breathing of the dog team and the distant otherworldly whine of wind in the rocks. Migatuk said to the two men, 'This is as far as I dare go. Beyond is the hut of the two-headed man.'

And in the next second Virga's eardrums reverberated with a *crack!* that made the dogs howl in fear. Migatuk spun around. Just ahead of the sledge a spiral of snow kicked up, ice chips spraying back into the men's faces. The sound of the shot stretched out loud and hollow across the plain, rolling on to the frozen sea.

Migatuk shouted, '*Maiksuk!*' and lashed his whip full into the side of the lead dog, at the same time wrenching bodily on the sledge to spin it around in the direction from which they had come. Virga, thrown backward and off the sledge, saw Michael also knocked to the ground by the sudden momentum of the dogs. Migatuk cracked his whip; the sledge shuddered fiercely, gathering speed. As the sledge reached the incline and started up Virga saw a knife in the Eskimo's hand, glittering in the light from the hut window. He was cutting their supplies loose to gain more speed. The equipment and the heavy canvas-covered thing were thrown off; they slid down to the base of the incline. Freed of the weight, the sledge took wings. Snow was thrown up by the churning legs of the dogs; in another moment the sledge disappeared among the rocks in Migatuk's headlong journey back to the safety of Avatik.

Michael rolled over on his stomach, his eyes narrowed, his senses combing the darkness. The sound of the shot had not yet died away; the men could still hear it moving like a thunderclap in the far distance. Over by the prefab hut there came a tremendous barking and baying of dogs.

Virga was lost. He stood looking around helplessly, knowing he made a perfect target but unable, somehow, to recall what it was he should do.

'Stay where you are,' said a man's harsh voice. The sound

191

reached them as a command but it had been spoken softly, almost casually.

Virga looked towards the source of the voice, off to his right. From the corner of his eye he saw a movement. Someone rose up from a prone position on the ice. Virga thought at first his legs were chopped off at the knee but then he realized the man had been crouched behind a small white screen. The man walked away from the camouflage and stood with a rifle aimed at a spot somewhere between Virga and Michael. He said something in Danish and waited. Then he said in English, 'You! Down on the ice with the other one. Both of you spread your arms and legs and don't move. Good, you speak the language. That's right, very easy.'

The man slowly moved towards them. Virga saw his boots, battered sealskin with a fringe of yellowed polar-bear fur. The man methodically slapped their waists and underarms in a search for weapons. Then, satisfied, he stepped back a few paces and said quietly, 'Turn over very slowly. I'll kill you if I don't like the way you breathe.'

They did as he said. In his furs and polar-bear pants the man was a shapeless, faceless bulk that towered over them. He was silent, examining their faces in the darkness. 'You're neither Eskimo nor Danish. Who are you?'

'We've come from Avatik to find you,' Michael said, and in his voice there was a strange soothing quality. 'We mean you no harm. We only wish to talk with you.'

The rifle barrel dipped down an inch or so. 'Some men came to talk with me once,' he said. 'They wanted my haul of bear-skins. Before they were through talking I'd killed them. What are you after?'

Michael said calmly, 'Your help.'

The man was quiet.

'Can we stand up?' Michael asked.

The rifle barrel swung up again and he stepped back. 'Stand up, then,' he told them. 'But remember that I can see in the dark.'

They got to their feet and brushed away the snow. Michael said, 'We can talk more comfortably out of the cold.'

'It doesn't bother me.'

'It bothers me,' Michael said.

The man grunted and motioned with his rifle. 'Walk ahead. But don't even think of trying to trick me. Don't even think it.'

Near the prefab hut there were dogs staked out on chain leaders. They were large beautiful animals with eyes like burning coals; they rose up, rumbling a welcome, as the men approached. An Eskimo-style sledge stood on one side of the hut and around it were empty tin cans and garbage, similar to the debris Virga had noted in Avatik. The man said, 'Stop,' and with his rifle still aimed in their direction, he walked around in front of them and pushed open the door. He stepped back to watch them carefully as they entered.

Inside, a portable stove hissed, flooding the hut with warmth. Two kerosene lamps emitted a dim yellow glow. A sleeping rack, covered with polar-bear skins, stood in one corner. The floor of the single-room dwelling was dirty and stained with blood. Across the bearskin-lined walls were strung pinup-girl posters. They lay in nude abandon on beds, on sofas, and on sun-warmed beaches.

'Ha!' the man barked abruptly. 'You like my little companions, huh?'

Virga turned to face him.

The man was shedding his great bloodstained coat. He was bear-like himself, huge and wide. Almost as tall as Michael, his head was within a foot of the ceiling. He had long unkempt black hair and a black beard that turned the colour of frost around his mouth. His eyes, cobalt-blue, glittered in a face ravaged by the elements. Lines traced his forehead and gathered around his eyes. Virga saw small, pitted scars that he thought were the remnants of frostbite sores that the man might have cut away himself. His eyes were narrowed slightly from years of squinting into the sun as it glanced dazzlingly off blue-green ice. There was a trace of Eskimo blood in the high cheekbones and tawny colour of the skin, but he was certainly a mixture of other races as well. It occurred to Virga that he spoke with a slight Russian accent, though his English seemed tinged with other, less identifiable, accents.

Michael said, 'We were expecting someone with two heads.'

The man nodded slightly. He put his rifle down in the corner but his cautious, intelligent eyes never left them. He eased down into a battered chair and threw his feet up on to the lip of the stove. 'The Eskimo have their own way of saying things,' the man said. 'You've found me now. Who the hell are you?'

'My name is Michael; this is Dr James Virga. And yours?'

'I'm asking the questions. What're you doing up here?'

'I've already answered. We were told about you in Avatik and we sought you out.'

'And almost caught a slug in the bargain,' the man said. 'You should be careful you don't catch one yet.'

'You saw us on the incline?' Michael asked.

'Saw you, hell,' the man said. He leaned forward slightly and stared up at the other. 'I smelled you.'

Michael grunted and looked around at the walls.

'My name is Rynn Zark,' the man said after a silent moment spent appraising the two strangers. 'You men are not ice travellers; you have no business here. Why do you search for me?'

Michael drew up another chair and sat warming himself before the stove. He said, 'We have information that helicopters flew over this area some days ago. We want to know where they landed.'

Zark's eyes narrowed fractionally. He said in a cautious voice, 'They were seen by a group of hunters from a settlement further north. The birds veered off to the east. Why?'

'We want to know where they landed,' Michael repeated in a flat, even voice, swinging his gaze from the stove into the eyes of the other man.

Zark held it for a few seconds, then grunted and leaned back. He reached in his parka and brought out a pipe that seemed to be a hollowed-out bone. In another moment he had filled it with a black, oily-looking tobacco, and blue smoke was curling from his mouth and nostrils. 'I don't know where they landed. I don't want to know where they landed. It's not my business.'

'We understood,' Michael said, 'that you were a man of wisdom, a shaman.'

'Shaman? Shit. I'm a good hunter and sometimes I tell the Eskimo where to look for the seal and bear. I hear the wind sing and I see the clouds that mean a storm on the ice. I know the land and I know men and most of all I know myself. But I am not a shaman.' He sucked vigorously at the pipe, looking from Michael to Virga and back again. 'Did you know that there are some Eskimos who follow me because they say that where I walk is a path of good fortune? They say I never have to find the bear; the bear will find me. If that were true I'd march down to Copenhagen and take them all with me. Shaman; I haven't heard that word for a long while.'

'If you know yourself you have more power than most men possess,' Michael said.

'Maybe. When I first came to this land, many years ago, I almost starved. The Eskimo saved me; they fed me and taught me how to feed myself. So sometimes when I go out for bear or seal I tell the Eskimo hunters where I believe they're going to be found. I always repay my debts.'

'Do you keep in contact with the rest of the world here? Do you know what's going on below?'

'The rest of the world? Ha! There is no other world but this.'

Michael said, 'A man has arrived here with those helicopters. That man has grave power; he has power to do what he wants with whomever he wants. That is the man we must find, and we must find him quickly.'

Zark had been smoking his pipe and listening. 'Why should I care? I can't help you.'

'But you can. You know the land. You've said so yourself. Dr Virga and I need someone to take us into the North-east.'

'What? Are you crazy? I'm not in the business of tourist guides. To make a journey with men who have no knowledge of this country would be suicide. Is this what you sought me for?'

'Yes,' Michael said.

'Then go back to Avatik. Go back to wherever you came from. I don't travel across the ice on the errands of fools.'

'I'll pay you.'

'I've said no.'

Michael glanced over at Virga and then back into the eyes of Zark. 'We have no way of getting back.'

'That coward,' Zark said. 'One bullet and he runs like an old woman. I should have shot him in the ass. All right, then. I'll take you in the morning to Sagitak; the Eskimos there will see that you return safely to Avatik. But you'll pay me for my time and trouble.'

'We seek a man named Baal,' Michael said after another moment. 'It is vital that we find him. We will not return. We will go on from Sagitak into the North-east.'

'Not with me. Maybe you can pay one of the Eskimos up there to go on with you. Give them a couple of bottles of good whisky and they'll do anything. Did you bring any with you?'

'No.'

'Well then,' said Zark, shrugging, 'you're in a shit of a shape.'

His eyes glittering, Michael opened his mouth to say something, but then he thought better of it and sat relaxed in the chair. He said, 'You won't help us?'

'I won't help you. I've got my own self to take care of. Look. That route you just came over from Avatik is a trade route; an old woman with one bad leg could get over it. But you get up higher than this, on rocks and pressure ridges and ice chunks as big as goddamned battleships, and then, my friend, you need good eyes and good lungs and you'd sure better have some ice experience under your belt.'

He stopped speaking abruptly and seemed to listen to the silence in the room. In a few seconds more the dog team staked outside began barking. Zark picked up his rifle. He whispered, 'We have a visitor.'

As Zark stood peering out the window, Virga could see nothing but total blackness. Then Zark stepped towards the hut door and opened it to admit a rotund but hawk-eyed Eskimo man with a scar across the bridge of his nose. The man shook snow from his furs and looked cautiously over at Michael and Virga. The Eskimo seemed to ask a question in his native language and Zark motioned to the two men and nodded his head. Then the Eskimo spoke again, fixing his eyes on the floor at Zark's feet and rounding his shoulders to appear humble, though he was obviously older than Zark. When he had finished his plaintive-sounding recitation he continued staring fixedly at the floor.

Zark turned to look at the two men. Then he nodded and said something to the Eskimo. The other man grasped Zark's hand and then went back out into the night.

Virga said, 'What was all that about?'

'The man,' Zark told him, 'is a hunter from an eastern settlement. His new bride wishes a child; he has sadly and regretfully lost the fire. So he's brought her here for me.'

'What?'

'Hell, I've probably got kids all up and down the Arctic Circle. I don't know; they seem to think it's some sort of honour if I can give their wives a child. The women aren't so bad. All that fat makes them like big soft pillows.'

'The man feels you have the qualities of a shaman,' Michael said. 'Since he feels disgraced at being unable to father a child he hopes a son with the qualities of a shaman will bring honour back to his name.'

'I guess that's it,' Zark said. 'Anyway, I don't mind. Well now, what's this? A young one.'

The Eskimo had brought his woman in from the sledge outside. He took off her fur-lined parka and put his hand beneath her chin to indicate her beauty. She was very young, probably only just out of her teens, yet her face showed the hardships she had already endured. She stood like the man had, staring directly at the floor, not daring to meet Zark's intense gaze. Virga supposed she was very beautiful indeed by Eskimo standards; her full lips were trembling though her round dark eyes seemed to reflect a remarkable inner calm. The girl's lustrous black hair, freed of the parka's confining hood, hung loose and full about her shoulders.

As the Eskimo spoke, Zark examined the girl's face. Zark nodded and the man beamed with happiness. The Eskimo touched her cheek gently, with scarred brown fingers, and spoke to her. Then he nuzzled her as if sniffing at her flesh. When he turned to leave she clung to his arm, but he spoke sharply to her and she let go her grasp. The Eskimo went through the doorway and in another moment the men heard his shouts as he urged his dog team up the incline.

The young girl stood trembling in the centre of the hut, her eyes downcast. Zark walked around her and said to the men, 'A fine-looking woman. Very fine. Good strong arms and thighs. Look at those muscles right there. You see? She hasn't yet got a lot of fat on her.'

Virga's face was reddening. He said, 'Are we going to watch this?'

Zark's surprised eyes left the girl's firm buttocks and looked up at him. He said, 'What else? You going to freeze your asses outside? Hell, I don't care. You can close your eyes if you like. You can have a go at her if you like. Do you want to?' He swung his gaze around to Michael.

'No,' Michael said, 'thank you.'

The man shrugged. 'Suit yourself.' He walked around and said something in a quiet voice to the girl. She didn't reply. He put his hand under her chin and raised her head but she still kept her eyes on the floor. Slowly and softly, Zark nuzzled her as the other man had, sniffing gently at her nose and across her cheeks and eyes. Finally, reassured by his caress, she raised her eyes to meet his and Zark smiled.

24

Virga stirred. Something was jabbing him sharply and repeatedly in the ribs.

He rolled over from his curled-up position on the dirty floor and after a few seconds recognized Zark standing over him. He had been nudging Virga in the side with the toe of his boot. Zark bent down and put a mug of steaming dark liquid in Virga's hand. 'Here,' he said, 'this'll wake you up.'

Michael was already awake, drinking from a mug and taking his clothes off a rack above the stove where he had hung them to dry the night before. Virga sipped at the beverage, finding it to be a brackish black beer, and saw that the Eskimo girl was gone. He'd barely been able to sleep for the noise they had made, rolling and thrashing on the sleeping rack like a couple of wild beasts. But he was grateful in one respect for having been able to find out something about Zark: before the man had lowered the kerosene flame to join the girl in the bearskins Virga had caught a glimpse of his broad naked back. Across it was a beautiful tattoo of the head of a Chinese ancient, done with such clarity and grace that it would have made Virga envious if he were an advocate of tattooing.

'Where's the girl?' he asked.

'Her husband came for her,' said Zark, cutting pieces of meat off a larger black slab he'd taken from an ice-packed oil drum at the rear of the hut. 'They're always a little jealous the morning after. You ever try walrus meat?'

'No.'

'You'd better get used to it.'

Virga and Michael took the pieces of black, tough-grained meat that Zark had cut for them. Michael ate his wholeheartedly, but the taste of it coupled with the beer was almost more than Virga could take: it was oily with a strong smell of fermentation. Nevertheless, he was glad to get something in his stomach. When he swallowed the last hunk without gagging he felt pretty damned proud of himself, but shook his head when Zark offered him a second piece.

Zark shrugged and tore into it himself. He said, 'What's that you brought along covered with canvas? Prefab materials in a crate?'

'No,' Michael said. 'It's some of my belongings.'

'Christ. You must have brought along everything you own. I walked out there and took a look at that junk the Eskimo cut off his sledge. You didn't plan to move very fast, did you?'

'We carried what was necessary.'

'Necessary, hell. All a man needs is a good solid sledge and eight strong dogs and he can go to the Pole and back, living off the land. You can forget about the prefabs and build ice shelters like the old hunters did. But you're *kraslunas* and you don't even know what I'm talking about.' He looked over at Virga. 'What kind of doctor are you?'

'A professor. Of theology.'

'What's that?'

'Religious concepts.'

'You live by the Book, huh?'

'I suppose I do,' Virga said, 'in a manner of speaking.'

Zark nodded. 'Yeah, there's always more room in the world for another holy man.' He took the leftover walrus meat back to the oil drum. 'Perverting everything, talking about things you don't even understand yourselves. You look at something and say it's bad in the name of God because you don't like it.' He took the drum lid off and wrapped the meat in newspaper before putting it in the ice amid other bundles. 'You use God as an excuse.' He snapped the lid shut.

Virga felt that this man was trying to pick an argument. He

said irritably, 'Some people do.'

The other man grunted and shifted his attention to Michael. He said, 'And I suppose you use God as an excuse, too, huh?'

'No,' said Michael, his eyes glittering in the dim kerosene-lamp glow. 'I only blame men.'

Zark stood looking into his face as if he were not quite certain of what he was seeing. His nostrils flared briefly, catching a scent. Then he smiled slightly and said, 'You ever killed anyone, boy?'

'Not to my knowledge.'

'You look like you could. You look like you could shoot a man down and never even wince. Killing a man is not so different from killing any other kind of animal, not really. Especially if he's about to kill you. Does talk about killing a man bother you, Holy Man?'

'I'm very broadminded,' Virga said.

'Good,' Zark said. 'That's good.'

Michael said, 'You won't reconsider about taking us into the North-east from Sagitak?'

'No. I won't reconsider. Now I'll go harness the team; you be ready to help me lift that gear of yours up on to the sledge when I get back.' He went through the doorway, admitting a blast of icy air, and momentarily Virga and Michael could hear him shouting to his dogs as he worked with them.

'What should we do?' Virga asked. 'Go back to Avatik and pay someone to guide us up? We're going to lose three days.'

'Yes, three days. Perhaps too late.' He looked directly at the other man. 'But if I'm too late here then there will be another place. I'll go on. What will you do?'

'I don't know. I haven't read a newspaper or heard a newscast in two days. I'm afraid to learn what's happening.'

'The worst' Michael said softly. 'Always prepare for the worst.'

'How did you come to be so desperately pursuing Baal?' Virga asked. 'How can you, how can we, do anything to stop him short of murder?'

'We must find him first. Then I'll deal with Baal . . . in my own way.'

The door came open again and Zark said, 'All right. I need some muscle.'

In the bitter darkness the three men heaved together to lift the shrouded crate on to Zark's weather-beaten sledge. He cursed violently and said, 'You're going to break the backs of my dogs with this goddamned thing!'

They lashed down the rest of the scattered equipment and then followed Zark back to his hut to gather up a few more things. Zark carefully cleaned his rifle and a rubber-gripped flare gun and stored ammunition and flares in a sealskin bag. Then he tied up a hunk of the walrus meat and checked one of the lamps to make certain the kerosene was brimming. Michael said, 'You're taking an ice-axe?'

'Yes,' Zark said. 'Why?'

Michael gathered his parka hood around his head without answering.

Outside, Zark rubbed snow all along the sledge runners and Virga had an opportunity to appraise his dogs as they stood in the glare of the lamp. They were broad and thick, powerful beasts that even now tugged at their rope leaders. The lead dog was a one-eyed black with numerous scars on his sides; the other dogs gave him a wide berth and, though they snarled menacingly among each other, never bared a tooth in his direction.

Zark checked the lashed-down equipment and cursed at its bulk. He said suddenly, 'We're moving,' and almost before Virga realized he had called to the dogs, the sledge shuddered and tore away up the incline with Michael running alongside and Zark cracking his whip over the head of the lead animal.

The beasts climbed the incline with a burst of power. They seemed eager and happy to be running in the snow. The sledge passed between the sharp outcroppings of rock and in a few moments they were running out on the open ice plain with the wind howling maddeningly about them.

Virga noted that Zark seemed much more skilled with his team than Migatuk had been. The man only occasionally used his whip or shouted to the team; they seemed to understand his commands even when his broad hands only tightened on the guiding handlebars. The man and the team were at one with each other, Virga thought, through long hard years of companionship. He'd heard stories of the fierceness of Arctic dogs, of their sudden savage attacks on both their own kind and Eskimo children, but here they were part of a beautiful living machine that awed him with its primal grace.

Michael did not seem disturbed at Zark's refusal to take them on, but Virga was downcast. He felt a childish frustration and a simmering resentment at the way Zark had tried to bait him at the hut. Zark didn't understand the importance of their search for Baal; probably he was the kind of stubborn man who would act no differently even if he did understand. But Virga felt useless and afraid. His long travel and the great expense it had incurred was now wasted because one man – one man – refused to show them the way. He cursed. If Baal could not be found how could he, Virga, return to the university and his day-to-day life knowing the full extent of Baal's power, knowing that for a brief instant he had almost been ensnared by that power, knowing that he could possibly still be. What could he say to Judith? What would he feel when he awakened in his Boston apartment in the middle of a restless night, more alone and frightened of the future than he had ever been before?

He glanced over and saw that Michael's sharp features had become a taut, determined mask. Here in this bitter land, travelling under skies as black as the door of death, there was no way to go but forward.

They reached a pressure ridge after a mile or so. Great chunks of ice were scattered in disarray like concrete blocks. Zark lowered his head against the wind and chopped with his ice-axe until he had cleared a narrow place for the dogs to struggle over. Then they were across the rough terrain and moving over smooth ice with the splash of the lantern leading them on. Zark corrected their course by a few degrees from time to time, though Virga could not determine how he sighted the path.

Sometime later, when ice had frozen in Virga's eyebrows and his new beard and he saw nothing but the dark wastes beyond, Zark waved a hand and slowly braked the team with his heels. 'We'll rest here for a while,' he said against the wind. 'This is the half-way point.'

Zark unpacked the bearskin tent and staked it out with

metal anchors, keeping it loose to absorb the wind's force. As the dogs voided themselves in the snow and Zark unceremoniously followed suit, Michael and Virga crawled through the tent opening with Zark's lantern and warmed themselves in its glow.

Inside the tent they were still cold but at least shielded from the harsh wind. Zark crawled in and lit his bone pipe, then checked his exposed flesh for frostbite sores. He held the lamp up to examine the faces of the other men and, satisfied that they had suffered no damage, he set the lamp in the midst of them, where it cast their broad black shadows on the walls.

Virga painfully rubbed the warmth back into his hands. 'How cold is it out there?' he asked Zark.

'Warm compared to some I've known. Maybe forty below but not any more than that.'

'How can you tell?'

Zark grunted. 'When it's forty below your piss freezes as it hits the ground. At fifty below it freezes on the way down. At sixty you try to piss and your dick falls off.' He blew a billowing cloud of blue smoke and watched as it rose to the conical top of the tent and hung there.

'You're not a full Eskimo,' Michael said after a few moments. 'What are you doing here?'

He rubbed his hands around the warmth of the bone pipe as if he hadn't heard the question. There was no indication that he was going to answer. Virga was about to ask him how the dogs withstood the weather when Zark said, 'I'm part Eskimo. Enough to feel the ice in my blood; enough to know I belong here.'

'You were born in Greenland?'

'Hell, I'm not a Dane. I was born in Gor'kiy. My father was a breed, Eskimo and Russian. My grandfather was an Eskimo and damned if I can remember his name, but he was a powerful hunter, a great leader in his tribe. I don't remember anything about him, but my father once told me he was lost in the bergs hunting narwhal with a bone harpoon. We had a small flat in Gor'kiy and my father was a welder; that place we had, that place was so small we couldn't even wipe our noses. My father couldn't stand it but he wanted to please my mother. He wanted to live on the northern coast and she loved the city.'

The smoke whirled around Zark's head. His eyes were cold and blue, glistening, Virga thought, like the ice must glisten beneath a white summer sun.

'He tried to please her,' Zark said, 'but you can't please women. You can't. And he started drinking and finally lost her. I remember him glaring at her, wild-eyed, in that place. She was leaving, she said, and he could keep the child because they were both alike. Both of them were wild and vicious and didn't belong around people. That was just after I almost killed another boy in a street-fight, but that's another story. And she was right. My father and I were alike; we shared a love of freedom. Inside us the Eskimo wanted a return to the ice.'

Zark was quiet for a moment. The north-born wind shook the tent; Zark seemed to be listening to it. He looked warily at the faces of the two men, uncertain as to whether he should continue.

'And so you both came here?' Virga asked, both interested in the man and fearful of returning into that cold blast.

'No,' Zark said. 'He went from place to place, from job to job, and I followed along. And every place we went was closer to the northern sea. There was where we were headed; he didn't have to say it. I knew it already. But before we reached the coast he took sick, something wrong with his lungs. I worked full-time at whatever I could find, which wasn't much but road-work and pouring concrete. I fought for a while in men's clubs. That was bare-knuckled fighting and I saw a lot of strong men go down. You ever see a bare-knuckle match?' He looked at Virga.

'No, I haven't.'

'I didn't think so. Too brutal for your blood, uh? Some of those men scarred their hands and let the callouses thicken until they might've been wearing brass knucks. They could punch into brick. Those fights would go on until neither of us knew where we were; we'd just stumble around looking for something to hit. The last man standing was the winner and the money was good in those days. But my father became worse. He was always coughing, always pleading with me to get him up to the ice. I found him dead one morning, just like he'd fallen asleep the night before. That was the only night he didn't cough until he'd choked, and I remember thinking that soon maybe he would be well enough to travel. It snowed on the day he was buried. Well,' Zark shrugged his shoulders and sucked furiously at the pipe to clear his vision, 'I reached the sea. I landed a job on a freighter hauling scrap iron. Holy Man, you ever work on the sea?'

'No.'

'It's tough work. But it teaches you a hell of a lot. It teaches you when to fight and when to lay back, when to plant your feet and when to run like hell. I worked in and out of the freight docks for a few years hauling on old buckets that almost came apart at the rivets out in the Baltic. I like the ways of the sea; it moves at its own pace. Nothing hurries it, nothing weakens that thunder. But then I landed a mate's slot on a tub hauling snowploughs from Riga up into the White Sea. I didn't get along with the bosun. He was a lying sonofabitch and a card cheat; I can't even remember what he looked like though God knows I had to look at him enough. He was always picking something, anything at all, to get at me. And damned if he didn't.'

Zark laughed suddenly, a hoarse bark that might have issued from the throat of one of the dogs. 'Damned if he didn't. I killed that man right on the foredeck under a half-moon. Two blows to the head. Two fine blows I would've been proud of in any ring.' He made the motion of a thrust with his huge fist. 'He went down like a fucking sack of grain. They were going to put me in the brig and head into Rusanova to give me up. But there were other men who had taken trouble off that bastard, and they were damned grateful to me for cleaning him off. So one night out in the Barents Sea they turned their backs and I lowered myself a lifeboat and headed out into the bergs. They thought I'd died out there, that maybe I was going out to commit suicide or some shit like that. Hell, no. I was getting away as fast as I could row.'

He regarded Michael and Virga through his whirling blue smoke curtain. Over the black bush of beard his eyes had become dark and hollow. 'You don't know what it's like to be alone in the sea, surrounded by nothing but ice, great huge pieces like frozen cities. Nothing around but the deep water and the bergs that blinded you with their colours: bone-white, deep blue, pale green. You could see the depths of the ocean reflected in that ice. And sometimes you'd likely as not hear a growl as ice crushed against ice and broke off into a smaller berg. Sometimes ice as big as my boat would rise up almost under me. That was maybe what I feared most: ice breaking up in the depths and rising to capsize me in that cold water.

'On the third day,' Zark went on, 'I was lost. I couldn't smell the wind. And then the bergs against the white sky looked like grey slabs of dirty concrete. I was going in fucking circles; everything looked the same. My food ran out. I went without anything to eat for three more days. There was never anything but the low clouds and the white sea and those berg mountains. And on the seventh day I woke up and saw him.'

Zark sat motionless, his pipe clenched between his teeth, his eyes black and brooding.

'Him?' Virga asked. 'Who?'

He shrugged abruptly. 'I don't know. I don't know who the hell it was but he was off my starboard between two bergs, an Eskimo in a kayak. I started rowing after him but he never let me get near enough to see his face. Never. But it was a man, all right; I could tell by the way he handled that kayak. Even though I grit my teeth and rowed after him until I was almost dead, he paddled Eskimo-style, always ahead of me. I followed that kayak for two days. He never said a word though I shouted and cursed for him to speak; he'd turn to make sure I was following and then he'd go on. He wound me through ice tunnels and bergs as high as buildings in Moscow. He knew those fucking waters, that's for sure. But after three days I lost him. He slipped away into a pocket between two bergs and when I rounded them he was gone. That's when I saw, over my port and far off, a group of Eskimos hunting from kayaks. They took me with them to Edge Island and I got a good meal of broth and walrus meat and slept for two days. When I asked them who had led me out they didn't seem to know. They didn't have any idea; they told me they knew of no hunter who had ever gone that far from land before. So I still have no damned idea who that was. I wonder about him.'

Michael was nodding. He said, 'The vision of a shaman.'

'Huh? Hell with that. Anyway, I followed the nomad Eskimos over the ice plains into Greenland and here I've stayed. The hunting is damned good and a man answers to no one but himself. That's as it should be.'

The three men sat for a while without speaking. Tobacco burned in Zark's pipe with a faint crackling sound. After a few moments he stirred and said, 'Time to move on. I want to have you at Sagitak in another couple of hours.'

25

Without warning the wind died away and was replaced by an utter calm that, oddly, played on Virga's nerves until they were as raw as the flesh across his wind-burned cheeks. Even the harsh breathing of the team quieted until all Virga could hear was the sound of runners on the ice, a smooth hissing as if they were nearing the nest of a coiled white reptile.

They continued on into the North, Zark correcting their course with only a slight movement on the handlebars. Looking up, Virga could see stars clearly and individually against a backdrop of total darkness. There was no moon, but the stars seemed to radiate a dim silvery glimmer that splashed down across the plain and painted it in deepest blue.

They reached a point where the land gradually began to slope down. Zark halted the team with a single soft command, and as the dogs milled about he stood with his lantern at his side and looked out to where the distance became a drawn curtain.

Michael stepped beside him. 'Is something wrong?'

'Be quiet,' Zark said. He was listening for something. He narrowed his eyes and swept them back and forth along the horizon. He looked briefly to the stars and then back at the far landscape.

'There are no lights,' Zark said.

'What?' Virga asked.

'No lights,' the man repeated. 'Sagitak is on the horizon. There should be lights in windows.'

'They're nomads? Maybe they've left,' Virga suggested hopefully. The man would have to take them on.

'Shit,' Zark muttered. He walked to the sledge and retrieved his flare gun and the sealskin bag. Virga watched as he popped open the breech and inserted a red cartridge. Holding it at arm's length over his head, he fired it with a soft *plop!* in the direction of the settlement. In another few seconds they could see, bathed in red light as the flare arced in the sky, the dim outlines of huts far away and something else, something like a dark semicircular scrawl. Zark tightened; Virga felt the response repeated in Michael. The hunter bent on one knee in the snow and waited for either a light or the reply of another flare.

There was nothing.

One of the dogs whined. Another answered. The black animal stood grim and unyielding; when another animal began to whine the big black snapped in its direction.

Zark shook his head. 'I don't know,' he said quietly, almost to himself. He said, '*Gamma!*' to the dogs and the sledge moved off again towards the lower plain.

In another fifteen minutes they had reached the flat. The flare had faded, returning them to darkness. Virga was aware Zark's breathing had become heavier. The dogs strained at their leads, perhaps recognizing by habit a place of food and rest. Virga tried to pierce the gloom but his eyes were not good enough. He cursed his weakness.

And suddenly the dogs yelped, stopping and then tangling together as if they had run collectively into a wall of glass.

Zark cursed. He tightened his grip on the handlebars and cracked his whip over the head of the lead dog. It wanted to go on and pulled mightily at its lead, but the other animals balked, thrusting their tails between their legs and digging in with their paws. Zark struck his whip directly into their midst, but still they refused to move.

The ground was rutted with the marks of sledges that had passed in the same direction, so Virga reasoned that they had not run into rocks or some obstruction. The settlement, if he had estimated the distance correctly, still lay some hundred yards ahead.

Throwing his whip down, Zark cursed the animals and retrieved his rifle from the sledge. He said to the two men, 'These animals are not moving. I'm going ahead. Are you coming?'

'What's wrong?' asked Virga, afraid to know. Beyond Zark

208

the darkness was awesome and absolute.

The man's eyes blazed briefly. 'I'm going to find out.' He held the lantern with one hand and followed its yellow track on the scarred snow. Virga and Michael followed behind. Zark stopped twice to bend down and examine the sledge tracks.

As they walked towards the settlement, the dogs still whimpered behind them. Zark stopped abruptly and sniffed the air, his face intent in the yellow light. 'Can you smell it?' he asked Michael.

'No. What do you smell?'

'Blood,' the man said. He raised his lantern and walked on.

Patches of it, black and frozen, were scattered about on the snow. Virga avoided it, feeling his heart hammering in his chest. They could no longer hear the dogs. Virga longed for any sound, even the wind's piercing wail.

Zark stopped again. He held out the lantern. Its illumination splashed on to the bloody snow and crept along a narrow path that broadened and broadened until it fell upon something that made Virga gasp and stiffened Zark as if he were suddenly frozen.

It was the body of an Eskimo, clad in bloody furs, bound with rawhide thongs to a cross of splintered wood. The cross had been hammered upside down into the permafrost, so the man's staring eyes were near ground level. Virga had a sudden recollection of having seen an inverted cross over a doorway, but the frantic rush of blood in his brain prevented him from remembering exactly where.

As Zark moved the lantern slightly its glow revealed a deep gash across the man's throat. Bone glinted; the blood made a black oily pool beneath a face open-mouthed in absolute, primal terror.

And he was not alone.

Zark swung the lantern to both sides. The three men saw a row of bodies, some disembowelled, some decapitated, hanging from obscene crosses and stretching on both sides into the darkness beyond the range of the lantern, seemingly into infinity. Virga caught the scent of blood that Zark had mentioned and noticed with a dulled sense of alarm that he was standing in a frozen puddle. The red snow covered his boots.

'Thirty-six men,' Zark said suddenly. He spoke as if he were totally drained of strength. 'Twenty-eight women. All of them have been murdered.'

'A barrier.' It was Michael speaking.

'What?' asked Virga, tearing his gaze away from those terrible agonized corpses.

'This is a warning to anyone who has reached this point. An example of what lies beyond for anyone crossing the barrier.'

'All of them,' Zark was saying. He shifted the lantern and looked, disbelieving, down the line of gruesome crucifixions. Faces caught the yellow light and stared back through ice-filmed eyes. Open straining mouths screamed at death blows. Curled fingers of out-thrust hands clawed at the last remnants of life. They had died in much pain and, worse, a terrible certainty of what lay before them.

Zark stepped forward and shined the light on an upturned face, here another, another, another. Some he touched gently. Some he stood over and spoke to, quietly, in their native tongue. Virga shuddered and, glancing towards Michael, realized that the man was looking beyond the row of corpses out towards the black wastes.

'These were good people,' Zark said. 'They were good hunters with loyal wives. And now . . .' He turned suddenly upon Michael. 'Who did this thing?'

'Baal,' Michael said softly.

'The man you seek?'

'The man we seek.'

'One man did this? One man murdered these people and left them staked out like dog meat?'

'He's not alone. There are others with him.'

'How many?'

'Three or four.'

Zark cursed bitterly. 'How can a man do anything like this?'

'They were your friends?'

'I knew them,' Zark said. 'They asked my advice. They trusted me. I knew them.'

Zark's anger was wild and churning behind his eyes; it seemed on the verge of breaking free. Virga shifted his weight, crunching through blood-caked snow.

'What kind of man,' Zark said, 'is this Baal?'

210

'The thing Baal has done here is nothing compared with what he's done below,' Michael replied. 'It's nothing compared with what he can do. We must find him very soon.'

The hunter turned, his eyes sweeping along the row of crosses. He shook his head at the awful carnage. 'This has the stink of evil,' Zark said.

'Yes,' Michael said in a voice Virga had to strain to hear.

Zark said, 'This is the final settlement before the great plain. I'll guide you along the route taken by their birds. But I must ask one thing. I want to deal with this man Baal.'

Michael regarded the other man and finally shook his head. 'No. That I can't promise you and I will not explain why. I know you want revenge. Revenge can be noble. But in this case revenge is a lost cause.'

Revenge. Revenge. Revenge. The word thudded inside Virga's head. He'd heard it before and it had terrified him. Where? Where?

'Lost or not,' Zark thundered. 'I'll have it!'

'No,' the other man said. 'You will not because you cannot.'

'Do you want him for yourself? Then I'll tell you something right now. You'll have to fight me for him. And I'll break you in half.'

'Perhaps.'

The two men glared at each other as if expecting a confrontation.

'We should be leaving this place,' Virga said. 'We can't do anything here.'

Zark blinked. His gaze flickered over towards Virga. He fired a last red stare in Michael's direction and then turned away. He stood for a moment, the lantern down at his side and blood all over his boots. 'Something is wrong,' he said. 'Damn me if something isn't wrong!' He stalked down the row of corpses, shining the light on agonized faces. 'There were over twenty children in this settlement. There are none here. There are no bodies.'

'We should be leaving,' Michael said.

'Where are their bodies?' demanded Zark, pacing up and down the barrier like a great hulking beast.

'Zark!' It was a command for attention, sharp and cold. The hunter stood in his tracks and very slowly turned his head

211

towards the lean, authoritative figure standing beside him. Michael put his hand on the man's shoulder. 'We are leaving now.'

Zark drew himself up to curse in Michael's face but, seeing the grim determination on the other's features, let his anger subside before he spoke. He shook the hand off and wheeled around in the direction of the sledge. 'We're leaving,' he said.

Walking back, Michael stepped beside Virga and said quietly, 'Prepare for the worst.'

'What do you mean?'

'The children's bodies were taken for a purpose, the same purpose for which children by the thousands were induced into Kuwait.'

When Virga did not reply Michael said, 'No matter. We shall see what we shall see. To attempt to explain to Zark the depth of Baal's power would be futile.'

Walking fifteen yards ahead, Zark turned and said, 'You talking about me back there? Come on. I'm not waiting for you.'

Zark cracked his whip into the left side of the lead dog to guide the team around the grisly barrier. The dogs were still shy but the ferocious head animal strained at its lead and growled until the others, sensing that they were not headed any further into that death-smelling place, shared the weight. The sledge tore away on a horizontal line a hundred yards beyond the barrier. Though Zark cursed and whipped them, the team refused to turn on a northern path for what seemed like almost an hour. Finally Zark cracked his whip over the lead's head and wrenched with all his strength at the handlebars. The sledge shuddered as the dogs began to turn and, minutes later, they had regained the correct course and left the visage of death behind.

They travelled in silence. Zark was grim and brooding, his eyes fixed on the indefinable, at least to Virga's untrained vision, horizon. The air was still and calm; it yet smelled of blood even though the settlement was far behind.

On all sides there was nothing but empty black and the ever-present stars. Virga saw the red and blue trails of particles streaking across the heavens, burning in Earth's atmosphere. Once a meteor flashed along the horizon and burned itself out in dazzling red hundreds of miles to the east. To primitive peoples, Virga thought, it would be a sign from God, perhaps a warning that the entity of the skies was displeased. The priests would sit over ceremonial fires for days debating the meaning of the flaming skywriting. Drought, famine, or even a war yet to come: the priests would argue as to which it was. And the mysterious result was that a great percentage of ancient predictions based on sky observation came about. There was no fall from heaven, the priests said, that did not foretell a fall on terra firma.

Another two hours – or so Virga thought – passed before Michael turned to him. 'Are you tired? Do you need rest?'

Virga shook his head. It was a lie but he didn't want to delay them. He felt weak and hollow-eyed but he didn't want to sleep. The images of the frozen dead faces were too sharp in his memory to allow peace; he knew he would dream of them and in his dream he would be one of them, struggling to escape over bloody snow but knowing always he could never get far enough away.

Several times Zark stopped the sledge and walked a few yards ahead, where he would bend down on one knee and just stare without moving, his eyes fierce slits. Then he would walk back and systematically make certain everything was still lashed securely to the sledge. He checked the rifle repeatedly and refilled his lantern with kerosene from a small metal container.

'How far would you say?' Virga asked.

'Can't say. Maybe one kilometre, maybe ten. Maybe one hundred. But I'll know. This is land that even the Eskimo avoids. There's nothing here.'

'You're sure we're headed in the right direction?'

'We're swinging east, the same route as the birds. You trust me and I'll trust these.' He touched the corner of one eye and his nose.

The stars disappeared. The harsh breathing of the dogs, the crack of Zark's whip became a regular rhythm. Virga, his eyes and limbs heavy, hung on to the sledge and let it pull him. Soon the terrain about them began to change; ice-crusted black rocks tore their way out of the permafrost and huge mountains of ice, veined in deep green, squatted like Eskimo attempts at skyscrapers.

The sledge began to slide, slowly at first then rollercoaster-like, up and over the slopes. Zark kept control by holding back on the handlebars and dragging his heels along the ground.

Then the ground simply fell away with breathtaking abruptness. Its runners hissing, the sledge came up a slope and hurtled down like a rocket-sledge over glimmering blue ice. Michael was thrown to one side, sliding down the incline on his belly. Zark scrabbled for a foothold but there was none. He lost his grip and fell, cursing.

Virga, hanging on, saw the dogs trying to scramble out of the way or, impossibly, outrun the vehicle with its overload of equipment. The sledge slipped to the right, throwing the team off balance and scattering them into their leads. A wall of snow and ice fragments collapsed over Virga's head, blinding him. He heard Zark shout, '*Jump clear!*'

At the base of the steep slope was a flat ice plain. The sledge was going to crash down on it. The dogs were yelping in fear. Virga released his hold on wood and threw himself to the left, wide of the hurtling sledge. He landed on his side and spun around and around on a surface of glass, trying to protect his injured hand. Below him, on the plain, there was a sound of metal grinding over rocks. Sparks flew up. The team whimpered, a chorus of pain. Then Virga slid to the base and lay there, breathing heavily, on his stomach.

Zark had regained his footing and was walking carefully down the lower third of the slope. Beyond him, Michael struggled to his feet.

Virga cleared his vision and cursed. Damn! Possibly three or four dogs had been injured. The dark hulk of the sledge lay ahead and the dogs, though still bound by their leads, were scattered everywhere. Most had already regained their footing to wait for instructions, but a few had not stirred.

And, as Virga counted the remaining uninjured dogs, he saw a light flash perhaps half a mile away.

He tensed. Michael had almost reached him. Virga stood, heedless of the new pain that throbbed in his hand, and motioned. 'A light,' he said. 'I saw a light out there.'

'Damn it to hell!' Zark said from behind them. He was brushing snow off his furs as he walked. Ice had completely caked his beard and made him appear an old man. 'That probably tore a fucking runner loose! And my dogs – '

'Zark,' Michael said quietly. He pointed into the distance and the hunter looked along the finger towards the flashing light.

The man grunted. He whispered, 'Could be another group of hunters on the ice. But hunting isn't good here. Still . . .'

'How far is that?' Virga asked. 'About a half-mile?'

'Maybe,' Zark said. 'No, more than that. You can be sure the sound of that sledge hitting bottom carried over there. Looks like someone with a lantern walking . . . moving too slow to be on a sledge.' He watched the light for a few more seconds and then quickly stepped to check his sledge and dogs. He moved among the team, speaking softly to them.

'You're all right?' Michael asked Virga.

'Yes. I'm fine.'

'Good. I believe that light is shining in Baal's camp. There is a possibility that Baal himself may already be gone. If that's the case I'll go back to Avatik and continue somewhere else. Will you go back to America?'

'I don't know. I don't know what I'll do.'

One of the dogs cried out sharply. They turned to see Zark raising his rifle and clubbing a second dog in the head. Then a third and a fourth. He bent down and with a knife from his coat cut loose the leaders of the dead animals. Then he carefully checked the runners and walked back to the two men. 'Three dogs with broken legs, one with a broken back,' he said. 'The sledge has a damaged runner. We'll be slowed but I don't have the means of repairing it. Both of you are okay? No broken bones? Good.' Zark gathered up a few supplies that had been thrown free and relashed them to the sledge frame. He coiled the whip around his hand and made certain all the leads were free. 'From here on in,' he said, 'I want no talking. None. Don't even breathe hard. Someone up there knows we're here. He may not know who we are or how many but he has heard us. We won't be showing our light.' He grasped the handlebars and said very quietly, '*Gamma*.'

26

When there is no sound for the brain to register it must invent one of its own, a fierce dry buzzing, to keep the nerves active, the electric impulses crackling.

In Virga's ears the buzzing had become a roar of deprived nerve endings. He and Michael walked a few dozen yards behind Zark, who would occasionally hold up his hand for them to remain still and then crouch down on the ice plain, sniffing the air, his head moving from side to side to catch any trace of sound.

They had left the sledge when the light beyond flickered and vanished. They had covered more than a hundred yards on foot and still there was no break in the blackness ahead. Virga felt his flesh crawling; fear had filled his mouth with the taste of blood. Beside him, Michael moved as quietly as a shadow.

Zark held up his hand, crouched and listened. Virga could hear nothing. Around them the rocks and upturned ice chunks were ominous markers on a path that fell off into the dark. They were large enough to hide a building; they were large enough to conceal any number of men who might be even now watching their progress. In fact, Virga suddenly had the feeling of being observed, though he thrust it aside as a fancy of his fearful imagination. Around him there was angry black rock and smooth glistening ice, nothing more.

Zark rose to his feet.

There was the sound of metal against metal.

At first Virga thought the sound had come from Zark but when the hunter turned his head violently to the left, Virga realized there was a man hidden in the rocks.

The men threw themselves to the ground even as the shot echoed back and forth, off blue ice and jagged stone. Ice kicked up less than a foot to Zark's left and the man rolled for cover. Michael was on his feet and running. He reached out and with one hand wrenched Virga up, dragging him along into an outcropping of ice-glazed rock. Another shot rang out. Sparks exploded over Michael's head. In another moment Zark, holding his rifle before him and crawling on his stomach, had reached them. He worked his way into a crevice so his entire body was protected. 'One man to the left,' Zark said, 'and another moving in behind us. We'll have to worry about the man on the left first; the other bastard won't be within range for a minute more.'

A rifle cracked. The bullet, whining wildly, scattered ice chips. '*Ha!*' Zark shouted, then lowered his voice. 'That cocksucker can't get us, but he's pinning us here for the man behind.' He eased up over the rock and positioned his rifle so the barrel was firmly supported. He did not fire; he was waiting.

The man on the left fired again. Virga could see the orange flame spit from the muzzle. The bullet sang over their heads and on towards the Pole.

'All right,' Zark said softly. 'Once more, you bastard. Once more.'

Fire exploded again from the man's rifle. Before it had vanished Zark had it pinpointed. Even as the bullet hit rock in front of him and screamed off, Zark's finger pulled the trigger. His rifle bucked. Then he whirled about, firing at the fur-clad man who had been climbing on the rocks behind them. The man, twenty feet away, was thrown backward and fell, open-mouthed, into a cluster of ice and rock. His rifle clattered down and slid, spinning, on to the ground a few feet from Virga.

Zark waited, his eyes narrowed and his senses throbbing. He said, 'That's it,' and stood up. He reached beneath his furs and felt for the kerosene lamp he was carrying from a short rope at his waist. The glass was cracked but no fuel had escaped.

'You knew they were there,' Michael said.

'I knew they were there. I had to offer myself as a target. And that bastard nearly blew my head off, too.' The man laughed abruptly at the expressions on Virga and Michael's faces. 'You can't shoot a man if you can't see him. If you can't see him you take the next best target – the muzzle flash. You care to stroll over there? I'll show you the hole at his heart.'

'I'll take your word for it.'

'I thought you would. All right. We're all in one piece.

217

Holy Man, if you'll pick up our friend's rifle and carry it along we can move on. It won't bite. Good. Just strap it across your shoulder.'

They moved onward around the outcroppings of rock. Everywhere Virga thought he saw black shadows sliding around them, men looking for clear shots. He had only fired a gun, a pistol, long ago and then only at paper targets. He understood very little about firearms but he felt somehow more secure with the weapon slung across his shoulder. Its weight reassured him.

No one spoke. Snow crunched drily beneath their boots. Around them the great slabs of ice grew larger. Here jagged fingers of rock swept up towards the sky; here skeletal blue ice, phantom faces, watched them pass. Zark still crouched and listened at intervals; Virga looked from side to side as Michael watched the rear.

Like an animal sniffing game, Zark stopped, Michael stepped beside him.

Ahead, as the great hulks of ice and stone gave way to a new smooth plain, was a long high-roofed prefab structure. The walls and roof were coated with ice. There were wide doors, like those of an aircraft hangar, that opened outward. The doors were cracked and there was a dim glimmer of light from within. To the right of the prefab structure was a thin-spired radio tower. Beyond that an ice pathway led off into a new burst of rock.

Motioning for the others to remain silent, Zark paused for a moment. He took the kerosene lamp from around his waist and relit it. Then he tied the lamp to the barrel of his rifle, holding it at arm's length ahead of him. They followed its light across snow pitted by many boots. Zark reached the long structure and carefully, quietly, pulled at one of the doors until they could slip through. Ice along the door seam cracked.

He stood on the threshold and shined the lantern inside. There was an unmarked black helicopter amid rows of stacked crates. At the far side of the structure was a small room, lit by three kerosene lamps, and the men could hear the crackling static of a transceiver. Zark took the lantern from the rifle muzzle and walked beneath the fan of helicopter rotors towards the radio room with the men following behind.

Virga's eyes were so accustomed to darkness that, once

inside the room, he squinted. A chair stood before the transceiver and there was a small table with a coffee pot and a cup.

Zark touched the pot. 'Still warm,' he said.

There came the sound of someone running across the hangar floor. Zark pushed roughly past the two men and stood in the radio room doorway with his rifle upraised. Beyond him a man had just reached the hangar entrance and was running out into the snow. Zark's weapon barked hollowly. The man cried out before he fell.

Michael reached him first. He rolled the body over and saw that the bullet had torn away the top of the man's head. The face was gaunt and terror-struck. It was no one he had ever seen before. 'Do you recognize him?' he asked Virga over his shoulder.

'No.'

'The bastard must have been hiding behind a pile of crates,' Zark said. 'That was the radio operator.'

'Killing him was unnecessary,' said Michael, rising to his feet. For the first time Virga saw a deep red glimmer of anger burning in his gaze. 'He could have told us where to find Baal.'

Zark was startled by the fierceness in Michael's face He regained his composure, his muscles coiling beneath his thick furs. 'Shit!' he said. 'If he's one of the men who destroyed that Eskimo settlement he deserved to die! I don't ask questions of dead men!'

'It seems to me,' Michael said firmly, 'that you do most of your thinking with your trigger finger.'

The hunter's face darkened. His hands curled into fists and he started to step forward.

'Baal is still here,' Virga said sharply. 'There's no need for argument. If the helicopter and radio operator were still needed then Baal is here.'

Zark looked at Virga for a few seconds and then back at Michael. 'He's right. So back off.'

The anger drained visibly from Michael. He seemed displeased that he had shown any emotion. He said, 'All right. If he's here we'll find him.'

Zark gestured towards the path that led away into the forbidding rocks. He started up it, mindful of his footing on the slick surface. They had gone no more than a hundred feet when

Zark held up a hand for them to stop. The hand trembled.

Ahead there was a maze of ice and prefab materials. Huge ice blocks supported a roof glazed with snow. Corridors wound off in all directions. It was a sprawling, nightmarish structure that seemed to have neither shape nor purpose; it was a winding labyrinth of ice-walled tunnels.

But it was not the structure itself that had stopped Zark. He had thrust his lantern forward; the light glared off the ice on both sides of the pathway. Now he stared wild-eyed past the light, unable to move.

Something was buried in the ice.

It was a small dark form; its shape chilled Virga to the marrow. He dared not look but was forced to all the same, hypnotized by its obscenity. Zark was stepping forward, the breath ragged between his teeth. He held the lantern against the ice. The yellow light showed clearly the open eyes, the gaping dark-spattered mouth, the curled fingers of an Eskimo child. And the light showed bodies to the right, bodies to the left. The ice was filled with corpses of children, frozen like butterflies under glass. The men had walked into a horrible museum of death. Virga felt weak and sick; he staggered backward before Michael turned and caught him. It seemed that the eyes were all imploring his mercy, the mouths shrieking the word revenge.

Revenge.

Revenge.

Virga shook his head violently to clear it.

'Christ!' Zark breathed hoarsely, putting a hand against the ice to steady himself and then jerking it away as he realized his fingers had covered a glaring pair of eyes. 'Christ!'

'I told you,' Michael said, still with a grip on Virga's arm, 'to prepare yourself for this. The ancient cults of Baal sacrificed children and buried their bodies in the walls of dwellings as a pagan protection from harm. I told you to be ready.'

Zark shook his head in disbelief. He couldn't tear his eyes away from the awful scattered forms. It was beyond anything in his experience. Caught off balance, his senses reeled.

'We must go on!' Michael said. 'They're dead and beyond help.' He took the lantern from Zark and continued along the pathway, then stopped to wait for the men to compose themselves. Virga was quietly sick. He wiped his face and then went on.

They entered the ice corridors. The lantern threw a solitary splash of light on the prefab floor and glimmered from the open eyes of the children on each side. Zark cringed from the bodies and kept to the centre. They continued on, reaching countless dead ends and retracing their steps through one death-littered hall after another. The corridors wound in circles, split into twos and threes, ended in empty vault-like rooms. The determination in Michael's face became more dark and grim with each blank wall they reached. And on and on they searched, avoiding the imploring faces, through the halls and through a hundred more until Virga knew they could never find their way out again. They would be lost forever, searching, and no man would find their frozen corpses even in a thousand years. Virga felt that the walls were closing in, the corridors steadily narrowing until the frozen fingers would reach from the ice and drag them into it with them. His nerve was breaking; he feared for his sanity. I can't go on, he said to himself. Oh dear God, I can't go on.

And then the corridor turned sharply to the right and there was someone sitting in a chair in a huge ice-gleaming room.

Michael stopped, the frozen breath bursting in clouds from his nostrils.

The man was sitting in darkness. Michael held his arm out and the lantern illuminated burning eyes above a savagely twisted mouth. He wore a heavy coat of dark fur. His hands rested along the arms of the chair.

Baal said softly, 'So. You've found me.'

'No, you sonofabitch!' raged Zark, bursting past Michael and raising his rifle to fire point-blank. '*I've* found you!'

'WAIT!' Michael said. The command rocked Zark back on his heels. He shook his head as if he'd been struck. Slowly he brought the rifle barrel down and stood looking across at Michael.

Baal laughed, a cold quiet laugh without mirth. 'Go ahead, Michael. Let him use his weapon. You! Come here!'

Zark stirred. He blinked his eyes and looked into Baal's dark gaze. He stepped forward and immediately Michael turned in front of him to hold him back. Michael said force-

221

fully, 'You will not go forward. Both of you will stand exactly as you are, do you understand? I want this very clear. You will always keep yourselves at a distance from Baal; keep myself between you and him. You will avoid looking into his eyes. You will by no means touch him or let him touch you. Do you understand?' He shook Zark. 'Do you?'

'Yes,' Zark said thickly. 'I understand.'

'And the same for you, Dr Virga.'

'All right. Yes.'

'Dr Virga?' Baal had looked in his direction but the other man cast his eyes away. He laughed harshly. 'Well, well. My good Dr Virga. I see you injured your hand. Isn't that unfortunate? You probably won't ever be able to use it again. Tell me, can you beat off with your left?'

Above the lantern Michael's eyes were glittering gold and alert. He said, 'Your time has finished. I've seen your name spread a burning evil trail. Now it is finished.'

Baal bent forward slightly. He said, 'Never. You're too late. Oh, you've found me. But now that you've found me, what can you do? Nothing, you goddamned whoreson fool, nothing! Even now my disciples are in America, Africa, South America; they spread the news of the Messiah's resurrection. In the Middle East the crowds clamour for war against the bastard Jews in retribution for what they thought was my assassination. Soon the superpowers will be involved. There is no way they can avoid involvement; the area is too strategically important, the oil fields too necessary for the continuation of their civilization. It will start with only a few rockets, perhaps, or a heated rush of infantry . . .' He smiled, slowly and mockingly. 'So you see? You can do nothing. I will have my pleasure dealing with the bastard Jews; my master will strike in the midst of chaos.'

'Who was the man sacrificed to the crowd in Kuwait?'

'An American Jew, a newsmagazine correspondent. We were able to "persuade" him to fire the shots Then my disciples spread the word through the mass that it was a Jewish-American plot. On the following day the television and radio networks released the news that Baal had died of two gunshot wounds at the hands of a Jew assassin. Response in Beirut was predictable anguish, peaking now towards holy revenge. The body – a body – was cremated and the ashes placed in a golden urn.

The Arabs are armed with what I taught them; there will be no stopping their fury at the death of the living Muhammad. No, Michael . . . you're too late.'

'I've come prepared this time,' Michael said.

Baal nodded. 'Yes? How?'

'Like all those who have given themselves to the dark forces, you cannot withstand the power of the Cross. It burns you with its purity. You're reduced, like all Satanists, to make mockery of it by inverting it.'

'Oh?' Baal said quietly. 'Watch yourself. You underestimate me. You judge my present strength by my past weaknesses.'

'I won't underestimate you,' Michael said. 'Not again.'

'What are you going to do? Burn a cross in my flesh? Stake me to one and leave me in the snow? No good, Michael. I wouldn't make a very good Jesus. I will only find a different method of approach.'

'I know that.'

Zark had recovered himself. He said in a still-weakened voice, 'Leave him to me. I'll rip out his guts.'

Baal laughed. 'Yes, Michael. Yes. Leave me to this stupid man. Then turn your back with the assurance that you'll never again have to deal with me. He'll do a good job, Michael.'

'No. You're coming with us. You're going to lead us out of here.'

'Why? I could refuse to go and let you wander here until you become too weak to go on. Then . . .' He grinned, his cold stare unyielding.

'You'll lead us out because one of your great weaknesses is curiosity. You want to know how I've readied myself for you.'

'When last we met, in Nevada, I was weak compared to this,' Baal said menacingly. 'I am warning you now. I have the strength of a million – no, more than a million. Are you very sure you wish to challenge me?'

Michael remained silent.

'Think,' Baal said. 'Think. If you were to aid me instead of opposing me. Think what we would have! Everything! Instead of being the mercenary of bastards like these, you would be the master! How can you turn your back on such power?'

223

'And what of your master? When you have given him what he desires do you actually think he will share the spoils with you? Do you actually think Israel will be yours for the taking?'

Baal spoke in a guttural growl. 'It will be mine again.'

'Stand up,' Michael commanded.

Baal remained seated. His black eyes began to take on a tinge of deep red. They glowed in his white skull-like face. Very slowly and carefully he rose from the chair, his gaze flickering between Zark and Virga. 'I am in need of amusement,' he said.

Michael stepped forward until his face was only a few inches away from Baal's. He said grimly. 'You will show us the way out of here. You will walk ahead of us.'

'And if I refuse?'

'Then the end will come here.'

Baal nodded. 'So finally you've decided it has come to that? Like the noble pissing martyrs you try to emulate, you would do it that way?'

'If need be.'

'You stinking sonofabitch,' Baal said in a low growl. 'You cocksucker, you coward.'

'I said you will move ahead of us. Dr Virga, step aside and let us pass.'

Virga gave Michael and Baal a wide berth. As Baal passed him he felt a terrible repulsion and, yet, a sudden sharp impulse to reach out and touch the man. Michael stepped beside Baal and Virga felt the impulse fade. Baal had seemingly been aware of the reaction he'd caused. He turned and grinned, his eyes bright and scorching-red, into Virga's face before moving out into the corridor.

As Michael held the lantern to watch Baal, Virga and Zark followed behind. Zark kept shaking his head, as if struggling from a daze, and muttering to himself.

'Are you all right?' Virga asked him.

'Leave him to me,' he said. 'Leave him to me.'

They reached the clean cold air outside the awful death-frozen maze. Passing the radio tower and hangar, they started through the rocks on the path that would lead them back to Zark's sledge. In the cold Zark's senses sharpened. He kept his rifle at the ready and watched the rear for another attack.

224

When they reached the sledge the dogs growled a greeting to Zark before they caught Baal's scent. Instantly they whimpered, backing away from the approaching figures. The dogs cowered, their tails dragging, and even the lead dog trembled.

Zark walked ahead to calm the animals.

'Beasts of burden,' Baal said. 'That's what you are, Michael. And you'll be a beast of burden until you have the courage not to be.'

Michael retrieved a canvas bag from the load of equipment on the sledge. From it he withdrew a pair of manacles joined together with a short chain. He approached Baal, who watched him incuriously and even thrust out his wrists to be bound. Michael clamped the manacles on and snapped them shut.

'You fool,' Baal said into Michael's face. 'You stupid, pitiful fool.'

27

Zark coiled his whip around his hand. He looked over at Michael. 'What did you say?'

'I said,' the other man replied, 'that we are not going back to Avatik.'

'Where then?'

'The sea. I want you to take us to the frozen sea.'

'What?' Zark asked. 'It'll take us at least two days to reach the coast. I don't want to travel with that man.'

'Don't be afraid,' Michael said. 'You need not be afraid so long as you do as I ask.'

'Why the sea?' Virga asked.

'Because it suits my purpose. That's all I'll say.' Beyond Michael, Baal was watching them, his eyes glaring across the ice.

There was still hesitation on Zark's frost-crusted face. He shook his head. 'I don't understand this. I don't understand that man you call Baal, nor do I understand you.'

'You don't have to understand. Just trust me and do as I ask.'

Michael held Zark's gaze for a few seconds. Then the hunter nodded and said, 'All right, dammit. The sea. But just to the coast and not on to the ice. Why not kill that man here and now?'

Michael didn't answer. He purposefully turned his back and neared Baal so as to shield the other men from him.

Zark cursed and cracked the whip over the heads of the team. The dogs started, pulling heavily at the sledge with its damaged runner. Virga saw that the sledge was leaving a deep, crooked track.

'I don't like this,' Zark said to Virga. 'We should kill that man here and leave his body. He deserves to die.'

Virga said nothing. He was haunted by confusion and insecurity; now, finally facing Baal, he wasn't sure that even Michael could control him. The sudden burst of panic he'd felt when Baal had glared at him still gnawed at the pit of his stomach. He would see those terrible red eyes forever. He couldn't even venture a guess as to why Michael wanted to reach the sea. He had the unshakable feeling that Baal's power was always on the verge of breaking wildly free, of turning on them all and reducing them to cinders. And at that point even Michael couldn't help them. He shivered though the sweat of fear burned on his face. He felt alone and helpless, wrenched from his life at the university, destined never to be the same again. And there were so many questions he wanted to ask, things that whirled around his head and left him staggering . . .

'You sonofabitch!' Baal was shouting at Michael where they walked off to the right of the crawling sledge. 'You fucking bastard!'

Virga rested his chin on his chest and grabbed hold of the sledge for support, trying to shut his mind to the awful obscenities that now poured from Baal's mouth. They did not stop but instead grew in both intensity and vulgarity. Baal was shrieking in Michael's ear and Virga wondered how the man could stand it. Then Baal's voice changed in pitch, changed from a low hoarse shout to the piercing scream of a small child: 'You cocksucker! You priest-sucking bastard! I'll kill you! You'll rot before you destroy me!' And then, incredibly, the voice of a young woman. Virga turned his head and Zark

226

made an effort to keep his attention on the ice plain ahead. 'Your eyes will fall from your head, you sonofabitch! I'll command you to go blind! Goddamn you! Goddamn you!'

Virga put his hands to his ears.

Zark whirled around. 'SHUT UP! SHUT UP!'

And the voices, Baal's voice, quieted. The laugh that reached them across the ice was low and lazy, gratified and pleased, as if from a man who has just won a game of chess.

The dogs strained, whimpering, on their leads; the sledge was dragging ice. As he walked Virga was aware of the hiss of runners on the snow, the grind against outcropping rock, the hiss, the grind, the hiss, the grind until his head was pounding with those alternating sounds. He could distinguish hard-packed snow and smooth ice plain, rocks the size of a fist and rocks with razor edges that could slash the paws of the team, all without opening his eyes, just listening to the sounds they made underneath the runner. Once, testing his newly developed abilities, he fell asleep while walking. When he jerked his eyes open he was looking to the right, towards Baal. With an effort he looked away, his nerves screaming alarm and new sweat freezing into his eyebrows.

When Virga stumbled and fell Zark halted the team. He helped the man to his feet and called to Michael, 'We've got to rest. The fatigue will kill us.'

Michael considered the request. After a moment he said, 'Very well. We'll rest here.'

Zark staked down the bearskin tent and crawled through its opening. Virga, his joints throbbing and his face a mask of painful cold, followed him and lay slumped against a wall, his breath coming in harsh gasps. Outside the dogs whined anew as Baal and Michael passed. Michael entered first and waited for Baal to crawl through, then he deliberately sat between Baal and the others.

Zark opened his package of walrus meat and cut a slice for Virga, who tore into it ravenously. He offered a piece to Michael, who refused it, and then cut a piece for himself before wrapping it away. Taking out his pipe and lighting it, Zark leaned back against the tent's firm wall, closed his eyes, and smoked.

Virga curled up for warmth and lay his head down.

Michael did not attempt to sleep. Baal's gaze was burning

into the back of his neck. He sat cross-legged and watched the two exhausted men as they drifted towards a deep, empty sleep.

And suddenly the tent was filled with a terrible rising scream that made even Michael's flesh crawl. His eyes bloodshot, Virga wrenched himself up because he thought he'd heard Naughton screaming from the shadows of an evil-smelling hall. Zark's eyes came open and in a blurred instant he had grasped his rifle and hurtled through the opening in a flurry of snow.

Virga shook his head when he realized where he actually was. The tent reeked of rancid breath. Baal laughed quietly from his corner, his teeth bared, his eyes coals.

In another few seconds Zark burst back in, his eyes rimmed with white and his beard ice-caked and dirty, and said, 'There was a bear outside! I heard it! Damn me if I didn't . . .' He stopped, hearing the mocking laughter, and his face flamed with rage. 'You sonofabitch!' he shouted, reaching across Michael for Baal. 'I'll kill you!'

Michael grasped Zark's arm.

The laughter abruptly stopped.

Baal said, 'Touch me. Go ahead. Go ahead.'

'Sit down,' Michael said.

'I'll kill him.' The breath clouds were fumed from Zark's nostrils and mouth. 'I swear I'll kill him!'

'Sit down,' Michael repeated, his voice sharp. He tightened his grip on the man's arm and Zark's eyes slowly cleared. Zark fell back against the wall and sat, motionless and drained.

'You won't sleep,' Baal whispered. 'If you try, the same thing will happen again. And soon your nerves will be shot and you'll be jumping at my every breath. Go ahead.' He grinned at them. 'Close your eyes.'

In Virga's frost-numbed mind was still the image of Naughton, lying on his back in a littered chamber, whispering something, whispering . . .

'Kill him now,' Zark muttered. 'Now.'

What was it? What had he said? What had he said?

'There is only one way. You! Eskimo! No, don't turn your face away. I need you. You and I together will leave this place . . . we'll leave both of them out here and we'll get back to Avatik. I'll let you sleep once we've left them behind. Listen

228

to me,' Baal hissed. 'Listen to me!'

Michael reached over and clamped his hand firmly about the hunter's thick shoulder. 'Stay where you are,' he said softly.

'You can't continue without sleep. You'll never make the sea. You'll fall dead in your tracks.'

Virga was trembling. He saw Naughton's mouth opening, opening, opening . . .

'Let me go,' Baal hissed.

Naughton whispered, 'Re . . .'

'. . . venge,' Virga said.

Michael looked over at him, his eyes blank and incurious. Baal was silent.

Virga said, 'What did you mean by that? It was something both you and Naughton said to me when I asked what Baal's purpose was. You said the word revenge.'

'Naughton?' Baal whispered from the corner. 'You found Naughton? Bastard! Cocksucking traitor! We should have torn out his eyes and tongue before we left him to die!'

'But,' Michael said, 'you didn't.' He said to Virga, 'Yes, that was what I said. That is the truth.'

'Your truth, perhaps. But beyond my understanding. And there are things here so far from my understanding that I'm afraid I'm losing my mind.'

Zark said, 'We should kill that man here and now.' He lapsed into a low, coarse muttering.

'I told you from the beginning,' Michael said to Virga, 'that there would be things beyond your understanding.'

Virga said, 'I want to know. I have to know.'

'Then know one thing first. You can never go back; you can never be what you once were. You'll be hung between life-in-death and death-in-life. If you choose to speak no one will ever listen; you'll be branded a madman.'

'I can never go back now,' Virga said.

Michael paused for a moment, searching the man's eyes relentlessly. Behind him Baal breathed like a beast in heat.

Michael said, 'You'll listen to what I'm going to say, but you won't hear. It will be beyond your comprehension. Do you believe in Jehovah?'

The question startled Virga. He said, 'Yes. Of course.'

'And then you also believe in Satan?'

Virga said, somewhat more uncertainly, 'Yes . . .'

'The great powers. The light and the dark. One patient and tolerant, the other reckless and cruel; but both of them warriors. Between them is a mixing of the elements, the All. There is a completeness in the combination of good and evil. Do you see? Without one the other could not exist – that is a Law. And balanced on that Law of All is the cosmos; to tip the balance of power would result in chaos and madness. It would result in what you see taking place at this moment.'

'Dog!' Baal whispered.

'Satan has never been a secondary power; he is the equalizing darkness to Jehovah's light. At the beginnings the cosmos was created by both Jehovah and Satan. The cosmos was, and is, a combination of celestial and demonic energy. Your ancestors were part of that energy. You are part of that energy. Baal is part of that energy.'

'The pagan god this man has named himself after,' Virga said.

Baal laughed quietly, a rumbling in the throat.

Michael said, 'No. What you see is a human body, but the entity itself is a formless mass of energy. He is Baal, within a form to make himself visually acceptable to those he wishes to influence.'

Virga sat motionless. Beside him Zark had closed his eyes and was breathing harshly.

'The light and the dark were not always enemies. As I've said, Satan is reckless. He is concerned only with the accumulation of power. If the Law of All is destroyed he is destroyed as well, but like a spittle-mouthed dog he cares only for the moment. At the beginnings the creation recognized only the god of light and the god of darkness, each equal. But Satan saw advantages in increasing his strength through the use of demons as pagan gods. Baal was one of the most successful; he was already strong, with an unreasonable lust for power and grandeur. Under Satan's influence Baal became a Canaanite deity, urging the sacrifice of children, sodomy and prostitution, the sacrilege of the temple. Satan was pleased with the result: he urged more and more of his demons to claim themselves as gods before a creation now confused and tormented. It was the only way Satan could claim more power than Jehovah. All these things Jehovah endured until Satan began to influence the Hebrews, Jehovah's chosen own, into darkness and black sorcery. Ths balance was overthrown. As an example He turned on Baal, the most successful of Satan's vanguard, and with the aid of the Israelites drove Canaan into the ground. His wrath was furious; He ordered His celestial armies to burn the wicked cities to ash, that the land should be fiery rock and nothing should grow. The idols and temples of Baal were destroyed; those who had worshipped the demon entity were wiped off the face of the earth. Baal was a combination of both powers, the light and the dark, but he'd betrayed one and now sought refuge in the other.'

'Lies,' hissed the figure behind Michael. 'Liesssss.'

'The damage was done. Satan had tasted blood. And so began then the battle that would determine the continuation or destruction of the Law of All. It rages here and now. Satan uses Baal to throw havoc into the creation; Baal seeks his own revenge, destruction of the Israelites who destroyed his kingdom of Canaan. He has existed in many physical forms, before this moment. And in each incarnation he's come a step closer to achieving both his goal and the goal of his master. Baal is a mad god, possessed by the forces of darkness.'

Virga was trembling. He was aware of it but he couldn't stop it. He tried to concentrate on stopping it. He said in a halting voice, 'Baal is a man . . . he's only a man . . .'

'Have it as you will,' Michael said softly. 'You asked, I answered.'

'Let me go,' Baal said in the voice of a child.

'We must continue. Can you go on?' Michael gazed at Virga.

Beside Virga, Zark had opened his eyes and was rubbing his neck and shoulders, working the blood.

'I don't know. I don't know. I'm so tired.'

'That's not what I'm asking. Can you go on?'

'They can't continue, Michael,' Baal said. 'Give it up. Let me go. Join me.'

Michael looked over at the hunter. 'Can you travel?'

Zark rubbed his hands together. He looked from Michael to Virga and back again. 'Yes,' he said.

'Good. Dr Virga?'

He didn't know. It seemed difficult to breathe. He said, 'I'm so tired.'

'I warned you. Didn't I warn you?' Michael said. 'We must reach the sea as soon as possible. You have two choices. You can continue with us or we will leave you here.'

Virga looked up, startled at the ultimatum. He ran his hands over his face. 'That's not a choice. I'll go on.'

Michael nodded. 'All right. Baal and I will crawl first through the opening. Then you and Zark.'

The bearskin tent was lashed away and the dogs, curled in tight balls against the cold, were urged to their feet by Zark's insistent whip. The team strained against their leads, the tautening ropes sending ice flying, and the sledge again began to wind its ragged way across the wastes. They walked as they had before, Zark and Virga close to the sledge and Michael shielding Baal far to the right. The cold ripped across Virga's ravaged face. It didn't serve to keep him alert but instead aggravated his exhaustion, and soon his chin was lowered to his chest again. He staggered on without knowing where he was.

Moments – or hours – later, someone whispered, 'Virga.'

He shook his head. He was dreaming. In the snow his boots sounded a continuous unbroken tattoo. He hung between sleep and wakefulness, fearful of both.

'Virga,' someone whispered.

He opened his eyes.

Zark stood at the front of the sledge, his back broad and bear-like in his furs. The dogs moved at their rhythmic pace, ice whirling beneath their paws. Virga slowly turned his head to the right, towards the two men walking in the gloom beyond. He couldn't see their faces. He narrowed his eyes.

Baal's red eyes were glowing fiercely over Michael's shoulder. The other man hadn't seen. Virga felt himself spinning, spinning, spinning down a great distance.

The red eyes, like terrible siren beacons, flashed.

'James,' she said. 'James.'

He called out, 'Who is that?' but he knew the voice and it choked him inside as if he were gagging on something lodged in his throat. His heart pounded with a violent intensity. I want to hear your voice, he told her. I want to hear your voice.

'James,' she said again, only now it was a pleading voice that almost killed him. Tears sprang to his eyes and he wiped them away before they could freeze. 'I'm here beside you. Can't you see me?'

'No,' he whispered. 'I can't.'

'Here. I need you, James. I don't want to go back.'

'Go back? Go back where?'

'Where I've been,' she replied, almost sobbing. 'A terrible cold place with grey walls. I don't understand this, James. I don't. I remember falling; I remember a hospital and people standing over me. Then nothing. Everything faded . . . everything turned to grey like the walls of that place. I can't go back. Please don't make me go back.'

He strained to see into the distance, but there was nothing. He couldn't see her. The bite of the cold reminded him that he was still awake but he moved across the ice sluggishly, as if it were turning into a viscous paste over the tops of his kamiks. It was her voice, yes, incredibly her voice. But where was she? Where was she? Her voice. Yes. Her voice.

'Answer me, Jamers,' she pleaded. 'Please let me know you hear me.'

'I hear you,' he called. 'Where are you?'

'Here beside you. I'm walking beside you but something separates us and I can't quite touch you. Oh God, you're so close. Why can't you see me?' The voice was on the edge of panic; it ate into him.

He turned and thrust his arms out in all directions, flailing, flailing, finding nothing. He choked back a bitter cry of rage and frustration. 'There's nothing here!' he said.

She began to dry. The tears overflowed and ran down his own face. 'I don't want to go back! I don't want to go back!'

'Then stay! Help me find you! Reach out and touch my hand! Can you?'

'Almost. I almost can. Something is between us. Help me!'

'How? How can I help you?' He looked around feverishly for her. The tears froze on his face, left thin crusts of ice in the lines around his mouth.

Her voice, moaning for him, died away. With a new determination he searched the darkness, his fingers grasping for a form that had seemed to be speaking just to the right of him.

And then she said, sobbing, 'They want me to go back, James. They say I have to and that I can't stay. Touch me. I don't want to go!'

His breathing was harsh and ragged. He cried out, 'I can't find you!'

'I do want to stay. I do. Help me!'

'Yes. How?'

'That man,' she said, her voice almost cracking, 'walking ahead of you. He keeps us apart. As long as he is there I can't reach through. If he were gone then they would let me touch you . . .'

The images of her were flashing kaleidoscopically through his brain. There was a roaring in his head; a tremendous weight was pressing down on the back of his neck. 'If he were gone . . .?' he asked weakly, a voice not his own.

She sobbed. 'Around your shoulder. The rifle . . .'

'Where are you?' Virga cried out. 'I don't see you!'

'The rifle . . . Oh God, they're calling me back!'

Virga was weak and off balance. He was afraid he would stumble. He saw the offered target of Zark's back only a few feet in front of him. The man was crude and cruel, a beast, a killer. Why should he live and make her suffer? Why should he live?

'The rifle,' she said. 'James . . .' Her voice began to fade.

'No! Don't go . . . not yet!' He hefted the weapon up with his injured hand and placed his finger on the trigger. The bastard was making her suffer! He was torturing her!

'James,' she said, calling from such a distance now that it made new tears course over his cheeks.

He took no aim. From this distance he couldn't miss. He squeezed the trigger.

Someone wheeled in front of him and wrenched the barrel towards the sky. The explosion of the shot deafened him and rocked him back. Flame exposed, briefly, Zark's incredulous face as the hunter dodged down to avoid a bullet that whizzed over his right shoulder into the darkness.

'Christ!' Zark said.

Michael wrenched the rifle away from Virga, his golden gaze unflinching. Virga felt his knees begin to give way but before

234

he could fall the other man caught him and lowered him gently. Beyond Michael, Baal stood without moving, arms chained before him.

'Has he gone crazy?' Zark said. 'That almost took my head off!'

'She was there,' Virga whispered to Michael, the hot tears of shame and regret already freezing down his face. 'She was standing right beside me all the time and I couldn't even touch her . . .'

Michael said softly, 'She was never there.'

'She was! I heard her! She tried to touch me!'

'No. She was never there.'

'She was . . .' he began, and the terrible sound of his pleading voice stopped him.

Slowly, with a hesitation born of deep and awful emptiness, Virga let her go. Her voice had been swept away by the rifle's blast but her image remained in his mind. Now, as he blinked away the tears, as he remembered who stood over him, he saw the beautiful face lose its colour and life. The light, gleaming softly from the eyes he remembered through a thousand dim nights alone in his apartment, that place that smelled of musty books and useless pottery and rancid smoke, faded until it was only a hollow shade of reality. And now she was receding back through a grey wall of mist and he felt the fear of losing her again throb at his temples.

He reached out a hand for her.

Michael grasped his wrist. 'She is dead.'

'No,' said Virga, begging. 'No.'

And beyond Michael, Baal laughed like the shriek of a woman.

Michael's eyes blazed. Virga instinctively cringed from the fire that seemed to glow from the man's face. The younger man rose up, up, towering as he walked across the ice, finally standing with his face inches from Baal's. There the two men, like cunning animals, weighed the possibilities of battle.

Michael's hands were curled into claws at his sides.

'Do it,' said Baal, grinning. 'Do it and destroy yourself too. You'd destroy yourself forever for the sake of an old man? No, I think not. Like me, you find this incarnation suitable.'

Michael's teeth clenched. A muscle spasmed in his jaw.

235

Where the gaze of the two men met the air seemed to glow white-hot.

'Do it,' Baal whispered.

Michael turned abruptly and disdainfully and walked back to Virga. He helped the man to his feet and gave him the rifle again. 'I want both of you walking side by side,' he told them. 'I want you to know always what the other is doing.'

'Coward,' Baal said over Michael's shoulder. 'You stupid bag of scum. You priest-fucking bastard.'

'You're all right now?' Michael asked Virga. 'You can continue?'

'Yes. I think I can.'

Zark said, 'For Christ's sake, watch him. I don't want a bullet in my back.'

Virga could now fully recognize his surroundings; he could remember why he was here. For a black instant he'd been caught in an amnesiac solitude. He felt weakened and drained as he'd never been before.

'You're very certain?' Michael asked.

Virga bent down and gathered up a handful of snow. He rubbed it across his eyes, then wiped it away with his sleeve before it could freeze his lids shut. His skin felt raw. 'I'm all right,' he said, 'but I swear before God I heard my wife speaking to me.'

'If you hear her voice again you'll recognize it for what it is. If you'd killed Zark, as Baal wished you to, we would have no guide to the sea.'

'My God,' Zark breathed. He glanced over at Baal. 'What kind of man are you?' He immediately lowered his eyes, remembering Michael's instructions.

'A better man than any of you,' Baal said. 'You think you're going to stop me, Michael, contain me, kill me? You know you can't do that. If anyone falls it will be you.' His eyes swept towards the other two men. 'And what will you do then? When I finish with him, where will you hide? Hear me well. There is nowhere on this earth you'll be able to go. I'll find you, and I have ten million eyes to help me search.'

Virga shivered. The man's voice cracked through the darkness and stung him.

'I've got a gun,' Zark said. 'You remember that.'

'On the contrary. I won't forget.'

'Move the team on, Zark,' Michael commanded. 'Remember, I want both of you walking side by side. That's right.'

The sledge continued its ragged course. The dogs seemed tired and Zark stopped repeatedly to feed them hunks of dwindling meat. Michael thrust his hands inside his furs for warmth and watched the men at the sledge for any sign of trouble.

'I won't be stopped,' Baal said. 'I've come too far. I've never been this strong before.'

'And that is exactly why I must stop you. You're on the verge of overpowering me. I realize that. And for that reason your time must come to an end.'

'I warn you,' Baal said very quietly. 'Watch yourself. You've thought all along you could master me. Me – one to whom hundreds of thousands have proclaimed their loyalty. And there will be more. And more. And then I will crush my enemies and take the place that was meant for me. You stupid cocksucker, you filthy piece of shit, you overstep your bounds.'

'I overstep mine to force you back over yours.'

'Too late,' Baal said.

'We'll see.'

'Damn you!' Baal spat at him. 'Hiding behind a cross of shit! You hope to win, knowing you cannot. You meddle with the future.'

'No. I preserve it. Their wars will come, yes. Their famines, their droughts. Their crops will turn to dust and their flesh will dry beneath a burning sun, but it will not be by your hand. You've begun the decay. I will not allow your power to warp them beyond all redemption.'

Baal's eyes burned, mirroring an insatiable greed and lust. He said mockingly, 'My master and I offer them hate. They take it gladly. They murder and loot and spit on everything you hold sacred. They take our hand and not yours. They praise our name and not yours. They are ours and not yours.'

'Be silent!' Michael said.

Baal laughed coldly. 'Ah. You smell the stench of truth.'

Michael didn't look at him.

Ahead the ice plains stretched to the lip of the sea.

28

The dogs were hungry. Zark could only lash his whip into the midst of the swirling pack as they turned on one of their number that had slashed a paw on jagged rocks. Fur flying and teeth bared, they bore the injured dog to the ground, while Zark shouted curses at them. The lead animal, now powerless to control against hunger, stood apart from the pack as if disdaining their cannibalism. The weaker animal fell beneath their combined weight but still guarded its throat with snapping teeth. The pack, their leads tangled around legs and throats, stood in a tight circle. waiting for an opening. And then a stout grey-flecked dog leaped in for the kill, followed by two more, and together they bore down with jaws straining for the jugular.

'Damn you!' shrieked Zark, laying in with his whip. 'Back off!'

But they were hungry beyond the comprehension of pain. There was a final cry from the dying dog.

Baal was laughing. 'The law of the world,' he said.

Zark could do nothing. He lowered his whip and shook his head from side to side, sickened. 'That was a good dog,' he muttered. 'A damned good dog.'

'How far to the sea?' Michael asked.

Zark shrugged. 'A couple of hours. Maybe more. If I lose any more dogs we'll never make it. Hell, I'm not so certain we can even make it back ourselves. Our food is gone; there won't be another refill for the lantern. We'll be moving in total darkness – very dangerous.'

Virga braced himself against the sledge, fighting off another wave of numbing exhaustion. His beard stubble was laced with ice and he had difficulty breathing, so sharp was the cold. Hours before, Zark had told him he had the first white patches of frostbite across his cheeks and, feeling his battered flesh, Virga felt them growing there like cold cancers. But there was nothing he could do. His feet, even in the sturdy dog-skin socks and kamiks, were rapidly growing numb. His fingers had frozen the day before. Now he kept walking only by a reserve of sheer will-power.

Nor had Zark escaped frostbite. It pocked his cheeks and the bridge of his nose. Ice matted his beard, the weight of it making him stoop over, as if he were ageing with every step. Virga had tried to keep a conversation going with the man in order to stay awake, but Zark seemed not to want to talk. He preferred silence, answering Virga in a low mutter that disdained communication.

Beyond them, far to the right and behind the lantern's yellow track, were the two dark figures of Michael and Baal. They would walk in silence for what seemed like hours, then Baal would suddenly spray a string of terrible oaths directly into Michael's face. And always, always, Baal would taunt Virga and Zark, reminding them that soon they would be his, that after he'd finished with Michael he would rip them to pieces, that after Michael could no longer give them protection they could never run far enough to hide.

'Virga,' Baal called suddenly over the growling of the dogs, 'you stumbling sack of shit, you're going to die out here, do you know that? You think I don't know you're slowly freezing to death? What good will you do your precious God when your body is a solid lump of ice? Answer me that.'

'Shut up, you bastard,' Virga said weakly, not knowing if Baal heard him or not. He raised his voice. 'Shut up.'

'Virga,' Baal said through the dark curtain that separated them. 'Virga, pray to your precious God that He freezes you to death before I can have my revenge. Come over here to me, Virga. I'll keep you warm.'

'God help us all,' Zark muttered. 'We should have killed that man a long time ago.'

'Zark,' Michael called out. 'Do you need help with the dogs?'

'No. I can take care of them.' He saw that they'd almost finished with the carcass. He took his rifle from the sledge and with the butt began to shove the animals back from the dead dog. He reached down and pulled the torn mass of flesh away. He waded among them, watching for any bared teeth or upraised tails, and calmly straightened the leads. The one-eyed black brute turned to face the rest of the team, ready if need

239

be to protect his master. In a few moments Zark had disentangled the leads and they were free to continue.

As they neared the coastal shelf the land began to rise up in winding hulks of rock and ice. Forbidding masses of stone, all agonized edges, suddenly materialized out of the gloom to bar their path. Zark corrected their course, taking a smoother but longer route to avoid any more injuries to his animals. A strong wind whined in from the sea; it began high above their heads, where they could hear it screaming, turning upon itself in blasting convolutions, and then dropped directly into their faces. Virga huddled for warmth but it was no use; he was slowly, as Baal had said, freezing to death.

They crawled against the wind through a wide black band of scabbish rocks to face a sight that froze the breath in Virga's lungs.

Balanced on the precipice of the ice-bound horizon was the moon, huge and blood-red, a bullet hole in ebon flesh. The ice reflected its brilliant crimson back on to the faces of the fur-clad men. For miles and miles the ground was smooth and bloody, bright and distant as a foreign desert.

Zark said over his shoulder, 'Melville Bay,' and Michael nodded.

There was no sea noise, no sound of breakers over rock; the thick layer of ice acted as a muffler. The only noise was that of the fierce wind, wailing now from the Pole, as it lashed across the bay and whirled through coastal rock on towards Greenland's interior.

Michael said, 'I want to find a place to cut through the ice.'

'What?' Zark twisted around. 'Now you want to go chopping holes? Christ!'

'How thick is it?'

'Several metres. This coastal ice is like iron except during summer thaw.'

'It's thinner ice further out?'

'Hell!' Zark said. 'My agreement was to bring you to the sea and no further. Not on to the ice.'

Michael ignored him. 'I seek a place of great depth. I presume that would be a kilometre or more out?'

Beside him Baal's eyes were burning slits. He looked from Michael to the hunter and back again.

'Maybe it would be,' Zark said. He swore. 'Maybe a kilometre or so.'

'Will you take us?'

Zark laughed harshly. 'Hell,' he said, 'do I have a choice?' He called to the dogs over the rush of wind and they pushed ahead, dragging the crippled sledge over a last fringe of rock-dappled land before reaching the bay's bleak smoothness.

'What are you going to do?' Baal asked.

Michael was silent.

'Doesn't the condemned man deserve to know?'

Michael fixed his gaze on the red-streaked horizon. The moon hung before him like a frozen sun.

'You bastard,' Baal said, barely loud enough to be heard. 'I warn you. Soon you can't turn back. Let me go while you still can.'

Baal waited for the other man to reply. Michael seemed not to be listening. 'You must want to be destroyed very badly,' Baal said. 'And what will it be for? Nothing. You will be scattered like dust in the stars and for what? Look at those two. Look at them! Fine examples of what you want to save. Weak, crawling, begging slabs of filth, no more. One already dead on his feet and the other soon to be.'

Michael turned his head slightly. 'You cannot save yourself.'

Baal's lips curled back in a travesty of a grin. He thrust his face forward, spittle shining on his mouth. 'And who will save you, Michael?'

The wind howled into their faces. Virga could hardly walk against its blast. The team was extremely irritable now that they'd left land behind. Zark's whip cracked continually over their heads; the lead animal, snapping and growling, bullied the others to keep them moving.

The sea ice beneath the mens' feet was treacherous. It was worse than glass, blue- and white-veined with deep threads of green. Virga, one hand always on the sledge for support, could feel a vibration through the soles of his boots. It was the sea thrashing beneath him, its tidal currents wrenching back and forth on the underside of the ice. He wondered at its depth, at its fury. He was gripped with a sudden fear of plunging through a weak spot to freeze almost instantly in the waters. His legs were shaking and uncertain. Go on, he told himself. Another step. Another. Another.

Walking on the other side of the sledge, Zark halted the team every few moments to chop at the ice with his axe. Then he would straighten and they would continue on a few more yards into the wind before he again knelt to test the thickness.

Beyond Michael, Baal burst into a wild scream that echoed around Virga's head like the whirl of wind. His scream grew in intensity and volume until Virga cringed to escape its terrible rage. It bore off into the distance; it vibrated against the far ice mountains. The dogs churned, whining.

Baal said in a low growl, 'I'll kill all of you slowly. So slowly, so slowly, so very very slowly. You'll cry out for death but it will be on my side. I promise you a century of pain.'

Zark stood up, his axe dangling at his side. 'This is as far as I go,' he said. 'I can feel the sea just beneath my feet. Further on, the ice won't support my sledge.'

Michael walked towards him, taking the axe and bending down beside the sledge. He chopped for a moment and then rose to his feet. 'How deep is the sea here?'

'Damned if I know. Deep enough.'

'And we cannot go on?'

'No. Too dangerous.'

Michael turned, contemplating the crated object still lashed to Zark's sledge. With an air of resignation he gave the axe back to the other man and said, 'The hole should be large enough for the contents of that crate to slide through. You begin it; I'll finish.'

Zark motioned at the canvas. 'What is that thing?'

Michael silently walked back and began working at the lashings, glancing up occasionally into Baal's gleaming eyes. Zark and Virga helped him slide it from the bindings and then Virga stepped back, breathing heavily from the exertion, to let Zark tear away the canvas covering. He began breaking it open with the axe. When he'd cut part of it away he tore feverishly at the wood and Michael helped him break open the sides to expose an oblong object inside.

A coffin.

But not so much a coffin as a simple chamber. It was dark and austere, plated with undecorated metal. There were no inscriptions, no flowing scrollwork, only a great dark bulk designed to hold a terrible, raging power.

Baal's laughter cut them to the bone. His mouth grinned below derelict eyes; his tongue flashed along the lips. 'You play games with me, Michael.'

'No games,' said the other. 'To destroy you totally would be my destruction as well. There are still your disciples with which to deal. They are demon entities within human bodies, carriers of your disease. You will be lowered into the sea and covered with ice. There your hideous soul will be trapped, unable to return in another Satan-seeded incarnation. No man will find you, no man will free you.'

Baal drooled saliva like an enraged animal. 'Nothing can hold me! You're a fool to think otherwise!'

'This can hold you,' Michael said. 'And this *will* hold you.' Taking off his mitten, he held his right hand motionless, fingers together, over the coffin's lid. Very slowly he moved his arm downward. Virga felt the hair at the back of his neck tingle, rise, rise, rise. Zark breathed a curse, his eyes wide and protuberant.

The man's hand was leaving a trail that melded, electric-blue and seemingly solid, with the metal. It glowed with enough energy to cause Virga to thrust a hand before his eyes and stagger back a few paces. Michael's hand continued downward in a straight, thick blue line the length of the coffin. Then he brought the hand up to the middle of the line and crossed it with another. There, pulsating on the coffin's metal lid, was an electric-blue crucifix, drawn from Michael's bodily energy.

Baal held both hands before his face, his chains clattering. He growled through gritted teeth, 'You sonofabitch! I'll kill you!'

But something was wrong; Virga sensed it. Baal's eyes glittered behind the hands. Michael let his arm drop and turned slowly, his eyes narrowed.

Baal backed away from the glowing blue crucifix. 'I'll kill you for this!' he shouted. 'All of you!'

'God in Heaven,' Zark whispered. His face, bathed in blue light, was tired and haggard. There were dark circles beneath the eyes. 'God in Heaven. You're not a man.'

Michael took the ice axe from Zark's hand. He bent down and, with tremendous force, steadily chopped at the sea ice.

Over to the right Baal cursed slowly, his voice intermittently rising and falling.

Slabs of ice scattered out around the sledge. Virga, watching Michael work, felt writhing within him a new fear from being so close to something awesome and intangible. His mind reeled at the recognition of the only possible link between Michael and Baal. The answer was in the form of a glowing blue crucifix shaped by a hand of flesh. Virga felt he had so much to ask, so much to learn. And so little time. He thought for a sudden terrifying instant that here, in this land of ice and barren plains, he stood poised on the brink of insanity.

The axe rose and fell, rose and fell. Zark stood dazed, his mouth moving but making no sound. And beyond the men Baal's eyes shined for a fraction of a second, bright and hideously red.

Michael, water-spattered from the sea that churned black and fathomless in the wide hole before him, rose to his full height. He threw open the latches on the coffin lid and opened it to expose a bare metal interior. He looked towards Baal. 'Come here,' he commanded.

Baal growled. 'You bastard!'

'Come here!' The voice shook Zark and Virga. Its power, like the report of a gun or the explosion of a cannon, echoed off across the frozen bay.

Even Baal seemed to tremble, but still he refused to obey.

And suddenly Michael's eyes began to change, to lighten through brown to hazel to hazel-flecked gold. In another instant, only time enough for Virga to draw a ragged breath, Michael's eyes were whirling gold, freezing and burning. Zark cried out and threw his arm over his face, staggering back into the cringing dogs. Virga's knees sagged. Something pounded at his temples. Again. Again. Again.

'Come here!' Michael said.

Shielding his eyes, Baal roared like an enraged animal. He took a step back, confused and wary.

And then Michael had reached him. He grasped the chain between Baal's wrists and flung him to the ground. Baal grunted in pain and began to crawl towards the sledge on his belly.

'Crawl,' Michael said. 'Crawl back to the pit, you thing of slime. Crawl!'

Baal staggered to his feet, hissing and cursing, and Michael

244

flung him down again, forcing him to remain on his stomach. Michael said, 'By the power granted me I force you to crawl as you have forced others, innocent ones, weaker ones. The brute blind force in both yourself and your master sickens me. You've murdered and burned, raped and ravaged . . .'

Baal reached up to grasp at Michael and the other man thrust his groping hand away.

'. . . you attack the weak, the mindless, the helpless. Never the strong.' Michael's eyes blazed. 'By the will of Jehovah your black soul will be confined for eternity.' They had almost reached the open coffin. He grasped the wrist chains and dragged Baal up. Baal's own eyes were fierce and red. It was an unbearable sight. Zark cried out again and Virga put his hands to his face.

Michael struck Baal across the cheek, a backhanded blow, and bore him down into the coffin.

Baal whispered harshly, 'My master will win yet. On the Megiddo plain. Sweet lost Megiddo.' And Michael slammed shut the lid. As he carefully latched it he seemed weakened by the confrontation. The blue glow illuminated dark hollows under his eyes. He staggered when he motioned for the two men to help him.

The three men heaved until they thought their spines would break. Slowly, slowly, the coffin inched over the edge of the hole and tilted towards the sea. Finally the sound of metal grinding over ice was no more and it slipped from their grasp and sank down into the black water. The crucifix remained visible for a time, shrinking until it had been swallowed in the maw of Melville Bay.

'Finis,' Michael said tonelessly. He ran a hand over his face. 'I'm tired. I'm so tired.'

'He's gone,' Virga whispered. 'Thank God.'

Zark stood peering down into the hole as if uncertain that all of it had ever taken place. 'Who was he?' he asked in a weak, listless voice.

'Someone who will never die,' Michael said, 'but will only wait.'

Zark looked towards Michael, the ice in his beard glittering red from the bullet-hole moon. With an effort he walked away from the other men and began to calm his dogs, checking to see that all the leads were untangled. 'We should be on our way,' he said after a moment. 'We've got a long journey.'

'Yes,' Michael said. 'We have.'

Zark cracked his whip over the team and the dogs, still nervous, began to stir. The sledge inched forward. Virga clasped his arms beneath his furs for enough warmth to get himself moving.

His eyes afire again, Michael twisted around towards the hole where dark water churned.

The dogs stumbled into each other, tangling themselves in the leads. The huge one-eyed black howled in fear.

Virga looked around, every breath a knife tearing his lungs. What had it been? That sound that sound that sound. What had it been? Beside him Zark stood motionless, his fisted hands white-knuckled at his sides.

And there it was again, that sound.

The sound of foot-thick ice cracking with pistol-shot intensity.

And then the crack that had begun at the lip of the hole widened, widened, veining out in blue and green, streaking across the ice plain beside them, behind them, in front of them, criss-crossing like jigsaw puzzle pieces.

The sea thrashed. Steam rose up, ghostly blood-red wraiths. Melville Bay, maddened black fury, overflowed the edges of the hole and sloshed around the men's boots. Virga felt its rage underneath the ice on which he stood. He struggled to keep his balance against a force thrusting against the frozen surface, threatening to burst through.

'What the hell is it?' shouted Zark, one hand on the sledge and his feet wide for balance.

But Michael would not, or could not, answer.

A great slab of ice cracked in half with a tremendous splitting sound and the coffin shot up from the water and bobbed once, twice. Its lid had been ripped away. The coffin turned on its side, filled with water, and sank again.

And then the ice at their feet exploded.

It lifted up around them, groaning with the sea's power. Black waves burst free. The veiny cracks widened into fissures, widened into gaps, widened into chasms. The men struggled for balance on pitching ice platforms, the sea crashing on every side. Virga, his arms flailing for some kind of support, staggered back and fell to his knees. The rifle around his shoulder slipped away, spun on the ice. Virga grabbed for it and saw it vanish through a fissure. Michael stood where he was on a wide slab, his fists clenched at his sides. Zark, hanging on to his sledge, muttered a continuous guttural cry.

They saw the fingers first.

Reaching from the hole where the coffin had gone down.

Grasping at ice, curling, the naked fingers thawed a hold, pulled from the black water forearms, shoulders, the top of a head. And Virga, on his knees, saw Baal's face break the surface, saw the red reflections of the moon in the eyes, saw the mouth grin wide and soundlessly in grim revenge.

And Virga knew. Hearing Michael cry out, he knew. And in knowing he knew the first seconds of death.

Michael was too late. Baal's power had doubled, tripled; he could overpower the Cross. He'd allowed himself to be brought to this place knowing that here there was no escape for them. Here he was the Messiah, and they disloyal.

Baal, steam swirling from his body, stepped free of the pitching waves on to solid ice.

Zark's footing gave way. Great fissures opened around him, the ice dividing with the noise of splitting timber. The dogs, scrambling for safety, wrenched at their leads. The sledge overturned, scattering equipment. Much of it, including Zark's weapon, went spinning by Baal's legs and into the sea.

Baal opened his mouth and emitted a high piercing shriek that threatened to burst Virga's eardrums. He clasped his hands to the sides of his head and cringed.

The huge one-eyed black, within range of Baal, leaped for the man's throat. Bound by the lead, the animal fell short, his slavering jaws gripping only empty air. But Baal, his mouth wide in the terrible shriek of vengeance, caught the animal around the neck and squeezed with both hands. The dog kicked and clawed. Virga smelled something burning. The one-eyed black burst into flame. It cried out once in agony and then Baal let the mass of fire drop. The other animals, with no leader now, pitched forward in the flight of terror, dragging the overturned sledge. The ice beneath them split open and, with a single terrible moan, the team fell through, borne down by the weight.

Someone, a hulk of furs, crashed into Baal even as the team disappeared. Baal staggered back, his eyes glinting. Trailing steam from his fingertips, he swung a blow that Zark dodged.

Michael started for Baal, weaving from platform to platform.

Zark struck Baal full in the face with the same sound as the blow of an ice-axe. Baal fell back only two steps before regaining himself, and this time he came up beneath another blow and caught the hunter around the throat. He lifted Zark bodily and held him at arm's length. Zark screamed, his eyes imploring Virga, before his furs caught fire. Then his hair. His body caught in a mass of yellow fire, the smoke of burning flesh mingling with steam from Baal's body. But Michael had almost reached them and, with the abrupt unconcern of a child turning to another plaything, Baal tossed the body to one side. Grinning, he whirled to face his adversary.

The two clashed with the sound of crunching bone. Michael drove his elbow into Baal's chin, knocking him back across the writhing plain. Baal's knee came up into Michael's stomach as the other man advanced. Then Baal struck a downward blow on Michael's head that resounded across to Virga, still huddled on his knees some yards away. Michael fell on to his hands and knees, and Baal struck him in the face before he could regain his feet. Michael shook his head from side to side, stunned, and as Virga watched in mind-reeling fear Baal's claw-fingered hands reached Michael's throat.

A red mist had fallen before Virga's vision. MOVE! He couldn't move. YOU OLD MAN! YOU WEAK PITIFUL OLD MAN, MOVE!

When he did it was with agonizing slowness. His muscles screamed. He searched about for a weapon. Something, anything, a jagged clump of ice, anything. Dear God, he shrieked, help me help me help me! Beyond him Baal's hands burned at Michael's throat. Michael clutched at him weakly, his eyes lost and defeated.

And then Virga saw the flare gun and cartridges that had scattered with the overturning of the sledge. They lay on the other side of Baal and to reach them Virga must pass him. He had no choice. He leaped up, moving low to keep his balance, and ran towards the two figures ahead.

Baal's head wrenched up.

His eyes blazed. He dropped his gaze around to where the flare gun lay. Virga knew that Baal already realized what he was going to attempt. Baal released Michael and spun around, his hands outstretched to destroy Virga as he had Zark.

At the last second, inches beyond Baal's grasping fingers, Virga dropped to his belly. He slid beneath the grip of the thing that walked as a man, slid with the ice spinning into his face, slid with his good hand groping for the flare gun. He reached it and grasped a cartridge, whirling to guard against an attack from behind.

Already Baal was almost on him, his teeth bared and his eyes bottomless pools of holocaustic energy. Steam swirled from his reddened fingertips.

Virga, in desperation, slammed the gun against the ice to open its breach.

Baal reached, reached.

Virga rammed in the cartridge.

Baal growled, thrusting out his arms.

Virga whirled, a finger on the trigger, and saw Baal's fingertips inches away. A blood-lust cry vibrated in Baal's throat.

And Virga fired point-blank into Baal's face.

The flare exploded in a mass of red and yellow incandescence, streaking across Baal's flesh into his hair. His clothes caught fire and he towered over Virga, his arms outspread, a single burst of flame in the form of a man. Baal grinned.

Fire leaping out of his black-scorched lips, he bellowed in expectation of what was to come. Still he reached for Virga's throat. Virga opened his mouth to cry out in helplessness, knowing he could never reload in time.

But there was a blur of motion to Baal's left and fingers entwined around the man's throat. Michael had recovered himself. They struggled in silence, like animals, and Baal gripped Michael's neck as they staggered back and forth over the ravaged field.

Something like electricity, white rimmed with blue, seemed to spark between the combatants. The two figures, still engrossed in fierce battle, were outlined by a glow that built in intensity, pulsating, pulsating, pulsating like the beat of a huge heart.

And then there was an explosion that seemed like the end of the world.

It lifted Virga up and threw him more than thirty yards over the ice. He grasped on to fragments, the terrible blast-thunder ripping at his eardrums, the sea crashing against him again and again. He gripped the ice until his fingers were bloody. Around him there was nothing but the white of plunging ice, the black of rising water. The sound of the blast would not die away; it echoed off to the distant coast and came back full force. He cried out against it. Great chunks of ice, raining back from where they'd been thrown into the sky, clattered down around him, some striking him and glancing off. He strained to hold on to his senses.

Slowly the sound of the blast died away. The sea fell back within its limits. Across the broken field huge fragments groaned as they crushed others. Then there was only the noise of the high wind and the sea as its tides churned about far below the surface.

After a while, Virga wet and freezing, struggled up. The ice was broken all the way to the horizon. Jagged holes gaped. A greater hole, the centre of the blast, was devoid of ice. He felt with dead fingers the burns on his face and realized, with a sudden strange humour, that he'd lost his eyebrows and stubble of beard. There were no corpses. It had seemed to Virga that, an instant before the explosion, he'd seen Baal and Michael simply swept away. Zark's body had probably been blown into the bay. No matter, Virga thought as he shivered with the piercing cold, I shall soon be dead as well.

He fell back and waited, his eyes closed. What did they say about freezing to death? That it is only like falling asleep, that one is indeed very warm when just about to die? Perhaps. He felt the folds closing about him. There were so many questions he'd wanted to ask. Now, very soon, he hoped to have those questions answered. The wind swept over him, whistling past his head, and he welcomed the first signs of death.

Baal's disciples.

Virga waited, poised with his last strength before slipping away. Someone had spoken, whispering close to his ear, but he didn't recognize the voice.

Baal's disciples.

There are more, Virga said. Baal is gone but they remain to walk as men, to spread contamination and brutality, blasphemy and war. They hope to deny man his mind, rob him of his thinking processes and in so doing rob him of his final chance. Baal is gone but they remain.

Something burned in his brain. He envisioned murders, gang warfare in the streets, jet fighters shrieking over flat plains where armies battled face to face, the high columns of mushroom explosions, the blasted bodies, the roar of wind through cracked city towers. Very slowly, very slowly, he climbed from the warm depths back towards the cold rim of life. He was aware, finally, of a noise over the screech of the wind. Something hovering above him. Thock thock thock thock thock thock.

He opened his eyes and they filled with tears.

It was a helicopter. A Danish flag was painted on the grey metal underbelly. Two men in heavy furs bent from the open cargo doors, staring down at him, and one of them lifted a bullhorn to his lips and spoke in Danish.

When Virga had neither stirred nor replied the man spoke again, in English. 'This is the Ice Patrol. Lift your hand as a signal. We will lower a lifeline.'

Virga blinked his eyes and lay still. His body felt old and useless, something that had been drained and discarded. He was afraid he would not be able to move and, realizing his fear, he realized also that he desperately wanted to signal. He wanted to cling to life.

Someone, whispering very close to his ear, said, *Baal's disciples*.

And Virga raised his arm.

BY DONALD F. GLUT, BASED ON A STORY BY
GEORGE LUCAS

THE GREAT NEW FILM SPECTACULAR!
THE EMPIRE RETURNS!
FROM A DISTANT GALAXY THE IMPERIAL
FORCES SET FORTH ON A DEADLY MISSION
TO DESTROY THEIR SWORN ENEMY: LUKE
SKYWALKER!

On the icy world that was planet Hoth, Luke Skywalker
and the Rebel Alliance found the ideal outpost. A lonely
wasteland at the outer reaches of the universe, the
perfect setting to conduct their war against the tyranny of
the Empire.

Or so it seemed.

Until Imperial forces, led by their dark warlord, tracked
down the Rebel base. And launched a ferocious and
devastating attack from space which threatened to destroy
the Alliance forever, and send Luke on a desperate
mission . . . with 'The Force' as his sole protection!

A STAR-BLASTING SPECTACULAR FROM
LUCASFILM, DISTRIBUTED BY
20TH CENTURY-FOX.

FILM TIE-INS   0 7221 5653 7   £1.00

WAR STORY

BY GORDON McGILL

Berlin, April 1945.

The city – and Germany – is only hours away from final defeat. Deep in the underground passages of the burning city a four-man British unit is fighting a desperate battle against time. Its top-secret mission: to bring a German general back alive, whatever the cost. And to keep one step ahead of the advancing Russian army.

But why?

Find out in WAR STORY

IT'S THE WAR STORY TO END ALL WAR STORIES

WAR FICTION   0 7221 5901 3   £1.00

A★RENA

BY NORMAN BOGNER

IN THE NEW WORLD THEY STARTED NEW LIVES, WITH NEW NAMES – AND A DREAM THAT WAS AS OLD AS MANKIND . . .

In the beginning there were the four families, driven together by a common enemy, united by the dream they shared. Together they fled to their 'promised land'. There, with new names and new hopes, they went their own ways but always connected by a chain of love and danger. And each would play a part in the intrigues, the dealing and dying, the loving and losing that meant –

ARENA

Sweeping from a daring bank raid in the heart of Hitler's Germany to a breathtaking bid for power at the topmost level of America's greatest sporting enterprise, from the pain and sweat of the fight business to the splendour and decadence of the movie industry, from the inevitable, brutal consummation of a merciless underworld vendetta to the tender consummation of a love that miraculously survived the most turbulent events of the Twentieth Century, ARENA is a genuine blockbuster of a novel from one of the greatest storytellers of our time.

GENERAL FICTION   0 7221 1733 7   £1.75

AIR FORCE ONE

BY EDWIN CORLEY

AIR FORCE ONE: THE FAMOUS PLANE THAT
CARRIES THE WORLD'S MOST POWERFUL
MAN. SOMEONE WANTS TO TURN IT INTO
AN AIRBORNE COFFIN . . .

A trip aboard AIR FORCE ONE amounts to the safest –
and most exclusive – journey there is. Luxurious, closely
guarded, superbly maintained, guided by a highly skilled
and dedicated crew, she is the Free World's airborne
nerve-centre, carrying the world's destiny as she flies.

Until one day, as she takes the President of the United
States on a routine trip, that nerve-centre and the people
aboard her have to face total terror. When a traitor strikes
on board. And the radar screen shows a fully-armed
World War II vintage fighter – HEADING STRAIGHT
FOR AIR FORCE ONE . . .

'Topnotch thriller . . . an explosive climax'
PUBLISHERS WEEKLY

ADVENTURE THRILLER   0 7221 0496 0   £1.25

A selection of bestsellers from SPHERE

FICTION

SNOW FALCON	Craig Thomas	£1.50 ☐
ARENA	Norman Bogner	£1.75 ☐
GOING HOME	Danielle Steel	£1.25 ☐
WIFEY	Judy Blume	£1.00 ☐
FIRESTORM	Robert L. Duncan	£1.10 ☐

FILM AND TV TIE-INS

THE EMPIRE STRIKES BACK	Donald F. Glut	£1.00 ☐
HUSSY	Rosemary Kingsland	£1.00 ☐
SATURN 3	Steve Gallagher	95p ☐
GOODBYE DARLING	James Mitchell	95p ☐
DAWN OF THE DEAD (filmed as ZOMBIES)	George Romero & Suzannah Sparrow	85p ☐

NON-FICTION

TRUE BRITT	Britt Ekland	£1.25 ☐
PIERCING THE REICH	Joseph Persico	£1.75 ☐
FOURTEEN MINUTES	James Croall	£1.25 ☐
THE NEW SOVIET PSYCHIC DISCOVERIES	Henry Gris & William Dick	£1.50 ☐
STAR SIGNS FOR LOVERS	Robert Worth	£1.50 ☐

All Sphere books are available at your local bookshop or newsagent, or can be ordered direct from the publisher. Just tick the titles you want and fill in the form below.

Name _____

Address _____

_____

Write to Sphere Books, Cash Sales Department, P.O. Box 11, Falmouth, Cornwall TR10 9EN

Please enclose cheque or postal order to the value of the cover price plus:

UK: 30p for the first book, 15p for the second and 12p per copy for each additional book ordered to a maximum charge of £1.29

OVERSEAS: 50p for the first book and 15p for each additional book.

BFPO & EIRE: 30p for the first book, 15p for the second book plus 12p per copy for the next 7 books, thereafter 6p per book.

Sphere Books reserve the right to show new retail prices on covers which may differ from those previously advertised in the text or elsewhere, and to increase postal rates in accordance with the PO.